Indentured Bonds

The First Generation, Circa 1715

A Novel

The first novel of

The Lovelys' Family Tree

series

MICHAEL KROFT

This is a work of fiction. The characters and incidents are products of the author's imagination or are used fictitiously and not to be construed as real. Any resemblance to actual persons, living or deceased, is entirely coincidental.

Copyright © 2020 by Michael Kroft

First Edition

PART I

CHAPTER 1
Virginia, September 1708

The lone crackling log in the fireplace and the five short, dancing flames of the iron chandelier failed to remove the somber and chilly feeling the young man was experiencing that evening. Sitting stiffly at the table in the whitewashed dining room, he occasionally forced a nervous nod to feign interest in what the large, round man in his mid-fifties was saying from the end of the table. Having finished a twenty-minute diatribe on England's politics, the man was then going on about local matters when the eighteen-year-old was reminded that starting the next day and for the next seven years less nineteen days, it would just be him working with the man, and he was instantly covered by a thick anxiety much like he had experienced when bedded down in the ship during the nine-week voyage there, though not as strong as what he had experienced during the ocean storms.

"And I say that's another reason to keep to ourselves the happenings on this plantation. They exaggerate and distort all if only for the attention they earn through the gossip," the man said before itching his chin's stubble and smiling, revealing several missing teeth. "I believe I've said that before, have I not? Though, it does no harm and possibly some good to repeat it." Pausing for a moment, he stared at his thin companion. "Move the hair from your eyes, stripling. I prefer to see them when talking to you." After watching the young man brush his brown bangs to the side, the man said, "Ben, we won't be harvesting Chalmers' field on the morrow, instead I'll send you to mine. I've business in Williamsburg and expect you're capable of working alone for the day. I don't expect to return before you finish hanging the bundles, so do be certain to hang them in the last curing barn. We don't want to confuse mine with Chalmers', do we?"

Replying with a nod, Ben realized his error and changed it to a shake of his head.

"That's correct — we don't. And I expect you to harvest most if not all. It's only forty acres... until I persuade that Huguenot, LaValle, across from it to sell his thirty. The man's so proud of his land one would believe he has a hundred, the LaValle Hundred," he huffed. "He's cleared only six. Six! Not near enough to feed and clothe his offspring, and it shall be years before he builds onto that shed he calls home, perhaps having to stack their bunks four high before then," he huffed again.

A young, barefoot Black woman in a stained frock of osnaburg cotton tied at the waist by a cord entered the dining room with a wooden tray. Placing it on the table, she began clearing the three sets of pewter dishes.

"Ann, don't distract us with such needless noise. It's bad enough we must see you. You need not force us to hear you as well."

"Sorry, Master Philpot," she whispered as she grabbed the last bowl from the table and gently placed it on another.

"You may nod your understanding! Next, you shall want to dine with us!"

"No, Master Philpot. My apologies, Master Philpot," she whispered, bowing nervously before turning to leave.

"Again, I require only a bloody nod!" he growled.

"Yes, Master Philpot."

As she left the room, he hissed to Ben, "It's too stupid *not* to talk back. As He is my witness, one day I'll fix it."

With the sounds of shoes coming down the hall, both looked toward the entrance to see a curly-haired woman no older than eighteen enter the room wearing an off-white apron over the front of her plain brown skirt and loose beige bodice.

Philpot forced a smile. "Ah, Margaret, we heard your shoes and expected Jeremiah."

"M-my apologies, Master Philpot," she whispered.

Struggling to pull his pocket watch from his tight-fitting waistcoat, he said, "No reason to apologize, my dear." Opening it and eyeing the time, his face showed his frustration. "I say if he wants to be in town before… before eleven, he must be on his way," he said, confusing Ben who wouldn't have expected the man to care.

"Is there anything more you require?" Margaret asked.

Pressing the watch back into his waistcoat, he asked, "It's been two months, yes?"

"Two months?"

"You've been with us for two months now, yes?"

"I have," she nodded.

"Then you know your duties well enough to make time to eat here with us rather than in the kitchen with them, and I say starting on the morrow, you shall share our table."

"As you wish, Master Philpot," she said, turning to leave

just as a husky man in his mid-twenties wearing an opened long coat appeared at the dining room entrance. Moving out of her way, he adjusted his eye patch that had an eye painted on it, which from a distance looked almost natural.

"Come in, Jeremiah. Come in, I say," Philpot said, forcing a smile as he stood up from the table with Ben following.

"Master Philpot, Ben, I'll be taking my leave."

"Yes, it shall be more than an hour's walk, and I do hope you don't think poorly of me. I would have Ben drive you, but it would be a two-hour journey there and back, not to mention the harnessing and then the stabling on his return. I say it's far too inconvenient for him, and more so when considering he shall need his full sleep for his first day alone on the morrow."

"I understand."

"And as I said earlier, it's best to go on a full stomach rather than an empty one, but I hope you're not leaving with that leather coat, the estate's coat. I only loaned it to you to protect your clothes in the field... and I say those new breeches fit you well, but then they should for the sterling I paid. Still, I didn't give you that fine coat to take with you. It's not part of the contract. The one before you used it, and this one shall use it after you. It's slightly too large, but he shall grow into it, I say. You can lay it over the chair if it pleases you."

"Certainly," an embarrassed Jeremiah said before taking it off to reveal a clean white shirt under a tan waistcoat that matched his breeches.

"I say I believe I'm doing you good by keeping the coat. The faster you walk, the less chill to fight off and the sooner you shall reach your destination." Forcing another smile, he shook the young man's offered hand and added, "I shall say also it was a pleasure having you here, and I'm confident you shall do well in South Carolina."

"I thank you, Master Philpot. It was a pleasure working with… for you."

"I'm sure it was, and more so when you're leaving with a small fortune, yes? One no indentured would see at the end of a contract, so do keep it close."

"Yes, I believe that's true, and I will."

Shaking Jeremiah's hand too, Ben said, "I wish you the best, and may He be with you."

"And with you," Jeremiah nodded. "Now, if you both would excuse me, I must be on my way."

"And the whip?" Philpot asked.

"The whip?"

"Have you taken it?"

With an awkward smile, Jeremiah said, "No, I'm certain that's the plantation's. I placed it on my bed. And I gave the pocket watch, pistols, and sword to Ben."

"Very good. Perhaps we shall cross paths in Williamsburg before you're off on your short voyage. But if not, as the French bastards say, bon voyage."

As Jeremiah left the room, Philpot remained standing as he hissed to Ben, "It shall surprise me if he finds South Carolina. He might go too far and have to learn Spanish, the idiot."

Ben nodded, reluctantly.

**

Comfortably hidden in the woods of tall and slender longleaf pines, Robert and his shorter brother, Stuart, stood holding their oil lanterns while impatiently watching their bowlegged brother shovel the last of the loose dirt into what was recently a rectangular hole. Swatting the back of his neck, Robert said,

"Harry, don't make a mound. We don't want someone believing there's treasure there."

Harry released an exaggerated sigh, threw the spade to the ground, and dropped to his knees to brush the fallen leaves impatiently over the filled hole. "I don't see whys I'm to do all of 'er!"

"Doing the last share isn't doing all of it," Robert said as he walked over to pat the dirt down with his shoes.

"Depends on who's doin' the last, don't it?"

"No, it doesn't."

After struggling to stand, Harry brushed the dirt from the knees of his trousers. "Still, we could've dropped 'im in the river and be done with 'im."

Joining them to help pat down the dirt, Stuart said, "He wanted him buried."

"Who's to care? We could've said we did and still drop 'im in. But no matters. We did as we said. Good boys, we are, and 'ow much gooder are we now?"

"Almost ten," Robert replied.

"Ten? That's not what 'e said!"

"Ten each. Near what he said."

"And what o' the clothes? They should fit me and Stuart with some work," he said, hobbling to a small pile of clothes lying near a stuffed flour sack. Quickly picking through them, he held up a white blood-stained shirt. "This 'ere's finished. Why put one in 'is chest?"

Stuart huffed. "As we said then, he heard your steps! They heard them in Williamsburg! If you had stayed with the horses, as we agreed, you would've profited from a clean shirt! We would've crept up on him, as agreed!"

"Would've crept up on 'im," Harry repeated, poorly

mimicking his brother. "Always my fault, is it? Look 'ere, ya ruined the waistcoat too, ya did. A waste o' fine clothes!" Dropping the shirt, he began going through the sack. "Would've ruined that long coat too if 'e was wearin' er." Then shaking its contents onto the forest floor, he raised his voice to say, "Bloody 'ell! I was 'opin' 'e packed 'er."

"Pack it all and we'll be gone!" Robert demanded. "And he wants the patch."

"The patch?"

"The eye patch. The one you pocketed, and it escapes me why you would want it."

"Why'd 'e want it? 'As no value."

"Perhaps to destroy it himself. Make certain there's nothing to identify him," Robert replied, swatting his neck again.

"Or as a memento," Stuart added. "Whatever the reason, we shouldn't concern ourselves with it... since it has no value."

"Memento? Robert, Stuart 'ere learned 'im a new word!"

CHAPTER 2
England, May 17, 1715

For the last two hours, with his back against the sideboard of the cart's small bed, a stuffed sack on one side of him, and his chubby eleven-year-old brother, Oscar, on the other, William had sat with his knees pulled in to give his two white-capped sisters across from him space to straighten their legs so their five-year-old sister bundled in a blanket could lie across their thighs.

Though content that the youngest could sleep through the rough ride rather than have to bear the boredom of it, he still found himself hoping the next bump or jolt would break or knock off one of the two solid wooden wheels, and he expected his father, who seemed intent on rolling over every large rock in their path, was hoping for the same thing. Then, after turning off the Roman-built stone road to take a shorter route between fields of young maize, the axle's whine for tallow and the additional bumping of the cart staggering in and out of the tracks left in the dried mud from the day before only added to his anxious state.

With the late morning's gray sky threatening to soak them and the cool spring breeze picking up, no one spoke of what was to come. Even Oscar, who had asked his parents one too many times how much further they had to go, said nothing out of fear his father would carry out his threat of making him walk behind them.

Wondering what his oldest sister was thinking, William looked across at her, and when she raised her fourteen-year-old head to return his look, her watery eyes caused a wave of guilt to splash over him. Needing to escape her look, he turned his head to his brother, who whispered, "How much further would you say we have?"

William shrugged and shook his head.

"Three?"

He shrugged again.

"Five?"

"Five miles seems correct," he said with a nod if only to pacify the boy.

"Five! At this pace, that's another hour!"

Fifteen minutes later, the boy whispered the same question and was disappointed by the same reply.

**

As the four-wheeled carts passed in both directions between the docked ships and row of limestone buildings, their heavy wheels thundering against the planks of the pier, the only ship showing any activity that Friday afternoon was *The Colonist*. Belittled by the navy ships moored on both ends of it and behind a day in loading its cargo because of the storm the day before, it rushed to fill its belly. With the line of full carts parked beside it slowly growing, the barefoot sailors in their off-white calico trousers, matching shirts, and red wool caps took a crate from the bed of the first cart in the line, struggled and cursed their way up the gangway hugging the ship's side, and once aboard, disappeared behind the main deck's short wall. Seconds later, they descended a rope hanging from the end of the bottom yard of the stern's mast to grab another crate.

Eight ships away, with the clouds darkening and the seagulls heckling them, the five did as their mother had told them and huddled together within a group of almost fifty people waiting near the opened double doors of a warehouse. It was their first time seeing ships up close, their first time being engulfed by a salty breeze that forced the three sisters to hold their cloaks closed, and their first time seeing sailors who stumbled in and out of what the siblings assumed was a tavern one block down.

When their parents entered the warehouse to mingle with the larger crowd inside, the five separated themselves from the group outside and the two youngest girls, with no interest in their surroundings, took advantage of hearing themselves speak by discussing the patterns of the fabric they hoped to find in the small textile village their parents planned to visit on their return home.

Where Oscar was excited to be at the pier, showing no concern for why they were there, William's anxiety smothered any excitement he would have had. With his bulging flour sack over his shoulder, he tried to distract himself from what was to come by listening in on his sisters, whose passion for fabric was beyond his understanding, and when his five-year-old sister screamed, "Brown is for boys!" and his ten-year-old sister replied, "It's for anybody!" he looked at his brother and tossed him a smirk and a raised eyebrow.

When Oscar replied with an eye roll, their ten-year-old sister caught it and asked, "What do you two think?"

"My opinion is worth less than nothing. I've never had reason to give women's clothes much thought," William replied.

"Mine as well. I only wonder how Willy would look in them," Oscar said with a grin, and as he turned to wander off, William pulled him back by the collar of his jacket.

"Willy is pretty in a gown, a green gown!" the five-year-old said with her usual excitement, causing the oldest sister, who hadn't said a word that morning, to replace her gloomy expression with a slight smile.

"William, how do you see me in a yellow dress with blue flowers?" the ten-year-old asked.

"With my eyes."

She huffed. "No! How would I look?"

"As you do now, with your eyes," he said, before grabbing at Oscar, who was just out of reach. "Oscar, come back!"

"No, *Willy*! I only want to see the ships in the harbor. I'm not going far and won't be long."

Not understanding why the ships in the harbor would be more interesting than those lining the pier, William shook his head, dropped his sack, and walked over to his brother. About to pull the boy back to his sisters, it occurred to him that doing as his brother wanted might distract his mind. "We'll do that, but only for a moment. We'll have to return before Mother and Father or you'll sleep tonight with yet another growling stomach."

"We will, and we'll see better from there," the boy said, pointing to a space further down between two ships.

As Oscar ran along the raised walkway dodging those in his path, William apologized to those he dodged as he ran after him, his heart skipping a beat when his younger brother failed to look both ways before running across the pier, barely avoiding a cart whose driver let loose several loud expletives. "Our apologies," William said to the man before waiting impatiently for that cart and two more to pass.

At the edge of the pier, near the large space between the bow of one ship and the stern of another, the two looked out at the ships floating in the harbor with their sails tucked into their yards, and as William expected, nothing was happening in the harbor bedsides the two men rowing a small boat toward them.

With the stronger breeze doing little to cool his anxious state, William unbuttoned his jacket and released the top three buttons of his shirt. Following him, Oscar released the straining buttons of his jacket that was a size too small, unbuttoned the top three buttons of his shirt, revealing his pudgy cleavage, and adjusted his breeches that were tight around the waist but ended two inches further below his knees than they should have.

As the small boat came closer, the brothers noticed it was towing a thick rope, and when it reached the pier, they stepped to the side as one of the two sailors climbed a ladder built into the pier, caught the thick rope thrown up to him and wrapped it around an iron mooring. After the man descended the ladder, the brothers watched them row the boat back to a ship almost two hundred feet away. Curious about the rope stretching, they soon realized that the ship, which was then lifting the small boat from the water, was pulling itself into the pier. With the ship creeping closer, neither mentioned to the other that they had expected the ships to sail into the pier, and after twenty minutes when it was only fifty feet from them, they heard muffled shouting from somewhere within it, and as it pulled itself closer, recognized it as singing.

Come hang, come haul together,
Horray, Horray!
Come, hang for finer weather,
Hang, boys, hang.

I'd hang a brutal mother,
Horray, Horray!
I'd hang her and no other,
Hang, boy, hang.

I'd Hang to make things jolly,
Horray, Horray!
I'd hang all wrong and folly,
Hang, boy, hang.

They call me hanging Johnnie,
Horray, Horray!
They call me hanging Johnnie,
Hang, boy, hang.

The ship's bow standing ten feet above them creaked against the pier, and when the singing stopped and Oscar's foot stopped tapping along with it, William said, "Come. We'll watch from the other side." Expecting his brother to protest, Oscar only did when William pulled him back by the shoulder, forcing him to wait for two carts to pass.

Standing on the walkway near the door of a limestone building, the brothers watched a sailor hang from the bow of the ship before dropping onto the pier. Catching a thick rope dropped down to him, he walked to where the stern of the ship would be when docked, and after wrapping it around a mooring, several sailors near the stern braced themselves on the deck as they heaved on the rope to bring its hull against the pier.

With nothing more to interest him, Oscar grabbed the arm of William's jacket and pulled him down the walkway until they were across from *The Colonist*, where they sat to watch the sailors remove crates from a long six-horse cart. The crates that clanged, William guessed, were cookware; those that clattered were wooden plates, and the few that jingled, he joked, were the King's jewels. Oscar guessed the lighter, silent ones were bundles of silk, and the heavier ones were bars of gold wrapped in cloth so their clanging wouldn't announce their precious presence.

"The crates would be much heavier than they are, and they would never send gold on a ship like that," William said. "It only has four things on its side. This one wouldn't be a challenge for pirates."

Oscar's grin accentuated his chubby cheeks. "Perhaps, or perhaps, that's what they're hoping we believe. If I were them, that's what I would do. Put it on a ship that no one would suspect... and they're called gunports."

After the emptied cart rolled away and another with a mountain of sacks moved ahead to take its place, a large, round man shouted from the deck of the ship, "Grab those hardtacks. Hurry now!" As two sailors climbed onto the cart's bed, the rest formed a line to have the two men drop a heavy sack over their shoulders, causing them to shrink slightly, and as they struggled up the gangway, one hand on the sack and the other on the railing of rope, several times it seemed one might stumble back and knock over those behind him, but none did.

When they carried the last of the sacks onto the ship and the cart rolled away without another to replace it, William's heart began beating hard and fast.

A few seconds later, a sailor on the ship yelled toward the waiting crowd, "ALL ABOARD WHO'S COMIN' ABOARD!"

William couldn't get to his feet.

His legs refused to move.

As his face went pale and he became dizzy, a hard tug on his shoulder rolled him onto his side.

"Come!" Oscar demanded, trying to pull his brother to his feet. "We have to leave or I'll not eat tonight. Come!"

"ALL ABOARD WHO'S COMIN' ABOARD!"

William forced himself out of his shock and to his feet, and with another tug from his brother, they ran toward their sisters.

When their parents emerged from the waves of people leaving the warehouse to pool on the pier, ignoring the curses thrown at them by the drivers of the blocked carts, Oink said, "The game has ended. Let's go home." But none seemed to hear him as all but the youngest focused their eyes on William, who was considering his brother's words when his father distracted him by pulling back his smallest sister who had turned to walk toward the blocked carts.

"No! I want to pat the horsey, the dark one there!" she protested as her father picked her up and stepped out of the way so William could take his teary-eyed mother's offer of a hug.

Kissing his cheek, she broke their hug and wiped an eye. "Listen to your master... and be safe." Trembling as she released more tears, she added, "We'll send letters."

"I'll do the same. I… I'll send one soon after arriving."

She hugged him again. "And remember, I love you… we all love you."

"I love you too," he said, fighting to control the pressure growing behind his eyes.

Forcing himself away from his mother, he faced his watery-eyed oldest sister, and after he hugged her and kissed her cheek, she whispered, "I hope you find what you're seeking, and I hope you won't forget about me… about all of us."

With the lump in his throat making his voice lower, he said, "Alice, I can't forget about you," and after he wiped his eyes with the sleeve of his jacket, added, "This salty air is hard on the eyes."

"Know this, William, I'll be thinking of you every sunset, hoping you're safe and hoping too that you'll return to visit. Even when I'm married with a dozen children, I'll always think of you as the sun goes down, wondering what has become of my big, brave brother with a heart bigger than his brain."

Only able to reply with a nod, he turned to his ten-year-old sister, who hugged him tightly and with the side of her face against his chest, said, "Goodbye, William. I'll miss you very much. Please try to return when your contract ends."

As she broke her hug, he bent down and kissed her cheek. "I'll miss you too, and I'll try… if only for a visit. And… and you would look pretty in yellow with blue flowers, though it seems impossible to be any prettier than you are now."

Clearing his throat, he looked down at his youngest sister who was looking curiously up at him and giggled when he picked her up. "I must go now."

"Be home on the morrow?"

"N-no, much later."

"Next week?"

"Later still."

"Two weeks?" she asked, holding up two fingers.

"Yes, I'll be back then," he lied.

"Bring me a horsey," she whispered in his ear. "Don't tell Father, and not a big one, a small one."

"I'll bring you a pony."

The child's eyebrows tilted in and her voice rose. "No! Did you not hear me!? I said a horsey! I want a small horsey! Bring me a *small* horsey... and don't tell Father!"

"I'll bring you back the best small horsey I can find," he said, breaking a smile that slightly reduced the pressure behind his eyes.

Causing her to giggle again by kissing her cheek, he set her down gently and turned to his father to shake the offered hand that had a weaker grip than he would've expected.

"This is it, then. As your mother said, listen to your master and be safe. Watch the weather and do as the others do. They'll know how to avoid the foul air," the man said, releasing his son's hand. "Do you have your paper close?"

William tapped the pocket of his jacket. "In my pocket."

His father pulled out a handkerchief, released a wet cough into it, and wiped his mouth. "Good. Watch your footing on the ship, and if there's a storm, as there's certain to be, perhaps as early as today, make certain you're below," he said before clearing his throat. "You've escaped the mines, but I expect this new life will also have its disappointments, and I expect it will change you enough to make you almost unrecognizable when I see you again. The voyage itself may change you too, and I hope the change is for the better… though how much better you could be is beyond my understanding. You're a good son, a great son. One any father would be proud of." Then surprising William with a hug, he whispered, "I will think of you always."

"And… and I, you," William whispered back.

Breaking the hug, his father said, "You must be off, but we'll stay for a last farewell. We'll wait to see you on the deck one last time." Pausing to collect himself, he added, "That is if this sky doesn't break and wash us into the sea."

"I'll see you then, but before I go, I want to give you this," William said, holding out a small leather sack that jingled.

"What's that?"

"What I saved over the last few years, five pounds six. I don't see any use for it there since they provide all."

"No, you'll need it. You've given much to the family and you'll never be wealthy if you continue giving away your sterling."

"I'm not looking for wealth. I'm looking for a life where I'm my own man, where I own land and work for myself."

His father swallowed and nodded. "And I'm more than certain you'll find it."

After William reluctantly pushed the sack back into his pocket, they shook hands again, both struggling to fight back tears.

"ALL ABOARD WHO'S COMIN' ABOARD!"

An icy chill went through William when he looked at those heading toward *The Colonist*, some carrying stuffed sacks slung over their shoulders while others were balancing small crates on them. Realizing by their trousers that he had overdressed for the occasion, he turned to Oscar, who had been shocked silent, and said, "This is it."

"No! No, it's not! You're not going through with it, Willy! You don't have to!"

"It is, and I am, and I'll write as often as I'm able."

"Then I'll never see a letter because you *can't* write," Oscar said while not understanding how it was possible that he could be sad, angry, and even frightened at the same time.

William forced a poor smile, one where his eyes contradicted it. "Perhaps I'll learn between here and there, and if I can't, I-I'll find someone who can."

Staring at his older brother for a moment, Oscar spat on his trembling hand and offered it out. "Then swear it. Swear you'll write… and swear you'll send for me when you're free from your contract."

Having never thought about sending for him and at that moment believing it possible, William spat on his hand before shaking his brother's. "I-I swear on it. I swear on both. I swear I'll write and swear I'll send for you."

"Good. I'll be expecting a letter soon and an invitation in seven years. That's if I don't take a contract myself before then," the younger brother said, hoping to fight back his tears until after William had left. "You should go. You… you don't want to miss your ship."

"True," William nodded. "But you have to return my hand."

After Oscar forced himself to release it, William wiped his hand on his breeches, picked up his stuffed flour sack, and flung it over a shoulder. "I'll write… I'll find someone to write the words for me after I'm settled."

With wet eyes, no one said a word as they watched him

cross the pier and walk toward the ship, consciously moving each of his reluctant legs.

"DON'T FORGET MY HORSEY… AND DON'T TELL FATHER!" his little sister yelled to him, and then looking up at her mother who was looking down at her with a subtle smile, she asked "What?"

"ALL ABOARD WHO'S COMIN' ABOARD!"

As his family watched William walk out of their lives, none noticed Oscar quietly release his tears as he walked off to mix in with those moving along the walkway toward *The Colonist*. Not able to take his wet eyes from his brother on the other side of the pier, he stepped into an alley across from the ship and watched him join the line of men ascending the gangway. On the deck, William presented his paper to a large bearded sailor, and after the man examined it and handed it back, he disappeared into the ship.

**

In the dim and dank passengers' quarters two levels down, William stood near several tight rows of bunks, each bed wide enough for two people. Across from the bunks were two long tables with built-in benches. Beyond that was what looked like a kitchen, and beyond that, sacks stacked to the ceiling and taking up half of the hull. The other half was taken up by barrels lying on their sides, piled three high and held in place by ropes stretched from small iron hoops in the floor to others in the ceiling.

Walking over to the first bunk in the first row where a man about ten years older was unfolding a coarse sheet, he asked, "Would you know where they have the private quarters?"

"Told ya that too, did they?" the man asked without stopping what he was doing. "Me and me mate there was told the same thing, the same lie. Treated like royalty, my arse! If I was ya, I'd be grabbin' a bunk quicky like and prayin' ya don't have a bedmate… and prayin' too that that was their only lie."

"Many thanks," a confused William said as he stepped to the side so a man could pass.

Finding it difficult to believe the kindly agent had lied to him, he decided to wait for the last of the passengers to board and then choose his bedmate from among them, but then it occurred to him that if he waited, he might have to choose from the worst and he made his way to a bunk at the far end of the last row.

CHAPTER 3
Virginia, May 17, 1715

Standing at a closed battened door while holding in one hand a wooden tray of only an empty pewter bowl and a spoon, she adjusted the clean apron covering her light-brown bodice and matching skirt before taking a deep breath and slowly releasing it.

"Who?" a woman groaned in response to her knock.

"It's Becky with Beth's meal."

"Enter."

Opening the door, she entered the room with its almost suffocating stench that she had yet to become accustomed to and didn't believe she ever would. "Good morning, Mistress Philpot."

The twenty-five-year-old woman lying on the top sheet of a small bed stretched out her legs from under her stained shift and moaned as she struggled to sit up against the headboard, revealing her long, curly brown hair and her pale, blotchy face that made her look forty-five. Setting a two-foot-tall doll in a pink dress beside her, she rasped, "Girl, only minutes ago Beth was telling me how hungry she is. Just look at her shrinking to nothing."

Becky nodded and placed the tray on the child-sized desk standing beneath the small window beside the bed. Pulling out its chair, she turned it to face the bed, and not yet prepared that morning to look at the sickly woman without releasing a tear, she looked at the doll. "Would you like to sit on my lap, Beth?"

"What's that you say, Sugar?" the older woman asked the doll. "You can answer for yourself. Be timid if it pleases you, but you shall receive no sweets after!" Offering the doll to Becky, who took it as she would a new born, the woman added, "Eat everything in your bowl, and perhaps I shall change my mind regarding those sweets."

Becky sat on the chair, placed the doll on her lap, placed the empty bowl on the doll's lap, and picked up the spoon. Dipping it into the empty bowl, she placed it to the doll's lips. "You're hungry this morning, Beth."

As Becky dipped the spoon into the bowl for the doll's second mouthful, Mistress Philpot said, "Girl, do not tell Charles, but I had the most wonderful dream last night, the most wonderful yet. Beth and I were in Alnwick, and with the sea between Charles and us, we were free to do as we wished, free to wander the fields. We had cheese and bread on Percy's hill, and Beth told her silly jokes and made her silly voices. 'Twas wonderful, simply wonderful. And afterward, we rolled down the hill as if in barrels. Is that how 'twas, Beth? Swallow before you speak!" Then looking up at the ceiling, she closed her eyes and cracked a smile. "She laughed so loud I can still hear it. She's not laughed such as that for a long time. Warmed my heart, it did."

Becky laid the spoon in the bowl. "It does sound wonderful."

"'Twas. 'Twas wonderful," the woman giggled with her eyes still closed.

"Perhaps you could take Beth to your village for a spell."

The woman opened her eyes and rasped, "Perhaps, but 'twould only happen after Charles passes. He would never allow us out of his sight for more than a day. Far too jealous."

The woman's response startled Becky who would've expected her to say she had booked a passage on the next ship, or planned to row herself there the next week, or even swim, but never that her husband wouldn't allow it because of his jealousy.

Reaching into the pocket of her apron, she pulled out a handkerchief and wiped Beth's mouth. "That's a good girl, Beth. I hope your appetite is as strong tonight," she said as she stood up from the chair to return the doll to the woman, who gently cradled it in her arms.

"Becky, before you leave, would you grab a doll from the dresser?"

Startled again by being addressed by her first name while being politely asked to do something, she couldn't help but stare at the sickly woman.

"Well, girl, why do you wait!?"

Becky bowed her head. "M-my apologies, Mistress." Walking to the group of smaller dolls neatly organized on the dresser against the far wall, she asked, "Which would you like, Beth?" Picking one up, she turned to face the woman. "This one in an orange dress?"

"I concur, Beth," the woman smiled at the doll. "The one in the yellow dress would be a pleasant change."

Exchanging the doll for the one in yellow, Becky handed it to the woman, who placed it between Beth's wooden arms.

"Mistress Philpot, I'll be back in a moment with your meal," she said as she picked up the tray of clean dishes.

"Good, and make certain 'tis you! That speechless Negro shall not be feeding me!"

"Understood," she nodded, not needing the hundredth-something reminder but accepting it as part of their morning routine. After she fed the doll, the women would remind her that the room was off limits to the slaves, and after returning to feed her, she would bathe her, brush her hair, put her in a clean shift, and try to convince her to take a brief walk outside, which the woman always refused to do. If there wasn't an *accident* to address, she wouldn't see the woman again until the midday meal, when she would again feed the doll first.

Leaving the room, Becky glanced through the hole in the seat of the wooden chair by the door. Expecting its bucket to need emptying, she was curious to find it didn't and hoped the woman hadn't relieved herself in the bed again, though there was no noticeable addition to the room's normal stench that she partly blamed on the fixed windowpane for blocking out the fresh air and in the afternoon, intensifying the stench by raising the room's temperature with the sun's rays.

CHAPTER 4
Trespassing

With his bottom resting on the side of an empty whale-oil barrel and his feet on a broken crate, he only realized he was rocking himself back and forth when the sun found an opening in the dark clouds and forced him to squint by brightening the stone walls of the alley offering him sanctuary from his father's disapproving eyes. After squeezing his eyes closed to force out what he hoped were the last of his tears and wiping them away with the sleeve of his jacket, he blew his nose into his sticky handkerchief and out of view of his mother, tossed it over his shoulder. He had to fight back more tears when William's leaving reminded him of the last moments with his grandfather who had struggled from his deathbed to share a final few words with him, but instead of being buried in the ground, never to be seen again, William would be sailed away, never to be seen again. Then with grief, anger, and fear fighting for supremacy, Oscar promised himself that when William appeared on the deck, he would shout out his love to him.

As the alley darkened again and a few raindrops fell, those inspecting *The Colonist* while waiting for their loved ones to appear on its deck offered him a better view of the ship when they disappeared to take shelter from what soon could be heavy rain.

A moment later, an overdressed couple crossed the entrance of the alley with a well-dressed Black woman following six feet behind as if pulled by an invisible rope. With the couple disappearing on the other side of the entrance to talk with someone, the Black woman stopped and his jaw dropped. Besides her dark-brown complexion, which he considered more attractive than blotchy white skin, her high cheekbones and full lips fascinated him, and when she looked at the red-eyed boy and gave a sympathetic smile, her large dark eyes impressed him. Returning the smile, he caught the warm roll she had snuck from her cloth-covered basket, and as he mouthed his thanks, the invisible rope pulled her past the alley. Struggling against going after her to ask where she was from, how long she had been in London, and if she had sisters as pretty as her but closer to his age, he only defeated the urge when he considered it might put her in trouble with the couple… and him in trouble with his father for acting on yet another impulse.

Taking a bite of the roll and forcing it down his dry throat, he realized he was hungry and blamed it on his mother. She should have insisted he finish his morning meal as she would normally do when someone didn't, but then no one had finished theirs that morning, including her. With his throat too dry for the bread, he stuffed the roll into his pocket.

Several minutes later, a group of sailors rushing about the ship caught the boy's curiosity. Raising a tall beam with an arm extending from its top, they dropped it almost eight feet into the deck so only about six feet remained, and when a sailor threaded a rope through a block hanging from the end of the beam and another sailor separated its two tangled loops, Oscar realized it was a block and tackle pulley system, which didn't interest him, and turned his attention to the hired coach stopping beside *The Colonist*. Impressed by its rare wheels of spokes, he watched the driver climb down and place a wooden block of three steps at its door so a redheaded man near William's age and dressed in an embroidered jacket with matching waistcoat and breeches could step out to assist a middle-aged woman down. "Mother, I will be fine," Oscar heard him say.

"I wish I was as certain," the fine-dressed woman said, her loud voice cracking as she stretched out her arms begging for a hug, and as she received it, added, "The wait for your first letter could put me in the ground!"

Her son kissed her cheek and broke their hug. "I'll write when I reach Virginia. It'll take months before I arrive and more for it to arrive here, but know it's on its way."

A long cart pulled by six horses stopped behind the coach, its cargo of heavy barrels rumbling as they rolled about slightly, and as several more carts rolled up behind it, a sailor on the ship shouted angrily at the coach, "MOVE IT ALONG!"

"That's if you make it to Virginia!" the woman sobbed as the driver removed a trunk from the top of the carriage and placed it on the pier. "If you're not wrecked before then!"

"Mother, look about. Do you truly believe they would load the ship if they didn't expect to complete the voyage? Of course, they wouldn't. Now return home and hug Father for me."

"I can't bear to let you go!" she protested. "This is all too much for my heart!"

As her son took her hand and turned her toward the carriage door, he said, "Mother, I can take care of myself."

"MOVE 'ER OR WE'LL DROP 'ER OFF THE PIER!"

"Do be careful, my dear Philip!" the woman begged as he closed the door behind her.

"Always," Philip assured her.

With the driver removing the block of steps and then driving the coach off, Oscar watched the young man struggle to pick up the trunk and then struggle up the steep gangway, almost falling back twice before reaching the deck where a husky sailor seemed to scold him for being late. After exaggerating a bow, the sailor pulled a paper from the young man's jacket pocket, examined it, and placed it back where he had found it. With the sailor refusing the young man's offer of the trunk, it took Oscar a moment to realize the sailor was making a joke when he yelled to the young man walking away with it, "Ya'll find yer quarters prepared as ya prefer, Yer 'Ighness!"

Minutes later, two sailors were standing on the barrels of the first cart, wrapping the lift's two large loops of rope around the ends of a barrel, and after two men at the lift pulled in the rope until the barrel was hanging above the deck's wall, another man used a rope attached to the lift's arm to rotate it and align the barrel with something beyond the wall.

Trying to come up with a faster way to load the ship, Oscar found he couldn't and blamed it on the occasion, telling himself he would give it more thought on the long ride home when his mind would be clearer and in need of something to fight the boredom.

Then growing impatient with waiting to see his brother, he

tried to distract his mind by watching the large crates, pallets of stacked sacks, and more barrels being lifted onto the ship, and in the crew's rush to load it, a rope slipped off an end of a barrel that dropped against the side of the cart and smashed against the pier, where its many gallons of yellow liquid drained through the cracks between its planks.

Two hours later and with nothing else falling from the lift, a cart rolled up with the largest crates yet that, by the sounds escaping from within them, held pigs, and as they lifted them onto the ship, the frightened animals inside caused them to swing, turn and shake so much that it seemed a rope would slip from them. And then one did. Falling several feet, it slammed onto the back of the cart and tumbled off to crack open a side, and to Oscar's surprise, a dozen squealing piglets rushed from it.

The sight of the small animals skirting in all directions and the sailors throwing curses as they chased after them caused Oscar to laugh so hard he almost rolled backward off the barrel, but he stopped laughing when two piglets with their little legs a blur ran toward the alley.

The shock of seeing one crushed under the wheels of a passing cart was quickly replaced by the excitement of the other entering the alley. Jumping up from the barrel to grab it, it squealed as it scurried between his legs. Then turning around, bending down, and pulling the roll from his pocket, he made several clicks with his tongue, and to his delight, the piglet stopped. Calming down, it cautiously approached him, sniffed the roll that he held out to it, bit into it, and squealed when he grabbed it.

As Oscar carried the baby pig by its belly, he fed it the rest of the roll and noticed a dark stain similar to a three-quarter moon on the small animal's side, and when he tried to wipe it off with the sleeve of his jacket, he discovered it was permanent, like the birthmark on the neck of one of his classmates that he tried to wipe away the first day they met.

At the broken crate and hoping to share a few words with the sailor who joined him with a squealing piglet under his arm, Oscar said, "They're difficult to catch."

"They're that," the sailor nodded as he placed his piglet into the crate, and then using his foot to keep the animal from escaping again, said, "Ya have yourself a quiet one there. Push him in if ya will."

"He calmed down with a bread roll. I think he was more hungry than scared," Oscar said as he bent down and pushed the piglet in. "And I saw a cart crush another one."

"Then that makes nine more to catch. Say, would ya be a good lad and keep the side closed 'til we catch the rest?"

Realizing his brother was somewhere on the other side of the hull that he could reach out and touch, Oscar considered sneaking aboard while the sailors were distracted, but in the next moment decided against it, since that would require sneaking off too. No, if he were to sneak aboard, he would do it for the journey... then another idea came to him.

"What say ya, lad? Keep the side closed while we catch the rest of the wee buggers?"

Forcing his mind back to the sailor, Oscar said, "I will," and then, pointing toward the alley, added, "And... and I saw two more run up there, up that alley."

"We need to catch those too," the man said before looking up at two sailors enjoying the commotion as they leaned against the deck's wall. "You two, we got more up the alley there. Come help!"

Without a word, the two men climbed over the wall, dropped onto the cart's crates, causing more squeals from within them, and hopped down onto the pier.

With the three running up the alley, Oscar looked about the pier. Everyone, including his family, was chasing after the squealing animals, some bumping into others like a Punch and Judy show, and with the few sailors remaining on the deck too enthralled by the commotion to look down and notice him, he dropped to his hands and knees, and hoping the oversized crate would hold his weight, pulled the side open enough to squeeze himself in while pushing back the pair of piglets. Forced to drop his head and bring his knees to his chest, he reached out to pull the broken side closed and noticed a pungent smell before realizing he was sitting in something wet and sticky.

As another sailor squeezed in a piglet, Oscar was questioning his latest impulsive act and wouldn't have been too disappointed if any of those squeezing in their captured animals had looked in to discover him, but none did.

Finally, with the side hammered into place and the eleven excited piglets unable to move about in the cramped space he left for them, the crate was lifted onto the ship with hardly any swinging and shaking.

As it was being lowered into the ship, Oscar peered through the thin gaps between the sideboards and watched as he passed several cannons lining the hull. Passing through the next level, he saw what looked like a kitchen, and as he passed through the level beneath that, saw several men stacking crates. Then as he passed through a level where two men were stacking sacks, he was wondering how many levels there were when the crate struck the floor, causing a painful jolt to his lower back.

Not noticing the boy's grunt, one of the two men stopped what he was doing to walk over to the crate, lift it slightly to remove the loops of rope, and shout, "ALL CLEAR!" As the shout was repeated on each level like an echo, Oscar's heart skipped a beat when the man dragged his crate to the other crates of piglets, but it calmed down when the sailor returned to his mate to help finish stacking the sacks.

Twenty minutes later, with the last crate of piglets lowered and the sacks stacked and secured, the two sailors ignored the crates to climb the steep, narrow stairs while talking about the women they were leaving behind.

When the hatch above the stairs closed with a bang and the double doors of the cargo hatches on each level slammed shut one after the other, Oscar's fear of being caught was replaced by the excitement of being on the ship. Kicking open the crate's broken side, he held back the excited piglets as he squirmed out through their waste. Kicking the side back in place, he struggled to his feet and let his curiosity take over.

In the open space between a wall of barrels at one end and a wall of crates at the other where a narrow passage at least thirty feet deep had been built into it, a fenced-in area for the piglets had been constructed, and like their crates, it appeared far too large for the small animals until Oscar realized they would grow during the voyage. Across from the pigsty were rows of stacked sacks, stacked bales of hay, and a wide and deep stack of firewood, all secured by ropes stretching from floor to ceiling, and near his feet sat the gibbous-marked piglet looking calmly up at him as if to ask, "What now? What's the plan, and would you have another bread roll?"

Oscar picked up the piglet and tried to cradle the squirming animal in his arms. "You're a persistent fellow. I think I'll call you Gibbous. No, that's too formal, like Kenneth. I know, I'll name you Gibby," he said and took the animal's snort as approval.

Then it occurred to the boy that his parents would panic when they realized he wasn't with them, but a second later, the joy of missing their annual purchase of dress fabric pushed aside his guilt, and a few seconds after that, the footsteps and voices nearing the stairs' closed hatch cut his joy short.

**

Where he should've been content with having the top bunk at the end of the last row to himself, William's mind was instead fixated on his family as he anxiously worried about what would become of them while he was gone.

Doing as they were told: wait for the heavier cargo to be loaded aboard the ship before going up to the main deck, William was ten minutes into the wait when a redheaded young man struggling with a trunk stopped near his bunk to look up at him before glancing at the older, scruffy man alone on the bunk across from William's and the lone older woman below it. Placing the trunk on the floor, he climbed the four-rung ladder to sit next to William and introduced himself as Philip John Smith the Third. With William only able to offer a nod, the two silently watched a sailor open the cargo hatch near their row of bunks, and minutes later, they watched the cargo being lowered through it.

Almost half an hour later, when barrels marked Salted Pork were being lowered into the ship, Philip smiled and nudged William with his elbow. "That's the gold they're bringing across."

Responding again with only a nod, William experienced a moment of déjà vu before remembering that Oscar had said something similar during what he then believed was their final time together, forever, and for the second time that day, the pressure grew behind his eyes.

"Not on this ship!" the old woman almost shouted from the bunk beneath them. "They use the navy for that!"

"And that's what they want you to believe," Philip replied, his smile growing as he leaned forward to look down at her bunk. "Pirates would never expect gold on this ship."

"'Cause they'd never put it in 'er!"

"Exactly, and that's more reason to do so. She's smaller, faster, and much less suspect than a navy ship."

"They'd never put it in 'er cause there ain't no need for it in Virginia. They need sterlin'," the woman said as she stood up to face them, revealing her medium, curly brown hair, her crow's feet, her pale complexion, and her bright orange dress. "Everythin' 'as to go through England, in and out, and that means payin' with sterlin'. They might send gold to England for it, but not the other way. My son writes me they're so lackin' of sterlin', they use those Spanish dollars, but England only takes sterlin', and since everythin' comes from England, they're always short it."

"I believe you're correct," Philip nodded. "The barrels are holding a fortune in sterling."

"Not on this ship!" the older woman barked. "They'd never send sterlin' with this ship! She'd be too easy to—" Stopping herself short, she shook her head and returned to her bunk. "Why bother explainin' somethin' to a striplin' that 'as to touch a flame to learn it burns!"

CHAPTER 5
Mary's Michael

Holding a tray of dirty dishes she exited the back door of the large two-story house painted a light gray instead of the more common white, and even though the wind blew her long, straight hair into her face and tried to lift the tray from her hands, she was thankful for it cooling that early afternoon's unobstructed rays.

The absence of the smallest children's shouts, screams, and laughter reminded her that the overseer of the plantation had stayed back from felling the trees and she expected him to soon ring for his midday meal, but having just fed Mistress Philpot and without Ben there to act as his audience, she would've appreciated another hour to prepare her mind for delivering it.

Working with a dozen other children within a large fenced-in garden to her left, a pockmarked Black boy no older than ten looked over at her and smiled, and as she returned it, the weighted door banging shut behind her caused him to drop his smile and return to his work. Looking behind her and seeing no one there, she assumed the bang reminded him too that Philpot was in the house.

Descending the few steps to walk a dozen paces to the red-bricked kitchen, the smells of roasting chicken, baking bread, and boiling stew welcomed her in while the heat assaulted her on its way out.

After almost seventeen months, the building's size still impressed her. On her right, next to a pile of firewood, a fire burned in a four-foot-wide fireplace where a ten-gallon pot dwarfed a smaller one hanging beside it. On the opposite wall, a chicken warmed on a spit above a smaller chest-high fire, and against the far wall, another burned near the bare feet of a thin Black woman in a stained frock who was removing several large mounds of bread from the dozen baking in the wide opening above it. Shaking them from the baker's peel onto a long chest-high shelf, she threw Becky a smile and a nod.

Becky returned both before placing the tray on the counter to her left.

At the large table in the center of the kitchen, a heavy Black woman about twenty years older than Becky stood slowly chopping carrots with a knife that had its point replaced by a small perpendicular metal plate, making it awkward to use for chopping and impossible to use for stabbing. Stopping her chopping, she looked over at Becky. "I have to say you look in need of a distraction."

"Then, Mary, I look about correct."

"How was she?" the woman asked as she adjusted the weathered kerchief circling her forehead.

"Well enough to feed herself, and while I waited for the dishes, I played with Beth."

"I have to say, I fear what would happen if that doll were to break," Mary said. "But if it pleases you, you may peel and slice onions for the stew."

"It does," Becky nodded as she joined her at the table and removed an onion from the basket resting on it.

"Ann, would you stir the soup?" Mary asked. "We don't want the master complaining it's been burned."

With her back to the two, the thin woman nodded as she slid the last three mounds of bread onto the shelf before walking over to the smaller pot hanging over the fire.

Returning to her slow chopping of carrots, Mary said, "I was just telling Ann about Doctor Richards marrying again."

Becky picked up a shielded knife from the table and peeled the onion. "I heard the same."

"My Michael heard the master telling Master Carlson he's marrying the one who caused him to murder his wife. She's expected to arrive from England next month."

Becky stopped her slow slicing to sigh and shake her head. "He didn't murder his wife. She died from consumption, and I expect Philpot... Master Philpot only believes he did because the man couldn't save her. The master tends to think the worst of people."

"I didn't say I believed it," the larger woman smiled. "He's a fine man, and I have to say he always offers a smile, a genuine smile. Looks directly at us he does, expecting us to look directly at him as if there's something familiar between us. Is that true, Ann?"

Stirring the soup, Ann turned her head slightly to respond with a nod.

As Mary placed the knife on the table and with some effort limped the few feet to rotate the chicken on the spit, Becky brushed the sliced onion aside, grabbed another, and said, "He is a fine man, and his wife was a fine woman. She died three years back, and it was obvious to all that they were still in love. It took several months before he could smile again."

Mary returned to the table, grabbed an onion from the basket, and began peeling it. "I never had the honor of meeting his wife. We see nothing of what occurs off this plantation, but I have to say I'm happy for him. He certainly deserves a woman to care for him, but I would be more pleased if he were marrying you. Would you agree, Ann?"

Stirring the much larger pot of stew, Ann nodded again.

"But we wouldn't want you to leave us, would we, Ann?"

Ann shook her head.

"That will do for onions," Mary said as Becky went to grab another. "In half an hour, it'll be ready to take out to Master Carlson."

Holding out her frock, the older woman slid the chopped carrots and onions onto it, and as she limped over to Ann to drop them into the larger pot, Becky went to the counter to take down several clean pewter dishes from a shelf above. She was about to grab a knife to cut a leg from the roasting chicken when the distant ring of an impatient bell caused the three to freeze as if stunned by the firing of a nearby cannon.

**

Charles Philpot sat at his oak desk as the bell's second ring echoed off the sparsely furnished room's log walls. Behind him stood two bookcases and ahead of him stood a tall clock with its pendulum patiently swinging. On each side of the clock was a glassless window with a pair of closed cast-iron shutters that would've blocked out much of the daylight if not for the eight-by-four-inch horizontal slots cut into one of each pair. The only other light in the room came from two candle lanterns hanging from iron hooks mounted on each side of the opened six-inch-thick door.

Impatiently shaking the small brass bell a third time, its ring bounced off the walls again as he placed it on the corner of his desk. Pulling a pocket watch from his opened waistcoat, he looked at the time on the pendulum clock and added three minutes to the watch before quickly winding it. With the sound of footsteps rapidly approaching, he dropped the watch back in his pocket, and as the steps slowed near the door, he slid a silver dish holding a small ceramic bottle of ink and a quill to the right and a closed leather-bound ledger to the left.

"Master Philpot, your meal is ready," Becky said as she entered the room. "And I tasted it," she added, answering the question before he could ask it.

"I thank you," he nodded, and after waiting for her to move the dishes from her tray to the desk, he moved his cup of cider further to the side and unrolled a cloth napkin to find a pewter fork, knife, and spoon. "I say I don't expect there to be, but I shall ask," he said as he pulled the soup closer, "Was there any change? Any sign of Margaret coming to her senses?"

"Not with this meal, but this morning, she used my name," she said as she picked up the empty tray.

"And that's good?"

"I believe it is. It's the first time she used it in more months than I can remember. She seemed to know me as she used to... if only for a moment."

The man looked down at his soup, dipped his spoon into it, and instead of dismissing her as she hoped, he said, "I say I'm not sure how much longer I shall allow this to continue. I'm considering sending her away, making her another's problem, though I expect I would have to make an excuse for her leaving, perhaps say she's visiting family. You're her friend… were her friend, what say you to that?"

Becky stiffened up. "I still consider Margaret… Mistress Philpot a friend, but it's not my place to have an opinion on such matters when it's between you and her. I'm neither a member of her family nor a physician, but speaking of physicians, have you spoken to Doctor Richards?"

"That murdering Royal College arse?" he asked bitterly. "I have, and what does he know? He tells me to spend more time with her as if that would help. All it would do is anger me by her refusal to come to her senses. I've tried being sympathetic, but with no results. Tried slapping it out of her too, but for a sore palm and her wailing, nothing came of that. No, my presence can do nothing to improve her state, and perhaps there's nothing to be done."

Wanting to end the conversation, Becky said, "It's your opinion that matters, Master Philpot, but I wouldn't want to see her leave, not when I believe she can recover."

"Becky, your constant hope, or is it faith, can make you appear as a fool," he snarled through the soup in his mouth. "And if I sent her away, I would be a bachelor again, be able to marry again, I say."

"Not in the eyes of our Lord," Becky said and then immediately regretted it. "Is there anything more you need?" she asked, desperate to leave the man to his meal.

"True, I would have to petition for a divorce, as difficult as that is, but perhaps I could look about before I was again a bachelor… if anyone would have this older man," he smirked. "Tell me, do you believe there could be hope for me, hope I might find love again? Would there be any takers? Would a woman perhaps share this house before we were husband and wife?"

Surprised by his question and finding herself preferring his usual *talking at* rather than this rare *talking with*, she wanted even more to end the conversation. "If still married, that would… that would be adultery, a sin while your vows are in place."

"A sin? That's not a sin. The holy book tells us to… commands us to. Look here." He dropped his spoon into his bowl, wiped his grinning mouth, and rose from his desk to search the leather-bound books on the shelves behind it. Pulling out a Bible, he skimmed it. "Not this one." Returning it, he pulled out a larger one. "Yes, this is it. Read me the seventh commandment. No need for all — only the seventh."

Humoring him, Becky bent down to lean the empty tray against the desk and accepted the Bible from the man who then stood with his hands behind his back as if trying to give a scholarly impression, but to her, it looked as if they were bound behind him. A look she felt suited him.

After quickly flipping through its pages and struggling to hold the heavy book on her forearm, she read, "Thou shall not commit adultery."

"Is that what it says? Read it word for word, slowly."

Having to use both arms to hold the heavy book that was growing heavier by the second, Becky read, "Thou–shall–commit—," and slamming it closed, as if to crush the words that had tried to bite her, she said, "That… that's not correct. That's a… an error."

The man's brief burst of laughter bounced off the log walls. "That's the first printing of The King James Bible," he proudly informed her before relieving her of it and placing it back on the shelf.

"That's an error," she repeated.

"Is it, or does the error lie with the others printed after it?" he asked as he returned to his chair. "Who truly knows if it's an error? Many would say man was not created for merely one woman."

"But not one of those men would be a minister."

He picked up his fork. "That may be so, but that Good Book tells us to commit adultery. Perhaps He had his hand in its wording, made it printed as it is. Perhaps all the following editions are going against His word."

Becky was considering replying that he was trying to benefit from an error in its printing, an error made over a hundred years earlier and since then corrected, when the rapid beating of hoofs and the violent rattling of a cart distracted her.

"Something's wrong!" Philpot growled as he stood up and hurried to a pair of closed shutters to look through the slot. Glimpsing an abnormally large figure sitting on the bed of a long cart as it disappeared toward the back of the house, he barked, "Something's happened! He has King with him!"

With Becky following, he rushed from the study and down the hall, each heavy step of his shoes booming like thunder.

To the right of the kitchen and in front of a semi-covered pigsty with its opened pair of large batten doors revealing a fence, Philpot pushed through a group of four anxious Black women (two graying and two pregnant) standing several feet from a cart parked in front of fourteen single-room log cabins organized into two rows that stretched along the dirt road. "Out of my way or I'll whip the devil out of you! You, Devil's Child! I told you never to be seen by me!" he yelled at the pockmarked boy standing among a group of children watching from a distance, most with a lighter complexion than the women. "Away, all of you!"

"It's Michael. He's hurt, hurt awful," Ben's voice cracked as he sat topless on the bed of the cart tightening a tunic around the thigh of a softly moaning Black man, causing him to moan louder. "His legs, they're ruined from the knee down. Failed to avoid a felled tree."

Standing a dozen feet back, Becky's eyes watered as she watched Philpot stare at the moaning slave whose blood-stained shorts exposed his mangled shins, and after he took a disgusted glance at the giant of a Black man in a blood-stained shirt and shorts sitting and holding the wounded man's limp hand, he grasped the cart's sideboard and released a large huff. Turning around, he raised both fists and shook them as he barked, "I said be gone, or as He is my witness, I shall enjoy whipping the devil out of each one of you!" With the children and the sobbing women scurrying away, he turned to Ben. "And King? Why's he here? Why's he not felling?"

"Thinks the fault's his. Refused to stay, and I dare not refuse him. Enjoy my head too much."

"And is it his fault?"

"He brought it down but can't be expected to know where everyone is when he can only perform one task at a time."

"Then I would say the fault is yours! Your task, your only task is to oversee them, and you failed!" Receiving an ashamed look from the twenty-five-year-old apprentice overseer, he continued. "Have King carry him into his cabin and then take the meal to the boys, ready or not. Lord knows they're sitting around watching those trees grow!" Pausing for a moment, he said, "No, it would be better to place him in King's cabin, and he can stand outside to keep him from being disturbed. Hear me, King? You're to keep all from disturbing him." Receiving a nod from the watery-eyed giant, Philpot turned to Becky. "Girl, why are you standing over there shocked? They're not your crushed legs! Go cover King's bed with flour sacks three deep to catch the blood before these two lay him down. We need not ruin a fine tick with this. After that, quiet the boy with a few gulps of rum, but not the red-glazed bottle, the guest bottle, the green one. He may empty it if he feels the need. After that, take a horse and ride to Richards'. Ben, why do you stand there? Carry him to the cabin… and where's your shirt?"

"Used it to tie off his legs."

"And where the bloody hell are your pistols, sword, and whip?"

Ben looked down at his waist. "I-I must have removed them to help him."

"You don't remember? Boy, I say you have the sense of a worm! How you've lasted this long is beyond me!" Philpot hissed. Then after shaking his head, he added, "Put on a shirt before you go. We need not have others thinking I don't clothe you. And when you take their meal, tell Mary to prepare me another. I shall not eat a cold one because of this idiocy, and I say I shan't be starving until the next!"

After placing a dozen empty flour sacks over King's bed and before riding out to fetch the doctor, Becky rushed to the kitchen, dreading having to inform Mary of the accident but preferring she heard it from her first.

Having heard only a little of what was going on near the cabins, Mary and Ann were eager to know what had happened and to whom, and when Becky entered the kitchen, they could tell by her state that the situation was bad and that it involved one of their men.

She didn't get beyond saying, "M-Mary," when Ann wrapped her arms around her shocked friend and uttered a short moan that stated everything she needed to say.

After Becky struggled to tell them of Michael's accident, Mary pulled her hand from Ann's, saying, "I want to be alone," and as Ann shook her head, spraying her tears, Mary raised her voice to say, "Yes, I need to be alone!" And then she confused Becky by whispering, "I must collect myself to tell my Michael goodbye."

Mary would never tell Becky to leave, but by ordering Ann out of the kitchen, she knew Mary wanted her out too, and after she reluctantly followed the thin, silent woman out, the older woman closed the door behind them, making it the first time Becky had seen it closed during the day.

Waiting outside the kitchen for several seconds, she quietly opened the door a crack to give the heat an escape.

**

A middle-aged man with a short graying beard that matched his head of hair entered Philpot's log-walled study and removed his blood-stained apron. "Well, Charles, it's done… they're done. I made the cuts four inches above the knees."

"Yes, even with the cabin that far off and with only its small window, I could still hear the boy's screams, but what had to be done is done," Philpot frowned as he set his quill in its holder and looked up from the ledger. "And his legs?"

"Wrapped in a sack and left outside the cabin to be buried."

"Good, the pigs shall have a treat today," Philpot smiled. "Why discard what can be eaten, I say."

Nonplussed, the doctor could only stare at him.

"Come, surely you know I'm making jest," Philpot said, losing his smile. "Now, what's to be done next?"

"Keep him inebriated to reduce his pain, and I shall return first thing in the morning to check on him," the man replied as he awkwardly folded the apron.

"Poor early or wealthy early?" Philpot asked as he stood up and grabbed his jacket from off the back of his chair. Putting it on, he hoped to impress the man with it stylishly skirting out at his large waist.

"At six."

"The morrow is Saturday. Let's make it wealthy early, and I shall see you at eight."

Doctor Richards took the offered hand and shook it. "As you wish. Have a blessed evening, Charles."

Philpot smiled. "You as well. Have a safe journey home, my blessed friend."

"And do pass on my condolences to Mary, if you would."

"Mary?"

"Your cook."

"Yes, but why?"

"Is Michael not her husband?"

"Husband?" Philpot asked, staring at the man for a moment before it occurred to him what he meant. "Yes. Yes, I say I do believe Michael is her husband… or mate, as I see it, and I shall inform her of your best wishes."

"My condolences," the doctor corrected him, "Regarding the loss of Michael's legs."

"Yes, that as well. Have a safe journey back and I shall see you at nine in the morning."

"At eight," the doctor corrected him again.

"Yes, eight. Until then, my friend, be well," Philpot said,

forcing a smile as he silently cursed the man for not commenting on his jacket.

CHAPTER 6
Leaving England

As Philip sat on the edge of the bunk watching the large crates that shook, turned, swung, and squealed as they were guided down through the hatch in the floor, William rested on the bunk staring up at the thick beam three feet above him, surprised to find he was already missing his family. He was missing his father, who spoke more through his eyes than his mouth as if it cost sterling to do so. He was missing his mother, who could be stern one minute and amusing the next, missing his two oldest sisters arguing about anything and everything, and he was missing his youngest sister ordering him about and regretting not being able to see her grow into a demanding woman. And then there was his brother, whose reins he had to pull in occasionally. He was missing him too but expected to worry about him more. With his parents placing most of their attention on his sisters and him not there to talk sense into the boy, his brother was sure to find more opportunities to release his boredom through what William considered impulsive and dangerous acts of amusement. Pulling his mind from his brother, he thought he might even miss his neighbors, even the Dangle brothers, who, until he began working in the mine, had tormented him whenever they found an opportunity.

Having tried over the last few weeks to focus only on the positives of his contract (escaping the mine, going to the New World, training for what he considered a profession, and eventually owning land and working for himself), he had refused to consider the enormous distance he was putting between him and his family, and although he knew the cost of travel was expensive (almost four times his yearly sterling as a miner), he had forced himself to believe he would visit his family once his contract had ended, but now, as the reality sank in, he believed it would take at least another seven years after his contract before he could afford the cost and time for the voyage there and back.

Boggled by the number of years before he could return home, the pressure again grew behind his eyes as he worried the years would fog his memory of their faces, and with their facial features changing over time, he feared that when he returned, they wouldn't recognize him and he wouldn't recognize them. Then wondering how their relationship would change after not being in their lives for so long, he questioned if it would be like passing a childhood friend on the street, exchanging pleasantries with little thought to the years they shared together as children. Expecting it to be like that with his ten-year-old sister, it occurred to him that his youngest sister might even forget he exists and he wanted to kick himself for not having had an artist make a pencil sketch of his face for them and sketches of theirs for him, but he gave himself a reprieve when he told himself he would include a sketch in his first or second letter to them and would include a pound sterling for theirs.

With the pressure behind his eyes beyond his control, he rolled away from the redhead sitting at the edge of the bunk and noticed they were less than ten feet from a wall of four chairs, each separated by hanging sheets and each with large holes in their seats and buckets resting beneath them. Rolling his watery eyes to the expectation that the smells would grow much worse, he questioned for the first time if he had been optimistically naive when he had signed the indentured contract and, hours later, proudly informed his family.

Early that Saturday evening, after everyone had finished eating and an hour before he had to work in the mine, he surprised his family by standing up from the table, laying several coins on it, and announcing, "I've some news. I've signed on to a Virginia tobacco plantation as an apprentice overseer, an overseer of their slaves, and that's the sterling for my signature. I'll be departing four weeks from yesterday."

With all sitting stunned while the room seemed to darken and its air seemed to thicken, he returned to the stool next to his oldest sister. Waiting for someone to break the almost painful silence, his eyes bounced among his siblings and parents until the one he didn't expect to, did.

"Why hushy?" whispered his youngest sister squeezed in at the end of the table next to her mother.

As his mother fought through her shock by stroking the child's curly brown hair, his father, sitting at the opposite end and struggling through his mix of emotions, cleared his throat and placed his muscular forearms on the table. "That is… that is quite the news." With all eyes focused on him, he cleared his throat a second time. "I expected something like this to come, but didn't expect it so soon," he said, nodding his disappointment. "Those shillings should pay for the loan of a cart on the day you leave… with a few to spare."

"Why not steal a horse and be sentenced to transportation? We could use a horse," his ten-year-old sister joked, trying to lower the tension in the room.

Nobody laughed and nobody noticed the five-year-old whisper, "I want a horsey," before their mother forced herself up from the table to clear it.

"Then who would know how many years of indenturement I would receive and where they would send me? And Virginia doesn't take anyone sentenced to transportation… and that would make it a better place, yes?"

"It's *indentured service*, not *indenturement!* At least know how to… how to say what you've signed on for!" his mother scolded him with a whisper as a tear escaped an eye.

About to take her husband's wooden bowl, the man placed his hand over hers and shook the small room when he coughed into a handkerchief. "William, I cannot help but believe I failed you, failed this family. A score and six or seven years back, when I was a boy, I too had my head filled with thoughts of adventure and would've joined a ship to see the world if not for my father beating that urge from me. I was barely older than Oscar here, and for years I resented my father for it, but as I aged, as I became an adult, I came to believe he was correct. I may merely labor in the mines, but I have a family, a roof over our head, and see enough sterling to feed and clothe us… but those mines disappoint you, nay, fall short of your appreciation." He coughed into the handkerchief a second time, and after wiping his mouth, added, "I pray it is good enough for Oscar here. I pray he sees it for what it is, an opportunity."

With all expecting a response from the boy, Oscar

confused them by looking down at his empty bowl while hoping his father wouldn't guess his thoughts.

"I could have easily perished with that ship and left no sign of my existence, much like you could in Virginia. I've heard the numbers dying there astounds the mind, and that's only from the diseases, and if we add that to the many more opportunities to die, like your ship sinking, you're putting your life completely in His hands."

Not able to hide his disappointment with his father's reaction, William replied, "Our life is always in His hands."

"You know what he means to say!" his mother whispered as his father released her hand so she could take his bowl. "It's best not to burden Him with all the responsibility, is it not?"

"I don't understand why this should upset us," Oscar said. "We all know he'll change his mind. This is Willy. He'll come to his senses, if not on the morrow, then the next day or the day after that. This is like three years back when he was telling everyone he was going to jump from Groaning's Point. For a week he talked about it, and then when up there, he couldn't do it! It's only fifteen feet, and he hasn't jumped from it yet, even after seeing me survive the splash thrice! Why take this seriously when we all know he's certain to back down from this too?"

"That's enough!" the patriarch barked, causing the boy to look down at his bowl again.

Picking up the boy's bowl, the mother looked at her oldest daughter. "Alice, that roll will not eat itself."

Passing the bread roll to Oscar, Alice said, "I heard they have to pull the plows themselves because they don't have horses."

After the youngest daughter slapped the table and yelled,

"I want a horsey! I love horsies," the second oldest added, "Henry's mother said the sun there turns people darker than a Negro, and it's so 'ot they cook on the rocks."

"It's *hot*, not *'ot!* Speak properly! We may be poor, but we need not announce it!" the mother scolded the girl.

Seeming not to have heard the girls, their father cleared his throat. "You're not nearly as impulsive as Oscar here, and I expect you've given this some thought before signing the contract, and if that's correct, why not discuss this with me... with us before now?"

"I've been considering it since the last time the agents came around... when I wasn't of age, and they gave me no time to reflect on it. Told me there were more than enough men applying. I also expected you to be proud when I surprised you with the news, and if not proud, then impressed that I took action to better myself. I'll learn a trade, and when my contract ends, receive two sets of clothes and six pounds five. I receive no land, but could easily purchase five acres to do with as I please. I would be a landholder. Your son would be a landholder."

"We would be proud and impressed if we weren't so worried," his mother said, defeated. "I've never heard of such an overseer, an overseer of slaves, but then we're far from the colonies and I expect there are different overseers there than here. What does one do? What does it require?"

"I watch over the slaves. The agent told me I make certain they're sheltered, fed, and in good form... safe, healthy, and happy, he told me."

His father coughed into his handkerchief. "I'll admit that such duties suit your temperament."

"If he can't look after himself, how can he be expected to

look after others?" Oscar cut in. "He even refuses to stand his ground! But then it makes no difference if he's going to change his mi—"

"Nevertheless, I can't help but feel you should've given it more time, much more time for consideration," their father continued. "There can't be too many interested if the agents must come this far from London."

"Perhaps, but it's done now," said William, who then volunteered the few details of his contract as he remembered them being told to him.

Since that evening, William's leaving had become a taboo topic. Even that morning, the last time they would sit at the table as a complete family, nothing was said about it, but then no one said anything. It was their quietest morning meal for as far back as William could remember.

With the hatches' double doors banging shut one level after the other, William sat up, swung his legs over the side of the bunk opposite the redhead, and dropped to the floor.

"You best wear your jacket if you're goin' up. It's promisin' to come down 'ard," warned the older woman from the bottom bunk.

"I'll not be long, Mistress," William said, heading to the staircase.

"It'll be a while before the sky breaks if it even does today," Philip contradicted the woman. "It rained far too hard yesterday to have much to spare today."

William only heard several seconds of the two arguing about the weather before their voices mixed in with those he passed on his way to the staircase so steep that the steps were more like wide rungs.

On the ship's deck, he made his way through the drizzle to the growing group of men lining the deck's wall facing the pier, chose a space between two older men shouting their final words to their loved ones, and looked for his family among those standing along the pier. Not seeing them in the crowd, he spotted his ten-year-old sister pulling his youngest along as she walked up the alley across from the ship. Believing he had heard her yell for his brother, the little one confirmed it with her frustration-induced high-pitched scream of, "OSCAR!" To his left in the distance, he recognized the swaying body of his father swinging his arms with each impatient step, and though he couldn't be certain, he thought he glimpsed his mother much further down on his right beyond two groups of sailors who appeared to be preparing for a fight.

William shook his head at his brother's thoughtlessness and guessed that something must have caught the boy's attention to draw him from his family, and he expected that somewhere at that moment he was annoying someone with his thoughts on how to improve whatever it was they were doing.

Though frustrated with his brother, William couldn't help but smile at the thought of Oscar's recent invention that the boy called a horse-stairs carriage. Using a stick to draw in the dirt in front of their row house, the boy described how horses would move a cart without having to pull it. He drew a wide leather belt of triangular wooden blocks that stuck out from the front of a cart at a forty-five-degree angle, making the blocks look like steps, and he described how two horses would walk up the steps while their weight rolled them to the bottom, where they would loop around the underside of the belt to roll up to the top, making them endless. One of the two men operating the cart would control the speed of the front wheels by the axle connected to the rolling steps, and the second would steer it by turning the rear axle.

After William pointed out that the carriage might be too heavy at its front and Oscar decided to balance it with bricks of lead at the back, he stopped himself from mentioning that a cart that heavy would be difficult to move, could be difficult to steer when the horses were blocking the driver's view and could be almost impossible to stop when descending a hill.

A drop of rain hitting his nose brought him back to the present, and with most of the families leaving the pier and most of the passengers leaving the deck, his heart raced, but then it calmed some when it occurred to him that his family wouldn't leave without a final farewell, with or without Oscar.

It raced again when two sailors on the pier removed the ship's ropes from the moorings, and it raced more when they returned to the ship and ordered the few passengers on deck away from the wall so a group of sailors could lift the gangway onto the deck. Watching them remove its roped railing before fastening the gangway to the inside of the deck's wall, William's stomach turned when they dropped back into place the small section of wall they had removed to make the opening for the gangway.

Then more than anything else he needed to wave a last goodbye, needed an opportunity to tell his brother to be smart while looking after himself, and he needed one last chance to memorize their faces. With his stomach becoming more upset, he anxiously walked the main deck searching the pier for his family, and after walking its length three times, his stomach had reached its worst and he rushed to the other side of the ship where next to a heavyset bearded sailor, he vomited bile over the side.

"Oi!" yelled one of two sailors in a small boat twenty-five feet below him, "Watch where yer pukin'! Gorge, move 'im along!"

With the sailor next to the upset one laughing hard as he readied himself to row the boat away from the ship, William tried to apologize to them, but all that came out was more bile.

"Now yer doin' it with purpose!" yelled the sailor, causing his mate to laugh even harder.

The heavyset sailor yelled down, "Better on ya than me, and 'twouldn't've 'appened if ya wasn't daddlin' about." Turning to William, he placed a hand on his shoulder and asked, "'Ave 'er all out of ya, do ya?"

Not sure if he had, William nodded anyway.

"That's a fast seasickness ya 'ave there. 'Aven't left and yer a'ready bringin'er up," smiled the sailor who then startled William by stomping his bare foot on the deck. "Release the slack! Let 'er out!"

Curious, William looked over the side to see a small anchor resting in the boat and the rope attached to it being fed out through a hole in the ship's bow near where the large anchor hung. As the rope piled into the boat, the sailor waved his fist up at him. "Oi! Not again, ya ain't! Ya'll not be wettin' me again with yer insides!"

Too embarrassed to say anything, William watched the men row away, towing the rope behind them, and then with his need to see his family dwarfing his curiosity, he returned to the other side of the ship where he was teased by the distant glimpse of his oldest sister turning into an alley.

After ten minutes of waiting for his family, he tried to take his mind off his disappointment by checking on the progress of the small boat some two hundred feet away, where one of its two sailors was standing and waving his arms.

The large sailor stomped his foot, yelled, "Haul 'er in! Haul 'er in!" and then with singing coming from somewhere below them, he wished William well and walked off.

As the ship gave a slight shake and its bow turned slowly toward the harbor, causing the stern of the ship to creak and grind against the pier, someone asked, "Ya findin' it interestin', are ya?"

"I-I am," William answered, drops of rain falling on his face as he looked up at the sailor standing on a shroud's ratline five feet above him.

"I expects ya thought we'd sail 'er out, eh?"

William nodded.

"Near impossible, and the other way's no more interestin'. A crew o' ten or more rows us. This's slower but less sterlin'," the sailor told him, obviously proud to educate the young man. "That's 'ow she goes, but ya best be gettin' below. The rains comin' and ya don't wants ta fall ill on yer first day."

"Will there be a storm, a storm on our first day?"

"Ya feel them winds tryin' ta push ya about?"

"No."

"There's yer answer," the sailor said, chuckling as he climbed the shroud. "The storm season's a month still, but that ain't ta say we ain't 'avin'em, but less chance o' the worstest until we nears Virginia."

Ignoring the sailor's warning, William remained on the deck until the small boat had again rowed the small anchor out and the ship had pulled itself further from the pier, making the few figures on it too small to recognize.

With the rain coming down harder, he reluctantly returned to the passengers' quarters where he excused himself through a whisper as he passed Philip pulling out from beneath the bottom bunk a set of permanently-stained sheets.

"I don't believe I introduced myself. I'm Philip John Smith the Third," he said, throwing the sheets onto their bunk before offering out his hand.

Having forgotten that Philip had earlier introduced himself, William shook the offered hand. "William… William Henry Lovely… the… the First."

"You're going to Virginia as an indentured?" Philip asked, continuing to grasp William's hand.

William nodded. "I am."

"I am too. I'm presuming all of us are, but I thought there were age limits," he said, with his eyes pointing down toward the woman resting in the bottom bunk.

The woman stuck her head out and barked, "I ain't goin' as one of ya English slaves! My son's paid me way! 'E owns a hun'red acres there! 'E'd be a lord if 'e 'ad the same land 'ere as there!"

"Slaves? We're not slaves," Philip said, looking for confirmation from William who said nothing as he took his hand back and stepped up onto the short ladder.

"You are that," the woman scoffed. "Give ya food, a bed, and shelter, and make ya work for nothin'! That there's a slave!"

Laying himself on the bunk before Philip could spread out the sheets, William stared up at the beams while trying to block out his disappointment with not having his last farewell. Closing his eyes, he tried to block out those around him too.

"But, Your Lady—"

"'Tis Mistress Burns to ya, Philip John Smith the Third, and if you're the third, I don't believe they 'ad it correct that there time too. Maybe with the fourth or fifth," she laughed.

"But, Mistress Burns, I've only signed on for five years, and the slaves have life. And after the term, I'll have two sets of clothes, eight pounds, and a trade."

"Pray ya live that long!"

"I will, and good fortune with the voyage," Philip said as he climbed up to sit on the bunk.

"Good fortune? 'Tis not like I'm swimmin' there!"

Two hours later, after Britain's coast had disappeared, the passengers were called up to the main deck where, as the sailors went about their duties, a tall, clean-shaven man wearing a closed long coat, shoes, and a stern expression approached the crowd of almost eighty men. Seconds later, he was joined by a barefoot and heavyset bearded sailor with his off-white calico shirt hanging over the straining waist of his matching trousers.

"The smart one looks as if he wants to kill us," Philip whispered just loud enough for William and Mistress Burns to hear.

"The other looks as if 'e want to eat us," Mistress Burns added, causing Philip to chuckle and William to recognize him as the sailor he had vomited near.

Without any greetings, the taller man said, "On behalf of Captain Humphreys of *The Colonist*, I, first mate Alexander Markus William Washington, also known as Cump, will state the rules of the ship." With several passengers talking, he raised his voice, "I'll state the rules only once with no leniency for ignorance if broken, so I would suggest you all listen with intent." As the group went silent and all faced the first mate, he continued, "While aboard *The Colonist*, you'll follow the rules of the ship put in place by Captain Humphreys. Break them and you are at his mercy. I'll start by saying the top deck is off-limits to passengers after dark. We want no one falling overboard unnoticed. The penalty for the first offense is one day in the orlop and meals of only rolls and water."

"What's an orlop?" a passenger asked.

"The lowest level."

"Then why not say that?"

"Then let me state it again. The penalty for the first offense is one day in the lowest level with the pigs and meals of only bread—"

"And pork," a passenger from the back yelled, causing others to laugh.

Ignoring the comment, Cump continued, "If you find the air in your quarters bad, it's far worse with the pigs. The penalty for the second offense is one week with the pigs. Next, there will be no inter—"

"What's the punishment for the third?" someone within the crowd asked, causing some to chuckle.

"And the fourth," yelled another from the back, causing William to wonder why so many men could make jokes when leaving their loved ones.

Then a man nearly ten years older than William pushed his way out of the group and rushed to the side of the ship to vomit, causing the heavyset sailor standing near Cump to smile and shake his head.

Ignoring the sick man and the few who joined him when their stomachs turned to the sound of his vomiting, Cump replied, "That is an unknown. No fool has ever broken it thrice, but you're welcome to put an end to your curiosity by being the first to do so. Also, you all should know there is to be no interference with a sailor's duties, nor any attempts to bribe them. The reward for the first offense is five strikes of the whip. The second is ten. There shall be no drunkenness, fighting, or smoking below deck."

"We can do all that up 'ere then?" a passenger asked, causing some to howl with laughter.

With his stern expression unchanged, Cump replied, "That is correct. We only permit smoking on the main deck because of the risk of fire below. Now, unless one of you fools feels the need to demonstrate the punishment for interfering with a sailor's duties, my duties, I would suggest you shut your flycatchers and listen to my every word. There will be no gambling on this ship. You may play games of cards, but not games of dice, and any found will be sent to the bottom of the sea. Anyone caught gambling will receive five strikes, ten for the second offense, and I can tell you that the punishment for the first offense of theft is to be thrown from the ship. I've witnessed it more than once, and for those wondering what the punishment for the second offense is, know that we don't bring you back onboard the ship after throwing you from it. Now then, George Thomas Keeper here will tell you what you can expect as passengers of *The Colonist*, and as he speaks, remember the rule regarding interfering with a sailor's duty."

As the man turned and without a farewell walked to the stern of the ship, Philip looked at William and said, "Well, that was a pleasant fellow. He must have discovered I bedded his sister."

Noticing William with a slight smile, Mistress Burns said, "That proved me wrong. I was thinkin' you and that Cump fella was related. Now don't ya start talkin' or laughin'. My 'eart mightn't take too many surprises in such little time."

The large sailor standing in front of them cleared his throat. "Now then, as Cump said, I'm George Keeper, but ya can call me Gorge. I'm the overseer of the sailors and ya lot, and I'm the ship's surgeon too," he said, straightening up proudly. "If ya need somethin' cut off, I'm always eager to practice the trade." Not receiving the laugh he had expected, he continued. "Now that ya know the ship's rules, let me tell ya what to expect while aboard 'er. First, let me start by tellin' ya that washin' your clothes is done up 'ere, but only when we tells ya. We don't want them blowin' overboard or havin' to dry below, makin' the air worser. We'll inform ya when we expect fit weather for both washin' and dryin', and we'll bring out barrels for just that. Second, everythin' but the rolls is eaten at the table, and since we're short of space, the meals are in two shifts. Pick one and stay with it. Third, there'll be no wanderin' about the two decks below yers or the one above it. 'Tis either in your quarters or 'ere, and durin' a storm, you're to be there. We don't need any of ya lot goin' overboard. Fourth, like on every ship, there're rats on this one too, but that's a good thing. They'll let us know there's a leak. If ya see 'em racin' up the decks in groups, let someone know. Don't be feedin'em and don't be eatin'em." Smiling proudly to the laughter from the passengers, he continued. "Ya might think I'm jestin', but come a month or more, ya might be considerin' doin' just that. And that brings me to the fifth matter, the difference betweens now and then. For the first month we'll eat well, 'avin' a variety, but come the second, things'll be scarce and we'll be eatin' a lot of the same, too much salted-pork stew and hardtacks — them heavy, dry biscuits we sailors sooo enjoy," he said sarcastically. "We'll be short beer, cider, and even water, but we always come through. I'm tellin' ya this cause there ain't no markets from 'ere to there and I don't wants to 'ear no complainin' from ya lot. Lastly, 'tis goin' to be 'otter than 'ell, much 'otter. It'll seem even 'otter down below, but ya'll grow accustomed to it, and like Cump said, ya ain't to be on top after dark, and that means no sleepin' up 'ere too. Now, knowin' what's comin', ya'll not be surprised when it does. Now with all that, any questions?"

"Where da women?" someone asked from within the group.

"Good question and the answer's there're none… or one. Sorry, Mistress." He said, bowing his head to Mistress Burns, who responded with an expression that he should be. "She's a small ship, so there ain't no separate quarters for women, and the captain don't believe in mixin' the two. 'E don't want no part in the women 'avin' years added to their contract seven to nine months after we reach Virginia and 'e don't want ya lot tempted to where 'twould require a 'angin' before bein' thrown to the sea, if ya understands me words. Don't take no children neither, no volunteers nor spirited. Captain Humphreys' a good Christian, a fair and kind one unless ya crosses 'im and then ya'll see the devil come out of 'im."

"Why don't we 'ave our private quarters like theys promised?" a passenger asked as he pushed his way to the front of the crowd. "They said we did."

"Because ya don't. We promised nothin' and can't be responsible for the promises of others."

"I wasn't promised me own quarters!" another passenger complained.

"Then it don't matter none," Gorge smirked through his shaggy beard.

"It bloody does! They was promised, but I wasn't!"

"Uh… oh, and the first shift of the comin' meal is at seven and the second's at eight, and for any of ya with a watch, don't bother with 'em. The ship's rockin' and the 'umidity take 'em off time even more. 'Ere we use a bell system for markin' the time, hours and 'alf hours, in a four-hour watch… uh, period. Ya'll soon find yourself familiar with it." Taking a moment to clear his throat, he added, "And that's all I've to say. A blessed afternoon to all."

After forcing himself to eat some salted pork on the second shift, William learned Philip was the oldest son of a middle-class family who expected him to work in the family business and eventually inherit it, but unlike his younger brothers, he had no interest in it. Instead, he wanted to be an artist, but since that paid poorly, he wanted to learn a trade that required him to use his hands, and when the opportunity came, he signed on as a blacksmith's apprentice in Virginia, which put more than enough distance between him and his disapproving father.

Philip's decision made William more comfortable with his own. If a middle-class and educated man had signed an indentured contract, William couldn't have made a huge mistake by doing the same.

Later that evening, as a distraction from the thoughts of his family, William listened to Philip proudly share his knowledge of Virginia, and when Mistress Burns cut in several times to correct him, the two would argue for a short time.

CHAPTER 7
Maimed Means Dead

Knowing she wasn't welcome in the kitchen that evening while her distraught friend cleaned it alone, Becky ate her meal on the back steps of the house while staring at the closed kitchen door, and with it still bothering her that she wasn't able to convince her friend that Michael had a much better chance of surviving than dying, she wished the sun would set faster and put an end to the day, though she didn't believe the new day would change anything. Her friend would go to bed that night believing Michael would soon die, and the next morning, she would continue to believe it.

Six hours earlier, Mary didn't react when Becky told her that Michael had survived the amputations, but later when she was picking up Philpot and Ben's evening meals and passed on to Mary that Doctor Richards had told her there was little chance of Michael dying, Mary did react, saying in an unfamiliar scolding tone, "I have to say you can be as naive as a newborn, but perhaps you haven't been here long enough to know that for us maimed means dead." And Mary was correct. Becky didn't know that, and with her friend's tone not inviting questions, she left the kitchen without asking why a maimed slave would mean a dead slave.

With the sweeping sounds sneaking out from the kitchen, she expected Mary soon to exit with two buckets of scraps for the pigs, and not wanting to make her friend uncomfortable by her presence, she picked up her plate and entered the house.

**

With the last of the setting sun's rays highlighting the wavy patterns in the panes of several small windows behind him and not ready to touch the roast chicken breast in front of him in fear of it coming back up, Ben was eating his vegetables at an unusually slow pace when he stiffened up to Philpot's fork clanging on his plate.

Having eaten with his usual aggressiveness, as if releasing his anger on the meal, Philpot sat at the end of the table, swallowing the last of his chicken. Releasing a burp, he said, "I do wish pigs could talk. I would like to ask them if they thought Michael's legs were as good as that chicken." With Ben's eyes enlarging, the man's laugh filled the room. "I jest, lad. They were buried behind their cabins. But I say it's strange how we can feed them the leg of a horse, but most feel it wrong to feed them the leg of a slave."

Ben laid his fork on his plate, fought to control his turning stomach, and was thankful when Becky entered the room.

As she placed a red bottle and two pewter cups in front of him, Philpot said, "Becky, I'm done with my meal. Ben, are you finished?"

Knowing what the man wanted to hear, Ben replied, "Yes, I... I'm finished."

"Becky, after returning these dishes, relieve the boy of some of his pain with the last three swallows for the night, or perhaps it would benefit him if he has six. I say that much should make him sleep. If he refuses them, use your way with King and have him help you force it down his throat. And after that, send King to Michael's cabin. I don't want him in our way when we check on the boy before bedding down ourselves. Nobody's fed him, correct?"

"Correct," she nodded.

"Good. It should have a stronger effect on him, I say."

After Becky removed the dishes and her footsteps faded off down the hall, Philpot poured rum into each cup and handed one to Ben. "Today was not a prosperous day."

"It was not," Ben said, shaking his head before turning his mind to the cup of rum that confused him since the man only served it during a rare celebration.

"To a better day on the morrow," Philpot said, raising his cup.

"To a better day on the morrow," Ben repeated, raising his shaking cup and following Philpot in downing the liquid through several quick gulps. Successful in holding back his urge to vomit, he failed to hold back his cough.

"I say that's a good thing. It shows you're not accustomed to it, didn't make it your second master," Philpot said as he again poured rum into their cups. Filling them almost to the top, he frowned. "I lost a boy today, lost labor... and sterling too. I need not tell you he was in demand. Always the first to be rented from what you told me, correct?"

"Correct," Ben nodded, finding it strange the man talked as if Michael was dead.

"It would have been better to lose him on the spot, I say. You should have let him bleed... and you also destroyed a good shirt. He may live, but he shall be a burden. Needs to be looked after and moved about by another, making it a loss of two today."

"I-I'm confident I can come up with something for him to do."

Philpot's eyebrows rose as he challenged the indentured servant with a stare. "And when he needs to relieve himself or has to move about?"

"We can have King carry him when needed."

"As I said, one broken slave costs me two," Philpot hissed before forcing a smile. "Lad, I think you're failing to see the obvious. We have to be rid of him, and before Richards returns and I see a second unnecessary expense come from this."

"You… you're saying we should end his life?"

"No, I'm saying we should relieve him of his misery."

"It's… it's the same thing and… and goes against the law. They… he has rights, and he's not yours to put down," Ben said, surprising himself with his assertiveness and then fearing it.

"Are you telling me what I cannot do, stripling!?" Philpot hissed. "He may not be mine to dispose of, but I'm acting on Chalmers' interest! As his agent, I do what must be done for the benefit of this estate!" Philpot took a moment to calm himself, before again forcing a smile. "And you say he has rights? Do they have rights? If that's true, then why do we hear nothing of it in the courts? Do you know why that is?" Ben shook his head meekly. "When no one knows of it, no laws are broken. Who would tell the tale? One of them? They can't bear witness. And this is not the first time I've had to put one down, not the first to be injured badly. I've put down two since your arrival. The younger ones. Both clearing branches. The one that hurt its back by a fall from the top and the other that lost an arm a short time before Jeremiah retired. Being children, I performed the mercy myself, and like the others, you believed they died in their sleep," Philpot said, pausing a moment to stare at Ben's shocked face. "I say this to you because what happens on this estate doesn't leave this estate, and you shall have to do the same with the next plantation's slaves you oversee. And what of that woman whose name escapes me, the one from the Isle of Wight? The one the bastard John Clayton tried to convict last year for beating her house boy to death. It was obvious she did the deed, but yet they acquitted her, though I expect it helped to have her husband on the court." Pausing to stare at Ben, he asked, "What does one do when a horse breaks a leg?"

"P-put it down," Ben replied, well aware of the point the man was about to make.

"Exactly, and you shall help me put this two-legged one down, this no-legged one," Philpot smirked. "And you should consider yourself fortunate you have to do it for the first time only months before you leave," he said, before raising his cup of rum. "So to an unfortunate event, and shall there be no more of them."

Feeling the effects of his first cup, Ben's shaking hand dripped his second cup of rum as he raised it and followed the man in emptying it.

"And one more for the courage to give mercy to the boy, but I say after this last cup, we may need reminding why we're drinking," Philpot smirked as he filled their cups again. Then sliding his small silver snuffbox over to Ben, he said, "But first, take two pinches. It too shall help calm you and make all smell like roses, literally, at least for a moment."

**

Carrying a green-glazed ceramic bottle, Becky used the

moonlight to guide her through what Philpot called Philpot Lane with its log cabins on the right and on its left, the semi-covered pigsty, a fenced-in chicken coop, several sheds, and a smaller log cabin, which was her destination.

"King, would you open the door for me?"

The wide giant sitting on the dirt with his back against the cabin's door rose to his feet. "Master me say one no come."

Becky sighed. "He wants to keep the others out, but I'm to give him his… his medicine, remember?"

After pausing for several seconds to consider what she said, King removed the beam barring the door, opened it, and followed her in, ducking under the opening to stand near the bed Michael was resting in.

Becky set the bottle down next to a burning candle and a wooden cup resting on a small tripod table. "Blessed evening, Michael," she whispered and then wanted to kick herself for saying it. There was nothing blessed about that evening.

"Good evening, Becky," the short-bearded Black man whispered back with a slight slur. "More medicine?"

"The last for tonight, but a double portion," she whispered as she picked up the wooden cup and poured some rum into it. Making sure not to look where his legs should have been, she bent down, gently raised his head, and placed the cup to his lips. "If you gulp it, as you did earlier, you can have it over with." With a nod from the man, she watched with pity as he struggled to swallow what she slowly poured into his mouth. After he coughed and cringed, she lowered his head and poured more into the cup, and when he coughed harder halfway through the second *dosage*, causing some to drip from his nose, she lowered his head, placed the cup on the table, and pulled the sheet up to his neck. "That's all we'll take of that tonight."

"Sleep well, Becky, King."

"You also, Michael."

Picking up the bottle, she bent down to blow out the candle but stopped when she remembered Philpot would be checking on him.

"Sorry me," King said to Michael. "Me bad."

"Sorry? Bad? No, it's my fault, my friend," Michael whispered. "If not for my carelessness, I wouldn't be lying here," Michael said before the two left him.

Outside of the small cabin, Becky looked up at King. "Master says you're to go to Michael's cabin until he's well again. Michael's children can share a bed."

"Come, you?"

"Not this evening," she said, and then moved by the disappointment covering his large, round face, she offered out the bottle. "Here. This might help you sleep better tonight. Could keep away the unpleasant dreams. Take two swallows."

The giant wrapped his lips around the bottle's stem and struggled to swallow the liquid rushing into his mouth. Forced to swallow four times, he pulled the stem from his mouth and gasped for air.

"It's difficult to believe we English drink it for enjoyment, yes?" she asked the giant, who coughed as he handed back the bottle.

"Burns," he said, pointing to his neck.

"It does, but it should help you sleep."

He lowered his hand to point at his stomach. "Burns."

"It does, and that means it's working."

Lowering his hand to point at his groin, his face showed his fear as he asked, "Burns?"

Becky had to hold herself back from laughing. "Not that I've heard, and I would've heard if it did."

With the fear leaving his face, Becky watched him turn and do his usual swaying side to side as he walked toward the log cabins, his giant, intimidating body reminding her of the shock she had experienced when first seeing his six-foot-two towering figure and his seemingly just as wide frame before she understood he was a creature of compassion rather than intelligence. A man who, if he was never told he would sink, would run across the water to save a drowning soul.

**

Certain that Becky had gone to her room and not noticing Mary leaving the small cabin to sneak off to the larger ones, the two quietly made their way toward it.

Following the large man into the cabin, Ben vomited at its entrance, and then with his stomach empty, closed the door behind him, stood where Michael's legs should have been, and stared at the door, hoping someone would enter.

"Mashter?" Michael slurred.

"Hush, boy. I expected you to be sleeping," Philpot whispered. "Ben, let us do what we must, and do it quickly." With Ben continuing to stare at the door, the man's voice rose. "Don't be turning into a coward, boy! Have to it! The faster we do this, the better for all."

With the rum still spinning his head, Ben continued to stare at the door.

"Boy, come to your senses!"

"shenshesh?"

"Not you!" Philpot growled. "Ben. Ben!"

"Whath're you doing?"

Ben turned nervously to look at Michael.

"Whath're you—"

Pinching Michael's nose with one hand and covering his mouth with the other, Philpot said, "Grab his arms, boy! Grab them now! I can't do this myself!"

With Michael's desperate hands trying to grab at Philpot's determined hands, Ben's shaking hands reluctantly held Michael's down.

Just after midnight, a baritone scream covered the plantation, and seconds later, it was followed by the wails of infants.

**

With her mind stuck on Mary's unwavering belief that Michael would die, Becky struggled to fall asleep, and when she did finally pull her mind away from Mary by convincing herself that her friend would change her mind once she saw him recovering, Becky's mind was stuck on her desire to unite with her family on an estate just outside of Boston where slavery wasn't nearly as prominent as it was in Virginia.

Like most others, Becky had once believed slavery was a necessary evil, one where Virginia couldn't function without it, but with her new duties requiring her to interact with the plantation's slaves to where she had befriended them, trusted them and they trusted her, she viewed slavery not only as an evil but as an attraction for it. It attracted people so cruel that she couldn't help but feel only those with a need for cruelty could be truly content in Virginia, but that would mean only a small portion of its population was truly content when she considered over half the souls in Virginia were slaves, a good portion of the English were indentured servants, or what Becky considered temporary slaves, and the larger portion of English who weren't indentured and didn't own slaves were in a constant struggle to exist.

Only a few months back, Becky had planned to leave Virginia with her fiancé, Peter. They were to marry three days after his contract ended, almost seven weeks from that night, and soon after that they would sail north, where they would begin their family.

An indentured servant to a printer in Williamsburg and with no newspaper in Virginia, Peter had accepted an offer as a typesetter for The Boston News-Letter to start almost a month after they were married, but he didn't finish his indentured contract. On a Sunday afternoon, while making his regular trip to see Becky, he was thrown from his borrowed horse when it tripped over a rope stretched across the road — an assumed child's prank. The horse broke a leg, and he broke his neck, ending their courtship that had begun several months before she took the position as governess to Philpot's daughter.

Becky still planned to leave Virginia, needed to leave it, but after Peter's death, she decided to stay to help Margaret recover from her illness, the only good that could come from her being there.

Waking for the fifth time from her light sleep, she gave up on it and decided to bring Michael his rum early and offer Mary an hour alone with him before the woman began preparing the morning meals.

In her inebriated-like state caused by her lack of sleep, she fought to keep her balance as she carried the bottle of rum to King's cabin where she presumed Ben had forgotten to bar it. Opening the door, she found Mary kneeling at the side of Michael's bed. "How is he?" she asked.

The older woman turned her head, revealing her red puffy eyes and the wet streaks running down her cheeks. "Maimed means dead," she whispered.

CHAPTER 8
Capture and Compromise

In the darkness near the back of the narrow passageway built into the stacks of secured crates, he cuddled the sleeping piglet while listening to the two sailors dragging each crate to the opened gate of the pigsty, prying off a side, and forcing the squealing piglets into the fenced in space. After the crates were emptied and stacked, he listened to them spreading the hay in the pigsty, pouring corn into some troughs and water into the others, and then after they extinguished four of the eight candles in the hanging lanterns, he listened to them climbing the stairs while complaining about having to clean the pigsty later.

A minute after the hatch above the stairs dropped shut, the hundred-plus piglets fighting for space at the troughs of kernels stopped to stare up at Oscar, who satisfied his thirst with several cupped hands of water before grabbing a fist of the dried kernels and swallowing several. With his growling stomach reminding him he needed to come up with a plan if he wanted to eat something besides dried corn, he sat with his back against the outside of the fence, fed kernels to Gibby, and decided that during the night, he would familiarize himself with the levels of the ship, and in the morning, would mix in with the passengers, find his brother, and hide day and night in his private quarters. He knew William wouldn't be happy with him coming along, but he knew too that after his brother berated him, he would give in.

With nothing around to interest him and the excitement of the day having exhausted him, the boy fell into a deep sleep.

He woke to the bored piglet softly chewing on the toe of his leather shoe, and not knowing how long he had slept in the windowless belly of the ship that was then gently rocking, he looked at a burning candle of a lantern for a hint, but it told him nothing since he didn't notice how tall it was before he had fallen asleep. And the two muffled rings of a bell from somewhere above told him nothing too since he had yet to know it was used to mark the time. Guessing it was somewhere between ten and midnight, he decided to explore the ship's levels.

As he grabbed onto the fence and pulled his stiff body to his feet, he heard footsteps and froze when the hatch above the stairs opened. He stayed frozen when the light of a lantern revealed bare feet on the top step, but when they were followed by the legs of trousers, he dove over the short fence to land among the snoring piglets who squealed when they woke.

A tall, thin sailor picked up the piglet protesting being left alone and placed it in the pigsty, and then watching it run through the crowd of piglets to what looked like a pile of stained clothes, he took a few seconds to make sense of it before unsheathing his long knife. "Well, well, well."

**

Lying on his side facing away from Philip, William struggled to sleep through the rhythmic creaking, the constant snoring, the occasional farting, and the lingering smell of that evening's meal mixing in with both the body odors and the fumes rising from the buckets beneath the four chairs. With the gentle rocking of the ship not hastening his sleep as he had hoped it would, he found he was missing his comfortable cupboard bed and even the lone snoring of his brother.

Having finally fallen into a light sleep, he woke to what sounded like his brother's protests, but when the sounds, the smells, the rocking, and his bedmate reminded him he wasn't home, he knew that couldn't be possible. Believing it a trick of the mind, maybe the start of a dream, he thought about the short scolding his brother would have received from his father and the not-so-short one his mother would have given him. He expected too that his three sisters would've let the boy know how angry they were with him for delaying their annual purchase of fabric, maybe even forcing their parents to postpone it, and he wished he were there to witness it, not because he wanted to see his brother being scolded, but because he wanted to see his family again, though he would've appreciated a chance to scold him for ruining their final farewell.

**

"Oi! Release me and I'll follow!"

"Come along, my two-legged pig," the sailor laughed.

With the sailor pulling him up to the main deck by his ear, Oscar ignored the cool breeze that he would've appreciated and failed to notice the clear sky with its innumerable stars scattered along the three-hundred-and-sixty-degree horizon that would've impressed him.

"Come, pig!"

"Better watch yourself! My father's an admiral!"

"He is, is he?" the sailor asked while pulling him along toward a door near the stern of the ship.

"He is! He'll have your head for this!"

"He will, will he? What's his name?"

"I just told you! It's Father!"

"I caught a regular Sir Newton. Come, pork chop."

"Eh, what 'ave ya there?" asked a sailor descending the shrouds.

"Caught a two-legged pig hiding with the four-legged ones. I'm thinking they packed one extra."

"I'm not a pig!" Oscar protested as the number of sailors following them grew.

"Enter," a baritone voice replied to the knock on the door.

"Captain Humphreys, I caught a trespasser," the sailor said proudly as he entered the captain's large quarters lit by six lanterns hanging from its walls. "Hiding with the pigs," he explained as he pulled the boy to the man's desk while seven other sailors entered to stand near the door.

Oscar's anger at being pulled by his ear was cast aside momentarily by his curiosity with the room that, besides having an array of curious oddities on its walls, had a large, neatly-made four-poster bed at the back near a row of three large windows.

Standing at the front of the desk, Cump straightened up from examining the map covering it, and with a stone face, moved to the side to reveal a middle-aged man sitting behind it. With his long salt-and-pepper hair in a ponytail and his clean white shirt unbuttoned at the neck, the man placed a small but heavy compass on the map before leaning back in his chair to look curiously at Oscar. "This is rather unusual," he said, and then, looking up at Cump standing at the side of the desk, he asked, "Would you agree, Cump?" With a nod from the stone-faced man, the older man rubbed his short, graying bearded chin. "In all my years, I have never had the pleasure of a trespasser, perhaps because they would starve before the end of our journey, and perhaps that is why a child is my first."

Oscar's eyebrows turned in. "I'm not a child!" he protested, and then looking at the sailor still holding him by the ear, added, "And not a pig!"

The captain flashed a subtle smile. "And it took all of you to catch one boy? He must be surprisingly fast for his size… and, John, you may release him. He can go nowhere with all of you blocking the door as you are."

"Aye, Captain Humphreys," John nodded before releasing Oscar's ear and flicking it with his finger, causing the boy to raise his fist and the sailors to laugh. "And it was only I who caught him, but I expect they want to see the show, see what comes of him."

"A show? Well, I hope we don't disappoint. He was hiding with the pigs, you say?" the captain asked, lacing his hands together and resting them against his flat stomach.

"Hiding in the pigsty, and since pigs don't wear no breeches, he wasn't difficult to notice," John grinned while the others laughed.

"Ha! You just said pigs wear breeches!" Oscar corrected him. "You used a negative twice, and that makes it contrary to what you meant!"

"I'll show you contrary," John growled, drawing back a leg to strike him.

"That will be enough," the captain ordered before looking past Oscar to a small, husky sailor. "Sledge, would you keep the time until John returns to it?"

"I would, Cap'ain 'Umphreys, but I'm on watch fer another 'alf hour."

"And what are you watching at this moment?"

"I... I... as you wish, Cap'ain," frowned the sailor, who bowed and left the room while releasing several curses under his breath.

"Now then, trespasser, come forward."

Oscar took a step forward to stand against the front of the desk. "I'm not a trespasser. I have my paper... had my paper," Oscar lied, unconvincingly.

"Your full name, if you please."

"I'm not a trespasser."

"Your name?"

"William... William Harry Lovely."

"'Tis a *lovely* name," a sailor laughed, causing the others to laugh with him.

"Age?"

"Eighteen," Oscar replied, and then, seeing the question in the captain's eyes, added, "A... a short eighteen."

"But not no thin one," another sailor added, causing the group to laugh again.

"William Harry Lovely, a short eighteen," the captain repeated back before opening a desk drawer and shuffling through several papers. Pulling one out, he said, "Well, let us see. Lovely... William Harry Lov—here we are. Lovely... William *Henry*, eighteen, born—" He cut himself off to look at Oscar. "You were brought into this world when?"

The boy thought for a moment. "January twenty... twenty-second, sixteen… sixteen ninety-seven."

"The month and year are correct, but the day is not. This states the twenty-seventh, not the twenty-second."

Oscar's face reddened. "I-I said the seventh. You heard the second, but I said the seventh."

Captain Humphreys looked at the tall sailor who had brought Oscar to him. "John, please find William Lovely and bring him here."

"Will do, Captain," the sailor nodded.

"But I am here!" protested Oscar, who was then more concerned about his brother scolding him in front of the sailors than what the captain would do with him.

"Yes, you are, but William Henry Lovely is not."

William woke to his name, but believing it was another trick of the mind, he tried to return to his sleep.

"Lovely, William Lovely," a man called out again.

"I'm William Lovely," he forced out, causing Philip to mumble something incoherent.

"Present yourself on the deck!" the man demanded.

"Shut it! Tryin' ta sleep 'ere!" a passenger complained from somewhere among the rows of bunks.

Confused and a little scared, William put on his breeches and tucked his nightshirt into them. Dropping from his bunk, he glanced at Mistress Burns, who was lying on her bunk looking up at him, and rushed off to the stairs in his bare feet.

"You're William lovely?" John asked as William joined him at the stairs.

"I am," William whispered as the sailor looked him up and down.

"The captain wants to see you in his quarters. Follow me."

William's face flushed as he stiffly followed John to the main deck and then to the stern of the ship. After he followed him through the door, the sailors, whose tight grouping magnified their body odor, moved to the side to create a short path to the captain sitting behind his desk. Nervously walking up to it, William didn't notice his brother through his tired and confused state until he was standing beside him. "Oscar? Oscar!" With a smile covering his face, he hugged his awkward little brother whose arms hung at his sides. Then realizing the strangeness of the situation, he released him and questioned if he had finally fallen into a deep sleep. "W-what are you doing here? How is it you're here, here on this boat? Why do you smell so... did you relieve yourself in your breeches?"

"It's called a ship, and it was the pigs," Oscar said, adding to his brother's confusion.

"And who would you be?" the captain asked.

"Uh... William Lovely... William Henry Lovely," he replied as he forced his attention from his brother to the man behind the desk.

"'Tis a *lovely* name," a sailor said, repeating the earlier joke that still caused laughter.

The captain raised his hands, and as the laughing stopped, asked, "Date of your birth?"

"January twenty-seventh, sixteen ninety-seven. What's happening here?"

"I am Captain Humphreys. Captain of this ship that your friend trespassed aboard and I now believe did so by hiding in a crate of pigs... piglets."

William shook his head. "He's... he's not my friend. He's my brother, Oscar... Oscar Harry Lovely,"

"Brother... I see. That makes more sense... if sense can be made of this."

Glaring at his brother, William said, "You're in much trouble! If Father and Mother haven't dropped dead from worry, I expect they'll hang, draw and quarter you when you're back home, but only once if He's watching over—"

"William, he will not be returning home. We will not be turning back because of a trespasser," the captain said, and then looking past the brothers to the group of sailors, he grew a smile. "But since you mentioned being hanged, drawn, and quartered, we must decide what to do with this extra pig, what to do with him as an example to others who might consider trespassing aboard this ship."

"I'm not a pig!" Oscar protested before silently scolding himself for possibly angering the man who was about to decide his punishment.

"What say you, men? What shall we do with Oink here?" he asked with a smirk.

Oscar was about to protest the name when a sailor behind him said, "I say we whip 'im. Find the whip an' 'ave at 'is back!"

"No," the captain said, shaking his head at the grinning sailors. "We had one several days back. Let us have something different."

"Let's dunk him!" demanded another.

The captain again shook his head. "No, we had that before our last whipping,"

"Tie 'im ta da mast fer a day or two."

"'Ave 'im walk the plank!"

With William and Oscar's eyes trying to escape from their heads, their jaws dropping, and the group of sailors fighting to hold back their laughter, the captain shook his head again. "Gentlemen, are we pirates? No, let us have something more creative, something he will remember for the rest of his days… if he lives to see more of them. What say you, Cump?"

Still wearing his stone face, Cump replied, "A keelhauling, Captain. It has been far too long since we were entertained by one."

"Aye, we 'aven't 'ad that fer so long, I clear forgots we calls it a 'aulin' and not a maulin'," a sailor laughed.

Those loudly agreeing to the keelhauling went quiet when Captain Humphreys raised his hand. "Oink, are you familiar with keelhauling?"

The boy shook his head, not caring that he was again called Oink.

"We tie a long rope to your wrists, another to your ankles, and pull you under the keel from starboard to larboard. You will hope to drown along the way, but you will not. If the barnacles fail to tear you open enough to bleed you dry, you will wake on the deck coughing out the water before going around again. It is a longer show than a whipping or a walking of the plank, and therefore more entertaining. What say you to that?"

Oscar could only shake his head as he released a tear.

"Come, you must have something to say about that."

With all waiting for the boy to speak, William forced himself from his shock to look at his teary-eyed brother before looking at the captain, who seemed either ashamed for upsetting his brother or ashamed to have to perform such a gruesome act. "Punish me. Killhaul me. He can take my place and I'll take his."

"No, you won't, Willy!" Oscar almost shouted as tears ran

down his cheeks. "Killhaul me, Captain! I trespassed! I'm to be punished!"

"I'm older! I'm responsible for you!"

"You left! You lost that responsibility! And you had no say in my trespassing! I'll take my punishment, but I won't stand in the way of your guilt! That's your reward for leaving me!"

"That's correct! I leave and you immediately do something stupid! That's my fault, and they should punish me for it, for not asking Father to tie you to him!" William countered, his eyes watering in response to his brother's. "I gave notice! I told them I was going! You, you just left on this boat without a word!"

"It's called a ship, stupid!"

"I'm certain they're going mad trying to understand what happened to you… because you were being *stupid*!"

"NO, YOU WERE, WILLY!"

"NO, YOU WERE!"

"NO, YOU ARE! YOU EVEN CALLED THIS A BOAT! IT'S A SHIP, NOT A BOAT!" Turning to the captain who was grinning at them, Oscar shouted, "IS THAT CORRECT, CAPTAIN? IT'S A SHIP, CORRECT?"

As the sailors released their laughter, Captain Humphreys dropped his grin. "Everyone, calm down if you please." Waiting for silence, his eyes bounced from brother to brother. "If you two have finished fighting for the opportunity to be killhauled… keelhauled. It is called keelhauling, not killhauling, and no one is to be keelhauled today. Oink, Willy, we are only jesting," he said, and then looking at the few disappointed faces among the sailors crowded behind the brothers, added, "Or some of us were."

Oscar wiped a tear as a bell gave a double and then a single ring. "It's Oscar, Captain, and he hates being called Will or Willy."

"It is Oink while you are on my ship. We give sea names as respect. Is that so, *John*?" With the sailor nodding meekly, the captain continued, "And seeing how you were brave enough… or was it stupid? There can be a fine line between the two and sometimes it is difficult to know the difference until some time has passed. Still, since you hid in a crate of pigs, I feel calling you Oink is appropriate. And while you were arguing with your brother, a thought came to me, and if you two would each unhook a chair from the wall and bring it here, I will share it with you. As for the rest of you, the show is over. You may return to your duties."

As William and Oscar, who was then flattered to be called Oink, each unhooked a chair and slid them over to the captain's desk, John whispered to the younger brother. "I've only been on this ship for a few months now."

"I've been on it less than a day… and have my sea name, *John*," Oscar grinned, causing the captain to smile.

After a red-faced John closed the door behind him and William and Oscar took their seats in front of his desk, Captain Humphreys stared at them for a moment before asking, "Oink, do you know much about our destination?"

"No, but for me, it's more about being with him than where we are."

Captain Humphreys forced down his empathetic smile, nodded, and said, "I see. You would like to join him with the same master with whom he has a contract?"

"Yes. Yes, I would," Oscar nodded, before realizing Cump was still there and hadn't moved from the spot at the side of the desk since the boy had entered the room. "Can I bring you a chair… uh, Cump?"

"No," the captain answered for the man. "He likes to stand while he works. William, do you have your contract with you?"

"No, but it'll only take a minute to find it."

"That will not be necessary. Do you remember the name on it?"

"Chalmers."

The captain's face went grim before he cleared his throat. "I know the plantation… know of it. Lord Chalmers owns a portion of this ship… owns part of the company that owns it. How long is your contract?"

"Seven years."

"And you are to be an apprentice overseer, an overseer of slaves?"

"Yes," William said, confused. "How di—"

"It is the only servant he contracts for, the only male servant he contracts for, since he has enough slaves to do the field work. Lord Chalmers is an absentee landowner, and Charles Philpot, his agent, oversees his plantation." Then looking at Oink, he asked, "Oink, how old are you?"

"Eleven."

"Eleven? You could easily be mistaken for twelve, which is what we will need to make him believe, but even at that age and with Philpot not needing another indentured, I doubt he would take a contract without making your term ten years… if he would take it at all." As the brothers' disappointed eyes dropped to the floor, the captain paused for a moment. "At this time, I only see two options. The first would be to place you in an auction in Virginia, but that would only mean you would receive an indentured contract, but not with Chalmers' plantation. The second option would be to lower the cost of the contract by lowering the cost of bringing you there, making it difficult for Philpot to refuse, and since we are a man short, we could have you two perform some menial but necessary tasks until we reach Virginia. With those two options, the only two that come to mind as I sit here, which would you two prefer, auction or labor?"

"Labor, Master... Captain Humphreys," William answered for the two of them.

With his eyes lighting up, Oscar slapped William's shoulder. "See, we can be together! See, I wasn't stupid!"

William wanted to throw some harsh words at his brother, but, instead, he forced a smile and nodded his head.

"You were stupid," Cump said, startling the brothers. "But you were fortunate as well. Another captain might only take you along if he witnessed you walking on water."

"Then labor it is, and, William, you may come to appreciate it. The voyage can be rather uninteresting," Humphreys said before taking a moment to look at the sheet of paper he had earlier pulled from his desk. "It states here you are from Kendleshire. Is that correct?" With both brothers nodding, he said, "On our arrival, I will send a letter there to inform your parents of your situation." Then taking a moment to stare curiously at the brothers, he added, "I believe I have a sister in your village, a mining village. Sarah Humphreys... or I should say Downing. Do you know—"

"Yes," Oink nodded.

"We know her and her husband, Richard Downing... and their six children," William said.

"Six now?" the Captain asked, his eyebrows rising with

his smile.

William nodded.

"He's Dick to us, and we *knew* her," Oscar added.

"Knew her?"

Ignoring William's foot striking his shin, Oscar said, "She died last winter. Caught the chills."

"Died?" the captain asked, his eyes bouncing from brother to brother.

"Last winter," Oscar nodded.

"Last Winter? I… I suppose I deserve to hear it this way by my jesting earlier… unless… unless you are returning my jest in kind. Are you returning my jest in kind?" the man asked, hoping for a positive response.

With William not knowing what to say, Oscar shook his head.

Then staring down at his desk for a moment before taking a deep breath and looking at William, Captain Humphreys said, "All… all is settled then. William, if you could shout for Gorge from the door, we will inform him of our arrangement."

William went to the door, opened it, and looked back at the captain, who was again staring down at his desk.

Cump said, "Yell, Gorge, the captain requests your presence."

"George—"

"Gorge," Cump corrected him, "And yell louder."

"GORGE, THE CAPTAIN REQUESTS YOUR PRESENCE," yelled William, who was surprised to hear it repeated in the distance and then again still further away.

Oscar asked, "Captain, why do you call him Gorge?"

Forcing his eyes from his desk, Captain Humphreys said, "That is his sea name, because of his size and the way he eats… I suppose. It has been a long time, and it escapes me as to when and why he received it… if it was even on this ship. Sea names follow us from ship to ship, and not all are flattering. Most are not, but as I said earlier, they are a term of respect, more than less. Now, if you would return the chairs to the wall, you will soon leave with him."

After returning the chairs, the brothers stood near the desk as the captain stood up from it to reveal his average height. "Enter," he replied to the knock at the door.

The door opened and the large, bearded sailor entered. "Ya want to see me, Captain?"

"I do. Seeing how we are short a set of hands, these brothers, William and Oink, will perform the simpler tasks… the safer tasks."

Gorge smiled at William. "Oi, 'tis ya again, is it?" Dropping the smile when his eyes questioned the presence of the boy, he asked, "Ya… ya want 'em feedin' the pigs and cleanin' up after 'em?"

"Yes."

"Cleanin' out the 'eads?"

"That's correct."

"Swabbin' the deck?"

"Yes, all that and anything more you feel is safe. They will labor six days a week and are your responsibility. They will sleep and eat with the passengers, but labor as sailors," the captain informed him while failing to notice Oscar's growing smile. "I will need you to pull two sets for each from the slop chest, and Cump will account for them later. That will be all and I thank you."

Reminded that Cump was still there, William and Oink thanked and wished him and the captain a blessed evening before the captain followed them to the door.

About to follow the brothers out, Gorge stopped to turn back and whisper, "Captain, who missed the ship? I thought we're all accounted for, with an extra to boot."

"We have one more than our full complement but do not tell them that. Also, if there is not enough work to fill their day, which I do not expect there to be, have them clean the floors, and perhaps by the time we arrive in Virginia, the lower decks' floors will look much as they did when the ship was christened."

"Will do, and, Captain, what's the young one doin' 'ere? I'd've remembered one 'is size."

"It is a tale that at least one sailor this evening can share with you," Captain Humphreys replied as he turned back to his desk. Then turning back around, he said to the puzzled man about to leave, "And have the smaller one put something in his stomach. I can't imagine he ate anything… unless a piglet is missing."

"Well do, Captain," the heavyset sailor smiled before closing the door behind him, saying, "Lads, me name's George, but everyone calls me Gorge on accounts of me 'ealthy appetite. And let me tell ya, ya two are fortunate to be slavin' for only six days a week. All but me do seven."

"All but you?" Oink asked.

"That's it," he smiled and nodded. "I do eight days. Nine if 'tis a leap year."

After telling the brothers to work barefoot so as not to slip on the deck and not have the salt water destroy their shoes, Gorge presented the brothers with two sets of calico trousers and shirts, and when Oscar asked about the wool caps most of the sailors wore, he told the boy that if he wanted one, he would have to purchase or trade for it from a sailor named Hemp, who also mended the sailors' clothes. Oscar laughed when he heard a sailor knitted them but checked himself when Gorge appeared offended for the man, and said "Bein' at sea can be as interestin' as watchin' trees grow. Forces all to find somethin' to pass the time with, but games of chance are the commonest." With his face then hinting that he may have said too much, he cleared his throat and said, "But we keep that to ourselves since it's not permitted on account of the fightin' that follows 'er." And then with his face hinting again that he had said too much, he added, "But we control that, so keep that to yerselves too!"

At the kitchen with only a single lantern's candle burning, Gorge offered each a hardtack (an eight-inch dry and dense biscuit weighing almost a pound) and after Oscar had accepted it and William refused it, the large man told them they would start their duties the next morning, half an hour after he woke them.

Then Oscar confused the large sailor by changing into his new sailor's clothes in front of him, and then impressed him by telling him he would sleep in them to be ready to start his duties first thing in the morning.

With Philip in his nightshirt, Mistress Burns in her shift, and both sitting on her bunk, William heard Philip say with some excitement, "Here he comes! We'll know in a moment who's correct."

After offering puzzled looks at the boy in his sailor's clothes with their legs and arms rolled up, the two discovered neither was correct when William, feeling he had no choice, introduced them to his younger brother, who told them proudly through a large smile that they were to call him Oink, that he had trespassed onto the ship, starting the next day he would be a sailor, and when they arrived in Virginia, he was going to be working on a plantation.

"We'll be performing the simple tasks on our way to Virginia," William corrected him.

"Ya should count your blessin's they didn't throw ya overboard," Mistress Burns laughed. "But after a week, when ya realize you're goin' from bein' a slave on the ship to one on a plantation, ya'll be wishin' they 'ad and want to do it yourself."

"For the love of God, shut it!" moaned a passenger a couple of bunks away.

"I'm not a slave!" Oscar whispered, and he was about to repeat that he was a sailor when William said, "It's time for sleep."

"That's correct. He's not a slave," Philip whispered to the woman.

After William told Oink that his and Philip's bunk was the top one and with Philip and Mistress Burns recommencing their earlier argument regarding indentured servants being slaves, Oink climbed up onto it, picked up Philip's neatly folded and expensive clothes resting at the foot of their bunk, and said, "Catch," as he dropped them to the floor.

Joining him, William said, "You should ask if he wants to change bunks."

"Why? By the sounds of it, he would rather be there than here. They can continue arguing if they share the same bunk," Oink said. "And you lied to me! You don't have your private quarters!"

"That's what the agent told me."

"Then he lied, and what other lies has he told you?"

"He didn't lie. He was mistaken."

"Then what else was he mistaken about?"

Lying next to his brother, who was eating the biscuit and carelessly dropping crumbs, William was content to have him along, and though he knew he would have to watch out for him, he felt it was the cost of having him there. He would've preferred not to have to work his way to Virginia, but he hoped it might distract him from missing his family. "Tell me, do you have any regrets about trespassing?" he asked.

Oscar swallowed what was in his mouth and, in a tone that implied it was a stupid question, said, "No!"

"Do you miss Mother, Father, and the girls?"

"Not now. Not at this moment. I'm sure I will, but now it's all too exciting, so exciting that I mightn't be able to sleep," Oscar replied, before crunching down on the biscuit. "You?"

"I do, but having you along should lessen it some."

"Hear that? Did you hear what you said?" Oscar laughed, almost choking on the biscuit. "I've been with you less than an hour and I'm already helping!"

"Still, coming on the ship was stupid."

"Or brave. Remember, the captain said there's a thin line between them and we might not know which at the time... but I'll call it brave."

From two rows away, someone demanded, "Oi! Shut yer traps!"

Another yelled, "KEEP IT DOWN!"

"OI! THERE'S OTHERS 'ERE TOO! STOP YER BLOODY BLABBIN'!"

"STOP THE DAMN YELLING, THE LOT OF YA!"

Several minutes later, William was in a deep sleep, and several minutes after that, with a half-eaten hardtack in his small, chubby hand, Oink was too.

From then on and for the rest of his life, Oscar would insist that everyone, including William, call him Oink.

PART II

CHAPTER 9
A Sailor's Life

Minutes after the bell's double and then single ring and not noticing the offensive smells surrounding him, the large sailor searched the rows of bunks for the brothers, and frustrated to find them at the far end of the last row, he gave Oscar… Oink a rough shake. When the boy mumbled, "Lose yourself, Willy," the bearded man slapped the shin of the short leg peeking out from the side of the bedsheet, causing Oink to sit up with his eyes still closed. "I said lose yourself!" Opening them, he yawned and was too tired to be surprised by Gorge pulling him off the bunk and standing him up against its post where, with the appendages of his sailor's clothes rolled up, he yawned again, rubbed his eyes with his chubby fists, and asked, "What's to eat?", causing the man's laugh to wake several passengers, and when Gorge reached across the bunk to wake William, the older brother rolled away, saying, "Another minute, Oscar," and took the sheet with him when he was pulled past his brother's side and over the bunk's edge, landing on the floor with the side of his head resting on Gorge's bare foot.

With a fresh bruise on his hip, William reluctantly

changed into his sailor's clothes, and minutes later, the brothers were at the long table, slowly eating their oat porridge that the cook, Crock, had prepared for the crew quartered above them.

On the next ring of the timekeeper's bell, Gorge returned and shook his head at the brothers asleep at the table, and with more enjoyment than a man should have with being their taskmaster, he roughly shook them awake. With their bare feet almost dragging behind them, he had them follow him down two levels where the hot, putrid air trapped in by the closed hatch forced them awake only to make them nauseous.

As the piglets woke, Gorge pointed to a corner of the pigsty where outside of it were two buckets, a shovel, and several smaller items, and in a stern tone that implied there would be no complaining, he said, "Ya'll be usin' that stuff to clean that there corner where they relieve 'emselves, the cause of this 'ere wonderful smell. Always choose that one, they do. And ya'll be usin' that shovel there to scoop the bad 'ay into a bucket there and emptyin' it over the side. Scrub 'er down with the brushes and that other bucket of soapy water. After that one's emptied, get the soap shavings from Crock for the next." Looking at Oink, he asked, "Ya hearin' me, lad?" And after Oink pulled his eyes from Gibby to nod his head, the man said, "Good. Now ya'll wipe it with a cloth and ring'er out in that there empty bucket. And you'll be tyin' those pads around your knees to protect 'em and your trousers. That's it for now, but this time next week, ya'll be replacin' all the 'ay there, but for now, it's only that there corner." Then looking down at the excited piglet, he dropped his stern tone. "'Tis rather taken with us."

"He's happy to see me. I met him when he escaped the

crate and named him Gibby because of that mark there," Oink said as he reached in and picked up the animal. Holding him to his shoulder as a mother would hold a baby, he laughed when the animal licked his ear.

"Ya did, did ya? Friended your food?"

"We're eating them… him?" Oink asked with wide eyes.

"No, these're goin' to Virginia. 'Tis salted pork for us, but when I've pig, I only name it when 'tis on me plate. Call it pork." Not getting a laugh or even a smile from either brother, Gorge frowned. "Now whens you're done there, ya scrub this floor with those there brushes. Fill up another with soapy water, pour'er over the floor, and give'er a good scrubbin'. I'm thinkin' a good dozen buckets of soapy water'll do it."

"Do we scrub all the floor?" Oink asked.

"Ya do and don't be missin' no spots."

"Is there someone to help us move the barrels and crates so we can clean the floor beneath?"

Gorge glared down at the boy before realizing it was an innocent question. "Ya take words for what they are, do ya?" he asked. "Ya scrub what ya can touch. This 'ere'll take some hours with the pair of ya workin' on 'er, same as the next one up, but the ones above that take longer, on account there's more of 'er, more ya can touch. But ya'll only do one a day unless ya ask more stupid questions. Now 'ave at 'er." Leaving the two standing there, he headed to the stairs, but before climbing them, he stopped and turned around. "And when you're done with the corner, fill up the troughs with water and feed from over there… and 'ere," he said, pulling two rolls from his pocket and tossing them to William. "Plug your nose with the inside of those. That's what we do to make 'er tolerable, and the bucket of dirty water ya be emptyin' over the side should be the one ya fill with the soapy water on the way back. That's 'ow the boys 'ere do it. Save ya from 'avin' to 'aul two around it will. And when you're done with that, ya'll give the floor a sweepin'. Now I'll be takin' four hours of sleep and see ya both again when I'm about."

With their nostrils then plugged with bread and while William patiently shoveled the soiled hay into a bucket, climbed the four levels of stairs to the main deck, and emptied it over the side, Oink fed Gibby the remaining pieces of the rolls, and when he discovered that if he chased after the piglet, it would run away from him, and if he ran away from it, the small animal would chase after him, Oink and Gibby chased each other around the space outside the pigsty while William emptied two more buckets of hay over the side, which he appreciated for the opportunity to air out his lungs.

As Oink stood catching his breath in the foul air, like someone drinking salt water to quench a thirst, William poured the soapy water around the bare corner of the pigsty and asked, "If you've finished playing with your food, would you help scrub this corner?"

Embarrassed for not noticing his brother had cleared the hay from the corner while he played with Gibby, Oink placed the animal back in the pigsty, tied the pads around his knees, picked up the second scrub brush, and as the piglet curled up to sleep, joined his brother in scrubbing the corner of the sty. When the two had finished, their eyes were watering much like they would when peeling onions.

During their scrubbing of the floor outside the pigsty, William informed Oink of the ship's rules as he remembered them, and since neither had witnessed a whipping and didn't understand how a thin leather cord could cause more harm than the stinging strike of a wet towel, he multiplied the punishment by five, and when he was done, both agreed that the worst punishment would be spending more than a few hours in the ship's bottom level with the pigs, maybe even worse than death if they didn't stuff their nostrils.

A couple of times, between the rings of the bell, the tall sailor without a sea name ignored the brothers when he entered the floor to check on the tightly secured crates, and both thought it strange that he felt he needed to do so when the ship's mild rocking offered no threat to them.

Neither expected to have to work through worse smells than they had just experienced, so both were more than disgusted to learn their next duty, a daily duty, was to empty what Gorge called the "heads" — the buckets fitted firmly under each of the four wooden chairs in the passengers' quarters.

The two again plugged their nostrils with the insides of a bread roll before pulling out the heavy buckets of gag-inducing sludge, and after they carefully carried them to the main deck by their cord handles, each removed their bucket's top that had a hole in its center a little wider than those in the chairs, gagged while pouring the disgusting contents over the ship's side, and then rinsed their bucket and its top by tightly tying a rope to each and lowering them into the sea, heeding Gorge's warning that they would go in after any they lost.

When finished, they exhaled hard through each nostril to shoot out the bread, took several deep breaths to air out their lungs, and joined Crock at the kitchen to scrub their hands in the pot of hot soapy water that the man had kindly prepared for them.

Then Gorge disgusted them again when he told them there were two more heads at the bow, two more in the crew's quarters, another in the captain's, and yet another in his and Cump's shared quarters above and slightly back from the captain's. The only positive was that the 'heads' on each side of the bow only had to have salt water poured through them since they emptied directly into the sea.

Not wanting any more disgusting surprises, Oink asked if there were more at the stern of the ship like those at the bow.

"No, but ya might think there was with the deck above me quarters bein' the poop deck," Gorge smiled, but then dropped it when neither brother was amused.

Reluctantly leaving the cool salty air of the deck, the brothers went one level down to the crew's quarters, where after their eyes adjusted to the little light being offered by every third candle lantern, they were drawn to the four black cannons on each side of the hull. Secured by heavy ropes, each had a long padded ramrod hanging above it, and beside each was a long wooden box holding what the brothers correctly guessed were iron balls. Touching the cold iron of a barrel, they were impressed by its size, and after examining its strangely small-wheeled wooden base and with nothing more to distract them from their task, they walked in the direction of the bow where two sickly buckets were waiting for them behind the door to the crew's quarters.

After William cautiously opened the creaking door to enter the room that, from what they could tell through their stuffed nostrils, smelled no worse but no better than the passengers' quarters, the two crept past a long table and through another door to come to a chest-high trough of soapy water near two wooden chairs with holes in their centers. Across from the chairs were three rows of four pairs of hammocks, one above the other, with a few of them holding weight and emitting snores.

Whispering that he would've preferred those rather than their beds, Oink agreed with William when he whispered back that the sleeping sailors must be the ones who had worked through the previous night, and when Oink crouched down to pull out a bucket from under a chair, William tapped his butt with his foot, and about to protest it, Oink looked up at William, who was gesturing with his head toward an opening further ahead.

Neither could make sense of what they were seeing. Lit only by the little light pushing past them, the triangular room had only a thick beam rising through its center, and not giving any thought to the four poles sticking out from it, their eyes followed the beam to the floor where it extended into the passengers' level.

Then noticing an intense body odor sneak past them, they heard, "Dat dere's de capstan. The worst part o' sailin' if ya asks me. 'Aulin' up the anchor, an' pullin'er ta port's backbreakin'."

Spinning around, the startled brothers discovered a topless gray-bearded sailor scratching himself under his stained trousers.

"Dey've dose boards on de floor dere fer grippin' when turnin'er, but makes fer a pai'ful fall, it does," the man said as he switched from scratching himself to patting down his graying beard. "Oi, I knows ya two. Oink an'is broder, eh?"

"I am and he is," Oink said, proud to be recognized.

"Was dere when theys found ya. Ya sightin' the sights?"

"We're to empty the buckets," William replied.

"Are ya? Dey 'ave ya doin' dat, 'ave dey? Give me but a bit an' ya can 'ave 'em. Come," he chuckled as he turned to walk toward the hammocks.

Doing as the man said, it shocked the brothers when he dropped his trousers and sat on a chair.

With Oscar and William looking at the floor while trying not to cringe at the sounds of the sailor's bowel movements that made them wish they had brought another bread roll to plug their ears, the sailor said, "Dang'rous too dose foot grips are. We 'ad one fall an' 'urt 'is knee. Walks wid a limp he does now. An idler now. 'Ave 'im cookin' are meals cause 'e don't move fast no more. Was de sailor in 'is time dough, but can't say dat now can we? But 'e lear'ed ta cook good, 'e did, an' now 'e's that, 'e is." Releasing a groan, he continued, "Been a sailor fer more dan a score an' eight or nine now. Don't reme'ber whe' I started but whe' she finds 'er way inta yer blood, ya can't get 'er ou'. The sea's de life if ya likes change." He released another groan. "Clear days 'ere, some rain dere, an' a storm dat'll make ya wishes yer dead, an' whe' it's done, ya be lovin' each minute fer a time, but dere ain't many dis season. No, 'tis a shame ya'll be missin'em, with de season an' all. An' let me tells ya too, wid ev'ry storm de boys are readin' deir Bibles fer a time," he chuckled. "Ya bring yers with ya?"

Overwhelmed by the uncomfortable situation and missing half of what the man said, William only shook his head.

"Would do little good. He can't read," Oink said, ignoring his brother's disapproving glare.

"Neider can most 'ere, but dey pretends dey can on de chance 'E migh' be watchin'," he said, chuckling again as he stood up from the chair to pull up his trousers. "Well, 'ave at 'em, lads. I'll be layin' me 'ead back down an' migh' be seein' ya on de deck dis evenin'. Pungy's de name."

As the man returned to his bunk, Oink grabbed the bucket from under the other chair, leaving the bucket with its fresh addition for William.

Being careful with the waste, they got none on themselves until the sailor without a sea name passed near the wall of the deck and bumped the bucket Oink had just removed the top from, causing him to splash its contents on his trousers' legs.

"By Jove, look where you're walking!" Oink scolded the man before gagging several times.

"My apologies, *Oscar*. I failed to see you, and it's John, not Jove," the man smirked.

"It's… it's Oink, *not* Oscar!"

"My apologies again, *Oscar*."

After Oink washed and changed into his second set of sailor's clothes, Gorge had them help Crock with the midday meal by chopping vegetables and mixing several large batches of dough.

As the brothers did their tasks, the bald cook contently limped about the kitchen telling stories of his years at sea, and as they neared the end of their kitchen work, appreciating the smell of the baking bread belittling the less appealing odors, he ordered them to slow down when he thought they might finish before his story did.

While the meal cooked, Gorge had them polish the ship's brass pieces, or what he called the brightwork, but instead of taking the time to point out where the pieces were, he made finding them part of the task.

With each carrying a bucket of water that smelled of onions, they searched for the pieces of brass and when finding them, used their soaked cloths to scrub the brass and their dry ones to polish it. After almost two hours of searching and polishing, Oink was polishing the large timekeeper bell he had left for last. Trying to ignore John as William had suggested, the boy had to put up with being told several times, "You missed a spot, *Oscar*," and then as he was about to leave, John told him he had to polish the inside too, which seemed an almost impossible task. Scrubbing the bell's rough interior while making sure the clapper didn't strike it and confuse anyone, he found he had to repeatedly rinse the dirty washcloth, and when he finally felt it was polished as well as it could be, both the washcloth and the polishing cloth were black. Realizing then that no one had ever polished the inside of the bell, he wanted to throw several curses at the man, but recalling none from their brief time on the pier, he could only walk away calling him a 'bloody louse.'

Whenever a passenger had passed him while he was polishing the brass pieces, the boy received a smile, a nod, or both, and he returned the same, and it was during the second shift of the midday meal when he learned that word of him working his way to Virginia had traveled among the passengers, who were curious with how he had planned to live undiscovered.

After they had eaten and were helping Crock wash the pots, wooden bowls, plates, and cooking and eating utensils, Oink bragged to William about being famous and suggested that because they were brothers, he was famous too, though not as famous.

"I don't want to be famous," William told him.

"So you only want to be rich?"

"No."

Oink looked at his brother as if he had lost his mind. "You want to be poor and infamous?"

"No, I only want an uncomplicated but productive life."

"You could have stayed home for that!"

"I'll add that I want an interesting one too."

Oink shook his head. "Considering what we're doing, you have a poor start with it."

"Perhaps, or perhaps not."

When the two finished washing the wooden bowls, the water in both the bucket of soapy water and the bucket used for rinsing them was so filthy that William suggested to Oink that when taking a bowl for their meals, they should take one from the bottom of a stack, one that wasn't washed and rinsed in the dirtiest of the water.

After ending their ten-hour workday by swabbing the deck, which both appreciated for its cool evening air and easy work of having only to push a mop over the salt water they had poured onto it, both brothers were sleeping profoundly through Philip and Mistress Burns' argument over that evening's orange moon being a sign of a coming storm, and when Gorge woke them the next morning with more respect than the morning before, both groaned as they forced themselves off the bunk.

It was the first time Oink experienced what seemed like every muscle from his neck to his ankles hurting, and it was the second time for William (the first being the morning after his first day in the mine) and neither was impressed when

Gorge told them that no matter how fit one was, any strenuous, repetitious movement that one wasn't used to would cause pain the next day, with the pain being the worst the day after that. "And the bestest way to deal with 'er is with more of the same."

After a week and no longer noticing the ship's rocking and swaying, Oink was still enjoying his life as a sailor, whereas William wasn't, but then he never did. He appreciated the work for taking his mind from his family, though he expected it also had to do with Oink being there, and he appreciated it too for distracting him from his anxieties regarding his coming duties in Virginia that had grown when Oink told Philip and Mistress Burns that he would be an apprentice overseer of slaves. It was the first time the two seemed to agree. With dropped jaws, they exchanged glances, and when he walked away, fearing what they might say, he heard Mistress Burns trying to whisper in her naturally loud voice, "He doesn't seem the sort, but I'll admit I could be wrong." And William also appreciated the work for fighting back the boredom that Gorge had mentioned could drive passengers mad and over the past dozen years had caused more than twice that to try to throw themselves overboard, with at least a few succeeding.

As the boredom grew among the passengers, it amused William to find some playing a variety of children's games both below and above deck, and he was no longer surprised to come across a passenger jammed into a tight part of the ship. Being careful not to give away the man's location during his game of Hide and Seek, William might exchange a discreet nod or subtle wave of the hand with him.

Unlike his brother, Oink wasn't amused by the men

playing children's games. Several times he had to ask those playing Leapfrog to move their game to another section of the deck so he could swab that area, and when a passenger demanded he work around them, Oink didn't do as his brother would have done (swab around them or come back to the area after they had left) but shouted that the man better respect his authority or face the whip for interfering with a sailor's work, causing the group to laugh as they moved out of his way.

Where some passengers played Crafts, Nine Men's Morris, Checkers, or Chess that a few had brought with them and lent out, Philip and Mistress Burns spent much of their time playing cards, sometimes using her collection of tin buttons as currency, and William believed they played the game for its many opportunities to argue. They argued so often that it caused Oink to suggest that since they were always arguing, were always together, and were sharing the same bed, "You two should have the captain marry you if you don't want to wait until Virginia." Philip's face reddened with embarrassment, Mistress Burns' reddened with anger, and William's reddened with a laugh that Oink hadn't heard for some time, and though he didn't understand what was amusing, it made him proud to make his brother laugh.

The only excitement the voyage offered was the occasional storm that the passengers waited out in their hot, humid, and pungent quarters, where the only thing to do was to watch the water drip in from the closed hatches above. The violent swaying from side to side and rocking back and forth made it impossible to sleep or play games. The vomiting of some made it even more difficult for the others to eat the hardtacks that were the only thing available, and the ship's groaning made most fear the hull would burst at any moment.

And just as Pungy had told the brothers, for a day or two after each storm, the passengers were ecstatic with relief and treated each other as if they were the best of friends.

Though William didn't enjoy the work, he was content that his younger brother did, and when Oink's enjoyment weakened that second week at sea, William tried to make it more enjoyable for him. As the two scrubbed the floor in the lowest level's growing heat while the pungent odor fought its way past their bread-stuffed nostrils, he challenged Oink with things to improve on. For a mousetrap, the boy decided not to improve on something that would kill mice one at a time but suggested poisoning them as a group with cheese mixed with hemlock. For a comb, he suggested they widened it to take several more rows of teeth, to which William smiled and told him he had reinvented the hairbrush, and for a cup, the boy took some time thinking before suggesting the addition of an iron door hinged to the top with a dozen small holes cut into it. When at sea, it would minimize the spills, and when on land, it would keep out the insects.

When William asked how he would improve himself, Oink caused him to smile by saying, "There's nothing wrong with me that needs improving," and he caused him to frown when he added, "But I would make you more confident, make you take control and question yourself less."

"I took control when I signed the contract."

"Because you felt forced. You wanted to leave the mines, and you ran from them, an easy run, or that's what you were thinking when you only had to sign your name."

Thinking his brother might be correct, William said nothing.

Where William passed his free time watching Philip and Mistress Burns play cards while listening to them argue, Oink spent at least an hour each evening playing with Gibby, who had grown twice as large since leaving London. The two spent most of their time playing fetch with a bread roll, and when the roll was soggy, Oink pulled it apart and fed it to the young pig. After that, Oink struggled to train Gibby to sit, stay, and, with two short whistles, to come, which he proudly showed off to his impressed brother. Feeling bad for the pig, Oink once tried to carry him up to the deck for some fresh air, but as he climbed the stairs with Gibby in his arm, a sailor spotted him and ordered him to return the pig to the sty.

After their playtime, Oink spent the rest of his evening on the main deck watching the sailors go about their duties, and when he came across Gorge, usually on the poop deck watching the crew work, he joined him and learned that Gorge was an officer on the ship but preferred to dress as a regular sailor, saying, "I started as one of 'em, and I'll dress as one of 'em to the end. Don't need no fancy clothes for respect."

Through Gorge, Oink learned they measured the ship's speed by dropping a buoy attached to a rope off the bow and timed how fast it floated to the stern. He learned that because of the eastern direction of the northern currents they didn't sail directly to Virginia but sailed south for a week and a half before sailing west across the ocean and then north to Virginia, but they sailed back to England with the current, nearly as the crow flies, taking almost three weeks off the trip. The boy learned too that they used a triangular device with a lead ball hanging from a string, or what Gorge called a quadrant, to determine the ship's location by the position of the stars, but he failed to understand how, and he learned they could sail into the wind at forty-five-degree angles, or by zig-zagging as Gorge called it, but also failed to understand how that was possible. When Gorge offered to explain how block and tackle worked, Oink brushed it off with, "It's only a pulley."

One evening Oink asked Gorge why all the sailors had tattoos on their arms, chests, and backs, and Gorge was more than proud to tell him, almost standing at attention when he said, "They tat the turtle when they pass the equator, and *only* if they passes'er. She's a tattoo of honor. 'Tis a long voyage it is, and 'otter than 'ell. And we take 'em seriously, we do. 'Eard of a man 'avin' one put on after too many rums and 'is crew makin' 'em cut it out cause 'e didn't earn it. Meself, I never went that far south to 'ave it, but I've the anchor 'ere." Pulling up his sleeve to reveal his tattooed shoulder, he said, "'Tis for crossin' the Atlantic, just like we're doin' now. And I got these. *Hold* here and *fast* here," he said, making two fists and pointing them at the boy so he could see the tattooed letters near his large knuckles. "We tat 'em for fortune, good fortune with grippin' the riggin', esp'cially durin' 'ard storms."

Fascinated by the permanent letters, Oink asked, "Who gives them? How do they do it? Does it hurt? How do I get one?"

"Ya don't until you're a sailor… a sailor by choice."

The next day during what was their weekly cleaning of the captain's quarters, Oink leaned the broom against the desk and searched its drawers for a quell and ink. After finding them in a deep drawer, the boy wrote a letter under each knuckle of his left hand, and then with his left hand, struggled to write more under those of his right. Proud of his work, he pointed his fists at William and said, "Look at my tattoos. What do they say?"

William took a moment to recognize the words. "Fast hold."

"Correct. What? No!" Confused, Oink turned his fists toward himself. "No, they say hold fast."

"To you, but to anyone else, they say fast hold."

Oink examined them again and saw his error. "I suppose as long as the words are there, the order doesn't matter."

"I expect that's true, but you should put that back before the captain discovers what you did and decides he wants you to tattoo his fingers as well."

"Do you believe he would?"

"No."

Near the end of the second week at sea, Oink asked Gorge for more important duties, and when the large man refused, telling him they required someone taller, he then asked how many more days before they reached Virginia. Gorge gave a guess, but after being asked the same question four times that third week at sea, the man's patience was exhausted and he put an end to the question by growling, "We'll arrive when we arrive. No sooner, no later. And if ya asks me again, I'll place ya in that cockboat there and pull ya 'alf mile behind us. You'll be wishin' then ya were cleanin' the ship." Looking curiously at the laughing boy, he added, "Ya won't be laughin' when you're out there floatin' about."

"I'm laughing at what you called it, called the boat. Mother would make you wash your mouth out with soap."

Gorge smiled. "Ya a Puritan, are ya? Ya want to call 'er a roosterboat too, do ya?" he asked, and as he walked away from the boy who was laughing again, he proudly added, "And speaking of mums, don't be tellin' mine what I said."

The next evening, after Oink had asked Gorge to explain again how they could sail into the wind, the man remembered that the captain had an important task for the boy: counting their store of hardtacks. Gorge brought Oink into his and Cump's quarters for a pencil and paper and told him that the captain could only trust him to take the exact count, but he would have to do it after his regular duties and he couldn't tell anyone what he was doing because they believed someone was *pinchin'* them. He also told him that if he lost the pencil, he would eat only hardtack until he found it.

After playing with Gibby, Oink spent much of his time near the kitchen counting the biscuits. Sack by sack, he separated the broken ones from the whole ones, and after counting the whole ones, he struggled to match up the broken pieces to form whole ones that he added to the sack's count. If a sack's quantity of biscuits was more or less than a hundred, he recounted them until he got the same number twice. Then, after finally finishing the count by counting the number of biscuits in the partial sacks, he went to the captain's quarters, where Captain Humphreys and Cump could only offer the boy confused stares.

"Six… six thousand, six hundred and… and forty-six at this very moment, you say?" Captain Humphreys repeated back, his eyes bouncing between Cump and Oink.

"With one sack missing one, three sacks missing two, and another missing four. I believe that's not bad for threescore and six sacks… and almost a half," Oink said. "I wanted to tell you myself to make certain none were eaten between Gorge hearing it from me and you hearing it from him."

"I… I understand, and I thank you," the captain nodded, before forcing an awkward smile. "That was very… very diligent of you."

"You did say it was a very important task."

"I did?" he asked before it occurred to him what Gorge had done. "Correct, I did. Yes, but next time, please inform Gorge first. We do not want him worrying longer than necessary."

"We thank you," Cump said in a tone that sounded more like a demand than a statement. "You may leave now."

"And Oink," the captain added, "If Gorge asks you to find and count the left-handed cutlery, see me before you do so."

"You have some?"

"Yes… I have some."

When Oink was some distance away from the captain's quarters, he heard muffled laughter, but since he couldn't imagine Cump laughing, he assumed it was coming from a couple of men in Cump and Gorge's quarters.

As the brothers were doing the dreaded emptying of the heads, John again bumped into Oink, who was lifting an almost full bucket to pour over the ship's side. Spilling some on his shirt, Oink let loose several curses he had heard the crew and passengers use, and as John was walking off smiling, Oink cursed him some more, laid down the bucket, and with two tight fists, was about to run after him when William grabbed him and pulled him back.

"It's the second time!" the boy protested.

"It is, but now that you know his game, it should be the last. He must know you'll be ready if he tries the same thing again."

After Oink had changed and washed up and William had cleaned the deck of the spillage, the brothers were emptying two more buckets when William took his brother's still-steaming mind from John by asking how he would change the way they collected the waste. Oink took much more time thinking about that question than he had with any of William's earlier challenges, and after they had emptied the buckets from the crew's quarters, he came up with what he thought was a better system. The idea impressed William, but seeing the twinkles in his little brother's eyes, he insisted he not bother the captain with it unless he came upon him by chance.

Minutes later, Oink was at the door of the captain's quarters, and when the captain answered his knock, he proudly entered and declared that after several weeks of removing the waste, he was an expert on the subject, and without giving the captain or Cump a chance to respond, he explained his idea of having the waste fall into angled troughs that would lead to a large barrel that each day they would lift by block and tackle and empty over the side. Oink was even prouder when he saw the captain was impressed — he couldn't tell if Cump was — but he was disappointed when Humphreys told him that was almost exactly how the navy did it with their much larger ships and their many soldiers, and he was disappointed further when the man told him that because of *The Colonist's* small size, they had to empty the heads as they did to save on space.

After the captain thanked Oink for doing respectable work of disposing of the waste and asked him to close the door on his way out, the chairs hooked to the wall gave the boy another idea, and he turned back to the two men. "We can place the chairs on the side of the ship and the waste can go directly into the sea. We could even face them away from the ship for privacy."

With Cump's bottom lip twitching uncontrollably, Captain Humphreys smiled. "That is a... a different idea, but I believe much too dangerous, and more so if one feels the need to relieve himself during a storm."

Oink was only a few feet from the captain's quarters when he was sure he heard both men laughing.

"What did the captain say?" William asked, pulling in his rinsed bucket as his brother joined him.

"He laughed! They both laughed at me!" Oink said as he wiped an eye.

"They laughed?"

"Yes! Not at me, not to my face. But when I left his quarters, they laughed!"

"Perhaps they were laughing at a story, perhaps the one I heard Sledge tell."

"The one about the horse and the pig?" Oink asked, fighting through his hurt feelings while aggressively tying a rope to his bucket's cord handle.

"No, I've not heard that one."

Oink lowered the bucket into the sea. "About the sailor and the minister?"

"Haven't heard that one either."

"The one about the Priest and the Pope?"

"Priest and Pope?" William asked. "No, this is about King George and the Archbishop of Canterbury."

"Haven't heard it," Oink said, letting the ocean rinse out the bucket. "But I want to."

"Uh, King George and the Archbishop of Canterbury are walking through the Royal Gardens and they... they come across what looks like dog poop. The king orders the archbishop to smell it, and the archbishop does. 'Does it smell like dog poop?' the king asks. 'Yes,' the archbishop says. Then the king orders him to touch it. 'What?' 'Touch it.' And the archbishop touches it. 'Does it feel like dog poop?' 'Yes, Your Highness, it feels like dog poop.' Then the king orders him to taste it. 'What?' 'Taste it.' So the archbishop tastes it. Then King George asks, 'Does it taste like dog poop?' 'Yes,' the Archbishop cries, 'It tastes like dog poop!' 'Then be careful not to—"

"Step in it," Oink said, finishing the punch line and shaking his head in disappointment.

"You said you never heard it."

"I didn't, and it was too long to be the story they were laughing at," Oink said as he placed the top on his rinsed bucket and left his brother standing there. "The one about the horse and the pig is better and shorter. I expect they were laughing at that one." And near the hatch to the stairs, he raised his voice to say, "And when you tell it again, it would be better if you make funny voices for them. Telling it as you did almost put me to sleep."

William couldn't help but smile as he picked up his rinsed bucket and walked to the hatch.

At the end of their fourth week at sea, when William and Oink were scrubbing the floors of the passengers' level, a sailor descended the stairs and ordered all to the main deck, where another sailor ordered them to stand across from the mainmast, and as the sailors grouped nearer to the stern, a shorter sailor whom the brothers recognized but had never exchanged words with was pulled out of the captain's quarters by a sailor on each side of him. At the mainmast, the two removed the shirt of the struggling and cursing man, revealing a chaotic pattern of two to three-inch scars on his back, and forced him to face the mast as they tied his arms around it.

Less than a minute later, Cump and Gorge exited the captain's quarters, and when they reached the bound man, Cump read loudly from a sheet of paper trying to escape with the wind, "For dereliction of duty due to inebriation, of which the penalty is five lashes of the whip, Jeremiah Alfred William Cline, also known as Frew, has been found guilty."

"I'm no more guilty than the other guysh, ya… ya landlubbersh! I'm ash Shober ash the day me wasssh born, ya crowd 'o scobberlotchers!" the bound man yelled before throwing several curses that were new to Oink.

"For theft from the stores, in this instance rum, of which the penalty is five lashes, Jeremiah Alfred William Cline, also known as Frew, has been found guilty."

"Give me allsh ya gotsh, ya son of a gun!"

"By the mercy of Captain Thomas David Humphreys, the combined sentence has been reduced to seven lashes, and every soul aboard *The Colonist* has been ordered to witness its execution."

Finished, the first mate left Gorge standing there to join Captain Humphreys near the sailors.

"Oi! Why not wait til 'e's walkin' straight and able to feel it?" one sailor shouted, causing his mates to laugh.

"And reme'ber it," another shouted to more laughter.

William and Oink only noticed Gorge was carrying a whip when he stepped back seven feet from the sailor and flicked it so the long cord rested on the deck in front of him. With neither having seen a whip, they watched curiously as he paused for a moment before sending it casually behind him.

Swinging it forward, the whip's loud crack caused the brothers' eyes to widen.

"Ha! Ya mished, ya saddle-goose!"

"Checkin' distance," Gorge said as he stepped back a few inches.

The second crack caused a scream and a three-inch streak of blood on the man's back.

Where William failed to hold back the terror on his face, Oink wasn't sure what to make of what he was seeing. He was fascinated by the whip's crack, confused by how such a light leather rope could cut the skin, and horrified by the man's scream.

Most of the passengers cringed at the next strike, and when William tried placing his hand over Oink's eyes for the third, the boy brushed it away. "They ordered us to watch!"

"Brutal!" Mistress Burns whispered to Philip.

"Not brutal to the sailors," Philip whispered back after the next scream.

"Not brutal to brutal men!"

"Brutal is relative."

"Ya 'ave a brutal relative, do ya?" she asked.

With the final strike delivered and with blood covering the man's back, William was sure he saw a hint of shame in Gorge's eyes as he coiled the whip, wiped his head with his palm, and without a word walked off to his quarters, and after they watched four members of the crew untie the bloody man and carry him below the deck, Cump shouted, "Let that be a warning to all who might consider taking liberties with the rules of this ship."

Finished scrubbing away the blood from on and around the

mainmast, William picked up his bucket of blood-tainted water, told Oink he was thankful he wouldn't have to use a whip in Virginia, and was taken aback when Oink told him he wanted to use one, not on a person but to understand how something so seemingly harmless could cause so much pain and damage, and for amusement, he wanted to make it crack.

CHAPTER 10
Becky

For three weeks after Michael's burial in the slaves' unmarked graveyard near the woods thirty feet beyond the rows of cabins and their privies, Mary barely spoke more than Ann, and when she spoke to Becky, she seemed to have to force herself, making Becky feel like she had become an enemy due to her association with the man whom Mary blamed for Michael's death.

Unlike her friend, Becky didn't believe Philpot was to blame for Michael's death. She had blamed Virginia for Peter and Beth's deaths, and now she blamed it for Michael's. She believed Virginia was cursed and looking for every opportunity to cause death and ruin, and she believed the reason for the curse was slavery.

**

Soon after Michael's death, Becky began to fear Philpot's paranoia would become a rational fear. Even with him requiring her to taste each meal, which she didn't bother to do, she knew that poison didn't always kill immediately after ingesting it. She heard stories of people slowly being poisoned to death over weeks or months if they ingested a small enough amount regularly, and she was sure that if Mary wanted to, she could do it over an extended period to minimize suspicion. But then she considered that if the man were ill for some time, he would believe he was slowly being poisoned, true or not, and would act on that belief, and if Becky was aware of that then Mary was too. Then pacified slightly, she was pacified more when she considered too that even though Mary might give her life to take Philpot's, she wouldn't want Ann implicated, which was sure to happen since they worked together. And Becky's fear completely evaporated when she considered Mary's worry about the next apprentice overseer being worse than Ben, and that worry would be far greater when it came to Philpot's replacement, who might be even crueler and might take liberties with the women of the plantation, as some slave owners and overseers did.

Then confident that Mary wouldn't attempt to poison the man, for days Becky struggled with how she might ease the woman's pain, and one evening as she was about to leave the morbidly quiet kitchen with her tray of two meals, an idea came to her. Placing the tray on the table, Becky picked up one of the two bowls of soup, and with Mary standing at the table slicing bread, held the bowl out to her and said, "Spit."

With Ann freezing where she stood while holding the peel of three loaves of baked bread, Mary's eyes enlarged as she took a step back from the table.

"Spit," Becky repeated as she took a step toward the woman. "Spit in it and make it a good one."

"I-I have to ask if you… if you've gone mad?" Mary's voice croaked with her lack of speaking that day.

"It wouldn't surprise me if I have," Becky smirked. "Now spit and I'll mix it in." With neither Black woman moving, she brought the bowl up to her chin, exaggerated a long snort, exaggerated a longer hawk, and spat into the soup. Holding the bowl out to Mary, she said, "Now you."

As the bewildered but amused woman's huge smile exposed her teeth, Becky's demanding nod gave her the extra push she needed to snort, hawk, and spit into the bowl.

"Ann, come and add yours," Becky said to the thin woman watching in awe from the corner of the kitchen.

Lifting her jaw back into place, Ann shook the bread onto the table, leaned the peel against it, and stepped toward Becky, who grinned as the woman took a long snort, a longer hawk, and spat in the bowl.

With Ann's eyes apologizing for the splash, Becky surprised the two with a laugh neither had heard for some time, a laugh that shook her body and spilled a bit of soup. "I should have poured out a bit before we started," she said through her smile. "Now I know for the next time."

Entering the back door of the house while still seeing in her mind the two women hugging each other as they bounced up and down like two children about to receive sweets as a reward for cooperating, Becky feared one or both of the men waiting for their meal might question her smile and she took a moment to force it down before making her way down the somber hall.

As Philpot ended his complaining about that day's rain, Becky entered the dining room, laid the tray on the table, and set the two meals out, giving the *special* soup to Philpot. Straightening up, she noticed Mary and Ann fighting for the small window behind him, and she had to fight back a smile when they decided to share the space with their cheeks touching. Wanting to see their reactions, she picked up the empty tray and stood with her eyes bouncing between the window and Philpot, who had switched to complaining about the minister. Pulling his bowl closer, he picked up his spoon and dipped it into the soup. "And that's all I want to say about him lest I ruin my appetite," he said as he was about to put the spoon to his mouth. Stopping, he looked at Becky. "Is there something else?"

"Yes, Mary… she… she adjusted the spices and would like to know your opinion."

"You tasted it… mine?"

"Yes."

"And what do you—" he said, stopping short when he realized he didn't care for her opinion. "I say give me but a moment." He put the spoon in his mouth, and to the bulging eyes and dropped jaws of the two women at the window, he swished the soup around in his mouth, and when he swallowed it, both struggled to hold back their laughter. "I taste nothing different. Have her make it more noticeable next time. And what is that bloody commotion?" he asked, looking back toward the window that the women had just vanished from as they released their laughter.

"The children," replied Becky, letting her smile grow as she turned to leave.

"Send those vermin to their cabins or I shall tear them down and give them tents! Let us see how they feel about that this winter!"

With a noticeable change for the better in Mary, the spitting in each meal that Philpot ate at the house continued, and by the next week, Mary was holding draws for the opportunity to spit in his meals. Becky had written pairs of numbers on small pieces of paper that Mary tore in two, handed one half to a slave to keep, placed the other half in a wooden bowl to use for the draws, and when a number was drawn, wrote it in the dirt beside the kitchen, informing all of it. Becky would know the winner by the slave's face peeking through the far dining-room window, and if she missed that, then by the one wearing the largest smile after their meal.

Several times, Mary had offered Becky the opportunity to spit in Philpot's meal, but she refused, preferring to leave it to those who deserved the honor more.

**

With Margaret resting in Beth's room and Philpot, Ben, and most of the slaves working the fields, Becky was passing the time at the kitchen table slowly peeling onions when Ann stopped stirring the large pot of stew to turn around and tap Mary on the shoulder, and when Mary looked at her, she pointed to Becky with her chin.

Stopping her slow chopping of carrots, Mary said, "I was waiting for her to mention it, though it's none of our affairs."

"Mention what?" Becky asked, knowing the two women valued gossip more than gold.

"Did he ask you again this morning, and did you refuse him again? I have to ask because he was impatient with the others when he's usually his quietest in the mornings."

Becky nodded as she began slicing an onion. "He did, and I did, but now he might finally accept my refusal. He was even bold enough to ask in front of Master Philpot. Told me it would be the last time he asked and didn't appreciate it when I asked him to add a promise to it."

As Ann giggled and returned to her stirring, Mary released a quick belly laugh. "In front of him? I have to ask what the master said."

"He laughed and told him to lower his expectations," Becky replied, cracking a smile at Mary's amused snort and Ann's louder giggle.

"I have to say, he deserves as much for asking in the master's presence. We know how much the master would hate to have you leave here."

Becky tried to ignore her stinging eyes as she sliced another onion. "I don't understand him, perhaps never will. I've never given him the smallest sign I was interested in him, and then with a few months remaining on his contract, he asks me to marry him. No attempt at courting, just a marriage request, as if asking me to pass the butter. I never saw it coming the first time he asked, and I suspect he mistook my moment of shock for a moment of consideration."

"That will do for onions, and don't become emotional over him," the older woman smiled as she held out the bottom of her frock and slid the chopped carrots and onions onto it. Limping over to Ann, she dropped them into the pot and returned to the table. "Who can understand men? They only see what they want to, hear what they want to, and maybe even smell what they want to. If he had no interest, he would see through you. That was how my Michael was. He never noticed me until Sarah decided on Paul. Saw right through me, he did. I waited years for him to notice me. I could have lit myself on fire and danced in front of him, and he still wouldn't have seen me," she said, straightening up as if suddenly remembering something. "Ann, we must use the last of those boiled eggs before they spoil. Could you take the basket out to the children? We know how they enjoy peeling the shells as much as they do eating them."

With a nod, Ann dropped the paddle into the pot of stew and picked up the basket of eggs resting on the counter near the chicken roasting over the chest-high fireplace.

Waiting for Ann to leave, Mary grabbed several turnips from a basket at her feet, placed them on the table, and looked curiously at Becky before whispering, "I have to ask if you're certain you want to reject him with you being on the far side of eighteen and with no prospects?"

"I'm certain," Becky nodded. "He doesn't interest me. He's an overseer of slaves and found an opportunity to oversee them in North Carolina, and I expect he only asked because he doesn't want to go alone." Grabbing a turnip, she joined Mary in peeling and then slicing them. "And who knows how he'll be in the future? He may avoid opportunities to be cruel, but will he always? Will he become like some and develop a habit of releasing his anger on them?"

"Perhaps a good woman would keep him from doing so."

Becky shook her head. "If a man needs a woman to remind him to be compassionate, I wouldn't want him. He shouldn't need to be told, and perhaps he would be just as harsh with me. No, if I were ready to court again, which I'm not, I would rather be alone than with a man whom I neither respect nor love... and who rarely speaks. He's twenty-five and speaks so seldom that I don't want to imagine how little he would speak after being with someone for several years."

Hearing the excited cheers of several children, both smiled.

"Perhaps it's too soon after your Peter, but I have to say he's not the cruelest, and that says something because he's not the sharpest. The less intelligent one is, the crueler one is, yes?"

Becky didn't agree with her friend and would've only had to use Philpot as an example of a cruel but intelligent man to prove her point, but not wanting to contradict her friend, she instead said, "He has the sense to avoid South Carolina since they're fighting with the Indians again."

Mary brushed the sliced turnip aside. "Still, Master Carlson's not like the one before him. Takes less pride in the whip and uses it as little as he can. He's no Master Philpot and I have to say again I fear the one replacing him will be far worse, so much so it worries me to see him retire, but not as much as it would if you were to leave… but if it would suit you, I would welcome it."

Becky found it curious that Mary regarded cruelty as relative, whereas she viewed it as an absolute — a person either was or wasn't. If they had the potential to be slightly cruel, then they could be very cruel if they believed the occasion justified it, and she was about to say so when the sound of hoofs splashing mud caught their attention. "That's three horses," she told Mary, who nodded back, fearful.

With Mary limping behind Becky, they left the kitchen to find three men in long leather coats and cocked hats sitting on horses, and with the swords hanging from their sides and the long muskets strapped to their saddles, both guessed why they were there. Then recognizing the three riders, the two were sure of it.

"Blessed afternoon, Becky? Is Philpot here?" one asked with a week's facial growth.

"No, he's out in the field. He should return in a few hours. What brings you and your brothers out this way, Robert… uh, Master Carter?"

"And Ben?"

"He's with Master Philpot."

Swinging his leg over his horse, Robert let his feet hit the mud with a splash. "I won't miss this constant mud this summer," he said as he tied his horse's reins to the eight-inch ring of the whipping post. "And I expected as much. We saw them out there yesterday." Then turning to his brothers, he asked, "What are you two waiting for? Do you require an invitation?"

Dropping from their horses, the long-bearded one displayed less finesse than the other and almost slipped in the mud. Cursing and with his legs awkwardly apart, he struggled for a moment to find his balance.

"We're looking for Joseph, Bradley's slave with the R branded on his cheek. Ran again."

Mary shook her head. "Not 'ere. Made no tracks 'ere, and 'e won't on accounts Master Philpot uses 'im for musket practice. Likes the runners, he don't."

Though she expected Mary to speak as she did so as not to appear above the men and give them a reason to strike her, Becky had to hold back a smile with the way the woman curled the side of her mouth to do it.

"If it pleases you, *girl*, we're not in the habit of accepting the word of no slave."

"But I ain't *no* slave. I *am* a slave."

"Ya tryin' to be amusin', girl?" the bowlegged Carter brother asked as he awkwardly shifted his weight for each of his two steps toward her.

"Perhaps you'll accept my word," Becky said. "The runaway's not here, and I would've noticed if he was. You'll have to return when Master Philpot is here."

"Don't worry about Philpot. You know we're his mates.

That's worth something, yes?" Robert said as he unstrapped his musket from his saddle. "Stuart, you check the cabins, barn, and stable. Harry, you check all on the left, and I'll check the curing barns. We'll meet back here… and shoot if you see him, but not at him. We want the full reward."

After Stuart, with his musket in hand, ran to the rows of cabins and Robert ran to the two rows of sixty-foot by twenty-foot empty curing barns following the river at the back, Harry unstrapped his musket from his saddle. "Why does I 'ave ta check the left?" he complained to no one before hobbling toward the small cabin beyond the sheds.

Becky shouted, "You're trespassing, and Master Philpot will hear of it!" and then looking at Mary, she whispered, "I'll return in a moment."

Several minutes later, she exited the house, struggling with four long muskets. After leaning them up against the door, she picked up one, pulled back its hammer, and noticed Mary fighting to get to her feet. "Mary, are you hurt?" she asked from the top of the steps.

"No, not the best push, but not the worst," she replied, trying to look behind her to examine the mud on her robe.

With a few women, including Ann, and over a dozen small children forced into a group in front of the cabins, Robert and Stuart returned, both breathing heavily.

"You'll *not* be checking this house!" Becky said as she raised the weapon to her shoulder. "You'll *not* enter uninvited!"

With her musket growing heavier, Harry hobbled out of the kitchen with his musket in one hand and a chicken leg in the other. "Oi! D-don't be pointin' that at me!" he yelled, causing bits of chicken to fly from his mouth.

"Harry Carter, you're trespassing! Don't force me to pull the… the thing here," she threatened, tapping her index finger against the side of the trigger before resting it on it. "There's a weak woman with the chills inside, and you three won't be disturbing her!"

Stuart readied his weapon at her. "Becky, if you're hiding a runaway, there'll be a whipping coming."

She swung her long gun toward him. "Bradley's runaway doesn't give you the right to search this plantation! And if you suspect Master Philpot of stealing a slave, I suggest you involve the constable!"

With his musket under his arm, Robert removed his hat and wiped his brow with his forearm. "We'll not be disturbing anything or anyone. Only want a quick look inside… for your safety."

"You'll *not* enter this house!"

"If ya don't move, we'll move ya!" Harry threatened.

Swinging the long gun toward the bowlegged brother, Becky's straining arms forced her shaking hands to grip the weapon harder, and with a flash from its slamming hammer and then a deafening blast, a small chunk of brick burst off the wall to the right of Harry, who dropped his musket, the chicken leg, and his jaw.

Trying to overcome both the shock of the blast and the painful kick against her shoulder, she forced a brave face. "The… the next one won't miss!" she said before realizing the weapon was spent. As the ringing of a bell from the second floor caught the attention of the Carter brothers, she dropped the long gun and quickly grabbed another. Wondering why it seemed to weigh much more than the spent one, she pulled back its hammer and pointed it toward the two older brothers.

"You've upset the woman, and you won't be upsetting her further with your presence!" she said while silently cursing her weak arms. "I expect the reward is near two hundred pounds of tobacco. Is your third worth risking your life at every plantation you trespass on?"

Frustrated, Robert shook his head. "Come. Forget about the house… for now," he said as he strapped his musket onto his saddle and untied his horse. "Harry, put yourself together!" And after a shocked-silent Harry Carter untied his horse and mounted it, Robert said, "Becky, if we don't find him, we'll be back, and pray we don't find him in that house."

As the three rode off to the front of the house, Becky let out a deep breath, and after her shaking hands struggled to release the hammer slowly, she leaned it up with the other two and sat on the back steps of the house to calm down.

Picking up the spent long gun, Mary limped over to stand it up with the others before sitting on the steps next to Becky. "I have to say one day your boldness will have the better of you. If you had killed any, they would've certainly strung you up."

"No, three trespassers trying to force their way into the house of a sick woman excuses my actions, even if one had been killed," Becky said, noticing her hands still shaking. "They're a strange group. Grown men playing soldiers as they chase after an unarmed slave, and if I were killed, it would be trespassing and murder against them."

"That may be so, but it's still a risk you should avoid. And I have to say, with it being this runaway's second time, he'll see far worse than another branding. They'll cut off his toes."

"They might," Becky nodded. "I don't know where he thinks he can go. It's not as if he can walk through

Williamsburg without being noticed. Eventually, someone will catch him."

"He's blinded by the chance of freedom and not too intelligent. Two things that make a man run to nowhere. He could hide with the freemen, but they'll be searched, and since they're near the Indians, they'll be as well."

Becky nodded before she stood up from the steps, picked up two long guns, and with her tired arms and sore shoulder, held both out as if she was aiming them as one.

"What are you doing?" Mary laughed.

"There should be a better way to protect yourself when there are more of them than you," she said as she leaned them up against the door. "They're much too heavy to hold together."

Then the bell rang again.

That night Becky told Philpot about the Carters' visit. He wasn't pleased to hear it, but when she forced herself to admit that she fired the long gun at Harry, instead of berating her as she had expected, he laughed and said, "I say if that doesn't push the message, nothing I say shall."

Later that night when thinking about their short conversation, she found it curious that Philpot seemed less concerned about them trespassing than he was about them seeing Margaret in her current state of mind, and she found it curious too that he thanked her for stopping the rumors before they started.

The next morning, after Becky set bowls of porridge, a plate of rolls and butter, and cups of cider in front of the two men, Philpot asked, "And how was she this morning?"

"The same, but ate only a little more than Beth," she replied as she laid the rolled napkins of cutlery in front of the two.

Waiting for Philpot to start, Ben, with his spoon in hand, said, "But the doll doesn't eat. Are you saying she ate almost nothing?"

"Of course, that's what she's saying! I say no one shall confuse you for Copernicus!" Philpot growled, before forcing a smile and turning his attention back to Becky. "Did you—"

"Yes, I tasted it."

"Good," he nodded. "I say she's been playing this game for almost a year, and I shall put a stop to it before rumor spreads I caused her madness. I shall feed this to her myself, but I'll be damned if I shall feed that doll!" Reaching out, he surprised Becky by taking her hand and slightly squeezing it. "I say this has gone on long enough."

Pulling her hand away, Becky's heart raced at the thought of Margaret eating his *special* porridge. "If you would prefer to eat with Ben before the porridge cools, I could bring hers when you're finished?"

"No, he can wait for me to return and eat then. Is that correct, Ben?" he asked as he stood up from the table, and not waiting for a disappointed Ben to reply, he placed his bowl and spoon on the tray Becky was holding and took it from her. "I shall be but twenty minutes."

Following Becky down the hall, he forced her to walk faster by almost walking on her heels, and when she turned right to leave the house, he turned left, stomping a warning of his coming presence on each steep step to the second floor.

Alone in the kitchen, Becky was halfway through her

porridge when Philpot shouted so loud that those still eating in their cabins could easily hear it. "I CARE NOT! YOU SHALL FINISH IT! EAT IT ALL! THIS HAS GONE ON FAR TOO LONG! ENOUGH IS ENOUGH! GIVE ME THAT BLOODY DOLL! I SAY GIVE IT TO ME!" With a shriek, a smack, and another shriek, he shouted, "IT'S A DOLL! IT'S NOT BETH, AND YOU BLOODY WELL KNOW IT! EAT AND WASH UP! UNHAND THIS DOLL!" With another smack came another shriek. "AND AS HE IS MY WITNESS, YOU SHALL SHARE MY BED TONIGHT!"

After the slamming of a door, there was silence.

With the shouting taking his mind from his cold porridge, Ben heard Philpot's angry footsteps coming down the hall, and when the man entered the dining room, he watched him walk to the fireplace and throw the large doll onto the single burning log. Both watched its dress catch fire, its hair turn to smoke, and its white-painted face turn brown as the flames grew to engulf it.

"That's the end of it, I say!" Philpot growled as he returned to his place at the end of the table just as Becky entered with her tray.

Neither man said anything as she placed a bowl in front of Philpot, and to Ben's thankful eyes, replaced his cold porridge with a warm one.

As she picked up the tray and Ben began spooning the porridge into his mouth faster than he normally would, both froze when Philpot said, "You shall wait ten minutes before collecting her dishes. She may eat more yet, may feed herself now that the doll is out of her arms."

"And I'll prepare her bath."

"Good," he smiled, and then startling her, he growled, "And collect every bloody doll in that room and destroy them! We've been too soft with her, far too soft, I say! Perhaps it shall bring the woman to her senses if there's no sign of the child."

Carrying the empty tray under her arm, Becky climbed the stairs and walked the few steps down the hall to Beth's bedroom door on the left. When the woman didn't reply to her knock, she knocked louder, and with still no reply, she took a deep breath to prepare for the expected scolding for waking the woman. Opening the door a crack, she looked in. On the side of the room that she could see, the four-candle iron chandelier was resting on the small desk, and in front of the desk, its small chair was lying on its back. Assuming Philpot had struck it in anger, she whispered, "Mistress Philpot?" With still no reply, she opened the door and failed to make sense of what looked like a stained white sheet floating near the toppled chair... until it slowly rotated to reveal long curly hair hanging down the front.

The tray slipped from her arm and banged on the floor.

CHAPTER 11
Another Funeral

As the dark clouds threatened to release a fourth day of rain, two men pulled ropes from the hole only two feet from a grave with its short mound still prominent. When the middle-aged minister closed his heavy Bible, placed it under an arm, and walked over to Philpot to shake his hand and exchange whispers, Becky and Ben took several steps back from Philpot

Then standing near one of the several young yew trees planted about the grounds, Becky recalled the many more mourners at Beth's burial and felt there should have been more than there were at Margaret's until it occurred to her that most came to support the family left behind. Thankful then that the small number of mourners said more about Philpot rather than Margaret, she noticed that the trees bordering the churchyard had thick beige rings around their dark-brown trunks from where someone had removed a strip of bark to slowly kill them over the next year. Wondering how many more graves the expansion would allow, she looked about to count the headstones and wooden crosses. With a hundred and twenty-seven grave markers in the fourteen-year-old churchyard, there were many smaller ones than larger ones.

Knowing that the buried children were English, she questioned if the English were even suited to Virginia's climate and if the situation was any better in the northern colonies — if mothers there also suffered the deaths of so many of their children.

Then wondering if children had a better chance of survival in England, she whispered to Ben, "How many children did your parents have?"

Startled that she was asking about his family, Ben took a moment before whispering, "Eleven that I'm aware of."

"How many survived past five?"

"Believe seven, but only four live now, four including me. I'm the youngest."

Then believing the English weren't suited for the world and not feeling she was strong enough to handle the death of her child, she questioned her wanting children. Why bring them into a world where dying of old age was a rare occurrence and dying young was almost expected?

"Yours?" Ben whispered.

Finding herself strangely content with not being married and even believing then that Peter's death was the best thing for her since it ended their opportunity to start a family, she worried that she had caught what Margaret had.

As she was hoping Peter wasn't looking down at her and hearing her thoughts as he sometimes seemed to when they were together, Ben whispered again, "And yours?"

Becky looked at him, confused.

"How many children did your mother have?"

"Five, but only two survived."

"Sisters, brothers, or one of each?"

"I have a brother."

Seeing the confusion on Ben's face, she explained, "I was one of the two who survived."

"Oh, of course," Ben nodded.

"Boy, bring the cart around while the minister and I talk some more," Philpot whispered as he approached them. "I'm beginning to believe I'm paying the man by the word!"

"I will," Ben nodded before he and Becky walked off toward the church where several carts were rolling away and several more were waiting with their drivers of either a well-dressed slave or an indentured servant.

"Churchyards are dispiriting, yes?" Ben asked.

"Not as dispiriting as a burial. Without them there would be no churchyards," Becky replied.

"Becky, Master Carlson," a reddish-skinned man dressed smartly in a long coat, breeches, and waistcoat greeted the two with a quick bow as he stood by a two-horse cart.

"Blessed afternoon, Daniel," the two said as they passed him.

"And how are you today?" Becky asked.

"Fine," the man replied. "Sad about Mistress Margaret."

"It is," she said as Ben helped her onto the back bench.

After untying the reins from the post, Ben drove the cart's two horses back a few feet from the minister's cart, the only one without a driver, and then moved them forward to follow the dirt road around the freshly painted white church with its two doors protruding out and its steeple topped with a cross. "Thought Daniel's servitude ended three years back," he said loud enough for Becky sitting behind him to hear.

"It did, but he put himself into debt again. He's with the Campbells now."

"Did it again? I'll never understand Indians and their

indentured contracts. One would think they would learn not to borrow sterling when there's little chance of repaying it."

"If the lenders didn't have the option of indenturing them, I don't expect they would lend it. I believe they do it on purpose, knowing they'll have them as an indentured within the year."

"Does he not have a family?" he asked as the wind picked up.

"Wife and four children past Kingsley Mountain."

Stopping the cart beside the graveyard, Ben turned himself sideways so he could talk to her without straining his neck. "Always surprises me to see an Indian dressed like us. Like seeing that cow dressed in a coat and pants they walk about every New Year."

"Does it surprise you too that he can speak?"

"It can speak?" he asked with wide eyes before his face reddened. "Oh, you mean Daniel. I meant to say I—"

"Remove your bloody shoes from the bench!" Philpot demanded. "And brush away that dirt before I sit!"

"My apologies, Master Philpot," Ben said meekly as he pulled out a handkerchief from the pocket of his breeches and wiped the seat next to him.

"There would be no need to apologize had you not chosen to dirty it, and I pray your handkerchief was clean," Philpot growled as he ignored the spot Ben had wiped to sit at the back next to Becky. "Let us be off before the man charges me for blessing the horses' droppings we're leaving behind. I say I shall not be the one paying for this funeral. Chalmers shall pay for it. She had two years left on her service and, therefore, his responsibility."

"Two years? I thought her contract ended before mine. Did

she not start two weeks before—"

"The child added two years, now drive!"

After ten minutes of uncomfortable silence, Philpot startled Becky by patting her thigh. "You've been with us almost two years, yes? Began as a governess and now performing Margaret's duties."

"Two years less four months," she nodded. "But I understand if you must release me from my position when Lord Chalmers finds another indentured to replace her."

"Release you? A new indentured? No, my dear, you shall continue doing as my wife did, oversee the house. I say you work well with Mary, and with the next indentured arriving in a few weeks, that's if he's on his way, I shall need you to help settle him in and familiarize him with his surroundings. If he's not here, if he's another three or four months away, then I shall need you even more with Ben retiring before then."

"You don't know if he's on his way?" Ben asked.

"How would I? The post of his coming would only arrive with him, but what I was meaning to say, Becky, before I was interrupted, is that with you no longer seeing to Margaret, you shall eat with us. It's balderdash to eat in the kitchen. From now onward, I expect you to join us at the table, starting tonight and every meal after that. It shall do me good to have a pretty face eating with us," he said, patting her thigh again. "Boy, hurry them along! We would prefer not to be soaked on our arrival!"

Not wanting to be there without Margaret, Becky's mind jumped to the letter she had received a month earlier from her brother, who had informed her of a governess position coming available in three or more months on an estate near where he and their parents had positions. Becky had put off sending a letter offering her service, but now with Margaret gone, she had nothing to stop her from doing so.

**

Not wanting him standing over her, reminding her of how considerate he was being by insisting she take Margaret's clothes when she expected he wanted only to rid his room of all signs of her being there, she waited for him to leave the house before forcing herself to enter his bedroom decorated by several paintings of himself at various ages and two charged long guns hanging by their shoulder straps.

With the opened cast-iron shutters allowing the sun to brighten the room and the air to cool it, she passed the large poster bed to open the double doors of the wardrobe, or what Philpot liked to call an armoire. Pausing at the depressing sight of her friend's clothes, she took a deep breath and began pulling out the heavy gowns, skirts, petticoats, bodices, shifts, and cloaks to make two piles: one for the few she liked and the few she didn't but would keep because her friend had cherished them and another for those she disliked and her friend had been indifferent to. The second pile she would give to Mary to pass on to the others, and a week later, each cabin would have colorful curtains covering their small glassless windows.

The pain of removing all signs of two people she cared about was too much for one day, so after removing the lighter garments from the dresser drawers and the pairs of shoes from the small shelves at the back of the room, she waited until the next day to enter Beth's room to remove her clothes and dolls, and a few days later, every young girl on the plantation would have a doll they would keep from Philpot's sight. A few days after that, Becky would notice the dolls' white-painted faces and hands had somehow turned brown.

Intending to donate all but one of Beth's dresses to a charity in Jamestown, the one she would keep for herself was the one the child had ripped. Fearing a scolding from her father, the child had tried to mend it herself with stitches so large they were more noticeable than the rip, and when Becky saw the child's work, she promised to mend it in secret, but four days later, Beth came down with smallpox and Becky forgot her promise. Then reminded of it, she intended to make good on it, but later while preparing to do so, she would slowly trace Beth's stitches with her finger and break her promise, preferring to keep the stitches the child had made, the only physical evidence of her existence.

**

With Philpot and Ben retired for the night, Becky stood outside the empty kitchen waiting for Ben's bedroom window to go dark, and when it did, she made her way through the moonlight to the small cabin on the left where she lifted the wooden beam barring its door, quietly leaned it up against the wall, and entered the room lit by its single candle.

"Blessed evening, King," she said to the topless giant sitting up in his bed waiting for her.

CHAPTER 12
Getting Their Sea Legs

By the fifth week of their voyage, the temperature had risen beyond what most of the passengers had experienced, and though Gorge had warned them about it during their first day at sea, it didn't make it any more bearable. At the passengers' level, the thick stale air seemed at least ten degrees hotter than on the main deck, putting all in such a state of irritation that a simple disagreement would lead to a fistfight, and with the growing heat, the putrid smells grew strong enough to mask the odor of a corpse, of which there were three.

There were no obvious mourners for the first two passengers covered in bedsheets, weighed down with stones from the ballast, and slid into the sea, but there were three for the third.

Just before the second shift of the afternoon meal, Philip discovered her passing when he went to wake her from a nap, and twenty minutes later, while sitting on the top bunk with the brothers, the three somberly watched a sailor place her belongings in an empty hardtack sack before replacing the bedsheet. On the deck and after learning her first name by Captain Humphreys' prayer, Philip broke the moment of silence between it and her body sliding into the sea by saying loud enough for all to hear, "She, Harriet Burns, was my friend. She may have been hard-headed, but she was soft-hearted. I shall miss her. Her family shall miss her, and anybody who has spent time with her shall miss her." He only allowed his tears to flow when the Lovelys placed their hands on his shoulders.

That evening when Philip confessed to William that he wished they could have done more to see her off, William shook his head. "If you told her that, you know she would've disagreed, saying something like, 'They bloody well did what they could! What do you expect them to do on a ship between nowhere and somewhere, invite the king?'" he said, poorly imitating the woman's voice.

With a slight smile and with tears pooled in the corners of his eyes, Philip nodded. "And if... if I thought they had done enough, she would've said, 'They bloody well could've done more! They could've toasted me and built me a casket so I wouldn't be fish food!'"

After her death, Philip spent most of his time in the passengers' quarters rereading several books he had packed away for the voyage, seemingly oblivious to the heat, humidity, and smells, and with the melancholic change in his friend, William spent more time with him. After he and his brother finished their duties, he would interrupt Philip, who was trying to isolate himself by either reading or sleeping, to insist they play cards, and during their games, he tried several times to make Philip talk by asking what he had been reading, but with William knowing little about the politics, places, and events that his friend stoically mentioned and not able to respond competently to start a discussion or an argument,

Philip would go quiet again. Then when William began fearing his friend might throw himself from the ship while they slept, he offended his brother by complaining about his snoring and then delighted him when he used it as an excuse to share Philip's bunk.

Having grown to almost four times their boarding weight, the pigs fared better than the passengers, with only two casually thrown over the side with neither prayers nor tears, though there would have been a boy with tears insisting on prayer if one of them had had a gibbous mark on its side.

With most of those on the ship going topless, William noticed most of the crew continued to wear their red wool caps in the heat, and when he learned that the Monmouth caps kept their heads cool during the summer by blocking the sun and collecting the perspiration, William thought it might slow his brother's growing bitterness with their duties and used a few shillings to purchase one as Oink's birthday gift. Afraid he might lose it, a delighted Oink never took it off except to ring it out when it was too soaked to keep the sweat from his eyes or to wash it when it began to smell.

Like the sailors, the brothers too worked topless, but not conditioned to the sun's harsher rays, their torsos and arms turned a painful dark red and they soon switched back to wearing their shirts... for about a day. With their shirts blocking the cool ocean wind while rubbing against their painful sunburns, the two were again working topless, and after almost two weeks of pain, itching, and then peeling skin, their torsos and arms browned, the pain and itching disappeared, and their skin stopped peeling.

Since the second time John had bumped him, Oink watched for him whenever he was emptying a bucket of waste over the wall of the main deck, and when the man was near them, would warn him to keep his distance, until one afternoon while they struggled to remove the tops that were stuck to their buckets by the dried waste, an irritated Oink spotted John walking toward him, but pretended he didn't. Getting the top off his bucket, he picked it up, and as the man *accidentally* bumped him, he turned and *accidentally* splashed him with its putrid contents.

Covered from the waist down in the sludge, John looked down and froze as it made its way to his bare feet.

Forcing himself out of the shock of seeing his brother splash the man with the waste, William stood up next to him.

"My apologies. I didn't see you there, *John*," Oink said while trying to hold back a laugh.

As he broke away from his shock, the sailor's face burned with rage and he brought his arm back to deliver a slap.

Pushing Oink out of the way, William caused him to splash more on the man as he stumbled to the side, and then dodging John's hand, the older brother replied in kind with a fist to John's ribs, causing the man to grunt and drop to a knee and William to groan from his inexperienced wrist buckling with the strike. When the furious man forced himself to his feet and slid his long knife from its sheath, both wide-eyed brothers instinctively took a step back.

"JOHN, WHAT ARE YA DOIN'!?" Gorge yelled. "Go wash that off! I'll 'ave someone keeps the time for ya, but onwards, give the lads some space!"

John looked at the large, frowning man who was holding a

long knife in his fist while standing ten feet behind the brothers. Then looking at each brother, John huffed and sheathed his knife before walking away.

Sheathing his knife too, Gorge nodded with a smile as he passed the brothers. "Good work, lads."

When the large man was out of hearing distance, Oink whispered, "That's a first! How did it feel? Good?"

"No. It hurt me more than him. It hurt my wrist," William said as he rubbed it and then slowly and painfully bent his hand back and forth.

"You need practice."

"There won't be any practice!" William whispered. "It was stupid of me and stupid of you!"

With his cap hiding his reddening ears, Oink growled, "It was him or me, and I prefer it being him!"

"He was about to strike you!"

"You should've let him! It would've proven he doesn't scare me!"

"He scares me! Did you not see that knife?"

Oink huffed. "Of course I did, but I never expected you to step in, never expected you to strike him! I would never have believed it if I hadn't seen it! Look at *passive* Willy punching a man to protect me! My big, strong hero!"

"I'm your older brother! I have to protect you!"

"Protect yourself! If you did, I wouldn't be here! I wouldn't have had to trespass and wouldn't be handling this shit and piss! And now I have to clean it off the deck too!" Oink barked.

"Stop being vulgar! If Mother heard you, her heart would stop!"

"It would too if she saw us cleaning people's shit and

piss!" Oink growled as he laid down the bucket. "I'm going to visit Gibby!" Walking away, he sang, "Shit and piss, shit and piss. Shit. And. Piss!"

Passing the boy on his way back, Gorge stopped and said, "That'll be enough of that sort of singin', lad… an' where ya goin' with no bucket? I 'ope you're not leavin' that there mess for your brother."

"I'm fine with it," William said, as he tied a rope to the handle of his emptied bucket.

Oink stopped and turned around. "He's fine with it."

"*I'm* not fine with it. Ya made the mess, and ya'll be cleanin'er. There'll be no dereliction of duty on my watch. I don't much like usin' the whip, but will when I must!"

Oink huffed and walked back to William. "I'll do it, but I won't like it!"

"I 'ope not. If ya did, I'd 'ave to check your 'ead for damage."

Two days later, while the brothers cleaned the floor one level above the pigs' and both too hot for any long conversations, William commented that the heat would be a little more bearable if there were a breeze. Oink agreed and took it as another challenge, spending much of the day searching his mind for a way to create one, and that evening while William was with Philip, Oink entered the captain's quarters and pitched his idea of a windmaker. The captain couldn't help but smile and Cump's jaw couldn't help but twitch as Oink suggested extending a set of rotating wings, like those of a windmill, out from each side of the ship, telling them that if the wings of a windmill could ground wheat, then they could easily rotate several smaller groups of wings mounted to the ceiling beams on each level of the ship. He admitted he didn't have the exact details of how it would work but expected it would use rods and leather belts to connect the two sets of wings extending out from the ship to the smaller sets in each level, rotating them all at the same time to push the air through the ship. And when he ended by saying that if he had a pencil and paper, he could figure out how to make it work, the captain had removed his smile, but Cump's jaw was twitching even more.

"That's a very interesting idea, very interesting," the captain nodded, sincerely. "But if you please, for any future ideas, discuss them with Gorge first, and if he feels I should be aware, he will make certain I am… and perhaps he will give you a pencil and paper to develop the exact workings. As it stands now, we will reach Virginia in only a few weeks and will not have the time to act on your improvements."

When he was only ten feet away from the captain's quarters, Oink again heard laughing, but this time from only one man, and he wished they would stop waiting for him to leave before telling their short and funny stories. He wanted to hear them too.

The next evening, as the sun's rays burned down on Oink while he swabbed the deck near the mainmast, Sledge and another sailor climbed down the shrouds near him.

"I'm changin' me mind. If I'm goin' ta be marooned, the one thin' I'll wants wi' me is Oink," Sledge said loud enough for the boy to hear, flattering him, until the sailor added with a laugh, "I'm guessin' by 'is size, I'll last a good two months on 'im."

"You're a… a… lubberwort! You both are… and

fopdoodles too!" Oink yelled as the two stepped down onto the deck.

With both grinning as they walked to the bow of the ship, Gorge approached the boy with a smirk. "Me thinks that's wrong."

"I do too!"

"Could last three on ya."

"What!? You too!?"

Gorge's smirk grew to a smile. "Yeah, me too. Why not? We insults ya cause we likes ya, respects ya."

"Insulting me isn't liking me!"

"It is if 'tis a sailor doin' the insultin'. We'd rather insult ya than talk ya up, but in a witty way. Now if 'e was truly insultin' ya, 'e might just say you're a lubberwort, a bobolyne, a saddle-goose, or even a fopdoodle," the man winked. "That's a large nose 'e 'as, but we wouldn't say it direct like. No, we might ask 'im if 'e stretches 'is sweaters tryin' to pull 'em over it, or ask to stick a note on its tip telling me mother I'll be there in a week." With the confusion on Oink's face, he added, "On accounts 'is nose'll reach Virginia a week before the ship."

"Is that true?"

"No, 'is nose ain't that long."

"No. About the insults, the way to insult!"

"That's true," Gorge nodded.

"Have to go," Oink said, dropping the mop and running toward the two sailors who were then near the bow of the ship.

Later that night, Oink asked his brother if the sailors had ever insulted him.

"Not directly, not where I could hear it," William replied. "Why?"

"I'm curious if they like you, but if they haven't insulted you, I expect they don't," he said, confusing William.

CHAPTER 13
Pirates

As they rinsed their buckets in the rough sea, both appreciating the strong, cooling winds and the dark clouds blocking the sun's rays, they thought they heard the ring of John's bell through the wind moaning in their ears, though it was a higher pitch and too soon since the last ring. When it rang again, both realized it was coming from above, and after ringing a third time and then seeing Sledge quickly descending the shrouds of the mainmast, the brothers hurried to pull in their buckets and join the growing group of sailors curious about the rare ringing of the bell in the crow's nest.

"I'll tells ya when I tells the cap'ain!" Sledge replied to the several questions thrown at him.

"Quiet down ya lot. The captain'll be 'ere soon," Gorge said as he joined the group and nodded a greeting to the brothers.

As the passengers began joining them, one asked, "Are we arriving? Was land spotted?"

Gorge looked up at the ominous clouds. "Ya see those birds flyin' about, do ya?"

"No."

"There's your answer. Now away with ya lot!"

"Oi, what about those two?" another asked, gesturing to Oink and William.

"What of 'em? They're part of the ship. I don't see any of ya emptyin' the 'eads, just addin' to them. Now lose yourselves!" Gorge growled, causing Oink to smile and nudge William, who also smiled.

To the relief of those eager to hear what Sledge had seen, Captain Humphreys and Cump joined the group, and before the captain could ask, Sledge raised his eye patch to his forehead, winced to the pain of the light rushing into his pupil, and struggled to control his voice to say, "I thinks 'tis pirates, Cap'ain. They're not waving a country considerin' none are black an' white.

"Could it be a Jolly Roger?" Cump asked.

"Could be, but can't tell from the distance."

"Could it be the ship you spotted heading north two days back?" Humphreys asked.

"Could be, Cap'ain. Ain't showin' much, just 'er bow. But like ya said then, they were searchin' fer a ship if they were 'eadin' north when they should o' been 'eadin' west. If it's 'em, then they'd've been givin' chase since then and 'ave ta be empty ta be closin' in on us so fast. But why chase us?" Then noticing Oink's wide eyes and his open mouth forming an excited smile, he released his panic. "Don't be lookin' so 'appy! They're not what yer expectin'! Not an honor'ble one among 'em!"

Embarrassed by the scolding, Oink dropped his smile, but not his excitement.

While the anxious sailors nervously whispered among themselves, the brothers watched the captain take the thick spyglass sticking out of Sledge's pocket and walk to the stern of the ship. On the poop deck, the others joined him as he stretched it out and aimed it behind the ship.

Looking at where the captain was aiming the spyglass, the brothers could only see a slight shape on the horizon.

Closing the spyglass and handing it back to Sledge, Captain Humphreys said, "It is unusual to be showing their independence, a Jolly Roger, this soon… unless they believe their prey is weak." Pausing for a moment, he said, "Put the wind at our back. Sledge, keep watch to see if they match our adjusted direction," and looking from Oink to William, he added, "William, stay close to the mainmast and let me know what Sledge sees when he sees it, and let us hope their presence does not concern us."

"What are we goin' to do, Captain?" a sailor asked.

"He said put the wind at our backs! Turn us thirty-two degrees larboard and straighten the sails!" Cump demanded. "Have at it, and after that, lock the wheel and every man waits at the guns. And send the passengers below. Tell them we're holding a drill and they're to stay out of our way, just as they did when we loaded the ship."

"Let's go!" Gorge said as he turned two sailors around by their shoulders and pushed them toward the poop deck's stairs. "If ya lot don't want yer stomach holdin' a pirate's blade, ya'll jump to it."

As Cump and Captain Humphreys headed down to the captain's quarters and the sailors scurried about the deck to adjust the sails, William and Oink had to adjust their balance to the steep angle of the quickly turning ship as they tried to keep up with Sledge rushing back to the mainmast.

"Are they intending to attack us?" Oink asked him.

"Don't knows why they be wantin' to. Always lookin' fer the Spaniards with their gold an' pieces o' eight, but if they're pirates, they might be starvin' fer anythin' they can finds. Not the first time we sees 'em in these parts, but woulds be the first they comes fer us, but that there's obvious by us standin' 'ere now," he said as he grabbed the shrouds and started his climb to the crow's nest. "Don't be movin' till I tells ya what they're doin'."

Waiting anxiously and impatiently for Sledge to yell down to them, Oink's mind was on the pirates, making him both excited and fearful. He wanted to meet one, but on friendly terms where he could ask questions, hear his tales, and form his own opinion of them. But he didn't want to meet one if they were intent on stealing the gold and killing for it. Then to address his fear that was slowly belittling his excitement, he struggled to come up with a plan to escape the pirate ship if it were chasing them.

William tried to take his mind off the pirates by watching the sailors struggle through the powerful winds to pull on the block and tackle as they straightened the sails, and when they tied off the ropes, his eyes followed them as they disappeared below deck. Having nothing more to distract him, he could feel his heart beating hard and fast, and when he looked down at Oink, who appeared to be in a daze, it beat even harder and faster.

The twenty minutes they waited for word from Sledge seemed like forever to each, and when the sailor finally yelled down, neither could understand what he was yelling through the wind until he shortened his message to, "TURNED! TWO HOURS! OI! TWO HOURS!" With the brothers then frozen as they tried to accept what they heard, Sledge yelled down again, "OI! TURNED! TWO HOURS! GO! GO NOW!"

With Oink struggling to keep up, William rushed into the captain's quarters to stop in front of the man's desk, and trying to control his panic, he said, "They turned and two hours!"

"He said two hours?" the captain asked as he sat calmly behind his desk while Cump stood stiffly at its side.

"Yes. He believes they're gaining on us, correct?"

"Of course he does!" Oink answered for the man.

"That will be all, and I thank you," Captain Humphreys frowned. "Please close the door on your way out."

Doing as asked, William stopped at the door to look back at Oink still standing at the captain's desk.

"We have to drop the cargo over the side to gain speed, yes?" the boy asked.

The captain nodded. "I expect they are only carrying what they must, and we would have to do the same to stay ahead, but it would take two full days to relieve ourselves of the extra weight. Now, if you would excuse—"

"Then we'll fight?"

"No, we only have four guns… four on each side," William answered for the man. "They have to have more seeing how they're… they're pirates. Come, Oscar."

"No, and it's Oink!"

Irritated, Cump said, "We are very much aware of our situation! Now, if you would—"

"How do you plan to keep the gold?" Oink asked as William walked back to the desk.

With Captain Humphreys' face turning a light shade of red, Cump raised his voice to say, "There's no gold on this ship!"

"The pirates believe there is."

"Perhaps the boy will only hear it from you, Captain. Hear it and be gone."

"Perhaps, but he is more than half correct," Captain Humphreys replied, causing the soft whistle of the wind entering through a crack in one of the large windows at the back of the room to grow louder by the sudden silence. "If there was ever a time to disclose it, I believe it would be now. It is not gold, but sterling, and much of it. My apologies, Cump. It was a secret, but word must have leaked and they are coming for it," he said before clearing his throat. "Tell me, Oink, how did you know?"

Then with Cump stunned silent, William answered for his brother, "He didn't."

"I did, Willy! I thought they would send gold on a ship no one would expect to be carrying it. One that couldn't protect itself… like this one."

"That is quite perceptive of you," the captain nodded.

Cump shook his head in defeat. "We're done for."

"So it seems."

"Can we give them the sterling and be done with them?" William asked.

Captain Humphreys cleared his throat. "I expect those beasts would go beyond taking the sterling. Pirates are cruel, if not evil, and the best we might hope for is they take our passengers to sell in The East, and that is if we have Him with us."

"You can both leave now," Cump said.

"We could leave it for them," Oink offered, ignoring the first mate while recalling Gorge's threat. "We could place it in the cockboat." With his brother glaring at him, Oink's eyebrows turned in. "That's what they call it, Willy! Captain, we could pull it a half-mile behind us, and when they take it, perhaps they'll stop the chase."

"Perhaps," the captain nodded, "But it could be for naught. They could keep coming, and I expect they would."

Exaggerating the clearing of his throat to get their attention, Cump gestured with his head for the brothers to leave.

Ignoring the man again, Oink said, "If we can't fight them one-on-one, then why not attack first? Instead of sterling, we give them a petard but make them believe it's sterling. We have the powder for the cannons. We can make it a big one like Guy Fawkes tried, but make them think it's sterling in the boat."

As the captain raised an eyebrow, an impatient Cump repeated, "You can both leave now."

"Just a moment, Cump," Captain Humphreys said before sitting back in his chair and rubbing his chin. "Sometimes it takes a fresh view, a unique perspective to address a problem, much like the lad's windmaker. What if it is possible to put a hole in the side of their ship without firing a gun?"

"Captain, with respect, we're wasting precious time with these two."

Captain Humphreys leaned forward in his chair and placed his forearms on the desk. "Are we? I am not confident we are. What Oink suggests could be our only option."

"This is all very strange, Captain. Are we even to trust this boy, these brothers? How do we know they're not part of this chase? It seems they're trying to reduce our powder by suggesting we float it off. The boy trespassed on the ship, admitted he knows we carry riches, and we even discovered him near the crates, where I expect the sterling is hiding and the reason for the passage within them that you requested. And then there's the older brother indentured as an apprentice overseer, an overseer of slaves. A peculiar contract and more so since his character seems unsuited for it, considering what I saw of his reaction to the whip. With all that, I can't help but suspect they put themselves on this ship to assist the pirates. We should bind these two, make certain the powder is dry, and check the cannons for blockage."

As William stood confused with what the man had said about his contract, Oink yelled, "I'M NOT HELPING ANYONE BUT US, YOU NINCOMPOOP!"

With Cump's face reddening and his eyes threatening Oink, Captain Humphreys asked, "William, are you and your brother working with the pirates? Was this planned before you came aboard?"

William shook his head. "No. My brother has a... an enormous imagination. That's the only thing he's guilty of... that and trespassing on this ship."

"Yes, I believe you are correct," the man nodded before looking at Cump. "And I believe too that I am a competent judge of character, and unless William here is a gifted liar who can fool a man who has experienced many, I can only believe what he says. I'm sure you recall Oink's shame when William found him where he stands now and William's surprise when finding him here. But, Cump, if you can believe neither and want nothing to do with their unusual but perhaps possible plan, then you may leave and I will judge you no worse for it, but as the captain of this ship, I see nothing to lose by it and would like to see it through, and if I am wrong about the Lovely's or the plan fails by our best attempt, it changes nothing. They will still come and they will still take us."

Cump's defeated eyes bounced between Oink and the captain several times before he said, "Perhaps the situation is causing my mind to believe things aren't as they are. First the pirates, then the sterling, and then these two knowing of it, or seeming to know of it and volunteering options that we never considered, would never consider. It's very unusual, very... very strange, but as you say, Captain, if it fails, it changes nothing." After he cleared his throat and the three let him think for a moment, he said, "As for the plan, it will be quite the task to explode a barrel of powder near their ship, making it a much greater chance of failure than success. They could easily sail away from it. After all, it would only be a barrel. And if it exploded near the ship, even against it, the damage could be little, if any."

"We make them believe it's sterling," Oink reminded Cump. "We put the powder in a chest that looks as if it's holding sterling, and we could use several chests for a larger effect. And if... if we lock them, they'll have to bring them aboard to open them, and that would be much better, yes?"

Captain Humphreys nodded. "Yes, locked chests of sterling... of powder in the cockboat, and opened on their ship for a better chance of damage. But do we pull them a safe distance behind us or leave them floating on their own... with a white flag to catch their attention," the captain asked himself. "Leaving them to float would be safer for us. The further we are from the blast the better, but the troublesome question is, how do we discharge them? Breaking them open should cause sparks, but only on the outside, and the use of fuse cord would be impossible for too many reasons to mention."

Finding the captain's consideration of Oink's plan surreal, William surprised himself and his brother by suggesting,

"Pistols. They don't have to be charged if all we need is a spark. If we rig each chest with a readied pistol inside, perhaps by a cord against their triggers, when they break one open and lift the top, the trigger is pulled, and its flint will spark."

"That could work," Humphreys nodded. "No, that *would* work. We would need to find a way to rig them, but I am confident we can."

With his usual stone face back in place, Cump added, "We'll also have to make the chests feel as if they're holding sterling. We mustn't give away the surprise before they're lifted aboard their ship. Perhaps weigh them down with stones from the ballast, pour the powder into sacks, stuff them on top, and pour some loose powder over it to catch the spark. But we would have to rig them some distance from us to avoid harming the ship if an accident were to occur during their rigging."

Captain Humphreys straightened up in his chair. "Good, we have a plan, but will need a volunteer to rig them." With William pulling Oink's arm down, he said, "No, Oink. We will need someone who has handled a pistol… and we can't afford to lose an officer. No, I think it best we use one who is not yet so important to the ship. Cump, could you choose several of our recent additions and bring them here?"

"Yes, Captain, and you two can join the others below, but say nothing of this."

"I believe they should stay. Knowing of the plan, we could still have a use for them, could need more of their unique perspective, and if nothing else, they should see their plan through."

"As you wish," Cump nodded before going to the door and yelling out four names to join them in the captain's quarters.

Not hearing his yell repeated, he left the room.

For the next two minutes, no one spoke until William, trying to relax his mind, said to Oink, "I don't know which will be worse, dying by pirates or surviving by your plan and hearing of it for the rest of my days."

Oink was about to say something when four anxious sailors followed Cump into the captain's quarters and pushed the brothers against the desk. "Oi! Don't be pushing!"

Standing up from his desk, Captain Humphreys wasted no time calmly but quickly explaining their plan, giving credit to the brothers and scoffing at the pirates believing they were carrying gold.

"Isn't this cowardly?" John asked. "Throwing a punch they don't expect and then running away."

"Is it?" Captain Humphreys asked. "I do not view suicide as bravery, and fighting them would be suicide, considering we are both outgunned and outmanned. We did not choose this battle, and to win it, we must be creative."

John cleared his throat. "Still, setting pistols among the powder on these rough waters could be suicide."

"Yes, it could be, but fighting them directly *would* be, therefore I am asking for a volunteer. Is there a man among you willing to take the challenge?"

As the captain waited patiently for someone to volunteer, Oink noticed him staring at the man standing directly behind him, and growing impatient with the silence, the boy looked down, saw a bare foot behind him, and stomped on it.

"Oi!" John yelled, causing the others to cheer and pat his back.

"You will do," Humphreys smiled.

As John tried to burn the boy with his eyes, Oink said,

"What? You're going to be a hero!"

"We will have to work quickly to prepare the contents of the chests, decide how to rig them, and then place them in the cockboat with John here. Take that empty chest there and find two more." Pulling out a large ring of keys from his desk drawer, he fiddled with one until he freed it. "Here is its key. Make certain you lock them when you have finished and pray the weather holds until they take them," the Captain said, handing it to John. "Cump, when we are ready to tow him behind us, have Gorge charge the guns and arm the passengers with what he can find. And if the plan fails, it is best to keep our numbers below board. Spread the passengers about in your quarters, my quarters, and the crew's quarters. When they hear Sledge ring his bell, they are to rush onto the deck ready to fight as best they can."

With the enemy ship less than fifty minutes away, Captain Humphreys leaned against the railing of the poop deck aiming his spyglass at a nervous John sitting in the roughly rocking boat being towed a hundred feet behind them. He watched him close the last of the three rigged chests and watched his shaking hands drop the key into the boat. Picking up the key, John locked the chest, straightened up to wave his arms, and then losing his balance, fell over the side. Then, without his body weight to counterbalance the weight of the chests, the small boat listed steeply.

"Pull him in!" Humphreys shouted through the wind.

With William and Cump pulling on the rope, several minutes later they had to put their weight into it, and a minute after that, Humphreys and Oink were helping the soaked sailor over the railing and onto the poop deck.

Unsheathing John's knife, Humphreys cut the rope tied to the railing, leaving the small boat behind, and after carefully cutting the rope tied around John's waist, he handed the knife back to him and patted him on the shoulder. "Well done, Powder. Now we wait and pray it does not rain."

"William, John has his sea name," Oink said loud enough for John to hear. "Now, it's your turn."

After a drenched John turned to Oink and said, "We'll soon know if I'll be keeping it," Humphreys put the spyglass to his eye, aimed it at the small boat that they left behind, and said, "Cump, she is listing far too much. With the waves as they are, she is certain to take on water."

With all looking out at the small boat growing smaller, Humphreys handed the spyglass to Cump, who aimed it toward the boat and after a couple of seconds, nodded. "Yes, the waves will flood her, but not before the ship reaches it, though the powder is certain to be wet when they take the chests… if they're taken."

Then in the morbid silence of the poop deck, William grabbed the rope that had been around John's waist and quickly tied it around his. "Pray for me, Oscar."

"It's Oink!" the boy barked as he pulled his eyes from the small boat to see his brother swing a leg over the railing and disappear over the side. "Willy!"

"Oink, grab the rope!" Humphreys demanded.

In his shock and confusion, Oink didn't hear the captain's order, so John grabbed it and wrapped it tight around his wrist.

During what seemed like too long a fall for only thirty-something feet, William questioned what he was doing and why he had been as impulsive as his younger brother when he should have waited for Cump or John to volunteer. Being sailors, they should've had far more experience swimming in rough waters.

Disappearing beneath the cool waves, he surfaced seconds later with the stern of the ship several feet away. Treading in the rough sea, he choked on a mouthful of salt water, coughed, breathed in more of it, coughed harder, and when he breathed in more and realized he was about to drown if the cycle continued, he forced himself to calm down and control his breathing. Searching for the small boat and not seeing it through the waves, he knew as much to swim in the opposite direction of the ship, and with the waves making it too difficult to breathe through his frantic front crawl, he changed to the breaststroke, and then finding it even more difficult to breathe, he carefully took a deep breath and swam the breaststroke underwater, where it seemed almost tranquil. On the eighth time coming up for air, he spotted the boat through the waves, and taking another deep breath, went under the water again before being yanked back by the rope around his waist.

As all watched William shrink in size as he repeatedly surfaced for air before vanishing under the waves, the rope tried to pull itself from John's hand. "He's reached the end!" he yelled.

After a moment of silence, Captain Humphreys told him to release the rope.

"NO!" Oink shouted as he went to grab the rope as it disappeared over the railing. "TURN US AROUND! WE'RE NOT LEAVING HIM!"

With sympathetic eyes, the captain looked over at the boy. "If we do that, the plan has failed and your brother's act would be for naught, but if the plan works, we will go back and search for him. That is a promise."

The man's words did nothing to pacify the terrified, sad, and angry boy, and as he struggled to climb over the railing that he was only a head taller than, John wrapped his arms around him and pulled him back.

"RELEASE ME!" the boy demanded as tears ran down his cheeks.

"If we could help William, I would jump into the sea to do just that," John said. "As it is, we're too far away to be any help. He must wait until we return."

"THEN, I'LL WAIT WITH HIM!" Oink yelled as he tried to squirm out of John's arms.

"The most you'll do is force him to help you. It's a long swim and one I doubt you could manage," John said, surprised by the boy's strength. "Tell me, do you believe in your plan?"

"I-I do," Oink nodded as he forced himself to calm down.

"Then you should believe that we'll be returning for him too, but we can't do that while they're close behind us."

Seeing the man's point, Oink calmed down more.

"Now, if I release you, will you stay with us?"

"Yes."

"Do we have your word?"

Oink tried to fight back his tears as he said, "Yes... yes, you have my word, my promise to stay here."

Releasing the boy, John watched him wipe his eyes with his fingers, dry them on his trousers, and return to the railing to look out towards the small boat that was almost too small to see.

Failing to untie the tight knot, William was struggling to

stay on the surface when the pulling stopped, and then realizing he was on his own, he continued with the underwater breaststroke while towing the rope behind him.

Finally gripping the bow of the cockboat, it took several tries of his exhausted shoulders before he could pull himself up to rest his stomach on its higher side, temporarily balancing it. Grabbing hold of the smaller chest on the opposite side and not giving any thought to the rigged pistol inside, he grunted each time he pulled it several inches toward him until it rested on his side of the boat. Not wanting to end up with his side then listing, he slid his stomach along the side of the boat, passed the much larger chest, and at its stern, groaned each time he yanked on the second smaller chest to pull it toward him.

As his side was then listing by his body weight, he lowered himself back into the sea, and after confirming the small boat wouldn't be listing too much on either side, he turned toward *The Colonist*. With no hope of reaching it, his tired heart skipped a beat, and when he turned to look for the pirate ship, it skipped another. It would be on the small boat in minutes, and knowing they would be on him too if he swam toward *The Colonist*, he swam away from the ships' path, and unable to continue the breaststroke with his aching and tired shoulders, he switched to the dog paddled.

Then his father's words forced their way into his head. *Your life is completely in His hands*. But at that moment, he was too exhausted to care.

"What's William doing?" Oink asked, breaking the silence on the poop deck.

Handing him the spyglass, Captain Humphreys said, "He balanced it and now is swimming from it. Intelligent lad. No good could come from swimming toward us."

After taking a moment to focus the unfamiliar tool, Oink searched the area around the boat and was relieved to find what he was sure was William's head above the water.

"He's fortunate it's bad weather," Cump said. "The sharks will be avoiding the—"

"Oink, what are the pirates doing?" John asked.

"The what?"

"The pirates."

Oink focused the spyglass on the ship with its row of ten muzzles peeking out from their gunports. "A man's hanging off the side near the water, and there's maybe two dozen on the deck," Oink answered with none of the excitement he normally would have had with seeing actual pirates.

"Good," Humphreys said. "They want the chests." Taking the spyglass from Oink, he asked, "And William?"

"I-I lost him. Lost him through the waves," Oink replied, tears building in his eyes again.

"Don't lose hope," John said as he placed his hand on the boy's shoulder. "Sink or swim, as they say, and it looks like he can swim better than I."

With Oink only able to nod before walking to the other side of the small deck to stand and stare out at the sea behind them, Humphreys lifted the spyglass to watch the pirate hanging from the side of the ship drop into the boat of chests and quickly secure a rope to it, and when his voice rose to tell the others that the pirates were lifting the chests onto the ship, the excitement that Oink, John, and Cump should have had with all going as planned wasn't there. "Let us pray they are three sheets to the wind and see the chests as an easy find." Then with the ship almost five minutes from them, he closed the spyglass and frowned. "That is if we survive this. They will be on us in minutes… sooner if they take the wind from our sails."

"I'm thinkin' from the silence they didn't take 'em," Gorge said as he joined them on the poop deck.

"They took them," John told him. "Now we're waiting for them to open one."

"Then let's pray they does. We've the guns charged and the passengers are ready with firearms and blades… and some blunt objects, but that jittery lot is far too anxious waitin' for the bell. I expect they'll be relieved to be fightin' if they must," Gorge said, before noticing Oink sitting alone in the corner of the small deck. "Why's 'e melancholic? Were they 'is chests?"

"His brother went over," John replied.

"Oh," Gorge whispered, his surprise quickly replaced by disappointment.

Captain Humphreys closed his spyglass. "Cump, when I give the mark, a sharp forty-five larboard and, Gorge, ready the larboard guns. We will attempt a broadside. How many shots do we have with the powder on hand?"

"Eleven, but that's includin' the guns on both sides charged and waitin'. That's to say, when we discharge what we charged, there's enough to charge only three guns."

"Then this broadside will have to do. I doubt we'll have the opportunity to show them our starboard."

"Aye, Captain," Gorge nodded. "Come, John. We've some fightin' to ready for."

"It's Powder now," John proudly told him as he followed him.

"Remind me when this is over."

Cump was about to leave too when he stopped and looked back at the boy. "Oink, come. You can help."

Oink nodded placidly before standing up and asking, "Will I get a sword?"

"There's not enough, but when the fighting starts, I'm certain you'll find a selection on the… it worked!"

Just as Captain Humphreys and Oink turned to see pieces of the pirate ship's stern fly from a cloud of smoke and flames, their ears rang with the sound of the explosion.

Then rushing from Gorge's quarters, the captain's quarters, and the deck's hatch while releasing excited battle cries, the passengers and sailors, with weapons in hand, gathered on the deck ready to fight, and not seeing the pirate ship alongside them, they silently looked around, confused.

When Gorge and John rushed to the poop deck to see the smoke rising from the pirate ship and the water around it splashing with debris, the large man had to push John away from him. "I never took ya as a hugger," he said as he walked over to a stoic Oink to place a hand on his shoulder. "I 'ear this was your plan. Fortunately for us, you're on our ship and not theirs."

As the passengers and sailors crowded the poop deck for a better view of the burning ship, only one passenger remained on the main deck. With a cutlass in hand, Philip stood near the hatch, and, much like Oink, seemed to have no care for what was happening around him.

"Lose yourselves!" Gorge demanded as the crowd of passengers and sailors forced him against the railing. "And be careful with those blades! By Jove, leave now or five lashes!"

"Captain," Cump said, "I believe we have a fireship heading toward us."

"It appears so," Humphreys nodded. "No time to turn. Keep as we are and pray their burning sales will put more distance between them and us before it explodes again."

"Come, lad," Gorge said as he took Oink's arm. "Ya lot leave this deck!"

Failing to pull his arm from the man's grip, Oink said, "No! William's still out there! We have to turn around and find him!"

Glaring at the boy for a moment, Gorge's eyes softened. "Come. She's burnin' and she's carryin' far more powder than we gifted'er. If ya wants to see your brother again, we go now."

"TAKE COVER!" the captain shouted just before the ship exploded and the shock wave smoothing out the rough waters knocked most off their feet, stretched the sails, and caused *The Colonist* to groan as its stern rose and its bow dipped. The incredible sound of the explosion that followed a split second later deafened everyone as burning debris began to rain down around them.

Forcing himself to his feet, Gorge yelled to Oink, "COME!" Then realizing that if he couldn't hear himself, no one else could either, he again grabbed Oink by the arm, and as the boy was struggling to his feet, pulled him toward the poop deck's stairs while knocking down others who were getting to their feet.

As debris tore through the sails, smashed into the deck, and struck some of those anxiously waiting in line to descend the main deck's stairs, Gorge was pulling Oink down the stairs when a short smoking plank struck the large man on the shoulder and the boy on the head.

And then the rain came.

From William's perspective, the burning ship looked as if it was about to take *The Colonist* down with her, and where he had only heard the first explosion, he felt the second as the shock wave rolled him over the sea, and where he was a safe distance from the debris of the first explosion, the debris launched further by the second began falling around him. Trying to avoid it, he did the only thing he could and took a deep breath before taking shelter several feet under the water.

As pieces of wood and metal splashed the water above him, like an arrow a six-foot-long, eight-inch-thick beam shot into it just inches from him, surprising him and causing him to exhale his air and inhale the water. As the beam vanished beneath him, he saw hundreds of twinkling stars as he began to lose consciousness and follow it down into the darkness. Then rising almost as fast as it had descended, the beam struck him in the stomach, forcing the water out of him as it pushed him to the surface.

**

His head hurt, but that didn't concern him so much when he realized he was wrapped tightly in a sheet and being carried by its ends. Expecting to be laid on a plank and after a quick prayer slid into the sea, he tried to free himself. "I'M NOT DEAD!" he yelled as he squirmed about. Opening his eyes to the plank ceiling, he realized he was lying in a hammock that was squeezing his arms to his sides.

"We know you're not. Everyone does now," William assured him as he sat in a chair beside the hammock. "Welcome back, Oscar."

Not noticing his brother using his given name, Oink grabbed the sides of the hammock and forced himself to sit up.

Feeling his head and finding a bandage wrapped tightly around it, he looked around the room and asked, "What happened? Why am I in Gorge's quarters? Why does my head hurt?"

"Ya near 'ad 'er knocked off," Gorge said, joining William by the hammock. "Been lyin' 'ere for near a month, ya lazy maggot, and your brother's been 'ere waitin' for ya much of that time."

"A month?"

"No," William replied, fighting back the smile that might encourage the man. "Close to a day."

"Now let's see 'ow your 'ead's workin'. 'Ow many fingers am I showin'?"

"You don't know? Were you hit on the head too?" Oink asked, causing William to let his smile out.

"'Ow's your arms feel?"

"With their hands," Oink smiled before dropping it when the man's face went stern. "Fine. Why?"

"I cut'em off," the large man said as the timekeeper's bell rang, and then with Oink's eyes enlarging as they darted to his hands grasping the sides of the hammock, he walked to the door. "They grew back, but since ya 'ad to check, ya'll be needin' more sleep, ya lazy maggot."

As the door closed, Oink asked, "What happened to you? I thought you were gone, gone forever."

"They came back for me. It was slow going with the torn sails against the wind and rain. Took a few hours. Now we're only going with the current while they make repairs."

"Do I need to tell you what you did was stupid?" Oink asked.

"It's a fine line between bravery and stupidity, remember?"

"Yes, and I still think it was stupid."

"Then I suppose that proves we're brothers," William smirked.

"Did I miss anything interesting?"

"More interesting than being chased by a ship that exploded twice? No, but to empty the guns, they discharged them into the sea, one after the other. Eight loud blasts, but nothing as loud as that ship's second blast, or even the first, and you missed the storm."

"I would have liked to have seen it."

"If you saw one storm, you saw them all."

"You know what I'm saying!"

"I do, but perhaps if you ask, they'll charge them again and fire them for your amusement."

"You believe they would?" Oink asked with some excitement.

"No. Stay here and I'll bring some food. They killed two pigs to celebrate the victory." Then, as Oink's eyes almost jumped out of his head, he added, "Crock wouldn't cook his hero's friend."

"They think I'm a hero?"

"Most do. Gorge spread the word of it being your plan."

"Anyone hurt besides me?"

"Some worse, most better. Two passengers were killed. The older man with the scar of a triangle on his chest and the one who's always... was always cursing and complaining. A sailor crushed an arm, and Gorge cut it off... but it hasn't grown back."

"And Philip?"

"He's fine. Still his quiet self," he said as the door opened and Sledge entered.

"I 'eard ya waked," the sailor said as he walked up to the hammock. "Welcome back. Did 'e tells ya we catched us a prisoner?"

"A pirate?" Oink asked, his excited eyes bouncing between William and Sledge. "You didn't tell me that. Did he fall onto the deck too?"

"No," Sledge chuckled. "Was grabbin' on the leaky boat. The fortunate devil was thrown off with the first blast. As fer the rest, who knows or cares?"

"I'll bring your plate of food," William said, standing up and heading to the door.

"Bring me one too, Fish."

With the door closing, Oink asked, "Fish? Did he earn his sea name too?"

"Yup, and 'twere me that gives'er to 'im," Sledge smiled proudly. "Not too creative like, but the firsts to offer'er, so she's as official as can be."

Staying out of the way of the dozen sailors attaching the mended sails to their yards and with his muscles aching much like they did that morning after their first day cleaning the ship, William was slowly swabbing the bow of the deck when Oink startled him.

"Have you seen him, talked to him?"

"Blessed evening to you too. Is your head still hurting?"

"Not so much. Have you talked to him, the pirate?"

"Only saw him brought aboard. Didn't talk to him and don't want to."

"Where is he?"

"In the captain's quarters."

"Good, I want to see him," Oink said, turning to walk to

the stern.

William dropped the mop and painfully hurried after him. "No one's permitted to see him."

"Are you forgetting who we are? We're the reason he's here!" Oink said in a tone that asked if William was stupid.

"You should sleep, but take your bed so Gorge can have his."

"I will, but I want to see this pirate first."

"He'll still be there after you've rested."

Oink stopped at the door. "How can you be certain? A lot happened in a few hours yesterday."

"Yes?" Captain Humphreys said in response to the knock, and setting his quell aside, he smiled as the brothers walked in. "Good to see you awake, Oink. What brings you two here?"

"I would like to see the prisoner. Perhaps have a few words with him?"

"If it were anyone other than you two, I would say no," the man with dark bags under his tired eyes said as he stood up, revealing his torn and slightly blood-stained shirt. "Come, but keep a distance. He can still bite and I expect he will if given the opportunity."

After noticing the dim room's boarded-up windows, the two noticed the long-bearded figure sitting with his legs stretched out at the back of the room a few feet from a chair with a hole in its seat. As they followed the captain closer to the man, William cautious and Oink excited, they noticed the opened wounds on his weathered face, his badly torn shirt, and his ripped leather trousers before realizing his ankles were tied together and his arms were bound behind him.

With William looking at him with disgust and Oink looking at him with fascination, the man, who appeared much too pathetic to be a pirate, looked curiously back at them.

"Excuse the state o' me dress. I'd've dressed proper like if I'd've known we'd be 'avin' guests."

"Are you a pirate?" Oink asked.

"Been called one. Been called better, been called worser."

"Have you killed people?"

"Straight ta the matter, eh?" he said, giving a quick laugh followed by a cough. "Killin's a good part o' wha' me does."

"Do you enjoy it?"

"As much as one can, sometimes more, but it depends on the weather."

"The weather?"

"Whether I'm in the mood fer 'er," the pirate laughed again.

"Were you surprised by the blast?"

"Lots o' questions, eh?" the man said as his eyes bounced between Oink and William. "Had no time to be. Woke in them waters. But that there wasn't honorable, not at all. Yer cap'ain's a cowardly one!" the pirate snarled as he glanced past the brothers to Captain Humphreys. "Still, if me cap'ain wasn't so eager, we would've waited til night ta close in on yas and tha' there'd never 'ave—"

"This is the one who came up with that plan. You were beaten by one with only eleven years behind him," Humphreys said.

"Aye, but, Humphreys, ya 'ad one with eleve' years fight yer battle fer ya. Which is the worser?"

"I'm twelve now," Oink corrected them.

"Good fer ya," the pirate said with a sarcastic smile.

"I did not realize that. Never too late to wish you well on reaching your next one, but after yesterday, I doubt the wish is necessary," Humphreys said, sincerely.

"Still, we were figurin' 'twas a game 'til yer mad sailor jumped ship ta take the chests ta 'is grave, maybe ta pay Saint Peter. 'Twas good fer ya ta keep that there game a secret from yer crew too. Mades it real, it did."

Both Oink and Humphreys glanced at William, who didn't appear to have heard the man.

"Come," Humphreys said. "We will not be making friends with this one. Let us leave him to consider the noose that will soon tighten around his neck."

"One moment, if you please," William said, startling both Oink and the captain. "If we gave you the sterling, would you have stopped the chase?"

The man took a moment to think. "Don't expec' so. Why stops there whens there's a cargo to boot?"

For a moment, William struggled to find the courage to ask what he didn't want to know but felt he needed to. "Would you… would you have sold us into slavery, slavery in The East?"

"Wha?" the man wheezed. "Nah, far too much trouble. Far too far. No, we would've just towed the ship."

"And what of us?"

"What o' yas? Perhaps a quick one. Run ya through if ya didn't fights. If ya did, we'd makes a game o' ya, keelhau' ya or somethin'."

With Oink's jaw dropping, William stood speechless as he tried to control his strange desire to strike the man.

Enjoying William's reaction, the pirate laughed. "Or we migh' skin ya! And if ya 'ad women, we wouldn't kill 'em, not righ' off. Nah, we'd 'ave some fun with 'em first, we would!"

Then, as an almost painful energy surged from William's

chest, making his arms and legs throb with each rapid beat of his heart, he considered grabbing the cutlass hanging on the wall and running the man through with it, but when his eyes fell on Oink, who was also shocked by the man's words, he fought against the urge.

"Come, lads. He is what he is. You will find no humanity in the likes of him. Worse than the Devil," Humphreys said while leading the speechless brothers gently toward the door by the back of their shoulders.

Struggling to control his anger, William forced out, "Y-you're certain… certain he'll hang?"

"I am," the captain nodded while looking curiously at William. "Does that agree with you?"

Thinking it too quick of a death, but wishing he was there to witness it, William nodded.

"Why's he here, here in your quarters?" Oink asked. "Is he a captain too? A first mate?"

"No, he is not, but it is the safest place for him. No less than half the crew and passengers want to offer him some punishment," the captain explained as he opened the door. "Have a good day, Fish and Oink. Oh, and I will no longer require you to clean my quarters or empty my head. Another will have that task on account of our visitor back there."

**

William failed to embrace his new sea name. While he put up with most using it, he refused to have Oink do so, and several days after the event with the pirates, when they were cleaning out the pigsty, Oink asked why he didn't want the name.

"When we reach Virginia, I want to leave this… this *adventure* behind us, and that includes being called Fish. I want no memento of this voyage."

"Because of the work?"

"Partly."

"The chase?"

"That too."

"The pirate, the prisoner?"

"Partly… but mostly because of what he said. I would rather forget that I came across evil and that we came close to death."

"You want to forget about Gorge and Captain Humphreys?"

"If remembering them reminds me of the pirate, yes."

"And Philip and me?" Oink asked with the hurt noticeable in his voice.

"I met him here, but he'll not remind me of here. He's not part of the ship. And you're my brother and remind me of home, not of this… unless you insist on talking about it when we're in Virginia."

"I'll want to, but I can keep it to myself," Oink said. "But it was a good plan, yes?"

"A great plan. Saved our souls… or at least our lives."

William didn't mention that he worried there would be another ship coming after them. Though he expected they could trick them too with the same plan, he worried they might be low on powder, worried that the small boat had yet to be repaired, and worried that if more ships came, they might come in groups and/or at night, spoiling the plan. He would worry until they reached Virginia, where he would trade those worries for others.

CHAPTER 14
Making Plans

Counting down the days wasn't a habit. The only other time she did it was when her mother had told her the number of days to her birthday. There were only four — easy for a six-year-old.

A month before Peter's death, the two had started counting down the days to their wedding, and after his death, she couldn't stop herself from continuing to count them down. It was the only thing she had of him to hold on to, but now that the day arrived, it put an end to it, and with no date set for leaving Virginia, there was nothing more to count down to, nothing more to hold on to.

**

With the younger children's shouts and laughter penetrating the house and with several sheets of paper in hand, she entered Philpot's study. Dropping the sheets on his desk, she sat down and pulled on the deep left drawer. Finding it locked, she realized her mistake and pulled out the middle one on her right to remove the tray holding the bottle of ink and a quill, and after carefully working the small cork from the bottle and with her hand slightly shaking, she dipped the quill into the ink.

For the last week she had been writing the letter in her head, but now motivated to put it to paper, she didn't know how to start, and growing frustrated with herself, she tapped the quill on the paper and made several small blotches, but she didn't care. She would use that sheet and the next two or three to test her words, and by the time she was ready to write the final version, she would do so with impressive penmanship.

Deciding to start with the name and address, Becky pulled a letter from beneath the sheets of paper and searched the writing. Not finding them on the horizontal lines, she rotated the sheet to search her brother's vertical lines of writing that saved him both paper and post. Finding what she was looking for, she copied them onto the blotched sheet of paper.

As a leg of pig slowly roasted, the stew boiled, soup simmered, and bread baked, Mary and Becky stood at the kitchen table quietly chopping vegetables, and with Becky's unusually quiet demeanor that morning continuing into the afternoon, Mary knew something was bothering her, and though she believed her friend would eventually mention it, she still had to struggle to hold herself back from asking.

With the shouts and laughter of the younger children suddenly stopping, both heard a horse approaching and each said to the other, "Jacob's here." When the horse stopped at the entrance, blocking much of the light from coming in through the opened door, a man no older than twenty-five and with a reddish-brown complexion bent forward from its saddle to look in from under the top of the door frame. "Good morning, my angels," he smiled before sliding down from the animal. Removing his cocked hat, he quickly finger-combed his black straight hair hanging to his shoulders and pulled a letter from a saddlebag. "Master Philpot has post," he said as he walked into the kitchen.

"Good afternoon, Jacob," Becky said, forcing a smile as she pushed her chopped carrots toward Mary's onions and wiped her hands on her apron. Taking notice of how attractive he looked in his clean trousers and shirt peeking out from his opened long coat, a rush of guilt swept over her as if her thoughts were betraying Peter.
"Sugar cane, I've a letter from Boston for the master. Eighteen pence for his share of the post, plus my one."

"Jacob, I have to say if we used a watch, we would set it by you," Mary said as she wiped her hands on her stained robe.

"Then I'm content you don't. I wouldn't want you putting it into practice, would rather not have the responsibility," he said. "More so when this morning's rain slowed my travel. Spent some time up near Conner's Creek helping pull a one-horse cart from some deep mud. Took two of us, and it wouldn't surprise me to hear it was stuck again."

"You're a kind man, Jacob," Becky said as she took the letter, and after fishing some coins from the small pocket of her bodice and counting out several, she handed them to him, her eyes enlarged, and she said, "Give me a moment. I have a letter for you."

"No need to write me a letter. You only need to tell me and save me the time of reading it," Jacob joked.

Becky didn't seem to hear his words as she rushed past him, almost slamming into the side of his horse, and flew up the few stairs to the backdoor of the large two-story house.

"Must be quite the letter for me," he joked again. "Mary, I can't understand how you can put up with the heat of three fires. This must be the biggest and hottest kitchen on this side of Williamsburg."

"I've become accustomed to it, to a point. Come and tell me how this stew is," she said, limping to the large pot hanging over the fire and grabbing a wooden spoon from the shelf above the fireplace.

Accepting the spoon of stew, Jacob blew on it before putting it in his mouth and exaggerated tasting it by swishing it about with his tongue. "It's as best as it could be," he said, handing the spoon back. "If Master Philpot wasn't in charge, I would join the plantation, if only for the food."

"I have to say, Jacob, I've never heard of anyone wanting to work as one of us," Mary laughed as she pretended to tap him on the head with the spoon.

"Don't be dripping stew on my head."

"I wouldn't be if you had cleaned off all that was on it," she said, laughing again while reaching for a cloth-covered basket on the table. "Here, take some rolls for your journey. They're a day old but still fine, I would say."

"I thank you, and I'll eat them on the way to Carter's place. It's best to have a full stomach when listening to the patriarch's complaints about my penny. He's of the mind that since I'm heading into town with or without his letters, I shouldn't be charging him for taking his," he said as he placed the two rolls in his trousers' pocket. "Tell me, how is she today?"

"Strangely quiet."

"I would expect as much."

"Why?"

"It's the day. Her wedding day. I had the honor of being invited. Perhaps after today, her heart will start to heal and she'll be able to put it behind her and start wearing her pretty smile again."

Fighting to control the sudden swelling behind her eyes, Mary said, "She mentions her man, her Peter, so seldom, so rarely, I... I forgot about their wedding day, though I have to say I'm never aware of the days of the month to know when it would arrive."

Becky rushed into the kitchen and held out the letter. "This is for Boston. I expect it's nineteen pence, including yours."

Taking the letter, Jacob examined the single sheet of paper folded in on itself and sealed by a wax stamp. "No, and no. It's only one sheet, making it fifteen pence, and the extra one we'll ignore."

"No, I'm paying you to bring it to the post," she insisted before nervously counting out the coins and holding them out to him.

Exaggerating a sigh, Jacob took the coins, and as he slid them into his pocket, Mary limped over and grabbed the letter from him. "What's this? Your stamp? Not the plantation's? How long have you had this? Look, Jacob. Two... two things back to back," Mary said, holding the envelope out for the man to see the imprint in its wax seal.

"Two R's," Jacob nodded.

"R's, yes. With a stamp as that, I have to say we'll soon have to call her Mistress Rowling."

If not for the contents of the letter, Becky would have been amused by her friend's boldness, but, instead, she blushed. "It was a gift... a gift from Margaret before she became ill, and I've never needed to use it until now." Realizing she may have said too much, she snatched the envelope from Mary and handed it back to Jacob.

"It is impressive," the self-employed postman said while

admiring the stamp. "But as much as I dislike it, I must bid you both farewell."

After the two women followed him to the entrance and watched him place the envelope in the saddlebag, climb onto his horse, and ride off with a shout of, "I'll see you sweets next week," Mary limped back to the table while Becky continued standing by the door, ashamed by what the stamp might have told her friend.

"I do worry about Jacob carrying all that post," Mary said as she held out the bottom of her frock, brushed the vegetables onto it, and limped to the large pot to drop them into it. "He's earned much trust, but I expect some English are not happy with him earning sterling by picking up and dropping off the post." Grabbing the wooden paddle, she stirred the stew. "He must earn almost a pound a month and should hire a second for protection. If not for being an Indian, if he was a free man, he would be dead on the road before now. As it is, few would touch him for fear of starting a war. Perhaps the only time being an Indian here is to his advantage."

Having never considered it, Becky was impressed to hear Jacob might earn as much as a pound a month, and then it struck her as odd that Mary would know the denominations of sterling until she remembered that when Beth had learned a fact, she might proudly pass her newfound knowledge on to Mary. And if she didn't, Mary might ask her what she had learned that day in the hope of learning from it.

Mary limped back to the table, picked up a knife, and then, as if not knowing why she had picked it up, placed it back down. "I think we're done for now." Looking over at Becky still standing near the door, she limped over to her and surprised her with a strong hug. Releasing her, she took

Becky's hands. "I know what today is. The significance of it."

Not sure what to say, Becky stood staring at the woman.

"And I know you would never use a stamp such as that for your family's letters. No, they're much too familiar for such a thing, and I want you to know I would never fault you for leaving us, but I would need to prepare my mind for it. We all would." With Becky standing there still not sure what to say, Mary continued, "I know you're not happy here. I know you have little reason to stay, and I know you were planning to leave with your Peter… and you did once tell me your family is in Boston or near it. I have to say that besides our friendship, I see little reason for you to stay where you probably shouldn't be and where you won't truly be content, can't be content."

As another wave of shame washed over her for betraying Mary by not mentioning her need to leave, Becky swallowed and said, "The… the letter is to a friend of the master of the estate where my family holds positions. My brother wrote he had learned they would soon have an opening for a governess, and I'm hoping to contact them before they find one. I-I didn't want to say anything until I received word back, but I do need to leave. I need to find something… something less… less…"

"Painful on the soul?"

Becky nodded.

"You need not explain your actions to me. I understand. We all do… except perhaps the Master, but I have to say this place will become darker without you, so much so I would rather not imagine it. I don't believe I have to say I wouldn't want you to retire from here, but it's more than understandable if you would want to, need to. You haven't been happy since the child's death and then there was your Peter's and then Mistress Margaret's illness… and her death." Mary looked down at the dirt floor for a moment before looking again at Becky. "Saying that aloud makes me want you to leave. I would hate to see you catch her state, and without Mistress Margaret and Beth, I expect the master will return to how he was before he married, and I wouldn't want you here if he does become as harsh as he was. But never mind that. Tell me, what will you do if they've found a governess?"

"I haven't yet committed my mind to anything. Since Peter's death, I've been living day to day," Becky said with her eyes beginning to water in reaction to her friends. "It will be a time before I receive a reply. A few weeks for the letter to reach them and at least that long for their reply. Still, there's little chance of being accepted. I might have delayed too long sending the letter, and if they haven't found a governess, they may not want me without a letter of referral, and I could never ask Master Philpot for one. I don't expect he would respond well to the request and can only hope my family's weak connection will be enough."

For a moment, Becky considered asking her friend to keep the news to herself, but she knew Mary wouldn't. It would spread among the slaves but go no further than there. Then she again found herself engulfed in the arms of the older woman.

Releasing her, Mary said, "Seeing how there is little to do until the meal is ready, why not give your mind a rest and lay your head down for a time?"

Then with an unusual desire to be alone, Becky nodded and left the kitchen. Even with Mary's understanding, she entered the house feeling as if she was deserting her and the others, and as she reflected on what her friend had said, she wondered what Mary meant by Philpot becoming harsher.

CHAPTER 15
Port Anne

William, Oink, and Philip joined the starboard wall of tanned torsos facing the ship-lined pier of Port Anne only two hundred feet away. Appreciating the early morning's cool breeze, the three said nothing for several minutes as they took in the surreal sight while wondering if they would have to get used to walking on land.

With their awe wearing off, some passengers speculated on how long it would be before they left the boring confines of the sweltering ship. Others discussed what they wanted as their first meal on land. Some expressed their joy with finally having the company of women, and a few questioned whether they would have to overcome landsickness, just as they did with seasickness, but none could answer it definitively since none were certain it was or wasn't an illness.

Of the three, William was the first to speak. Looking over at Oink on the other side of Philip, who had yet to regain the sparkle he had brought with him when boarding the ship, he asked, "Oink, are you happy to be here, to be leaving the ship?"

Not wanting to admit his disappointment with their

adventure ending, Oink replied with a nod

"One adventure ends, and another begins," William said as if reading his brother's mind, and as Oink grew a smile when realizing his brother was right, William nudged Philip. "And you?"

"Yes," Philip replied with a slight smile that surprised the older brother. "It's overwhelming that we're here, almost unbelievable."

With the three again silently staring at the pier in the distance, they didn't notice Cump leaving the captain's quarters with a smile so out of place that it would have looked sinister had they seen it. After ordering all to form a group near him, he diluted their excitement by saying, "Don't be expecting to leave the ship today. Word of our arrival will be sent, and you'll be released to your masters on the morrow or the day after. If you have clothes to wash, you may do so today, seeing how the weather permits it." Then he seemed to grow two inches taller when he stiffened up, pushed his chest out, and added, "Now if any of you have the fool's intention of jumping ship, we'll be guarding against it. Soldiers are watching the pier, and the crew will be on constant watch here. Anyone caught attempting to leave without being signed for will be punished."

From somewhere within the group, a man asked, "How's that?"

"How's what?"

"What's the punishment?"

"Planning on jumping?"

"No, only curious."

"The same as that of a runaway indentured: a minimum of five lashes and two years added to the contract," Cump replied, and then addressing the group again, said, "On the morrow, most of you will be called as your master receives you. If the weather permits, you'll wait near the bow while they wait at the stern to sign for you. If it doesn't, you'll wait below. Those remaining, those not received then, will be called the next day, and if you're not received then, we'll find new contracts for you."

"What? Auction us as slaves?" a passenger asked at the front of the group.

"If that's how you wish to see it, but now that we've arrived, tonight we'll eat like the King of England. There will be chicken, ham, and more. We'll eat, drink, and be content, and if you can't find a spot at the tables, you may eat wherever you sit. The deck will be open for eating. Have a blessed morning."

With his last sentence temporarily making up for the disappointment caused by the ones before it, some passengers were brave enough to pat him on the back as he made his way through the group to the stairs' hatch.

"May we indulge in a bit of rum?" someone asked.

Cump stopped, turned around, and again disappointed the group. "No. With your contracts about to begin, we'll be following their rules. Most, if not all, are not to consume spirits unless offered by your master. Oh, and for those who want it, Gorge and Crock will offer haircuts and shaves. Some of you could use both," he said, looking at William before continuing toward the hatch.

Seven hours later and still in his sailor's clothes but with his sparse facial hair removed and his hair shortened to the length it was when he had boarded the ship, William stood guard over his and Oink's clothes drying over the railing of the poop deck. No longer required to work, he watched Sledge and another sailor empty the waste buckets into the harbor where he expected the stench of their contents to linger for a period, causing him to worry it might invade the clothes he looked forward to putting on, the first in months washed in fresh water, making them less stiff and coarse and not causing rashes on parts he would never mention.

Over the last two months he avoided much of the anxiety of what was to come in Virginia by not thinking about it, at points almost forgetting why he was on the ship, but now being there, he looked out at the pier anxiously considering what was to come. Would his master be pleased with seeing him? Would he be somebody whom he would enjoy working under? Would the position be one he would learn quickly? Was he expected to know his tasks? Then reminding himself that he was to be trained, the man would have to assume he was arriving knowing little to nothing about overseeing slaves, and he was sure there was much to learn since it had to be more complicated than working in the mine. Then he wondered how long it would take to adjust to the climate. He assumed, like Britain, it was at its hottest point of the year, but he wasn't sure since Philip had told him the night they first met that there were only two seasons in Virginia: winter and summer. He thought his friend was joking, but he wasn't sure.

"Anything of interest?"

Appreciating the interruption, he turned his head to his capless brother standing a head taller than the railing with his eyes puffy and red. "You'll have the morning with him too. And if we're not received on the morrow, then that evening and the next morning too."

Not needing or wanting his brother's reminder, Oink again asked, "Anything interesting?"

"Only that cart," William said, gesturing with his head toward the pier. "It's been there since I laid out the clothes. Two soldiers came over from it, but nothing happened since they went into the captain's quarters."

Oink looked at the wharf jutting out from the end of the pier to see two tiny figures in red cocked hats and red jackets standing near a cart with a large, windowless square box built onto its bed.

"That's new too," William said, looking down the side of the ship.

Standing on his toes, Oink looked down over the railing to discover the steep gangway hugging the ship's side, and at its end, two sailors whom he didn't recognize waiting in a small boat. "I should have expected that. Saves us from using a rope ladder."

Seconds later, a tall sailor dressed impressively in a red long coat highlighted by dark-blue cuffs, lapels, and collar caught their attention when he stepped out of the captain's quarters saying something loud but from where the two stood, incoherent. When two red-jacketed soldiers holding their long guns across their chests stepped out to join him, Oink said, "You said two."

"I must have missed the one in the long coat," William replied before three pairs of sailors struggling with heavy crates left the captain's quarters to join the soldiers. "Do you suppose that could be—"

"That's the sterling!" Oink almost shouted.

Watching as the soldiers led the sailors toward the gangway and then looking over the railing to watch them direct the sailors to set the crates in the boat, Oink thought he might want to be a soldier when his indentured contract ended. Their uniforms, long guns, and swords at their sides were impressive and intimidating, and if it had been soldiers guarding *The Colonist* in London, he would never have considered hiding in the crate of piglets.

When the eight returned to the ship, the two soldiers joined the taller one standing with Cump near the hatch, and after Cump and the tall soldier exchanged a few more words, the four returned to the captain's quarters.

Curious, the brothers said nothing as they moved to the poop deck's stairs for a better view, and they didn't have to wait long before the two soldiers exited the captain's quarters, one pushing along the pirate, who had his hands fastened behind his back by iron clamps joined by a short chain. The few sailors also watching responded to the pirate's curses with cheers and clapping, and as a soldier forced the broken man down the gangway, the sailors offered him their worst wishes. Then returning to the railing to look down over the side, the brothers watched the pirate being pushed into the boat to sit with a soldier on each side of him.

"He finally has the sterling," Oink grinned.

"He does," someone said from behind them.

Turning around to face the tall, clean-shaven soldier in the long red coat, the man smiled as he gave them a moment to recognize him. "I'm displaying my colors," John... Powder said.

With William too confused to speak, Oink asked, "You joined the Army?"

"Always been in it, or I should say, I've never been a sailor. I was tasked with watching the sterling. Joined the ship here under the guise of a new sailor," he told them as he reached into the inside pocket of his coat. "Only the captain was aware of my true reason for being here."

"You were protecting the sterling from the pirates?" Oink asked.

Searching in one of the lower pockets on the outside of his coat, he replied, "No, I was protecting the sterling from the crew. We can only speculate on what they might have done had they come across it. Greed makes people do evil deeds, as we witnessed, and I appreciate neither of you mentioning the sterling after the incident." Finding what he was looking for in a third pocket, he pulled out his fist. "I didn't want to leave without saying farewell and without giving you these." After taking a moment to separate the two leather cords, he held them up to reveal a key hanging from each. "I saved these for us," he said, offering them out. "I'm wearing mine for good fortune."

Taking one, Oink said, "I thank you," and excitedly hung it around his neck as William, still at a loss for words, took his.

"I'll admit I didn't expect your plan to work, but I suppose it proves that greed makes fools of some. I thought the better plan would have been to drop the sterling overboard and fight to the end, but that's probably because of my soldiering. But your plan was better in the end, and it left me with a memory I'll keep to my end and a sea name I'll admit I'm rather proud to possess. From here, I'll be going to Boston for four years. That is after we investigate who and how word leaked about the sterling onboard, and because of that and with piracy here growing, I expect they'll stop using merchant ships for the sterling, making it a longer wait between the navy's deliveries, that is until they cast coinage here as they do in

Massachusetts. And with that, I pray we meet again. I very much want to see what you make of yourselves."

Oink shook Powder's offered hand. "I pray too that we'll see you again."

"I-I too hope we meet again," William forced out as he shook his hand.

"I must depart but know that what we experienced joins us together for a lifetime, joins us all as any fight would. You, me, Cump, Gorge, the Captain, and the rest, but perhaps not the pirate," Powder grinned. "So be well until we meet again."

With the brothers still taken aback by the man's revelation, they watched him walk down the two flights of stairs to the main deck and then to the gangway. After returning Powder's wave, they watched the three soldiers and the pirate being rowed to the wharf where the waiting soldiers took several trips to carry the crates to the cart's secured back before forcing the pirate into it too. After the cart rode off, the brothers continued watching the shore for several minutes, neither saying a word.

With nothing more to interest him, Oink stuck out the palm of his hand to William, who placed his leather-corded key into it. "Do you think they'll hang him soon?" Oink asked as he added William's key to the other one around his neck.

"Why would they hang Powder?"

"No! The pirate!"

"I expect they will after a trial."

"Do you want to see him hanged?"

"No," William lied. "You?"

"No," Oink lied.

"Master Lovely, Oink Lovely," Gorge said in an exaggerated aristocratic accent and bowing so deeply that he was looking down at the planks of the poop deck, and when he straightened up, almost lost his balance. "The cap'ain… Captain Humphreys requests your presence in his quarters if you would."

Oink returned the exaggerated bow. "I thank you, my good man. Please inform him I will be there momentarily," he said in a poor aristocratic accent before walking toward the stairs.

"If by chance you arrive before I and if it pleases you, inform him for me that you will be there momentarily, My Lord," Gorge said as he put his arm out to block William's way. "Sorry, Fish. The man asked only for 'im, only for Oink there."

Wondering what the captain would need with his brother, it occurred to William that Oink would have to sign his name to the contract, just as he had done months before.

Gorge put his hand on William's shoulder, cleared his throated and added, "But allow me to say, and I think I speaks for all the crew 'ere… no, I'm sure I does when I say I… we appreciate your work, and if not for ya and Oink there, we mightn't be 'ere. I should say too that bein' at sea for a stretch, we rather undervalue ya landlubbers, but ya and Oink 'ave given us a new appreciation for 'em, at least for a bit."

"I thank you," William said, noticing the rum on the man's breath.

The large man cleared his throat again and followed it up with a burp. "No, we should be thankin' ya. On the morrow, me and most of the crew'll be takin' leave for a couple days before dockin' and unloadin', but I expect I'll be seein' ya before then to say our farewells, but even then, not our final ones. No, I'm expectin' we'll meet again before the year's done."

Watching Gorge turn and slightly stagger to the stairs, William hoped he wouldn't be caught intoxicated and sentenced to several strikes of the whip, but then realizing it would be Gorge delivering them, he smiled at the thought of the man trying to whip himself in his intoxicated state.

With his shirt partially unbuttoned and its sleeves rolled up, Captain Humphreys sat behind his desk pouring rum from a ceramic bottle into a tin cup resting on the desk with two others. Setting the bottle down, he was about to pick up the cup when the door opened.

"You asked to see me, Captain Humphreys?"

The man smirked and pointed to the two chairs in front of his desk. "Take a chair, if you please." As Oink sat in one, the man continued smirking. "In the future, you should knock and wait for a response before entering. Imagine how awkward it would be if I were entertaining a woman, dancing with her on the bed."

"My apologies," Oink said, not understanding why they would dance on his bed, and then confused by the man's slight slur, he noticed the ceramic bottle, the cups, and several wet rings on the desk. "You asked to see me?" he repeated.

"Yes, yes," the captain nodded, seemingly shaking off his smirk. "On the morrow or the next day, you and your brother will join your master. Are you welcoming it with pleasure?"

"I suppose I am."

"I see," he nodded again before taking a moment to rub his chin. "I must tell you I am reconsidering what we should do with you, what would be best for you and perhaps for us as well."

Panicking, Oink said, "We decided I-I would go with

William. We-we worked to pay down the journey, to lower the costs, to make it… to make it tempting to his master. You said you would make it an offer he couldn't refuse."

"That is correct, and it remains an option, but that was decided during our serendipitous encounter."

Not knowing the meaning of *serendipitous* and assuming it was a bad thing, Oink's heart raced faster.

"That was before we were acquainted with you. Before we developed respect for you," Humphreys said, taking a moment to rub his chin again. "I am concerned with what will become of you, and that depends on what happens to you, and what happens to you depends on the choices you make." Seeing the confusion on Oink's face, he paused for a moment, "I beg you to consider my words. When you were first discovered, we had decided you would work down the cost of the voyage, and you and your brother did, but now, Oscar, I am reconsidering what is best for you." With Oink trying to hide his panic, the captain picked up his cup. "It is customary for the captain to uncork the finer rum when we drop anchor at our destination. We do not patronize the taverns, but we have this, our more intimate celebration among the officers, and now more significant considering the predicament we have survived. We even gave several drinks to our guest, if only to make him more manageable… seeing how it is the end for him." He was about to place the cup to his lips when Oink's panicked stare caused him to smile. "Would you like a bit?"

Not hearing much of what the man had said through his panic, but recognizing his last sentence as a question, Oink nodded, causing Captain Humphreys to take a moment to stare back at the boy whom he had expected to refuse the offer. Then believing he was being called out on his jest, he added two splashes of rum to a cup, set the bottle down, and leaned forward to hand the cup to a confused Oink. Standing, Humphreys held his cup out. "Cheers to our arrival and prayers for our safe journey back."

Standing to tap his cup against the captain's, Oink said, "Cheers," and impressed the man by placing the cup to his lips and sipping the rum that burned the inside of his cheeks before he forced it down his throat. A second later, he was struck by a coughing fit that caused the captain to release a short laugh that the boy didn't appreciate. Recovering, Oink tried to save face. "My apologies. I believe I might have caught the chills."

"It will burn less on the next sip," the man said through a smile as they both returned to their chairs.

Taking his words as a challenge, Oink wiped his eyes with his shirtsleeve, took a second determined sip, and discovered the man was correct. With the liquid then warming his stomach, he followed him with yet another sip.

Captain Humphreys dropped his smile and straightened up as if suddenly remembering where he was and who he was. "Now back to the topic before us. I will start by informing you that our return to London will be my last voyage with this ship. Once in London, I shall take command of another." After he took another sip from his cup, the boy did the same and placed his empty cup on the desk. "I am telling you this because I would like to offer you the opportunity to join my crew as a timekeeper. I have never made this offer to someone as young, but you are twelve now and would earn a pound and a half each way. A respectable yearly sum for a timekeeper traversing the ocean four times per year. What say you to that?"

With his head feeling slightly foggy, Oink said, "Yes!"

Then remembering his brother, he said, "Perhaps," and then thinking about it more, he reluctantly shook his head. "No. I can't. I can't accept the offer."

Disappointed, the captain stared at the boy for a moment. "I expect the reason for your declination is that it would separate you from your brother, and I can appreciate that when considering you trespassed to be with him. I would have liked to have offered a position to William as well, but he has a signed contract." The man picked up the bottle and was about to pour more rum into his cup when he stopped and placed the bottle back on the desk. "I suppose I should ignore the other option: delivering you back to Kendleshire. But there is yet another option, that of sending you out on your own. That is to say, we would consider your voyage paid… but I would fear for you in this nearly lawless land, even with two pounds in your pocket, or perhaps more because of it. It's only worth half here, but a pound is a pound to a robber, of which Virginia has more than its share."

With the rum having relaxed him, numbing both his surprise with the option to be free in Virginia and his confusion by the two pounds, Oink said, "I would prefer to be with my brother. Being near him is not being with him." With the captain's nod relaxing him further, he added, "And I don't have two pounds."

"My apologies. It seems the rum has slowed me down," he said before pulling out a drawer on his right, lifting a small sack from it, and laying it on the desk. "Gorge insisted we contribute to your new life in Virginia, so this is yours — two pounds, three shillings, and seven pence. A considerable sum and one I would keep to myself if it was in my possession." Oink's dropped jaw caused the captain to smile and say, "I should admit I had little hope for the plan's success."

That's the second time today someone said that!

"But it was successful, and we are here because of it, and the crew wanted to show their appreciation. It has been honestly gained and properly deserved. And I believe we need one more to celebrate."

Joining the captain in standing, Oink watched as the man poured a bit of rum into each cup, and after each took a cup, said, "Cheers," and clanged them together, Oink followed him in downing it. Then as his stomach grew warmer, his ears did too.

"Now with what we had decided being decided yet again, I will have the contracts for your indentured servitude ready by the morning and Cump or Gorge will have you put your name on them. I hope to see you once more before you depart, but if not, allow me now to shake your hand and tell you that in the years I have left on this earth, I do not expect to come across another character quite like you."

Oink placed his empty cup on the desk, and as he shook the man's hand from across it, Humphreys told him he would miss him, and releasing his hand, reminded him to take his sack of coins.

Doing as he was told, Oink forced it in the pocket of his sailor's trousers, and after bowing slightly, he turned and headed to the door. Then an idea came to him and excited by it, he spun around. "Captain?"

"Yes."

"With my newfound sterling, may I purchase Gibby?"

"What's a... a gibby?"

"A pig, a pig I befriended. He has a gibbous mark on his side, and I would like to buy him if I may."

"A pig," the man smiled. "You made a pet of a pig?"

"Yes, and I consider him a friend rather than a pet."

After taking a moment to consider the request, Captain Humphreys frowned. "If the pig were mine to sell, I would certainly gift it to you, my friend, but sadly, it is not. They are accounted for, more than accounted for when considering we lost several and ate two."

Disappointed but honored that the man had called him friend, Oink nodded his understanding before turning to the door, and then realizing he may never see him again, he looked back at the man returning to his chair. "Captain Humphreys, it was an honor being in your company."

Humphreys cleared his throat and looked down at his desk as if needing to avoid eye contact. "It was mine also, Oscar Lovely, much more mine than yours, of that I am certain." Revealing his wet eyes as he looked over at Oink, he added, "Oscar, I... I expect word will spread of our adventure, making your plan impossible to repeat, but still, you might want to keep it close to you, only disclosing it to those who come to know and respect you, of which I'm certain there will be many. Sadly, I expect those not yet familiar with you may not believe the tale, and it might do you more harm than good. I mean to say with their initial impression of you."

"I will do that," Oink nodded, disappointed with the man's advice but understanding his reasoning, though it changed nothing since for his brother's sake, he wasn't planning to speak of it.

On the poop deck with several other passengers escaping the heat of the ship's insides, William watched the last of the fresh meat and vegetables from the small boat docked at the bottom of the gangway get exchanged for a sack marked Post, and as he watched them row the boat back to the wharf, Oink appeared next to him.

"Did you write your name on the contract?" William asked.

"No, I'm going to do it on the morrow."

"On the morrow? Why did he want to see you now?"

"He asked me to join his crew, to be his first mate."

Noticing Oink's breath matching Gorge's, William forced himself to ignore it and asked, "His first mate?"

Oink nodded. "His first mate... after a period as his timekeeper."

"And what did you say?" William asked while trying to hide his panic.

"I told him I couldn't leave you, seeing how you need me with you. You do, correct?"

"I do," William admitted if only to keep Oink from changing his mind.

"You do *what*?"

William smiled. "I need you... need you with me."

Oink returned the smile before picking up his red Monmouth cap drying on the railing.

"It's still damp," William warned him.

"Then it'll cool my head faster," Oink said as he pulled it down over his ears. "I prefer it damp and cool."

PART III

CHAPTER 16
An Adventure Ends and Another Begins

Unable to come up with a plan to sneak Gibby off the ship, Oink was temporarily distracted from his concern for the pig when Gorge told him and William they could keep their sailor's clothes, and he was further distracted from it when he found that the clothes he had boarded the ship in were not as tight as they had been.

**

Oink, William, and Philip stood with the other passengers at the bow watching the well-dressed and not-so-well-dressed men board the ship. They watched Cump record their names, direct them to wait near the stern of the ship, and after there were almost a dozen waiting, he called one into the captain's quarters. Several minutes later, both returned and Cump called the name of a passenger.

After six men had met with the captain and ten passengers had left with them, some going happily and others stoically, Cump called out, "Master Burns." Recognizing the name, the three watched a man dressed casually in trousers and a shirt with its sleeves rolled up enter the captain's quarters, and a few minutes later, left carrying a sack.

Without a word, Philip left the group to walk toward the stern. "Master Burns," he said as he approached the man.

"Y-yes?"

"My name is Philip John Smith the… Philip Smith. I had the pleasure of meeting your mother and I'm hoping you'll permit me to say she was very proud of you and eager to see you again, to be with you again."

The man stared at Philip for a moment. "I-I thank you, Master Smith. I appreciate your words. It's been far too long since I last saw her. Close to a score since I saw her face and it means much to hear she's proud of me." As the two shook hands, Master Burns said, "Again, I thank you, and I hope you find good fortune here," and then looking him up and down, added, "And good fortune with your servants."

"Uh, I thank you."

As Master Burns walked down the gangway, squeezing to the side to make room for a man making his way up it, Philip returned to the brothers.

"What did he say?" Oink asked.

"It's been a long time since he last saw Mistress Burns… and I'm overdressed."

Half an hour later, Cump called out, "Philip John Smith the Third."

"This is it," Philip said, forcing a brave face as he shook hands with William and Oink. "We'll meet again, and until we do, be well."

"We will," both nodded.

"And you too," said William, who helped Philip pick up his heavy chest and watched him struggle with it to the other end of the ship.

The brothers couldn't hear what the two said, but they could tell Philip had failed to impress the man. The husky blacksmith tugged at Philip's jacket while saying something that by his expression wasn't friendly, and he squeezed his arms and said something else that must have been even less so. After being pushed to the gangway and then onto it, Philip stopped halfway down to look back at the brothers looking over the side at him, before another push caused him to stumble and fall facedown near the waiting boat. With one hand, the large man picked him up by the back of his jacket and dropped him in the boat. Grabbing the chest with such ease that it appeared empty, he dropped it on Philip's lap and the pain on the young man's face proved it wasn't.

**

Coming over the top of the hill, Becky was glad to see the green water beyond the wooden buildings, and knowing she would soon be alone on the cart while Philpot and Ben received the new apprentice, she released a sigh of relief.

For the last hour, she had to endure sitting next to the man who over the rattling cart and the beating hoofs habitually barked orders at Ben, who impressed her by his patient responses of only, "Yes, Master Philpot." But then she realized he had spent much more time with the man than she had and had likely become used to his barking, much like she had become used to his body odor, sometimes so heavy that she could tell which room he had been in by the smell it left behind.

"Boy, you barely missed that large rock!" Philpot barked.

"What rock? I didn't see a large rock."

"I'm aware of that; otherwise, you would've struck it. Slow down at the end there and turn them to the right."

"Yes, Master Philpot."

Making their way down the wide wooden pier toward the wharf jutting out into the harbor, Philpot ordered Ben to rest the cart behind two others.

"I say that's what not being in a hurry does for a man. We would've had to park the cart further from the wharf if we had arrived earlier, and we would've wasted time waiting for the boat," Philpot boasted as Ben stepped down from the cart to tie the reins to a post, and as he went to help the sizeable man down from the back bench, Philpot stepped down and extended his hand to Becky. "You'll wait here, boy. Becky and I shall board her."

Becky realized then why Philpot had ordered her to join them and why he had insisted she wear her *inherited* gold-threaded flower-patterned dress, which she thought was too pretentious for such an occasion. She was to be an accessory for Philpot, who wore his seldom-worn white curly wig under his cocked hat and wore his latest fashion from France where the breeches were slightly longer than the current English fashion and its silver and gold stitched flowers glowed from its dark-gray fabric.

"If he's with her, I expect I'll do well," a passenger said, breaking the silence of the group watching Becky and Philpot stepping onto the deck.

"Would be for naught. I don't expect you're his sort," another said, causing the group to laugh, including Oink and William.

"I hope they've come for me," another said. "I wouldn't be complaining much if I had her to admire between waking and bedding."

"Wouldn't be complaining *at all* if you had her to admire between bedding and waking," another grinned.

With all silently agreeing, they watched the couple walk to the stern.

Recognizing Philpot's name as the proxy on Oink's contract with Lord Chalmers, Cump looked him up and down suspiciously, like a father meeting his daughter's suitor for the first time.

Becky noticed him sizing up Philpot and assumed it was because of Philpot's poor reputation preceding him.

Philpot noticed too and assumed it was because the man was envious of his clothes. Then recognizing one of the few waiting at the stern, he pulled Becky along to exchange greetings with him.

Seeing Philpot coming toward him, the man's eyes darted from side to side as if looking for an escape, and as Philpot extended his hand to him, Cump called out, "Master Jackson."

"Blessed day, Charles," the man nodded before hurrying to the captain's quarters.

"After all I've done for him, he couldn't give me but a moment," Philpot hissed to Becky. "He rents a third of your father's old plantation, the portion with the house on it. Do you remember that two-level house?"

"Do I remember it? The house I lived in much of my life?"

"That's the one. He talks about clearing those last three acres to the road but has yet to do so. He even had the gall to complain about the Carter boys I sent him. Complained they were lazy and worked as a single man but received the sterling of three. He even rents several of my boys every Saturday, but yet he's still behind," Philpot huffed. "I say my thirty per centum shall be near nothing this year. I shall see more from renting the boys than from the land."

Several minutes later, Cump and Master Jackson left the captain's quarters. Cump called out three names, and Master Jackson was off with three indentured servants. Leaving the ship, he offered Philpot another nod of the head.

Philpot returned the nod before adding a huff and whispering to Becky, "Three? What's the fool thinking? I say he shall have to sleep with an eye open or have his throat cut as he snores. Three living together in an unfamiliar land, forced into labor they don't appreciate, and then complaining to one another every free moment they have makes for a deadly situation."

"Perhaps he feels if he treats them well, they'll work well, rather than treating them poorly and having them behave poorly," Becky replied, not bothering to whisper.

"That's the thinking that shall see him killed!" Philpot snickered. "Proves he thinks like a woman!"

As the two waited to be called, Philpot watched those boarding the ship, huffing with each he didn't recognize, and after six more were waiting, Cump called his name. "Only you," he said, shaking his head at the man pulling Becky along.

"Master Philpot," Captain Humphreys said, forcing a smile as he stood up from his chair to welcome the large man into his quarters. "It has been a long time."

Shaking the captain's hand, Philpot also forced a smile. "Yes, my friend, it has been too long. You're looking well, and that's a fine waistcoat you have, fine indeed, and if I may say, that's quality stitching on your shirt's collar as well."

"You may. Please have a seat and you will soon be on

your way."

With the captain returning to his chair, Philpot took the seat in front of the desk while trying to hide his disappointment with the captain not reciprocating the compliment.

"I believe you know Cump."

"Cump?" Philpot asked, looking at the stone-faced man sitting to his left.

"Or Compass, as he was called several years back."

"Oh, I beg your pardon, Compass… Cump," Philpot said, forcing a large smile that revealed his missing teeth. "My apologies. I failed to recognize you, though your height should have given it away. Yes Compass, because you can guess the direction of the ship within a few degrees, they say. I suppose soon you'll be called Dump, Mump, or maybe Lump, because of the rhyming we English enjoy too much," Philpot laughed. "Or maybe Lumpy, like Will for William, and then Will-Bill, and then just Bill, or Billy to his friends, yes?"

Receiving no response from Cump, Philpot dropped his smile and turned back to the captain who cleared his throat before saying, "I expect he will be called Captain Washington when he takes control of this ship in London, as I shall be taking on another yet to be christened."

"Is that so? Congratulations to you both," Philpot said, looking from the Captain to Cump, who responded with a nod.

"I thank you," Captain Humphreys said as he pulled two sheets of paper from a drawer of his desk. "I must inform you we have a rather odd situation with your man."

"Strange?" Philpot asked, straightening up in the chair. "Was he wrapped, weighed, and slid?"

"No, nothing such as that, rather the contrary. He seems to

have multiplied," he said, smiling at both Philpot's obvious confusion and Cump's unusual smirk. "He has with him his younger brother. The boy trespassed and we only discovered him after leaving port."

"I see, and how does that concern me? I say you could have thrown him overboard, yes? Trespassing is a crime, yes?"

With Cump's stone face turning red, the captain cleared his throat again. "No, I do not throw souls from my ship, not breathing ones, not for that, but what I would do and did do was make both Lord Chalmers' indentured servants by reducing the cost of passage by having both work their way here. They proved their mettle and earned the crew's respect, which should please you, and if the boy had accepted it, I would have him as part of my crew. But since he prefers to be with his brother, the reason for his trespassing, I offer him to you as a seven-year indentured for the sum of a mere pound, but I must add that his contract is not transferable, making him yours for the full term. He is twelve now, making him more than capable with menial tasks."

"A pound, you say?" Philpot asked. "A pound for seven years?"

"Yes," Captain Humphreys nodded.

"Then I say I would be mad to reject it. I can surely find something for the boy to do, and it would be a pleasant change to have a young one on my estate."

"And together the two come to eighteen pounds twelve shillings."

Philpot pulled out a small sack, counted out the coins, and placed them on the desk. "That should be it, exactly."

After quickly counting the coins, Humphreys slid two back to Philpot, swept the rest into his palm, and poured them into a drawer of his desk. Pulling out four pieces of paper, he had Philpot sign them, had Cump sign them as a witness, and handed two to Philpot to take with him.

After the two shook hands, Philpot wore a grin as he headed to the door with Cump following.

"Master Philpot, one moment more, if you please."

"Yes, Captain?"

"I must say, I would do you, the brothers, and my crew a disservice if I failed to mention we had grown rather fond of your indentures... Lord Chalmers' indentures, and if any harm were to come to them while under your charge, something out of the ordinary, something unnatural, the crew might hold you accountable."

Philpot lost his grin as he glared back at the man. "I shall consider your words, though as unnecessary as they are. Virginia is not London, my good man. There are many more ways to die and even more ways to be maimed, and most, if not all, would be out of my control."

Growing self-conscious as she waited near the captain's quarters, Becky found the source of her discomfort and put the mainmast between her and the dozens of men staring over at her from the bow of the ship.

With his eyes bouncing among the faces of the passengers, Oink whispered to William, "They all want to do the same thing with her."

William's initial shock at his brother's words quickly turned into curiosity, and he asked, "And what would that be?"

"You know... kiss her," Oink said in a tone that asked if his brother was stupid. "What did you think? Hold her hand?

Maybe they would, but only while they were kissing her."

William held back his laugh but failed to hold back his smile. "And what do you want to do with her?"

"Talk to her and then kiss her when I win her heart," Oink replied before adjusting his Monmouth cap and walking away.

"You can't go over there."

"I can. Have you forgotten we're sailors?"

Where William would've normally gone after him, he decided against it and stepped behind the group of passengers to look out beyond the bow of the ship, hoping that if his brother tried to point him out, he wouldn't be able to see him.

Standing in front of Becky, Oink found himself strangely nervous and could only stare at her for a few seconds before fighting through his uncommon state to say with a poorly forced baritone voice and an even worse aristocratic accent, "Greetings, Mistress. A blessed day to you," and as Becky offered a smile, he added, "It's my pleasure to make your acquaintance."

"I thank you," she replied, deciding not to reciprocate his poor accent or baritone voice. "Welcome to Virginia. I'm Becky, and you are?"

"Master Oscar Harry Lovely at your service, Mistress Becky," he bowed. "But most call me Oink."

"It's a pleasure to meet you… Oink," she said, offering her hand and holding back a laugh when instead of shaking it, he gently turned it to kiss the back of it.

Continuing his poor accent and baritone voice, he said, "Since recognizing that you're spoken for but yet alone, I feel it's my responsibility to protect you from those who have not seen a woman for several months. But permit me to admit my action is not completely selfless. My father, the dear old man, used to say that to make the acquaintance of many beautiful women, one need only make the acquaintance of one, and more were sure to follow," but he left out that when his father had said it, he was referring to the boy's mother and sisters.

Where Becky would normally take offense to a man admitting he was using her to meet more women, she couldn't with the boy. Instead, she was amused, and her smile grew as she asked, "Oink? That's an unusual name. Is your business swine husbandry?"

Offended, Oink dropped the baritone voice and accent. "What? No! It's my sea name!"

"I see your brother's preparin' the lass for your introduction."

It took William a moment to recognize the large, clean-shaven man in a white shirt, waistcoat, breeches, and even shoes.

"It's me landlubber look," smiled Gorge, who then spun around to show off his clothing. "I'm off ta see the family in Jamestown for a spell."

"Jamestown?"

"That's it. The first town 'ere. I'm a third-generation, I am," he proudly informed him. "Now let's go meet us that lass your brother's preparin' for ya."

"I don't expect he'll appreciate being interrupted while he's making his introduction. He's not timid when it comes to women... or anything I'm aware of."

"Is 'e now? Tryin' to catch a whale with a needle and thread is 'e? No, 'e's far too young, but you've the years. Come," the large, well-dressed man said as he took William by the shoulder and almost dragged him toward the mast. "If nothin' comes of it, the practice will do ya good."

"Mistress, is this *child* disturbing you?" Gorge asked, making certain to pronounce his words properly as he interrupted Oink about to tell her about his hiding in the crate of piglets. "He escaped his guardian here and it will be no bother to take him away."

Becky's eyes jumped from Gorge to the awkward-looking but attractive young man with him. "He's not disturbing me, and he was about to entertain me with a tale."

"He was, was he? Well, I'm confident it's a tale to be told, but better told by an impartial party, and by good fortune, Master William Lovely here can tell it better than most, and if he'll permit me to say, I'm confident it will be his pleasure," Gorge said, smiling when Oink shot him a glare after recognizing him. "Oink and I shall leave you two to become better acquainted, won't we, lad?"

As Gorge was about to pull a reluctant Oink away, Cump called out, "Fish and Oink. Uh, William and... and Oscar Lovely." Spotting the brothers standing near the stern's mast, Cump pointed out the two to Philpot, who went to them still steaming about Humphreys' warning.

Turning toward Cump's voice, William and Oink straightened up when they saw the large, overdressed man coming toward them with an unwelcoming expression.

Surprised with both being Chalmers' indentured servants and wondering if they made a mistake, Becky looked over at the disappointed passengers to check if there were any remaining that were around William's age. Not seeing any, she turned to Philpot, who introduced himself to the brothers, shaking their hands roughly while forcing a smile. When he reintroduced the two to Becky, the new apprentice overseer of slaves instantly became unattractive to her, but Oink amused her when he proudly corrected the man with their names, telling him he preferred Oink, his sea name, and his brother preferred William, not Will or even Fish, his sea name.

Not appreciating being corrected, Philpot hid his annoyance when he noticed Gorge's threatening stare. "Then… then Oink and William it shall be. Collect your belongings and we shall be on our way."

"I 'ave ta go too, but I'll be back in Decem'er for two months, and I'll make me an effort to find yas to knows 'ow ya two are farin'," Gorge said before smiling and adding, "And, Oink, I'll be bringin' me second oldest with me, seein' 'ow she's closer to your age."

Shaking his hand, William said, "Until we meet again."

Shaking his hand too, Oink smiled, "I'll be waiting to meet her."

Dropping his smile to shoot a quick glare at Philpot, Gorge walked toward the hatch of the stairs.

CHAPTER 17
The Plantation

Sharing the bench near the bow with his brother, William felt smothered by the uncomfortable silence of the small boat, and to make the situation worse, he felt forced to look past the two rowers to Becky sitting at the stern next to Philpot who continued to steam over Humphrey's warning. After finding nothing around them that he could fake an interest in, he looked at Philpot looking down at nothing, and when he looked at Becky, she was smiling at Oink who was using the silence to amuse her by pretending to grab one of his eyeballs from its eye socket and while keeping the eye closed, pretended to put it in his mouth and by poking his tongue against his cheeks, faked moving the eyeball around in it. If not for William's nervous state he would've been amused by Oink, who instead of pretending to spit it back into his hand, return it to its socket, and open his eye again, as he would normally do at the end of his trick, he extended it for his captive audience by pretending to drop it into the boat and then in a panic, look around for it. Playing along, William closed his eye when Oink pretended to steal his eye, push it into his own eye socket, and open his eye with a grin, and as they came to the wharf, William relaxed slightly when Becky's smile grew with Oink pretending to find the lost eyeball near his foot and pushing it against William's closed eye, replacing the one he had taken. When William opened his eye, Oink took a quick bow and nudged William to do the same, but he wouldn't.

With it feeling strange to be walking in shoes and even stranger to be walking on land that seemed to rock when they knew it couldn't, the newcomers followed Philpot and Becky to the cart, where the large man broke the silence by telling a confused Ben to place their sacks on the bed of the cart.

After doing as he was told, Ben found Philpot gripping the reins with Oink sitting next to him, and having to take the back bench, he forced Becky and William to move to the sides as he sat between them.

The horses' quick start down the pier pressed them against the short backrest, and seconds later, all were gripping the edge of their seat when Philpot's sharp turn tried to slide them right. After passing several blocks of wooden buildings that ended with several tall and wide double-door structures that the brothers guessed were warehouses, Philpot slowed the horses to a trot and followed the road up a hill and through a section of forest where the then dirt road had two wide ruts worn into it. Then after traveling along a stretch of straight road separating fields of wheat and corn, Philpot took a crossroad, and ten minutes later, and to the curiosity of the brothers, they passed deep fields of waist-high green plants with their large leaves being worked in the distance by dozens of Black men and women.

When Humphreys' warning had finally faded away, Philpot looked at Oink, and over the creaking cart, the soft rattling of its solid wheels and the slapping of hoofs, said, "That was far less painful than when I took charge of Ben seven years back. I waited long, too long, I say. Waited far too long for the boat, waited more to sign for the boy, and waited more for the boat to return me to the wharf. I say I'm not fond of waiting and less fond of water. But I heard they plan to extend that pier, and if that's so, in another seven years the indentured's ship could be docked when I take charge of him. As it is now, those in the harbor must wait for the docked ships to empty and head to Port Mary to take on what they're bringing to England. The use of two ports isn't convenient for the ships, but it is for the merchants and agents."

"They use two ports?" Oink asked if only to force an interest in what the man was saying.

"That's correct," Philpot nodded. "See there? We're less than an hour from the plantation. We follow York River on our right there. You shall see the water soon enough, but for now, know that it's before those mountains. The plantation runs along its banks. It's much more convenient to send the hogsheads, the larger barrels, by river than by road. We only roll them onto a barge and they're floated to a warehouse. Now if we stay on the main road, we would be in Williamsburg, the capital. Used to be Jamestown," he said before surprising Oink by spitting to the side as if the name left a foul taste in his mouth.

Startled by phlegm barely missing him as it flew past his face, William looked at Ben, who looked forward as if nothing had happened, and when he looked past him to Becky, she dropped her smile and looked forward too.

"That devil town burned twice, twice! A sign from Him, I say."

"Is Jamestown a bad place?"

Seeing Philpot spit again, William pressed himself against the bench's backrest as phlegm again flew past him.

"The worst. Is that so, Ben?"

Ben leaned forward between the man and the boy. "Yes, it's the—"

"You lads won't be going there. It's forbidden to you, and you have no reason to when the other is nearer. You shall see Williamsburg soon enough when you're fitted for your field clothes."

"We have sailor's clothes," Oink proudly informed him. "William brought extra clothes, but he has sailor's clothes, too."

"Sailor's clothes, like that cap? No, they're too much like what the boys wear."

"Boys?"

"Slaves. Still, those shall do for now, but since you mention sailors, do tell me how you earned your rather unique name, your sea name."

As Oink began proudly telling the story of his sneaking onto the ship, Becky leaned forward to listen to the tale he had wanted to tell her earlier, and noticing her listening in, he told the story with more energy than Philpot appreciated and exaggerated much of it by telling how he had planned the crate's fall, lived well on the ship for several days, and when he was finally caught, it was by three sailors armed with swords. After knocking two unconscious, he was subdued by the 'largest and meanest of them,' and the only reason he wasn't sent overboard was because the captain recognized his extraordinary skills.

Taking advantage of their distraction, William took a

prolonged, unhindered, and discreet look at Becky's profile. Hoping she would turn her head toward him so he could glimpse her eyes again, Ben did instead, his eyes stating his disapproval before he leaned forward to block William's view of her.

As Oink was describing the work he and William did on the ship, Philpot interrupted him, "I say you were fortunate to find a weak captain. Another would have thrown you overboard, with or without your *extraordinary skills*, or sold your service to the highest bidder, not caring who you went to. But it is an interesting story, if only because most men would never consider trespassing on a ship. It takes an exceptional level of desperation, I say."

Disappointed with having failed to impress the man, Oink was more disappointed when he considered the man's use of *desperation* as an insult.

"You were also fortunate the crates were large, fortunate they used those to hold the small beasts, or we wouldn't have the pleasure of your service. I expect they're the same they use for unloading the grown beasts when they arrive," the man said, tossing Oink a genuine smile that made Becky think the boy might soften him. "And making the pig, Dibby, your dog was unusual too."

"Gibby, because of the gibbous mark on his side."

"Gibby, yes, I believe that's what I said."

"I'll miss him," Oink admitted as he fought back the sudden pressure behind his face.

"Perhaps I can find you a dog to take his place."

Oink shook his head. "It wouldn't be the same. Would be like replacing William. It can't be done." Then needing to change the subject, he said, "I find it strange that they would bring pigs from England. Don't you have them here?"

"They do, but it's less coin to buy a respectable number of piglets there and pay for their care and passage here, and when they arrive, they're almost fully grown. None here would sell a drove, only slaughtered ones, and if they would, it would cost more than twice what it would cost to bring them from England. They're afraid of competition, afraid they might be bred and their offspring sold. I breed them only to eat them and try to keep one male per six females." Glancing at the field of tobacco plants to their right, he said, "We're thirty minutes from the plantation. That field there and the forest on my left are Lord Chalmers'. He has twenty-eight hundred acres. I say it seems like much to a newcomer, but there are only eighteen hundred cleared, and that means only nine are useful. Do you know why that is?"

"No," replied Oink, who didn't care for the answer and didn't know why the man was bothering to tell him.

"We only use the ground for three seasons, can only use it for three. After three, it must sit for another three to strengthen its soil. We use half the land if we want constant production. It's a difficult crop. Besides being hard on the soil, it requires much maintenance, too much of it. We spend our time clearing land and growing tobacco. Myself, I have close to eight hundred acres cleared. I rent more than half and have another hundred still to clear. Tell me, how many acres of land can I use at one time?"

"Four Hundred… including what you rent?"

"Good boy. It shows you were listening — listening and learning."

Nodding to the man who seemed far too interested in something so boring, Oink wondered if he sat and watched the plants grow too.

At a thick patch of forest on their right, Philpot steered the cart onto a narrow dirt road cutting through the woods, and a few minutes later they came out passing between two rows of tall, vibrant purple bushes that seemed out of place with what they had seen on their way there.

Both William and Oscar were instantly impressed with the two-story stone structure that to them would have looked like a mansion if not for the log cabin sticking out from its side, making the rest of the house look like an overly zealous expansion of it. The path to the front door was hidden by unkempt shrubs, weeds, and wildflowers, and when they passed the side of the house, the brothers noticed that the structure's stone walls were an illusion caused by the vertical lines carved into the planks, but the log cabin was real and stood out like a large bulbous mole on a person's otherwise smooth cheek.

Philpot grin. "She's impressive, yes?"

"Yes," the brothers nodded.

Driving the cart beyond the house to pass the double row of seven cabins on their right and the row of sheds on their left, he said, "Your chambers face the back. William, you shall take the extra bed in Ben's chamber, and, Oink, you have a smaller chamber for yourself. You may have Ben's larger bed after he retires, but I say the one in your room shall do for now."

With not a slave in sight, he stopped the cart at the large barn next to the stable where two long carts rested and where the brothers' eyes were drawn past the small log cabin on their left to the row of eight enormous barns stretching away from it. Pulling their eyes away from the buildings, they discovered in front of them a wharf extending twenty feet into a river.

"Ben, remove the beasts, count the boys and girls, and join us in my study. Lads, grab your sacks and follow me."

Following behind Philpot and Becky, neither noticed the dark faces peeking out at them from between the colorful curtains in the small front windows of the cabins, and when they passed the few pigs curiously looking out from behind the fence of the pigsty's covered section, William tried to lighten his nervous state by whispering to Oink, "Perhaps you can make another friend."

"Maybe," Oink whispered back, serious. "You want to kiss her, yes?"

"I have no interest in kissing a pig," William smiled.

"You know who I'm talking about!" Oink hissed. "Perhaps we should duel for her."

"If you wish. You take a sword. I'll take a pistol, and we'll fire at ten paces."

When Philpot opened the back door, entered the house, and left Becky to hold the door for the newcomers, he said "When we're finished familiarizing you with the house, Becky shall show you about the grounds."

Following William in, Oink glanced behind them at the red brick building with its three smoking chimneys and failed to make sense of it.

Upstairs, after Philpot pointed out his bedroom as being the closed door on the right near the steep, creaking stairs and facing the front of the house, he stopped at the first door on the left and directed Oink to his bedroom facing the back of the house, and doing as the man said, the boy dropped his sack next to the small bed and was impressed to find a small desk beside it. "There's no fire?"

"No. The heat comes up from below those vents there,"

Philpot said, pointing to the iron vents on the floor. "The winters are milder than you're accustomed to, just as William's forehead tells me you're finding the summer harsher."

At the next door down, William found his bedroom to be much larger than the one he had shared with Oink. A small table beneath its one window separated two beds, and across from them was a dresser and wardrobe. When he looked at the far wall, the only one with anything on it, he was taken aback by the coiled whip hanging next to a sword and was taken aback more when he noticed a belt of two pistols resting on a deep shelf.

"That stripling hasn't emptied his pot again!" Philpot hissed to no one. "How complicated can it be?"

Following the man down to the first floor, on the right side of the hall there was an unused room next to Becky's, and the room across from hers was, to the curiosity of both brothers, called the bathroom, and to their fascination, it contained an iron bathtub with a cork in the bottom to discard the dirty water through a hole in the room's planked floor. Besides the tub, the room had only a polished pewter disk hanging on the wall, a small shelf holding a single brick of soap, and an exterior door that Philpot told them was always to be barred when not bringing in the bath water.

Glad not to have to share a bucket of water as he did at home, an idea came to Oink and he went with it, saying, "We could raise the tub and place a small fire beneath it, a fire on bricks to heat it."

"A fire under the tub?" Philpot laughed, making his stomach shake. "We might do that if we were in the practice of boiling people alive."

Offended by the laugh, Oink countered, "We would put the fire out when the water's hot."

Releasing his annoyance through a huff, Philpot said, "No. That would cause smoke, and by the time the water was hot enough, you could've added ten pots of boiling water from the kitchen to the cold water already in it, instead of the single pot we add to it in the colder months. But I say you shall not want to add boiling water to it for a few months yet. I expect you shall appreciate the cool water during the summer, and I *expect* you both to bathe once a week or more and from your smells, starting tonight. I bathe weekly, I do, and Becky here bathes most evenings before bedding down, but then she's a woman. And you shall find the washcloths in the cupboard there near the door."

Disappointed with himself for not thinking the idea through before mentioning it and more disappointed by the forced bath to come that night, Oink silently followed Philpot, Becky, and William out, and when he caught William staring at the back of Becky's head, as if admiring her long, straight hair, he lightly elbowed him and whispered, "That's my wife-to-be you're drooling over."

"Here's the dining room," Philpot said as he passed it on their left to stop at an entrance on their right. "And this room here is the most important, my study."

Becky and the brothers followed him into the room of log walls, which to the brothers appeared to be as out of place on the inside as it was on the outside, and when Philpot told them no one was to use the room, neither had a problem with that. "And there's only one situation that shall require you to be here. We have over ninety slaves on this plantation, over sixty adults, and that shall be over fifteen to one when Ben retires...

and here he is now, tardy as usual." All could hear the rapid footsteps coming down the hall before Ben rushed in and stood next to Becky to catch his breath. "Ben and Becky are well aware of what I mean to say," he said, causing Oink and William to guess what the man was talking about. "It has happened in other colonies and shall happen here. And of course, I'm speaking of an attack by the slaves." Walking behind the desk, he said, "Oink, join me."

With both brothers taken aback by the possibility of the slaves attacking, Oink exchanged a look with William before joining Philpot, who pulled the chair back to reveal a short lever coming up through the floor from under the desk.

"Push that lever forward. You may use your foot if you prefer."

Curiously stretching out his leg to push it forward, a loud snap surprised the newcomers and the echoing bang of the door slamming stunned them.

Philpot laughed. "If you were standing in its way, it would break a limb, perhaps even take it off. It's heavy and thick to keep them out, and it locks in place by those bolts at the top and bottom there. This, lads, is our battle room. I pride myself on being prepared for the worst, and that is it. Now once we're in here, we close the door and fight. Those slots in the shutters are for discharging the guns. If the savages try burning us out, the log walls give us a few hours before the flames reach us. And there's that hatch to the left of the door there. We unbolt it and crawl under the house when we must," he said before turning to the two narrow bookcases behind his desk. "And this is our armory," he said proudly as he pushed on the side of a bookcase, rolling it back by several hidden squeaky wheels to reveal a collection of hanging long guns, pistols, swords, and daggers. "Everything we need to defend ourselves is in here. The balls, powder, and stuffing are on the left there," Philpot said with a smile, mistaking their shock for being impressed. "Have you experience with guns?" With the brothers shaking their heads, he frowned, "Then we must give you some. Ben shall show you how to charge and use them before he retires from the plantation. Is that so, Ben?"

Ben nodded. "I'll teach—"

"And include Becky. The more practice, the better, I say." Rolling the bookcase back into place, concealing the firearms and blades, he turned around to face the four. "Now Becky shall take you about the grounds before we eat. The meal shall be early since we missed the one before it to claim you two. But before you leave, you two can help Ben open the door."

Then Philpot watched with amusement as William pulled the top bolt down, Oscar lifted the bottom one, and Ben grunted as he strained to pull on both of the door's iron handles. After he opened it an inch, William pulled on a door handle, and when they had moved it several more inches, Oink prayed they had a firm hold on it as he squeezed his small hands between the door and its frame to pull on the door's edge. When they had opened it almost forty-five degrees, Oink stood behind it and pushed until the door's bottom bolt clicked into a small hole in the floor, locking it open.

Before the three could catch their breath and Oink could ask how the man had rigged the door to shut with so much force, Philpot left the room.

Following Becky out, the brothers were impressed by the sixty-foot-long garden on their left surrounded by a two-foot-tall picket fence, but they gave no thought to the field behind it where several cows grazed.

When Becky brought them into the kitchen where the harsh heat splashed over them, the brothers salivated at the aroma of the baking bread that reminded them they had missed their midday meal, and both stood awestruck when they saw the two Black women in stained frocks standing at the table slicing mounds of bread.

"Blessed afternoon, Becky," Mary said, and then looking up and seeing the newcomers, added, "M-Mistress Rowling."

"Mary, Ann, this is Master William Lovely. He'll be replacing Master Carlson, and this is his brother, Master Oscar… Master Oink Lovely. William, Oink, this is Mary and Ann. They're charged with the meals."

"W-welcome, Master Lovely and… and Master Lovely," Mary said while Ann nervously nodded her head.

Being the first to pull himself from his state of awe, Oink nudged William, who then smiled nervously and said, "Call me William, if you please."

"And I'm Oink, just Oink, and this is an enormous kitchen."

"It has to be. It has to feed over ninety people," Becky told them as the two women stood at the far end of the table, staring at them.

"Did they forget to put it in the house?"

"No, its heat would be too much, and more so in the summer," Becky smiled. "Come, there's more to see."

As Becky turned to leave, William walked over to the table and extended his hand. "It's a pleasure to make your acquaintance."

For a moment, the two women stared at the hand before their eyes jumped to Becky, who, after bouncing her confused eyes between William and the two women, nodded they should shake his hand.

"The… the pleasure is ours," Mary said, wiping her hand on her frock before shaking his hand.

Ann too wiped her hand before cautiously taking William's as if she was placing it near a flame.

A second later, Oink was standing beside his brother, excitedly shaking the hands of the women. "It's a pleasure to meet you, Mistress Mary. And a pleasure to meet you, Mistress Ann."

"Have a… a blessed day, Master Lovely and… and Master Lovely," Mary said.

"Just William if you please, and you as well."

"Have a blessed day, and it's just Oink."

Leaving the two stunned women in the kitchen, the brothers followed Becky outside where she stopped and whispered, "I expect relations between Master and slave are casual in England, but here they're formal. A slave addressing you by your given name will be whipped if Philpot was to hear of it."

Blushing, William and Oink nodded their understanding before following her to the rows of sheds and cabins.

"What's the use of that post with that ring?" Oink asked as they passed it.

"That's the whipping post, and that's where the hands are tied," Becky said, trying to sound matter-of-factly. Staying to the left, she pointed out the pigsty, pointed out the chicken coop, the laundry shed, the milking shed, the butcher shed, the small smokehouse, the shed with a fireplace that they used for such things as preparing preserves and making candles, and lastly she pointed out the barber's shed, telling them that two women gave the slave's haircuts and shaved their faces, but she would cut the brothers' hair once a month and shave William every Sunday before church service.

Stopping at the door of the small log cabin, she knocked on its closed door.

"Here me," a baritone voice replied.

Wanting to see their reaction to the huge man, Becky opened the door and gestured for the two to enter the cabin, where they found a startled King standing awkwardly over them.

"King, this is Master Lovely. He'll be replacing Master Carlson, and this is his brother, also Master Lovely. William, Oink, this is King."

Pausing a moment to take in the man standing almost a foot taller than him and almost twice as wide, William offered his hand. "It's a pleasure to make your acquaintance, Master King."

Noticeably frightened by the hand, King looked at Becky, and after she nodded he should shake it, he extended his hand.

Confused by the hand extended next to his, William took it and shook it.

Doing as his brother did, Oink took the giant's hand, shook it, and found it strange that the large man never grasped his, and when they were outside the cabin, he whispered, "For a giant, he seems timid, but he must be important if he has a cabin to himself."

"He is," Becky nodded, and then pointing at the eight large barns further to their left, she said, "That's where the tobacco cures."

Both brothers thought it but only Oink asked it. "They're sick… get sick?"

Puzzled, Becky could only stare at the boy until it occurred to her what he meant, and she gave a quick laugh before explaining, "That's what we call drying… to make certain they don't attract mold." Then seeing the embarrassment that her laugh had caused him, she said, "But I agree. It's an unusual name for it."

Moving across to the other side, Becky pointed out the stable and the barn, telling them that the barn must be locked at all times since it stores the axes and such, and then heading back to the house, she pointed out the slaves' two rows of cabins.

"May we meet them?" William asked, feeling he should meet his wards sooner rather than later.

Nonplussed, Becky stopped walking. "You want to meet them?"

"I would like to."

"I would too," Oink nodded.

As they stood at the open door of the first cabin, blocking out much of the daylight, it took several seconds for the brothers' eyes to adjust to the room lit by a single candle. On the left wall was a small fireplace. Taking up the back wall and a third of the floor were wide bunk beds stacked three high. On the right wall was a set of shelves holding clothes made from osnaburg cotton, with the top one holding a small pile of shoes made from flour sacks. Beside the door was a small window and beneath it, a large chamber pot, and in the middle of the room were five fearful souls: a man, a woman, two small girls, and the boy with the pockmarked face, whom the brothers would learn was named Thomas. As Becky introduced each, Oink confused the family by offering his hand, and after she signaled for them to shake it and the father did, the rest of the family cautiously did the same.

With each cabin they visited, which included the handshaking, William became more stressed by the number of names he would have to learn. He tried memorizing each by using them in his greeting, saying them several times in his head, and using them again in his farewells, but he knew that in his nervous state, it would be mostly for naught.

At the second last cabin in the second row, Oink was taken with a girl near his age, and when she fearfully shook his hand, he flipped it to kiss the back of it, causing Becky to giggle, William to roll his eyes, the shocked girl to quickly pull her hand back as if he tried to bite it, and Oink to blush.

On their way to the house, Oink whispered to William, "I like Sophie."

"I didn't notice," William smirked.

"You may have Becky if she'll have you."

"I appreciate your permission."

With Oink's hungry eyes bouncing between his pewter bowl of soup and his plate of boiled vegetables and a chicken breast, he forgot about Philpot scolding him minutes earlier for taking the seat at the end of the table that the man said was reserved for the woman of the house.

William had hoped the meal would be relaxing, but with Ben sitting rigidly next to him as they waited for Becky to arrive with the last of the meals, he didn't think it would be, and attempting to relax his mind by breaking the awkward silence, he asked, "You don't use oil lanterns?"

Eyeing the newcomer for a moment, Philpot cleared his throat and said, "No, much too dangerous. One minor accident and that damn whale oil turns a house into an inferno. I say that liquid fire should be outlawed. Only last year, the

Chapman home burned to the ground because of it. Lost a few splendid horses, he did."

"And his wife," Ben added. "And two chil—"

"That's not much of a concern, boy! They can be replaced without cost, and he still has three other rats!" Philpot growled, and then catching a shocked William exchanging looks with Oink, he softened his tone. "Can't replace those horses, though, not here. Several years back, I made an offer for them, offered more than their value, but he wouldn't take it, and I'm certain he wishes now he had."

"I know the concern," Oink nodded. "At home, we live so close to one another that the village has to work together to put out a fire or their homes will burn too. We had two fires that I remember, but they never went beyond where they started."

"That may be, but here we're isolated and rely on ourselves. We grow our vegetables, keep our animals, build our edifices, mend our clothes, and even make our candles. There are the boys and girls for all that, making little need for Williamsburg but for our clothes, the material for the slaves' clothes, and grain and cheese and such. We don't buy lumber, but have our felled trees sawed into planks for the mere sum of a few extra logs."

Entering with two sets of meals, Becky placed them in front of Ben and Philpot, and after leaning the empty tray against the wall, she sat next to Oink, forced a smile across the table at William, and offered a genuine smile to the boy.

"Enjoy, lads."

"Shouldn't we pray first?" Oink asked.

"Pray?" Philpot asked, startled by the question. "No, we don't pray. I see no reason for it. We have a better chance of Him reading our letters than listening to our prayers mixed with all the others. We use the church for that and the table for meals," Philpot told him. "I ask you this, did you pray on the ship?"

"We couldn't without the others throwing food at us."

"And if you pray at this table, you might experience the same," Philpot smirked. "Now let us eat."

Oink picked up his bowl of pea soup, and as he drank it, noticed a woman lifting a child up to the window behind Philpot so it could peer through the wavy glass. Lowering his bowl, he smiled and nodded a greeting to the little girl.

"What are you doing?" Philpot hissed as he was about to put his first spoonful of soup into his mouth. "We use spoons. We don't drink soup. If we did, it would be in a cup!"

"My apologies," Oink blushed as he placed his bowl back on the table, and licking the bit of soup from the corners of his mouth, he grudgingly picked up the pewter spoon and dipped it into his soup.

Philpot turned to Ben. "Why are you grinning? You did the same with your first meal here," he said before turning to William. "It's good to see you both speak well, properly pronouncing your words. Ben here with his 'ads, 'ems, and ain'ts and such had to learn proper English. When he arrived here, one would have thought by hearing him talk he had just staggered out of a tavern in Jamestown," he said and then spat on the floor. "The slaves spoke better than him. Some still do, but then they're expected to speak like their master. Looks bad on us if they don't. But the big one speaks like a two-year-old, so I say it's a good thing he rarely speaks."

With Philpot finally putting the spoon into his mouth, a child's laugh brought Oink's eyes back to the window to find the child gone and its laughing fading off into the distance.

For the next twenty minutes, all ate in silence, and when Oink finished first, he stared down at his empty plate, impatiently waiting for the others to finish.

Being the second to finish, Philpot wiped his mouth with a napkin and placed it over the plate. "I expect you two haven't had a meal like that for some time."

"We had a feast when we arrived yesterday, but *little* today," Oink said, trying to throw a hint.

"Is that so? They fed you well, did they?"

"They did," William nodded, and then trying to compliment the man, added, "But what my brother calls a feast was not as… as appetizing as this, and only a feast if compared to the last couple weeks of mostly hardtack and salted pork."

"Is that true, lad?" Philpot asked Oink.

Tossing an annoyed glance at William, Oink nodded, "Yes."

"Yes, I expect it is," Philpot smirked.

"And today we *missed* our midday meal," Oink added with the hope the man would catch the second hint.

Ignoring the boy, Philpot said to William, "Finish, lad. Becky must clear the table."

As William hurried to finish his vegetables, Becky picked up the tray and slowly piled the dishes onto it, saving William's for last.

"May I be excused to visit the privy?" Oink asked.

"You may but hurry back. It's at the side of the house, and Becky shall show you to it."

With Oink following behind her, Becky stopped near the entrance of the kitchen where the last of the slaves waiting to be served formed a short line. "It's to the left," she told him.

"Uh, I don't have to go. I was—"

"More?" she asked with a smile.

"Yes, if I may," Oink nodded, his face turning slightly red.

"Come. There's no chicken, but there's stew."

When the two entered the kitchen, Mary froze as she was handing a slice of bread to a man holding a wooden bowl of stew; Ann froze as she was emptying a ladle of stew into a frozen young woman's bowl, and the four men standing behind the woman froze with their heads toward the boy and their eyes toward the floor.

"Mary, Master Lovely would like seconds," Becky said, struggling not to grin at the living statues. "And, Master Lovely, you'll have to eat it quickly."

"It's just Oink. Master Lovely's my father," the boy smiled.

"M-Mistress Rowling," Mary said, "If you would hand Master Lovely a bowl from the shelf, Ann will serve him."

Becky handed him a wooden bowl, and when he turned to leave the kitchen, she asked, "Where are you going?"

"To wait in line."

"You don't have time. Master Philpot expects you to hurry."

"You can come to the front, Master Lovely," Mary said, her eyes jumping from Oink to Becky.

Realizing Becky was right, Oink thanked Mary and then apologized to those he cut in front of.

"Ben, you shall take him with you when renting the slaves. William, on Saturdays we rent our slaves out to other plantations to help with their crops. Labor is scarce here, and some will rent one for a day," Philpot said. "I say, Becky, you were longer than expected."

"My apologies, Master Philpot," Becky replied, placing a red ceramic bottle and a pewter cup in front of the man before placing bowls of rice pudding in front of each.

As she sat down, Oink, with stew stuck to the corners of his mouth, rushed in and sat next to her.

"As for you," Philpot said to Oink. "You shall oversee the garden. Becky, you shall introduce him to it. Also, William, I expect you have never used a whip, and before Ben retires, you shall need to become competent with it."

Hit by jealousy and not noticing his brother's face paling or considering why he would need to use a whip, Oink asked, "Will I need to be competent with it too?"

"Would you like to?"

"Yes!"

A smile covered Philpot's face. "Good, very good. Then yes, you shall also learn to use it. I shall have Becky purchase a shorter one for you, and Ben shall teach you both how to use them." Then, while drinking his rum and letting their rice puddings wait on the table, the man was pleased to have two fresh pairs of ears hear about his position as the overseer of the plantation that he held for over twenty years and how he had grown the 'estate' significantly by increasing the acreage of the cleared land by over a hundred percent and had grown the number of slaves by over two hundred percent. He told them how he had grown his own land over that time from only a hundred acres to hundreds of acres, and he compared his growth to his neighbors' while several times going off on tangents about what he felt were his neighbors' shortcomings.

After emptying his cup three times and to Oink's relief, he told all to eat their desserts, and as he left the table, added that William and Oink should settle themselves into their rooms, take their baths, and go to bed early to be well-rested for their first day.

In William's second nightshirt and hoping to beat him to the bath, Oink held it up so he wouldn't trip on it as he rushed down the steep stairs and through the dark hall, only to be disappointed by the bathroom's closed battened door. Noticing a light coming through a tiny knothole two feet from the bottom, he kneeled to peek through it, and seeing Becky pouring a bucket of water into the tub, he was satisfied it wasn't his brother. But then unable to pull himself away from the knothole, he watched her place the bucket on the floor, close the outside door, bar it, and as his heart sped up, watched her loosen the laces of her bodice.

Fully dressed so Becky wouldn't catch him in his nightshirt and hoping to beat Oink to the bath, William rushed down the stairs and then down the hall to stop near his brother kneeling at the bathroom door. "What are you doing?" he whispered.

"Uh, nothing," Oink whispered back. "What are you doing?"

"Hoping to bathe."

"You'll have to wait," Oink said as he got to his feet.

When a curious William kneeled to see what Oink was looking at, Oink pushed him over and walked away asking through his laugh, "Do you intend to wash your clothes at the same time?"

Hearing the laugh, Becky went to the door and pulled it open a crack to see William getting to his feet. "May I help you?"

"Uh… no. I was… I was buckling my shoes."

"That's impressive."

"Impressive?"

"Yes, because you're not wearing any."

"Yes... I... I... enjoy your bath," William said before rushing off, red-faced.

A few minutes later, Philpot left his study, and avoiding the hall's floorboards that creaked under his weight, he stopped at the bathroom door to kneel and peek through the knothole but was disappointed to find Becky had stuffed it with a cloth.

**

Bathed and in his nightshirt, William reached out from his bed to snuff out the candle on the small table between his and Ben's beds. "Sleep well," he said to Ben as he pulled the sheet up to his neck and looked up at the ceiling to reflect on the day's events.

"She has no interest in you," Ben whispered.

"My apologies," William whispered back. "What was it you said?"

"Has no interest, no interest in you."

"Who?"

"Becky. She has a lover."

"She's with Master Philpot?"

"Whisper!" Ben hissed as he brushed his sheet aside, got out of bed, and looked out the small window. "With King, the enormous idiot. Wait and watch."

Curious, William left his bed to join him at the window.

"In a moment, she'll go to his cabin. Only have to wait and watch."

They didn't have to wait long. With the help of the light from the full moon, they could see the young woman walking past the kitchen, and when she turned left, she disappeared past the pigsty to reappear seconds later at King's cabin, and from their elevated angle, they watched her remove the beam barring its door before entering it.

"Same thing every night. Waits for my snuffing before visiting his cabin."

"She had a book with her?"

"Sometimes yes, sometimes no. Perhaps a Bible to pray for forgiveness. Prefers to be around the slaves more than us. Been doing it even when engaged to marry. Not a jovial girl. Rarely smiles and never laughs."

"She's engaged?"

"Was. He died four or five months back. A horse threw him. But she still has King, who by her good fortune has a cabin to himself. What I find more curious than her need to be with him is his need to scream during the nights when she doesn't visit, which is seldom since she visits often," Ben said as he returned to his bed. "Do you know what'll happen if she has his child?"

"No."

"She'll be whipped, and her child'll be a slave for a score and ten years."

Reminded that he wasn't in Kendleshire, William returned to his bed, finding it strange how Becky's intimate rendezvous with the giant concerned him much more than he felt it should have. He expected, since he knew nothing about her, it was because he was more attracted to her than he should've been. Yes, she was pretty, and yes, she seemed gentle, but he didn't know her enough to appreciate her personality and opinions. Then it occurred to him that being in the company of men for two months might have heightened his attraction to women until he had become accustomed to being around them again, much like how an unusually warm day during the coldest days of winter always feels warmer than it is.

**

Becky went to bed reflecting on the day's events, and after thinking about Philpot being his strange self on the ship, she thought about the two brothers they had brought back with them. She liked Oink, couldn't help but like him, and she smiled when she thought about the brothers introducing themselves to the slaves and Oink kissing hers and Sophie's hands, and her smile grew when she thought of him intending to wait in line with the slaves for a bowl of stew and then apologizing to them when he moved to the front of it.

Unlike Oink, she wasn't sure she liked William, but she was sure she didn't want to. He was initially likable by being Oink's brother, but he was still an apprentice overseer of slaves and would've had to have chosen that specific contract over the much more common and less severe ones that she was sure were available, and that choice belittled any likable qualities he may have displayed that day.

Then recalling the respect the two had shown the slaves, she could only believe that the slaves in England received much more respect than those in Virginia, and curious to know how long it would take William to adapt to Virginia's harsher treatment of them, she wondered how long it had taken Ben and made a mental note to ask Mary.

**

In his new environment, without the constant noises, the pungent odors, the intense heat, and the rocking in every direction, it took Oink less than a minute to fall asleep after laying his head down.

CHAPTER 18
The First Day and the Worst Day

William had slept profoundly and he could've easily slept for several more hours if Ben hadn't woken him. It took him a moment to realize who was looking down at him, another to realize he wasn't on the ship, and another to relax when remembering where his brother was by the boy's snoring. Out of habit he put on his sailor's clothes and had to be reminded to wear stockings and shoes before following Ben down the hall past Oink's room, where Philpot's sonorous snoring was trying to drown out the boy's.

Outside, William shadowed Ben as he removed the beams blocking the cabins' doors and counted the heads in each, and at the sixth cabin, Ben scolded him for 'teasing' the slaves with his wishes for a blessed morning. "How blessed can it be? They're slaves!"

Opening King's cabin last, Ben informed William that while Mary and 'the mute' made the morning's meal, the slaves would milk the cows and clean the stable, chicken coop, and pigsty, and with their large number, their tasks didn't take over forty minutes.

Following Ben into the stable, William looked about to see

fourteen of its sixteen stalls occupied.

"Harnesses are over here," Ben said as he removed a harness and a bridle from a double row of hooks near the door, and when William followed him into a stall, Ben turned to him with a question mark on his face. "We're taking six. You can take another harness and bridle," he said in a condescending tone, and when William returned with the harness and bridle, Ben looked at him with an even larger question mark and pointed with his thumb to the stall beside them. "Put it on the horse there, unless you prefer to wear it."

In the next stall over and after he sorted out the web of leather straps, William confirmed what he had expected: he didn't know what he was doing. Peeking over the short wall to see what Ben was doing, he learned which end of the harness went where, but couldn't figure out how to put it on the horse, and after the annoyed beast bit him twice, he peeked over the wall again and Ben noticed. "Have you never harnessed one?"

"No, never," William said, embarrassed.

Ben huffed. "Give me a moment."

A few seconds later, Ben joined him, and talking to him like he was an idiot, he slowly explained how to attach the harness.

Wondering if they had expected him to know how to harness a horse before he arrived, and then worrying about what else they expected him to know, William asked, "Did you know how to do this before you arrived?"

"No, but didn't pretend to either. It's easy once you know how. Grab another set and I'll watch you harness the next one."

With Ben huffing and shaking his head each time he had to correct the newcomer, with the last horse, William didn't receive any head shakes or huffs, but Ben had to tighten the girth that William had left loose so as not to cause the animal discomfort.

After they attached the six horses to a long cart, they harnessed and attached six more to a second one that Philpot would load with slaves to take to one of his own fields.

With Philpot sleeping in late Saturday mornings, Becky served Ben and William their morning meals before disappearing into the kitchen, where Mary and Ann rapidly served the slaves who formed a line from the kitchen to King's cabin.

In an uncomfortable silence, the two sat across from each other at the dining room table drinking cider and eating boiled eggs and bread with preserves, and when finished, William asked, "Will Master Philpot be seeing us off?"

"No, be up in half an hour," Ben replied as he dropped his napkin onto his plate and stood up with William following. "With those clothes, someone might want to rent you," he said. "And we leave those for her."

"We're heading out, yes? Passing the kitchen?"

"We are," Ben replied with his face taking a stern posture. "And *those* will wait for her. We all have our tasks. She doesn't perform ours and we don't perform hers."

Fearing Becky would feel he was being inconsiderate, William reluctantly placed the dishes back on the table and followed him to the back door, content with Ben not carrying a whip.

"Oh," Ben said, stopping at the door. "I'll be a moment."

Rushing up the stairs, a minute later he returned wearing a

long leather coat that seemed too heavy for the day's coming heat, and peeking out from one side of the unbuttoned coat, making William's heart skip a beat, was the handle of a coiled whip.

At the rows of cabins, Ben removed the whip and startled William with two loud cracks that caused the slaves to leave their cabins and form two lines: one of topless men in shorts and another of frocked women.

King was the last to join them, and unlike the others, he wore a short-sleeved shirt and carried a stack of empty wooden buckets, two bulging water skins, and something rolled up that looked to William to be a small net. Ignoring the lines, the giant climbed onto the back of the cart to sit with his back against the bench.

"We take a score and a half. A score of boys and a half of girls," Ben told William as he began walking down the row of men, tapping the shoulders of some while counting aloud. "Usually pick the same ones, the stronger ones unless they have an injury, and our *Lord* Philpot takes the rest."

While the tapped men wearing somber expressions climbed onto the back of the cart, William tried to hide his shock by the two to three-inch scars on some of their backs.

Unlike the men, the woman whom Ben tapped seemed pained by it, and after sitting tightly together on the cart's bed, they clenched the hands of those closest to them.

"Master Carlson," a thin man in his thirties said nervously from the cart. "Liz is with child."

"Is she?" Ben asked as he walked to the side of the cart. "Stand, girl."

A woman around twenty years old nervously stood up.

"Turn around."

She nervously turned around.

"Sit down," he ordered. "Boy, it'll do you well to keep your mouth closed. When she shows, she stays."

After dismissing the remaining slaves, Ben climbed up onto the bench, and with William joining him they slowly rode off. Passing by the side of the house to take the road through the woods, they reach the main road several minutes later where Ben stretched out a cheek with his tongue as he turned the long cart onto it, and after passing a thirty-minute section of tobacco plants and then a small section of woods, Ben shook the reins, and with the horses trotting, his body seemed to relax as they came to smaller tobacco plantations on both sides of them. "That was Chalmers' second half of his field. Eventually, you'll clear that small portion of the woods we just passed. Owns the forest across from it too. Follows his land on the right, but doesn't go as far back," Ben told him. "Do you read?"

"Some. I've had little practice."

"Good, then you don't write either, and you won't have a reason to for the next seven years. But mind my words. It's best you tell our *Lord* Philpot you do neither. Here, guide the horses." Seeing William's panic as he held the reins out to him, he laughed, "You can't drive horses either?"

William blushed. "Never had the opportunity."

"Do now. Easy since they follow the road until you turn them, and we'll not be turning for a few minutes yet. Take them so they don't drop behind the horses."

While William held the reins, Ben pulled a small sack from his pocket and began counting its coins. "A pound," he said before sliding the coins back into the sack, closing it by its string, and taking back the reins. "Use it to break their sterling, and we only take sterling. None of those Spanish dollars for us.”

“Dollars?”

“Pieces of eight. Never heard of them?”

“Yes, but never saw one. To me, they’re like leprechauns,” William joked.

“You’ll see them soon enough. Not leprechauns, but pieces of eight,” Ben said, almost shocking William with his smile. “More common here than sterling, seeing how we’re closer to the Spanish colonies than England. We only take sterling and everyone along the route knows it. A shilling per slave. Virginia doesn’t make its sterling like the other colonies, so it’s British sterling for us.”

“A shilling a slave? Once a week? That’s over… over two pounds a year for each, almost half of what I received after a year of working the mine.”

“You’re good with mathematics for someone who can’t read.” Ben smiled again as he glanced at William. “But we only rent them for eight months, and sterling here always seems more than it is to newcomers until they need to purchase something. And I expect you might just fall off the cart when you realize how much sterling you’ll receive from renting them. Ask me how much I’ve received since I’ve been here. Go on and ask.”

“How much?”

“Almost a score and two pounds, or that’s what I saved,” and with William’s face showing his surprise, he added, “You’ll see as much too.”

“How? I was told we receive sterling at the end of our contract, and far less than that.”

“This isn’t our usual task, not one that’s expected of us,

and I don't expect Lord Chalmers would approve, seeing how it takes away from them working his field. We keep this task to ourselves and receive three shillings a week because few will rent them from Philpot directly. Most want nothing to do with him. He could have his friends rent them, the Carter brothers, but not one of the three can be trusted. Would only see half the sterling if he's fortunate, but still a great sum, considering he's renting Chalmers' slaves and keeping the sterling for himself. Again, mind my words when I say we keep this to ourselves."

Finding what Ben said strange and wanting to ask several questions, William instead only nodded his head.

"Should know too that sterling's rare here, but not so rare in the smaller coins. Everyone has a little, but few have much. Philpot likes to say a man's true wealth is measured in sterling, not dollars. There's too much bother with those dollars. They cut them into wedges, eight per coin. Each is worth almost six shillings, but that could change on the morrow. And some wedges are smaller than others, so best to stay away from them, understand?"

After William nodded again, he had to hold on to the bottom of the bench when Ben took a quick, wide turn to guide the horses down a road dividing two small fields of tobacco. "Used to be the Glendale One Hundred, but he split it into portions of ten and sold them for more than he would've received as a whole," Ben told him as he turned the horses left and stopped them in front of a wide log home. "More takers for ten acres of cleared than for a hundred. More buyers to offer more sterling."

"Bless ya, Master Carlson!" an older, clean-shaven man said as he exited the cabin in only his trousers. "I'll be needing four if ya can spare'em."

"And blessed be you, Jeremiah. But alas, you mightn't be as blessed this morning. Only brought what you took last week, two."

Jeremiah's face flashed his disappointment before noticing William and smiling. "You must be the new lad, yes? Taking over for Ben, will you be?"

Before William could reply, Ben said, "Jeremiah White, permit me to introduce you to William Lovely."

"It's my pleasure to make your acquaintance, Master Lovely."

"And yours, mine, Master White."

"If you would choose two from the back, we'll be on our way," Ben said. "But if girls are capable, you may have two of those."

"They are, and I will. Seeing how they'll be topping, women are more than capable," the man laughed.

"So be it, my friend. Take two, but it's still a shilling each, four for all."

"That it is," Jeremiah said as he reached into his trousers' pocket, pulled out some coins, and examined them for a moment before handing several to Ben. "I thank you, Ben, Master Lovely."

While Ben pulled out the small coin sack and added the coins to it, William stretched his neck to watch the man walk to the back of the cart to select two younger men and two younger women, and after the two men stepped down from the cart, they assisted the two women, who exchanged their melancholic faces for relieved ones.

"Jeremiah, have a blessed day and I shall see you again near eight. Bless Mistress White for me too and let her know the smell of her morning bread is teasing my nose," Ben said, and as he turned the cart around to head back to the main road, Jeremiah said he would and thanked them again.

Driving toward the road, Ben glanced at William. "I could have spared the men, but when I have the opportunity, would rather rent the women for field work and keep the men for stronger tasks."

Noticing a mosquito intending to drink from the back of his hand, William swatted it and realized it was the first one he had seen since the summer before. Then reminded that there were no insects during their voyage to Virginia, he was disappointed that he failed to appreciate it, and then surprised to be thinking about the voyage, he tried to take his mind off it by asking, "What's topping? That's what Master White called what he's doing today, yes?"

"Cutting the tops from the plants. It forces the leaves at the top to grow larger. A simple task," Ben said. "You've no experience with tobacco, but have you any with slaves?"

William shook his head. "No, I rarely saw them unless they were passing through with their masters. None work the mines. I expect it costs far too many pounds to lose one. If they lose a slave, they lose all they paid for him, but if they lose a miner, they only have to move his family out and bring in another."

"I too had little experience with them before I arrived here. My home is on an estate twenty minutes from London. My father works its grounds, and I only experienced the slaves there. They help maintain the estate and need no driving. I befriended one too. One I consider smarter than most and more civilized than some English." Then surprising William, he laughed. "I used to jest with Joseph that if he lost his color, he would easily be mistaken for an English, a better class of English."

Impressed that Ben had lived on an estate, if only in a servant's house, William asked, "Do you miss it, miss home, miss your father, your family?"

Ben's face went cold, as if William had brought up a taboo subject, and he said only, "Yes," and with Ben then seeming to have lost interest in talking to him and William not daring to ask any more personal questions as they rented fourteen more men and five more women, William tried to memorize their route in the unfamiliar land. Then, when Ben finally spoke to him again, he confused the newcomer by saying, "Don't expect to find a woman here. Aren't enough and our association with Philpot hinders the search."

William was about to ask why their association with the man would work against them when a skinny topless man a few years older than Ben and riding full gallop toward them slowed his snorting horse beside the cart. Even from six feet away, his body odor spoke louder than he did when he ignored William's presence to say, "I was growin' old waitin' for ya!"

"Blessed morning to you too, Master Benton," Ben said coldly as he stopped the horses. "And from what I understand, we're all growing old by the second." Catching the shilling the man tossed to him, Ben added, "It's two shillings this week, and if this one's bruised too, it shall be three next week."

"Two? They're less in Jamestown!"

After spitting away from William, Ben said, "They're four there, but if it pleases you, you may ride there."

Benton's face reddened, and his voice rose. "That I may, but not before I beat some respect into ya, Carlson!"

Calmly twisting on the bench to face the man, Ben brushed

his opened long coat aside to reveal the grip of a pistol on his hip, surprising William. "Attempt if you must, but remember I'm Philpot's man."

"So be it," Benton said as he calmed down and reached into the pocket of his badly stained trousers to toss a second shilling to Ben.

"Choose one and we'll see you in ten hours," Ben said coldly. "And be warned, any roughness with this one and it's three next week and perhaps a visit by Master Philpot."

William watched as the man rode to the back of the cart, slid off his horse, and stepped onto the cart's bed. Looking over the women, he grabbed what looked like the youngest and dragged her off of it, and with tears streaming down her cheeks, he grabbed her bottom and laughed before lifting her onto his horse. Joining the grieving young woman, he turned the horse around and galloped off ahead of the cart.

William was questioning what he had just witnessed when Ben shouted, "A blessed day to you too, Master Benton," and moving the horses onward, he said, "I should have said four shillings. Men like him are the reason we arm ourselves, and it's best not to show the pistols until we must, and best to have two." Giving a soft shake of the reins, the horses walked on. "Some folks here would run you through for a dollar, run you through twice for sterling, and with the likes of Benton, one never knows when he'll change his bark to a bite. Was indentured here. His contract was shortened by six months when his master drowned in the York River. Rumor is he killed the man, his master, but there's no proof. The man was a widower with no children, and normally Benton's contract would go to the purchaser of the land, but seeing how it was Philpot buying it, Benton saw his retirement clothes and sterling. He bought a few acres and has been struggling to clear them since.

"Philpot owns almost a score of plantations himself. Rents most for sterling and a share of the harvest, but the rest he works, or I should say we work it for him. Few here would work for him, and of those who would, Philpot wouldn't want them to — hence why you and I are here. Word rides fast around here. Can make or ruin a man depending on if it's good or bad." Glancing at William, he added, "But some can use their poor reputation for their benefit, even if only a rumor, like Philpot. Make men fear them by the rumors that follow them."

Ben looked at William as if waiting for him to ask what he meant, and William might have asked if his mind wasn't on something else.

"What of the woman, the one he rented?"

"Yes, need pistols here," Ben nodded. "A man could kill us in front of the slaves and never answer for it. The most they'd receive is a rumor. Slaves can't bear witness... much like horses can't."

"What of the woman?" William repeated as if he didn't hear Ben's attempt to avoid the question. "The woman Benton rented."

"The girl? What of her?"

"Is she doing his cooking and cleaning?"

Ben shrugged.

"Sh-sharing his bed?"

"I don't believe he has much of a bed, but I expect so," he said as his face reddened, and then with William's heart seeming to shift in his chest, Ben straightened up on the bench. "You'll come accustomed to it," he whispered, "If you try not to give it much concern."

Not believing he could do that, William asked, "Have you?"

"King, hand me the water."

William took the water skin from King, uncorked it, and handed it to Ben, who took several swallows and handed it back to William, who took several needed swallows, corked it, and handed it back to King. "I thank you," he said, confusing the giant. Turning to Ben, he asked, "Is it… is it not going against the law to have intimate relations with a slave, or is it only English women?"

"Going against it? Who's going to witness it? What evidence would there be? It's different for a woman to bed a slave. If she has a slave's child, she'll be whipped and the child made a slave. Only happened once that I know of, and she was married. Philpot says she was whipped and divorced." Then noticeably more uncomfortable with the conversation, he paused for a moment. "But for a man, he can't give birth. And when the girls have an English child, Philpot says it's better for the numbers. A mixed slave is a better slave, more obedient and more intelligent… or so Philpot says. He sees it as breeding a mare with a stallion of some pedigree. And mind my words, you'll do well to keep some distance from them. Regard them as only horses. We're not renting women, only horses."

"It's difficult to accept the two being the same," William said, unaware that the slaves nearer to them were eavesdropping. "Horses don't speak, don't show their feelings as we do, don't look like us."

"We? Us? Slaves are not like us, and as I said, you shouldn't regard them as such. And mind my words again, never have Philpot hear you say such things, never. And it's not like they have souls."

"I… I'm not certain I agree. I tend to believe all things of flesh have souls."

"Why would He waste one on them? And it doesn't say they do in the book."

"It does… or I believe it implies it. The Jews were slaves, and they have souls; otherwise, it defeats much of the teachings, yes?"

"They were a different slave, and don't mention Jews around Philpot either," Ben warned with his voice showing his growing frustration. "Mind my words. It will do you no good to consider they have souls. Must rent them or bear Philpot's wrath. Have no choice. He's not someone you want as an enemy. Can make your seven years even more unbearable than they'll be… than they could be. Again, mind my words."

William wanted to push the conversation, but with Ben's tone telling him to drop the topic, he reluctantly did.

When they rented the next woman, William wanted to close his eyes and pretend it wasn't happening, but instead, he forced himself to look for a sign that the man intended to bed her. Not seeing one, he still felt as if he had lost a part of his soul, and to his relief, the last two rentals were for men.

Ten minutes later and with only King and three others sitting on the back of the cart, Ben drove between two long fields of tobacco where the field on the left extended so far back that the men working the rows were almost unnoticeable while the field on the right ended at a tree line three hundred feet away, and after another ten minutes, Ben turned right to take a short, narrow dirt road to a two-story stone house resting on four acres cut into the field. Guiding the horses to the back where there were two rows of three huge curing barns, Ben stopped the cart to find a white-bearded man in boots, clean trousers, and a pressed shirt exiting the house with a basket in his hand.

Ben smiled. "Sammy, I have three for you today, a boy and two girls."

"Ah, Master Carlson, you're a fine sight for these worn-out eyes, and unless they're seeing double, you've brought along another lad. Samuel Harwood at your service, young man," the man said as he slowly made his way to stand on William's side and offer his hand, "But those familiar with me call me Sammy."

Appreciating the man's cheery mood, William shook his hand. "I'm William Lovely, and it's a pleasure to make your acquaintance, Master Harwood."

"I expect you exaggerate, Master Lovely," Sammy smiled as he continued to grasp William's hand, "Making me state with confidence that the pleasure is more mine." Releasing William's hand, he asked, "Would it be fair to assume you'll be taking charge of this fine lad's duties?"

"It would."

"Wonderful! Not wonderful to be losing Master Carlson here, but wonderful that his replacement will be another strong young lad who looks as moral as he does intelligent," he said as he made his way around the horses to stand at Ben's side of the cart. "Ben, my friend, here is a gift from my overseer." Seeing the confusion on William's face, he laughed. "That would be Mistress Harwood, or Charity, as you will come to know her, or perhaps even Charry, as you become familiar with her."

Ben reached out and took the basket. "Much appreciated, Sammy," he said before looking back at the slaves. "You three, join Master Harwood."

As the three slaves stepped down to leave King sitting with the stack of buckets between his legs, William followed Ben as he stepped down from the cart.

"Sammy, we may be longer than usual. Have to teach the newcomer here how to trap them."

"Then we'll free the horses while they wait, and may both He and good fortune be with you."

"They always seem to be," Ben said with a smile as he walked toward the woods at the far end of the tobacco field with both William and King following.

"You don't take his sterling?" William asked, deciding to avoid any more surprises by asking questions as they came to him.

"I don't," Ben replied as he walked between rows of tobacco plants. "I give him what we have remaining since we're crossing his land. I never rent them all, and though he can afford it, he doesn't believe in owning slaves. He's a Quaker. But he takes more than a few indentured servants each year, perhaps as many as ten. He treats our slaves well, feeds them well, doesn't work them too hard, and I expect he even gives them a few pennies too, not that they could do anything with them. He's as gentle a soul as any here, and there are only a few."

"A Quaker? I've never met one before now. I didn't know there were any here."

"The last of his kind here. Years before I arrived, his children left for Pennsylvania to be with their kind. Folks here don't appreciate Quakers, but Sammy keeps to himself — no trouble to anyone. Most put up with him, even those in Jamestown," Ben said before spitting.

"You didn't give him King."

"Can't. Not to be rented. Not right in the head. Prone to fits of anger, and only one person can calm him."

"Becky?"

Ben nodded. "Used to be Margaret. When he becomes agitated, Becky whispers in his ear and he relaxes. Don't know what she says to him, but it works." Then Pointing to a tobacco plant, he said, "See the tops there? See how they're cut off? That's the topping I told you about earlier. Remove the buds to make the leaves grow larger. They'll grow two feet higher yet." Stopping, he bent down to pick something off a large leaf of a tobacco plant, and straightening up, he held it out to William, who recognized it as a brown caterpillar. "Sammy'll have them pick off these tobacco worms. Some can be difficult to spot, but with practice, it comes easier. This is one of several sorts." Continuing on his way to the end of the field, he asked, "Did you notice the lack of flying insects? Not the mosquitoes that disappear when the sun's at its hottest, but the other kinds."

"No," William replied, looking about for them.

"There're almost none among the crops. They avoid the plants. It's the strangest thing, and when you leave the field at dusk, you'll walk through a wall of them at the edge of it."

Then walking in silence, ten minutes later William and King followed Ben through the woods to come out at a clearing near a shallow stream almost twenty feet wide. After King dropped the buckets, water skins, and net onto the tall grass and Ben removed his pistols, whip, and coat, William followed him in removing his shoes and stockings and rolling up the legs of his trousers, and doing as Ben had told him, he sat on the stream's bank to watch Ben and King enter the stream to roll out the net, and with each holding an end, crouch down to push it to the bottom. After a few seconds, they brought the ends together, lifted the bottom of the net in a scooping motion, and shook out onto the grass six fish that frantically wiggled and flipped about, and as the two returned to the stream, Ben told William to put them in a bucket.

Back in the water with King, it amused Ben to see the newcomer struggle to grab the slippery fish and carry them one at a time to a bucket, several times dropping the wiggling fish and struggling to pick them up again. "Bring the bucket to them," Ben yelled through his laughter. "You've never touched fish? They don't bite."

Embarrassed, William yelled back, "I haven't. They're dead at the market."

"Grab them by their gills. It's their handle."

After watching them trap fish several more times, filling a bucket and a half, William's mind wandered back to the rented women. His heart picked up speed when he realized he would have to do the deed with Ben again next week, and it beat faster when he considered he would have to do it alone every week after that. Then desperate for a distraction from his thoughts, he surprised himself with his assertiveness. "King, sit if you please. I'll take your end. No, don't sit in the water. Sit over here."

William quickly developed finesse with the net, and as he and Ben trapped the fish, Ben told him they only swam the stream until September, but he still gave Sammy slaves until November, when he stopped renting them. He told William that he suspected Philpot charges Chalmers for the fish they bring back, and he told him that when he had first met Philpot, he was a crueler man. His marrying Margaret, after they discovered she was having his child, had calmed him, and with her acting as his conscience, checking his cruelty toward the slaves, he calmed more. Then Ben told him about the death of the couple's child, told him how Margaret had gone mad, told him about her death, and told him how he found it strange that after their marriage, Margaret had two more years added to her indentured contract because of the child. "Philpot would've been the one to add the years, and it was his child!" When Ben told him that some indentured women might hang themselves when they discovered they were pregnant, told him it was often rumored that their masters had raped them, and added that some of those rumors included a rumor that the women's deaths were made to look like suicides, William wished Ben would stop talking.

Seeing King enter the stream to drink water from his cupped hands, William took it as an opportunity to interrupt Ben by reminding King that they had brought two water skins.

"They're for us," Ben said.

"Then he may drink from my portion. King, take it from a skin."

With King continuing to drink from the stream, Ben laughed and shook his head. "Won't do it. Does only what we've trained him to do, like a horse. He's never used a skin."

Half an hour later and with the buckets full, the three sat on the tall, cool grass where Ben and William shared the cheese, bread, and the ceramic bottle of apple cider that Sammy had gifted them. With King sitting motionless while seeming to stare at something that wasn't there, Ben watched curiously as William sliced several pieces of cheese, grabbed several pieces of bread, and leaned over to offer them to the large man. When King leaned away from him, as if William was about to stab him, William smiled. "They're for you. Take them, eat them." Cautious of the newcomer, he looked for permission from Ben, who grinned and said, "Eat them. Do you require a plate?" With King then eating them, Ben stood up with the bottle of cider and walked past William to hand it to King. Telling him to have a drink, Ben grinned as the giant licked the stem, and liking it, he placed the whole stem into his mouth, turned the bottle up, and gulped down the liquid. "Take your time."

Sitting next to William again, Ben told him it might be the first time King drank from a bottle, and after going quiet for a moment, he said, "I... I only realized now why Sammy gives me so much cheese and bread each week. Sammy, being Sammy, must have believed I would share it with him. Been filling my stomach with his share all these years, and Jeremiah before me did the same."

"I expect it would be much like wasting bread and cheese on a horse," William said, and when he noticed Ben's face covered in shame, he regretted saying it.

The three ate in silence for several minutes before Ben decided it was time for them to leave.

On the ride back to the plantation, with only King and the buckets of fish on the back of the cart, William found it strange that Ben talked about his predecessor rather than himself. He told William where the man was from, describing the place as it was described to him, talked about the man's family, his exceptional skill with firearms, his love for hunting, and how he went south to oversee the slaves of a tobacco plantation so large that it required several overseers.

When they reached the edge of Chalmers' plantation, William found it strange too that Ben stopped talking mid-sentence to go back to his quiet self.

**

Oink woke to a man shouting. He thought it was coming from somewhere on the bottom floor, but hearing it again, he realized it was coming from the grounds. With the third shout, he jumped up from the bed to look out to see what the commotion was about, and with the wavy pattern of the window's pane blurring his view, he searched the garden on the left, where more than a dozen small figures were working. Assuming the shouting wasn't coming from there, he strained to look to his right where he glimpsed past the kitchen a long cart of dark figures rolling out of view. After watching for another few seconds and hearing nothing more, he guessed Philpot was the one doing the shouting and guessed too that he was the one driving the cart.

Putting on his sailor's clothes and red cap, he went to check on his brother, and after opening William's bedroom door a crack and seeing the beds empty with their sheets neatly covering them, he decided to soothe his growling stomach.

As he passed Philpot's room on his way to the stairs, he stopped and took two steps back to open its door a crack. Peeking in, he found it strange that there was a cast-iron bracket on the inside of the door frame, and stepping in, he found it stranger that there was a pair of open, rusty iron shutters attached to the bedroom window, much like those in the man's study. Ignoring the oversized poster bed and the painted portraits of the man hanging on the walls, his curious eyes were drawn to the dresser, where two pistols rested between two large brass candleholders, and as if not to spook the triggered curiosities, he crept toward them to touch one of the cold iron barrels. Giving into his urge, he gently picked it up with both hands to feel its weight before taking hold of its wooden grip and stretching his short finger around its trigger. With his hand shaking with excitement, he pulled back the hammer and pointed it at the window. "Surrender, pirate!" Then wondering if it was loaded, he looked down the barrel, but seeing only darkness, he shook it and listened for the sound of a lead ball. Hearing nothing, he decided it was empty and again pointed it at the window. "Drop your sword!" he growled before pulling the trigger.

Placing Philpot's dirty dishes on the tray, she was about to wipe down the table when a blast filled the house. Pulling herself out of her stunned state, she wondered who could've caused it when no one was there, but then remembering Oink was still there, she rushed down the hall and hurried up the staircase to Philpot's room. Recognizing the odor of burnt gunpowder that she had experienced several weeks before, she froze at the sight of the red-capped topless boy standing with his back to her while the pistol lightly smoked near his bare foot.

"Are you hurt?" she asked, trying to control the panic in her voice.

Oink turned around slowly, revealing a fresh cut between his eyebrows, his nose bleeding, and a tear crawling down his cheek. "I didn't do it," he said, and then dropping his eyes to the floor, he whispered, "I-I did it, but I didn't know it was charged. It flew at my face!"

Becky walked over and picked up the pistol. "They're

always charged. It's wise to assume they are. Master Philpot believes that just as a knife should be sharp, a firearm should be charged," she said, trying to pacify the boy. "It was very loud. I froze when I heard it."

"I-I heard louder… much louder, so loud it knocked men off their feet."

Assuming the boy was exaggerating to save face, Becky placed the spent weapon back on the dresser.

"Please don't tell my brother," Oink begged in a whisper.

"You should be asking me not to tell Master Philpot. I expect his reaction would be harsher than your brother's."

"He might yell at me as he yelled this morning, but William wouldn't yell, wouldn't say much, and it's what he wouldn't say that's worse."

Becky held back her smile. "I'll tell neither if you've learned a lesson, learned to assume all are charged as they always are… and not to be handled."

"I did."

"Good. Now, where did the ball go? Did it damage anything?"

"Out the window. I pointed it at the window."

Becky walked over to the window and noticed a fresh gouge in the rust at the edge of an iron shutter. Curious, she turned around and noticed a small, dark hole in the whitewashed plank wall behind him, a little to his right and at his chest level. "That's… that's a good thing — no holes," she lied.

"Should we charge it?"

"No, I expect it will go unnoticed. When he carries one, he carries six."

Not wanting to eat alone in the dining room, Oink joined Becky in the kitchen, and remembering what she had told him about slaves not addressing him by his given name, or sea name, he startled the two women and amused Becky when he greeted them as Mistress Mary and Mistress Ann.

After Mary offered the young master bread, preserves, and two boiled eggs while fighting back her desire to ask Becky about the gun blast, Oink shook his head and surprised all by asking for some of the remaining bean porridge drying in a large pot, and standing at the table, he ate it under the curious but discreet stares of the two slaves, whom he amused when he complimented them on it and asked for seconds.

When he finished his second bowl, Becky brought him to the garden, which seemed much larger when standing just outside its fence, and after she pointed out the obvious: the first half contained over a hundred rows of vegetables and fruits and the second contained stalks of corn, the boy's heart skipped a beat when he saw Sophie among the other children, including the pockmarked boy named Thomas, carefully picking up the last of the cabbage leaves scattered along the inside of the fence. Mistaking the boy's attraction to Sophie with being impressed with the garden, Becky told him they were removing the weeds and insects, and picking up the cabbage leaves they used to catch the snails and slugs.

"Do we eat them, the… the slugs?" Oink asked, fearing the answer might be a 'yes.'

Becky cracked a slight smile and shook her head. "No, we burn them in the kitchen and later they'll sprinkle ashes around the plants, ashes from the pile there," she said, pointing to a three-foot pile of ash near a large spit at the side of the kitchen. "Shall we walk the length and see what's here?"

As Becky told him the names of the vegetables they passed, Oink recognized the many rows of cabbage and the rows of turnips, onions, carrots, parsnips, and cucumbers, but the various beans and various squashes, which Becky called the largest pumpkins, were new to him, and when she pointed out the rows of strawberries and raspberries, the boy forgot he had just eaten and salivated.

"What should I be doing?"

"You oversee them, make certain they're working."

"But they are working… without me overseeing them."

Finding the statement curious, a thought struck her, a thought that would explain the brothers' apparent respect for the slaves. "Have you never seen slaves driven?"

"Of course. All the time," he lied, finding it strange that she would ask him about the carting around of slaves, and then thinking he would impress her with his brother, he added, "William drives them about faster than most. He's famous for it in England."

"He is?" Becky asked, thinking it strange that someone would be famous for overseeing slaves.

"He is," he nodded.

After she left Oink to oversee the garden work, the boy stood outside its fence watching the children pull weeds from the ground and insects from the plants, and fifteen minutes later and with nothing to interest him, he walked around the garden's fence pretending to watch for beasts that might carry away the children.

When he passed Sophie picking weeds, he was disappointed when she didn't seem to notice him, and as he continued to walk the fence line, he began to feel he was being watched, and the feeling was correct. Every child, including

Sophie, was fearfully and discreetly watching the English boy, and when he quickly turned around to confirm he was being watched, he caught several of the younger children turning their heads away from him.

Having walked around the garden nine times in a little over an hour, he opened the small gate, walked to a row of vegetables that hadn't been worked, and began pulling out the short weeds around them. Then feeling eyes on him again, he looked over at the others and again caught a few heads turning away from him. Returning to pulling out weeds, he waited almost half a minute before spinning around to catch a boy no older than six staring at him. "Ha! Caught you!" he laughed, but he stopped laughing when the boy wetted the front of his shorts.

Having reloaded the pistol after stuffing the small hole in Philpot's wall with bread dough, making it look like a knot in the wood, Becky spent some time curiously watching Oink from his bedroom window. She was pleased that he didn't bark at the children to work faster, which they could have easily done, and she found it as strange as the children did when he helped with the work, pacing himself by their speed. Then when some of the children noticed he was keeping up with them, they began working faster and the others soon followed, and then when Oink noticed they were working faster than him, he worked faster too, causing them to work faster and the newcomer to think it was a competition.

With the cycle continuing until their arms were blurred more than they normally would be through the window's wavy glass, she was impressed by Oink's method of overseeing the slaves and assumed the boy had learned to lead by example from his brother, and that would explain why William had never used a whip. Knowing Philpot wouldn't allow him to oversee the slaves in such a way when a painful snap of the whip could have the same result, she was again curious about how long it would take William to adjust to Virginia's way… until it occurred to her he would probably embrace it quickly since it required less effort.

Then fearing the children working as fast as they were might faint under the sun's growing heat, she went out to the garden where Oink and the other children watched her join them in weeding it, and with his cap soaked and no winner yet declared, Oink slowed down his pace to match hers, and the others soon followed.

Three hours later, Oink was disappointed when the children formed small groups and without an invitation or any goodbyes, disappeared into their cabins for the day.

******

After William, Ben, and King took the buckets of fish to Mary, who later that day would fry them for the English and make a stew of them for the slaves, they helped Becky load a large, half pot of stew, forty wooden bowls, and a metal domed-covered dish onto the cart, and when she and King rode off to deliver the midday meal to Philpot and the slaves, Ben taught the Lovelys how to use the whip.

Reluctantly doing as Ben had shown them, William practiced the forward strike, the simplest and the same strike he had seen Gorge perform, and after hitting himself several times, to the amusement of Oink, and causing the occasional loud crack, he passed the whip to an excited Oink, who also struck himself several times while not cracking it once.

Then with Oink's ear stinging from his last swing of the whip, Ben took their training to the next level by grabbing several onions from the garden and forcing one onto the head of the lone spike sticking out a couple of inches from the whipping post at about chest height. Scattering it with his first strike, he left William and Oink to practice their aim on another onion while he took a nap.

After more than two hundred tries at the onion while cracking the whip most times, William never once struck it, and with just as many tries and never cracking it once, Oink had lightly slapped the vegetable several times, but by his reaction, one would have thought the slap had burst it with a loud crack.

As Ben and William were about to leave to collect the slaves, Oink asked William if he could go too, but his brother refused, telling him they each had their duties and collecting the slaves was not his, and then when Oink asked Ben, the assistant overseer impressed William by saying, "Your brother spoke for the two of us."

Almost an hour after William and Ben had left, Philpot returned with his cart of slaves. Not impressed to find Oink barefoot, he disappointed him by sternly telling him that from then on he was to wear shoes, and when he told the boy he could only join them at the table that evening after he had washed his feet and put on stockings and shoes, Oink asked innocently, "Where do I eat if I don't wash my feet?"

CHAPTER 19
Sunday

When Ben went to wake William, he found him looking up at the ceiling, and without a word, the newcomer did as he was told and put on his better clothes.

William didn't sleep well. He had woken several times in a panic as if from a nightmare that he couldn't remember, and after the sixth time, he waited in bed for almost an hour and a half for Ben to get up. He had gone to bed dwelling on the women they had rented, and he didn't expect to be able to look them in the eyes after that first day, didn't expect to be able to look any of the women and men in the eyes.

Desperate to rid himself of the guilt, he had tried blaming Ben, but a second later, was covered in shame for doing so. Being there and doing nothing to stop it made him guilty too, and the only thing he could come up with to put it right would be to stop renting the women, but with Ben warning him of Philpot's wrath, by refusing to rent them he would be putting his brother at risk too.

When sleep did come, he was wondering if Becky knew of the women being rented for bedding, and if she did, it would make her much less attractive.

Picking up their chamber pot, William entered Oink's room where his jealousy of the boy contently snoring was replaced by his disgust with the room's sour smell. Picking up Oink's chamber pot with what must have been two night's contents, he assumed the boy had yet to have his nose cleared of the pungent smells they had tolerated during their voyage, and with a chamber pot then in each hand, he struck the bed with the heel of his foot, causing his brother to mumble something incoherent before rolling over. The second kick of the bed caused him to sit up, rub his eyes, and growl, "I heard you the first time!"

"Put on your better clothes. We're going to church."

A few seconds before Philpot took his first spoonful of oatmeal porridge, Oink noticed a man's dark face looking through the window. Curious as to why the man whose name he couldn't remember was looking in on them, he turned to ask Becky and was startled by her hand tapping his knee, and when he looked down at it, she waved it. Taking it as a signal to say nothing, he ate his porridge.

William, with two days of stubble on his face, stood with Oink outside the shed waiting for Becky to finish shaving Ben, both finding it odd that, except for Mary and Ann, the slaves remained in their opened cabins. After a clean-shaven Ben exited the shed and told William he was going to hitch two horses to the smaller cart, William entered the shed, and with Becky stropping what looked like a small meat cleaver against a strip of leather hanging on the wall, he nervously sat on a stool. As he unbuttoned the top two buttons of his shirt and folded back its collar, Oink entered and sat on the other stool.

Worried that his younger brother would notice his nervous state and bring attention to it, William was about to ask him to wait outside when Becky asked Oink if it was his first shave.

"No," he said, shaking his head, and then blushing, he nodded, "Yes."

Taking his chin in her hand, she exaggerated examining his face as she turned it left and right. "It could use one, but only once a month." Then, with William looking at her as if she had gone mad, she added, "With it being your first, you'll have to close your eyes to avoid flinching. It's necessary until you're accustomed to it, perhaps during the next three or four shaves."

"I'll be fine," Oink said as he unbuttoned the top of his shirt and folded back its collar as William had done.

Becky laid the razor on the small table beside Oink, placed a small towel around the base of his neck, and taking a small block of soap from a bucket of water, rubbed it in her hands until it created a thick froth. "That's what they all say... the first few times, but I must insist. It's a sharp blade and one flinch could take off an ear. You only have to ask One-Ear Roy in Jamestown to know I'm speaking the truth."

William watched curiously as Becky lathered his brother's face with the froth, told the boy to close his eyes, and with Oink doing as he was told, used the back of the razor to remove the froth from his left cheek, from under his nose, from around his chin and then from his other cheek.

"How was that?" she asked as she used the towel around his neck to wipe his face dry.

"Great!" he answered as he rubbed his hands over his face. "It's smoother!"

"It should be," she said, and then looking at a smiling

William, added, "That's something I learned from Grace, one of the two who shaves the men, shaves and cuts their hair."

"What did you learn?" Oink asked as he buttoned his shirt and fixed his collar.

"To have you close your eyes the first few times."

After Becky placed the towel around William's neck, her heart began to race as she lathered his face with the froth, and not understanding why she was nervous about shaving another Ben, another overseer of slaves, she tried to calm down by trying to imagine she was shaving Ben.

As his heart raced with her touching his face, William tried to calm down by imagining his mother doing the shaving, and when Becky brought the blade to his cheek, her face inches from his, he closed his eyes so it would be easier to imagine, but it wasn't. Her soft breath against his neck made it almost impossible.

Taking a deep and discreet breath, she found it helped that he closed his eyes, and wishing she could do the same, she took another deep breath and slowly exhaled as she gently slid the razor down his cheek.

Not noticing Becky's slightly shaking hand, Oink found it curious that William had closed his eyes as if it was his first shave too, and it surprised him to see her nick his chin, and after she apologized, nick his cheek and then his neck, as if it was her first time shaving a face.

Finished, Becky apologized again before handing him the towel around his neck. "Next Sunday I'll remember to be more careful around that dimple."

Patting his neck dry, William noticed several tiny spots of blood on the cloth. "Is there a dimple in my neck too?" he asked with a smile.

"There is," she nodded with a straight face.

With it being his first familiar place since leaving England, William found comfortable sanctuary in the church that seemed purposely hidden within a section of forest separating two plantations.

Sitting in the second pew that announced Philpot's status within the congregation, the church reminded him of the one in his village. It had the same tall and narrow windows, the same tall, white walls, and it had the same two rows of pews leading up to the same two-level stage. To the left of the fenced-in altar taking center stage, a well-dressed man sat at an organ. On the lower stage, the minister in his black robe stood at the left while an older clerk in a white robe stood at the right, and after the hundred-plus parishioners had found their pews and whispered greetings to one another, the clerk moved to the center and raised his hand. As the organist began playing, William and Oink recognized the song, *All Praise to Thee, My God, This Night*, and feeling as if they were home, both stood with the others and sang along.

When the song finished, the minister took the clerk's spot at center stage, lowered his head, and said a prayer, and after the many soft amens had filled the church, he didn't read a short piece of scripture and follow it with a homily, as the brothers expected, but instead began preaching about the fifth commandment, *Thou shall not kill*.

While the minister spoke loud enough for all to hear, William looked on, but because of his lack of sleep, he took in little of what the man said until he raised his voice to almost yell, "Man purposely kills in war, in defense, in revenge, kills in anger, greed, fear, jealousy, and even in grief, but the one state he never kills in is in a state of happiness."

As Oink sat next to him with his head back, eyes closed, and mouth open, William struggled to stay awake as the minister preached about achieving a state of prolonged contentment by reducing one's wants and expectations while identifying real needs rather than perceived ones, and using several examples from the *Old Testament*, he preached about appreciating and enjoying what one has and what one has achieved while not comparing one's achievements to those of another. Finally losing the sermon, he raised his voice again to say, "If one is truly content, then every commandment can be followed without exception, unless one is content with breaking them," and followed it with a prayer.

After the clerk read out several announcements and gave an update on the health of two absent members of the congregation, the parishioners approached the stage to exchange a few words with the minister, and thinking he would do the same, William stood up from the pew hoping for the chance to ask the man if he believed slaves have souls, but the chance never came. Philpot hurried them out to the cart, where he took the front bench, told Becky to sit next to him, and taking the reins, rode off while complaining about the man's simple cure for the world's problems. "I say he should practice what he preaches! If he were truly a content man, he wouldn't continue asking about that six hundred pounds of tobacco! More than a month since Margaret's death and a year since Beth's, and the bugger still feels the need to remind me of what I owe for their burials! If there's no chance of him shutting up about it, I say I shall have to deliver it with this crop!"

"Who are... were Margaret and Beth?" Oink whispered to

William.

"I'll tell you later," he whispered back.

Before riding off on a horse that Ben had saddled for him, Philpot ordered the brothers to practice with the whip, telling them that when he returned that evening, he expected both to be able to crack it consistently.

Soon after Philpot left the plantation and while the slaves were doing their Sunday chores and the smaller children were running around playing, Ben told William he could find the whip in their room, and ten minutes later and without any goodbyes, he also rode off on a horse.

After a dozen misses, William, who couldn't have cared less each time he missed the onion stuck on the whipping pole's spike, handed the whip to his excited brother, who impressed himself when he finally cracked it after two dozen attempts. Looking about to see if he had impressed Sophie, she wasn't around and neither were any of the other children who had disappeared when William had first cracked it.

It took almost two hours for William to burst his first onion, and though he saw it burst with his eyes, his mind saw a three-inch gash appear in flesh. Handing the whip to his brother, he replaced the onion and was thankful when Becky announced that their midday meals were ready.

Becky was thankful too. The two hours of cracking the whip had annoyed her and stressed the slaves, and after the brothers had eaten stew in the dining room and she had eaten in the kitchen, she had to endure the cracking of the whip for several more hours.

When William's sore shoulder confirmed he had practiced enough, he left Oink to practice by himself while he took a short nap, but because of the lack of sleep the night before and the heat of the day, he fell into such a deep sleep that when Ben returned, he had to wake him for their evening meal.

**

Believing the others had gone to bed, Becky was leaving the house when she almost bumped into a drunk Philpot staggering up the steps with his waistcoat opened and his dirt-stained shirt unbuttoned halfway.

The large man's red face lit up with a smile. "There she is! Waiting up for me, were you? Worried about me? Concerned for my safety?" he asked, forcing himself to pronounce each word properly before he belched and laughed. "I'm flattered, but I say there's no need. I can care for myself better than most. Now, give me a blessed night kissy," he begged as he walked to her with arms out.

As Becky walked backward into the house, he kept coming, and when her back hit a wall and he tried to embrace her, she dropped and crawled out from between it and him.

"Sleep well," she almost yelled while rushing to her bedroom, where she closed the door and placed her foot against it.

A moment later, Philpot was at the door. "One kissy and I'll be on my way, merely one."

Turning her head away from the door, Becky hoped her voice would sound as if it was coming from her bed. "Sleep well, Master Philpot. I will see you in the morning."

After a few seconds of silence, she heard him stumble down the hall and found herself reflecting on that night's earlier visitor.

She had been sitting with her back against the bed's headboard reading a book by candlelight when Ben knocked softly on her door, and when she opened it, he blurted out that she had to come with him or spend the rest of her days and nights with Philpot. "I don't expect you're fond of the man, but I know he is of you. Doesn't say it, but I've seen it in his eyes. And when he comes for you, he won't take rejection as well as I do." Not seeing the response on her face that he had expected, he added, "I know of what I speak. Witnessed it with Margaret."

If she believed what he was saying, his anxious words would have covered her with a chill, but believing he was saying it only to frighten her into leaving with him, she tried to ignore the insult from his expectation that she would give herself to a man she wasn't attracted to as an escape from another she wasn't attracted to by saying. "Ben, I appreciate your warning, but you're going south and I would prefer going north."

"That's also what I must tell you. It's a lie. I lied. I'm returning to England. Can't tell you why, not now, but will when we're gone from here. I've more than enough for our passage and can promise you we'll live on a grand estate and work for an honorable man."

With his returning to England then making less sense than his warning about Philpot, she said, "Another promise? How can I believe you'll keep it when you've broken your first?"

"What promise have I broken?"

"The promise of not asking me again to be with you," she said as she closed the door on him.

"Then… then if you please, keep what I said to yourself," Ben pleaded from behind the closed door. "To yourself until I'm gone."

"I will if you stop this annoying request."

"Then consider it stopped," he said, defeated.

After Ben had walked off, Becky stood at her closed door trying to make sense of what he had said. She struggled to recall any obvious signs of Philpot's strong interest in her, and then giving up on that, she struggled to understand why Ben would go back to England, how he would have the sterling for his and her passage, and why he would've come to Virginia as an indentured servant if he intended to return to England after his contract had ended. Then thinking of England, she considered that if Philpot wanted a wife badly enough, he could contact an agent there to send him one, as was still occasionally done by the wealthier bachelors.

Then standing behind her closed door for the second time that evening, she again considered if there was something to Ben's warning, but then shaking her mind from it, she excused Philpot's behavior by him being intoxicated.

**

As a baritone scream resonated through the outside wall of their room, William woke and immediately knew who it was.

"I expect he spent the night alone," Ben whispered to him through the darkness. "Hear that?"

"The children crying?" William whispered back.

"No, the snoring. Philpot can sleep through anything."

"That's my brother."

"No, that's a different snore, a lighter snore. You'll soon tell them apart."

"Sleep well," William said, not understanding why he should care whose snore was whose.

CHAPTER 20
Williamsburg

Becky had been looking forward to a quiet day, one where she wouldn't have to hear the cracking of a whip for several straight hours, but that Monday morning at the dining room table, after exciting Oink and shocking William by his waistcoat with three pairs of pistols holstered at its front, Philpot told her to take the brothers into town to be measured for their clothes. "And not soon enough, I say. You two look like someone or some two I would see crawling out from a tavern. After you have your field clothes and boots, I don't want to see those clothes on you two again. Wash them and put them away for the next seven years."

"May I wear this cap?"

"That cap!?" Philpot growled before reminding himself the boy was only twelve. "I shall say yes. I shall accept it, but only because it's you," he smirked. "And Becky, bring the boys with you to the field when you bring the meals."

After Ben and Philpot had ridden off two long carts packed with slaves, William tried to impress Becky by harnessing the horses to the smaller cart while she helped Mary and Ann clean the kitchen, but he failed. She assumed he knew how to do it before he arrived, so she wasn't impressed when she noticed the horses' girths had to be tightened.

Not comfortable having the older brother sitting next to her, Becky delighted Oink by telling him he could steer the horses, giving William the back bench to himself, and after she took a minute to tell him what to do, the younger brother's cheeks expanded with each excited exhale as he guided the horses away from the house and down the narrow road through the woods.

After turning the small cart left onto the dirt road that went straight for a few miles, Oink asked Becky if he could make the horses trot and was disappointed when she told him that until he had more experience with the cart, it was better to get there safer than faster, and since it was early, they didn't want to reach Williamsburg too soon and have to wait for the shops to open.

With no effort needed to drive the cart on the straightaway, Oink took more than a few minutes to ponder on how he might ask Becky if she was courting or engaged without having her realize he was asking for his brother's benefit. Finally deciding to work it into a conversation, he asked how long she had been in Virginia, and after she told him she was born there and that her father arrived as an indentured servant when the crown was still offering land as part of their contract, he asked, "Are you courting?"

"No."

"Have you ever?"

"No," she lied, hoping to avoid any more questions on the subject.

"Neither have I, and William hasn't either. He's courted no one. He has no one at home. The mine kept him from it. He worked until six in the morning and slept during the day. Is that so, William?" With William not able to hear him over the rattling cart and the beating hoofs, he raised his voice, "William, you worked six until six in the mine, correct?"

"I did," William said, and then curious about what the two were talking about, he leaned forward to add, "Six in the evening until six in the morning."

Confused, Becky said, "I thought he was an overseer, an overseer of slaves."

Oink shook his head. "His first time, but our father believes it's a proper position for him. He says it suits his character."

"Yes, it does take a certain character."

"He has the character for watching over people, to make certain they're safe, healthy, and happy."

"Safe, healthy, and happy?" she asked, offering a confused look at William still leaning in.

William blushed. "That's… that's what the agent told me."

"He also told him he would have private quarters on the ship, but he didn't."

"The agent said you would keep them safe, healthy, and… and happy?"

"Yes, and that's exactly… *exactly* what I'm to do," he said for Oink's benefit.

Then more confused, she turned her head toward the road. "There's a cart coming. Keep to the left to give it space," she said, appreciating the opportunity to change the subject, and with their cart bumping about as its left wheels rolled over the rocks at the edge of the road, she said, "Too far. Gently guide them back." And as the boy did as she said, she was amused by his cheeks puffing out with each nervous exhale. "That's it.

See why I said we shouldn't hurry?"

Oink nodded and then relaxed after the cart passed them.

After another few minutes on the straightaway, Oink proudly informed her he was an inventor. "I've invented nothing yet, but I have many ideas," he said and then went on for some time about his horse-stairs carriage.

Becky didn't understand how the steps turned the axle and she held back her smile when she imagined the horses climbing an endless loop of steps, but she couldn't hold it back when he told her how the driver would use a grappling hook to stop the cart and she imagined it catching people and dragging them along screaming.

When the boy asked her what she thought of his invention, she wasn't sure what to say, so she looked back for help from William, who said, "Tell her about your windmaker."

"Winemaker?"

"No, wind. His windmaker."

"Wind? Flatulence?" she asked, causing William to smile.

Oink huffed. "No, not farts! Wind! Wind inside a ship or a home," he said, and then described how he would use the rotating wings much like that of a windmill to rotate a group of much smaller ones attached to the ceiling beams of each room in a house.

The idea impressed Becky, and she saw nothing amusing about it, agreeing with Oink that if the wind could turn at least a ton of stone to grind flour, it could create wind too.

As they rolled past huge fields of wheat toward a town visible from almost a half-mile away, Oink told her how he would connect several small sets of rotating wings on different floors, control their speeds with levers, and how he would disengage them when they weren't needed during the cooler months.

Entering Williamsburg by a gravel road, Becky directed Oink to turn the horses right and to take the next left down Boundary Street, where they passed several carts and pedestrians.

Impressed by the two-story stone houses' lawns of chamomile, thyme, and the much rarer weeded and recently scythed grass, William was disappointed when the pleasant smells disappeared after they turned left onto the wider Duke of Gloucester Street, where his little brother straightened up proudly as he drove the cart past several wooden houses before passing on their left the three equal sections of the large grass lawns leading to the three-story, red-bricked Governor's Palace, and on their right, the white-stone Town Hall with its whipping post and two pillories mounted on a large stage extending out from its left side. Continuing toward the merchant shops and taverns where the smells were the most disturbing, William noticed the town was much smaller than he had expected and the buildings weren't packed as tightly together as those of the London streets they had traveled through on their last day in England.

Passing Colonist Street, Becky took the reins from Oink and parked the cart, and when the brothers joined her as she tied the reins to a post, Oink pointed further down the road and asked William, "Do you expect that blacksmith sign down there on the other side of the street is the one Philip's indentured to?"

"I don't know. Perhaps we can inquire later," William said, looking at Becky for permission.

"I'll be renting a few books from this shop, and if you would like, we can meet here or there when I'm finished."

With the three agreeing that if they weren't at the shop when she left then she would meet them at the blacksmith's, she walked up the steps to enter the shop with *Library* painted above its door that dinged when it struck a small rusty-green bell.

Walking down the wooden sidewalk toward the blacksmith's shop, William asked Oink, "How do you feel about Chalmers' plantation?"

"With my hands," Oink grinned.

"I expected as much, and what's your opinion of it?"

Oink took a moment to consider the question. "The gardening is simple enough. Becky is kind. The others seem kind too. I haven't been around Ben enough to have an opinion of him, and I don't have one of Master Philpot. He seems angry, but then sometimes he seems nice. He's not like Gorge or Captain Humphreys, but maybe he's like John — rough and rude until we know him better. And I have no opinion of the slaves yet, but I think I frighten them. They don't say a word to me."

"They'll need time to form an opinion of you too, I suppose. Do you miss Mother, Father, and the girls? Have you thought much about them?"

"I do sometimes. You?"

"The same," William nodded, "But I fear I'll forget their faces and plan to send a pound for pencil sketches of them."

Oink had never considered that he might forget his family's faces. He thought of his father's face and saw it clearly, but when the man's eyes scolded him for leaving, he thought of his mother's face. Hers was clear too, and when her eyes scolded him, he thought of his two older sisters who had the same scolding eyes. Lastly, he thought of his little sister, whose eyes scolded him as she screamed he was a bad boy. Shaking his head clear, he said, "We'll have to insist they smile for them."

Nodding, William said, "We should send a letter soon to let them know we've arrived."

"We should," Oink nodded back. "I'll write it out in pencil and ask Becky to fix it so it's worded well. If she reads, I expect she writes too. But we need to decide what to say. Should we tell them about the pirates?"

"I think not. They may not believe us. We don't want them thinking we're telling grand tales in the first letter we send them and have them question what we tell them in the letters to follow."

"Should we tell them about Sophie and Becky?"

"Don't mention Becky. *Don't* tell them we'll be marrying," William said while trying to remember who Sophie was.

"You want it to be a surprise?" Oink asked with a smile covering his face.

"We should probably not mention practicing with the whip or Master Philpot's battle room. We don't want to give them a reason to worry."

"The battle room I understand — it's for fighting the others if they attack — but why not the whip?"

"It has one use, and we saw that on the ship."

"So do swords and pistols, but having them and practicing with them is not the same as using them."

"Perhaps, but people have them to use them, and for one to use them well, one must practice with them."

"Or one has them on the chance that they may have to use them, not that they will or want to."

Surprised that he was losing an argument with his little brother, William changed the subject. "Tell me, did you hide in the crate to avoid the mine? You would've begun work last month if you stayed home."

"I didn't want to work in the mine, but it's not the reason I'm here. I never considered it until you mentioned it now, but I would rather be here than there."

Stopping across from the blacksmith sign, they waited for a small cart and then a covered carriage to pass before crossing the street to follow a stone path between two buildings toward another further in with its two opened battened doors offering a view of the man who had received Philip just days before. Topless, wearing an angry expression, and already glistening with sweat so early in the morning, he placed a glowing-red piece of metal on a waist-high anvil and barked something to someone.

Instinctively, William stopped just past the two buildings and pulled Oink back.

Startled by the unusually aggressive pull, the boy was about to protest when he saw Philip appear in trousers and a stained, half-buttoned shirt to hand a hammer to the muscular man who took it, barked something else, and poked him in the stomach with it so hard that it knocked the air out of him.

When the man slapped Philip with the back of his hand, William tightened his grip on Oink's shirt to hold him back from going to their friend's aid. "We'll return when he's… when he's settled in," he whispered.

"When he's settled in? He's being attacked now!"

William turned and pulled Oink along with him. "There's nothing we can do. Interfering will only make it worse for him."

"But he's being attacked!"

"Give it some thought!" William demanded, stunning Oink with his tone. "He won't maim him, not bad enough that he can't perform his tasks. He didn't pay his way here only to maim him. No, we'll return when Philip's familiar with his duties and settled in. When he knows what he's doing and… and not being beaten."

While William tried to fight back the anger that seemed to grow from every part of him, the two silently walked back to the shop, and when they were almost across from the shop that Becky had entered, a man about twenty feet away with a stained and ripped shirt, which made him look like he was on the losing end of a recent fight, hobbled toward them growling something at an older couple wishing him a blessed morning. Reaching the brothers, he said, "Oi! Ya sailors are startin' early this mornin', are yas? Celebratin' survivin' another, are ya?"

Flattered to be mistaken for a sailor, Oink pointed to Becky leaving the shop across the street. "No, we're waiting for our friend over there."

"Looky 'ere! A little one too!" the man laughed before looking over at Becky, and surprised to see her, his eyebrows curled in. Turning to the brothers, he pushed Oink aside and grabbed William by the throat. "That one's not for the likes of ya. She's property of me mate, Charlie, and ya don't want to cross 'im. Ya two bests be lookin' somewheres else," he warned, tightening his grip on William and following him when he took a few steps back.

Then behind the man, Oink saw an opportunity and kicked him between his bowlegs.

With the man groaning, William felt like he was looking at

himself from a distance when he punched the man in the nose, forcing him to the ground.

Both shocked and ashamed by what felt like a sudden burst of anger, William questioned why he reacted as he did. Was it the man grabbing him by his neck? He doubted it. Though harsher than a grab of a shirt, it wasn't threatening enough to cause him to punch him. Then wondering if it had anything at all to do with the man, he questioned if it was an opportunity to release his anger at seeing Philip beaten or release his anger for renting the women and having to do it again, and again, and again. Was it because he had been misinformed about what he would do in Virginia, or was it because Oink was there with him when he no longer wanted him there with him, or was it because the pirate's words were still in the back of his mind? With the number of reasons coming to him at that moment, he expected there were more he had yet to consider and was thankful he only hit the man once. Then another question jumped into his head: who was this Charlie?

"Why strike him!? And don't say you were protecting me because my kick finished it!"

Unable to explain himself, William just stared at his brother.

Seeing the brothers across the street standing over Harry Carter, Becky took a moment to accept what she was seeing before rushing across the street. "You attacked a lame man!"

With William too ashamed to speak, Oink said, "He started it, and I finished it."

"Not finished yet!" Harry growled, causing the blood from his nostrils to bubble. Pulling a six-inch blade from the sheath on his side, he was using both hands to get to his feet when

Becky stepped on the hand holding the knife, bent down to pull it from his hand, and placed the blade between the pages of a book so only its handle was visible.

"Harry, it's finished, and you can see Master Philpot about this knife."

"Always my fault, eh?" Harry complained as he got to his feet and hobbled off. "Not this time, and Philpot'll 'ear of it!"

"I don't see how he couldn't when you have to see him for your knife!" Becky countered, and then shaking her head, said, "You two are sticking with me. You go off once and you cause trouble. I'm not sure how it is in England, but that sort of trouble will find you dead here. Harry's one of three, and the other two *able* Carter brothers won't appreciate you striking him. It could be all Philpot can do to calm them down when they learn you're indentured to the plantation."

Hearing *Carter brothers*, William recalled what Ben had said about them, and he worried for his brother. A man might forgive someone for striking him in the nose, but he wouldn't forgive them for striking him in the groin.

"He attacked us for no reason!" Oink protested.

"I expect the reason was alcohol," Becky said. "And I expect he's still inebriated from last night, perhaps took a room above a tavern for a few hours."

"But that was Sunday."

"The taverns are open every day, and to some here, the day has little meaning."

Then as an idea came to her, she lifted her skirt with her free hand and ran after Harry, and with the brothers watching curiously, she caught up to the slow-moving man and after a few words and some aggressive posturing between them, handed him back his knife.

When she returned, Oink asked, "Why give it back?"

"If I give it to Philpot, I'll have to explain what happened, and when Harry comes for it, he's certain to exaggerate it. By giving it back, I made him promise to say nothing of it."

"Will he keep it, keep his promise?"

"I don't know, but a man his age being knocked down by a young man and a boy might not be something he wants people to know about. Now you two stick to me like molasses. You're not going off on your own again today!"

Having calmed down after she considered who they had fought with, she still played angry to make her point. She said nothing to them when she took them to the tailor where they were measured for shirts and trousers, and she said little when she took them to the cordwainer to be measured for boots. She said even less when she took them to a shop where she purchased a shorter whip for a delighted Oink, and when Oink asked to carry it, she said he could as long as he didn't crack it. After taking them to a shop where she purchased a pewter snuff box for a pound and a half, she nodded to Oink's request to take them to the printer where William purchased a dozen sheets of paper, but when Oink asked her to bring them to a place that sold quells and ink, she refused, telling him they could use Philpot's if they never let him know they did.

Twenty minutes later, as Oink was driving them between fields of wheat, he asked Becky if she liked to read, and with his brother sitting on the back bench unable to hear them clearly, she only nodded.

"William can't," Oink told her. "Oi, here's an idea. Why not teach him to read?" he said, trying to sound as if the idea had just come to him.

"I don't teach," the plantation's ex-governess lied.

Oink was going to say that it wouldn't be like teaching him to write, which he was certain required more effort, when a copperhead snake slithered out from the left side of the road and frightened the two horses that neighed and darted ahead, pulling the cart along the right side of the road.

When Becky grabbed the reins from Oink and pulled back on them, the horses' heads went back for only a moment before the panicking animals forced them forward, almost pulling her forward with them, and with her heart then beating as hard and as fast as the slapping hoofs of the horses rushing further to the right, the cart's furiously spinning solid wheels bumped along the road's edge of rocks and boulders, and when the horses finally responded to Becky trying to turn them to the left, the right side's wheels pressed against the boulders and a second later and with a loud snap, the cart returned to the road and bounced about as if trying to buck them from it. As she again pulled back on the reins, the horses stopped, the cart dropped forward, and she and Oink tumbled to the ground behind the animals.

After almost being thrown over the front bench's backrest, William jumped from the cart, and ignoring Oink's hand, he first helped up Becky, who was annoyed by it, and then as he inspected the front wheel resting on the clean break that made it look as if it was partially buried in the dirt, his little brother brushed the dirt from his trousers and said to Becky who was brushing the dirt from her skirt, "My apologies for that."

"It's not your fault. It's the snake's," she said as she adjusted her dress before walking over to the horses to calm them with several pats and a couple of whispers.

With Oink running off to search for the broken section of

the wheel, William, curious about what she was whispering to the horses, joined her and was disappointed when she stopped.

A minute later, Oink returned with the missing section of the wheel. "We can't repair it ourselves," he said, "And we can't drive it with what's there."

"No, we can't," Becky agreed. "And there's no chance of using our carpenters. Philpot took both. We'll have to walk into town to have a man from the cabinetry shop come and give it a temporary repair."

"I can go," Oink said, seeing an opportunity to leave the two alone. "There's no reason for all of us to walk back in the heat."

Becky would have preferred to be alone with Oink rather than his brother, but the boy's enthusiasm forced her to agree, so after she told him the directions to the shop, annoyed him with a warning about the snake they had passed, and William annoyed him further by telling him not to dawdle, Oink was walking back to town with his whip in hand, easily and proudly cracking it along the way.

William followed Becky onto the cart, and when she laid herself back on the front bench and pulled her knees up, he did the same on the back bench, and after ten minutes of both staring up at the clear sky, the rays of the morning sun tired him, reducing his inhibitions, and he asked, "Which books did you rent?"

"Three: The Diary of Samuel Pepys, Don Quixote, and Perrault's Fairy Tales."

"Do they cost much?"

"A shilling each for six weeks."

"One of the books is about fairies?"

"A book of children's stories called fairy tales, but not all involve fairies."

"You like them… fairy tales?"

"Not so much, but a friend does. I read them to him," she replied, hoping his questions would stop.

William hoped that was what she was doing with King when she was visiting him with a book in her hand, and since that might make his new world slightly less eerie, he couldn't stop himself from asking, "King?"

Becky's eyes enlarged. "What!?"

"Do you read to King?"

Sitting up on her bench to look back at him, she asked, "How… why would you ask that?"

William blushed. "I-I saw you going to him, going to his cabin one night when I was bedding down, or it seemed you were going in that direction. It was difficult to tell by the angle, but you had something in your hand, something like a book."

"It is King," she nodded. "I read stories to help him sleep, to give him something to dream about. He has nightmares and the stories keep his mind from them, usually."

"That's… that's very kind of you," he said, relieved.

"Not sure how kind it is. His nightmares cause him to scream out, and even in the small cabin with only a small window, his screams still disturb everyone, including me," she said as she laid herself back on the bench.

"Still, I think that's kind of you."

"Was that what you thought I was doing with him?"

"I-I expected you were reading to him."

Becky smirked. "I think you're lying."

"I am. I'm lying on the bench."

Ignoring his bad joke, she asked, "Did you know he's been

castrated?"

"What!?" William almost shouted as he sat up.

Becky had to hold back laughing at his bulging eyes looking down at her from over her backrest. "He has. Next, you're going to ask me how I know. Mary told me, and I have no reason not to believe her. Years ago, Philpot had him castrated to calm him down, but he can still lose his temper when he witnesses men being cruel… sees the English abusing slaves. The only thing that seems to calm him is to tell him the abuser is going to hell," she told him. "Can I trust you to keep this to yourself and not mention it to anyone, especially Philpot? I expect he wouldn't want me reading to him."

"You can, and you can believe that," William said as he again laid himself down on his bench. "Do you know a Charlie?"

"Yes, and you do too — Charles Philpot. Why do you ask?"

"That man, Harry, mentioned him, and speaking of Master Philpot, how is he with the slaves? Has he used those pistols in the waistcoat he was wearing this morning? Does he use the whip on them?"

Finding the questions coming from an apprentice overseer of slaves curious, Becky took a moment before saying, "I expect he has whipped them, though I haven't seen it myself. I've only been on the plantation long enough to see the results of past whippings, and I expect he only wears the waistcoat of pistols as a warning. I've never heard of him using a pistol on anyone, but there're many stories about him, but mostly rumors." Finding it strange how easy it was to talk to William when not looking at him, she continued, "I don't enjoy spreading rumors, but I will say that one of the milder ones is that he was part of the plant-cutting riots of the eighties. Over a hundred plantations were destroyed by some trying to raise the price of tobacco by reducing the number of crops. They hanged some men for it, and rumor is Philpot helped organize it, but they could never prove it. He would've been just over twenty then. But as I said, it's a rumor and a milder one."

"It's an old rumor, and even if it's true, he was young and people change," William said. "I like to think people are good, though I'm not sure how good I am since I would like to hear more of these rumors."

"No, you don't. Some are far too evil to be true."

Finding it strange with how easy it was to talk to her through the back of her bench, William said, "We almost met true evil during the voyage here, and I refuse to think about what would've come of us had we met it."

"On the ship?"

"On the sea."

Not sure if she should believe what he would tell her, she said, "Do tell," and he did.

Staring at the clear sky and feeling as if he was thinking aloud, he told her about their ship being chased by the pirates and why, described the plan, and gave Oink all the credit. He told how the pirate ship continued to come after them after taking the sterling, or what the pirates thought was sterling, told how the ship exploded twice, with the second being much larger than the first, and he told her about Oink's wound and the capture of a pirate, but he didn't mention their conversation with him.

When he finished, Becky continued looking at the sky. "That's quite the story, but I'm not sure if I should believe it, especially about that small ship carrying all that sterling. But

I'm not surprised about the pirates. I read in the paper that they were growing in number near the Spanish colonies. Some even use several ships now and fly their own flags, as if they're proud of it. They even have a name for them, Holly Roger."

"Jolly Roger. That's what I heard on the ship. Does Virginia have a newspaper?"

"No, they won't issue a license for one, but the Boston paper is here. It's late by two or three weeks and sold in secret. Philpot reads it in his study after the evening meal," she told him, and then with a smile, added, "Perhaps you should tell your tale to King, but add some fairies to make it believable."

William smiled. "If you don't want to believe it, don't ask Oink to tell it. He's certain to lie and tell the same story."

With the sound of an approaching cart ending the conversation that both were starting to enjoy, they sat up to see a lone driver in a short two-wheeled cart stop beside them, and after exchanging greetings, the older man offered them a ride.

"We thank you, but we're waiting for a cabinetmaker," Becky smiled back.

"I'm not that," the man chuckled as he drove off. "That's rather specific, but I hope by chance one passes. Have a blessed day."

With the momentum of the conversation lost, both lied down again, and not knowing what to say to the other, they said nothing and were soon asleep.

It was half an hour later when Oink and a man in his late thirties rode up in a small cart. The man greeted the two, and with Oink annoying him with questions, he attached the broken piece by bolting iron plates to each side of the wheel.

Heading back to the plantation and with the reins in her hands, Becky said, "Oink, tell me about the pirates chasing your ship."

"Pirates?" Oink asked with surprise, and when he turned to look back at his blushing brother lying on the bench, he said, "You told her about the pirates!? *You*, who asked me not to mention it! *You*, who wanted to forget it happened! You strike a man and now you tell her about the pirates! Who are you because you're not the brother I know!" And not getting a response from William, he said, "Tell me to tell the story, *Willy*. I need to hear you say it, *Willy*."

William forced out, "Oscar, tell the story."

"It's Oink and I will, *Willy*!"

And he did, adding the details William had left out, like William's swim, the ship going back for him, the passengers and sailors killed or hurt by the second explosion's shock wave and falling debris, and John's true reason for being on the ship.

They were twenty minutes from Lord Chalmers' plantation when he finished the story by showing Becky the two keys hanging from his neck. "One's mine and one's William's, but I forgot whose is whose. Not that it matters since William doesn't want his."

"I found your version of the story much more interesting than your brother's," Becky told him. "He left out much, including the part where he swam to the small boat."

"They call it a *cock*boat," Oink grinned, "And I wouldn't call it swimming. From what I saw, he can float well in rough water. His sea name is Fish because of it, but it should've been Cork. If I had given it to him, it would have been Cork. It suits him better, yes?"

"It does," she said, looking back at William lying on his back and coyly smiling back at her.

Reminding herself that the newcomer was a slave

overseer, she flicked the reins, and when the horses went from walking to trotting, William was rolled against the backrest. Then when she pulled back on the reins, the horses stopped and he rolled forward, wedging himself between the two benches. Flicking them again, the horses walked on. "My apologies, Master Lovely," she smirked while looking forward. "Oink, did you see what I did?"

"You made the horse trot with a flick of the reins and then stopped them with a quick pull."

"That too, and if I wanted them to run, I would have flicked them rougher at least twice more, like this."

Getting to his feet and wishing she would let Oink drive the cart again, the horses' sudden running forced William over his bench's backrest to land on the cart's bed, and then their sudden stopping slid him against the bench.

"My apologies again, Master Lovely. I should be more careful with that damaged wheel."

CHAPTER 21
Overseeing

Hoping to distract her mind from her confusing feelings toward William, Becky joined the women in the kitchen, and after a few minutes of being there, Ann gestured to Mary to ask their young friend about her time with the curiously strange brothers and Becky obliged, telling them what had happened that morning and what she had learned about them, but leaving out the story about them being chased by pirates since she considered it something Oink should tell.

Both Becky and Anne agreed with Mary when she worried that if William was naive enough to believe what the agent had said regarding his duties as an overseer of slaves, it could work in Philpot's favor, possibly over time making him more accepting and therefore more malleable to what the overseer of the plantation expected from his apprentice, and after the three agreed William could be molded to become crueler than the last two apprentice overseers, Becky had no problem tossing him out of her mind… until she left the kitchen and found him dirtying his hands in the garden with Oink and the other children, who were sneaking curious glances at him.

After the Lovelys helped her load the large pot of stew, seventy-plus wooden bowls, two covered meals, a jug of cider, and a half dozen buckets of water onto the bed of the small cart, they joined her on the cart, and during their ride to the field, Oink silently cursed himself for forgetting his whip on the back steps of the house.

Almost twenty minutes later, they stopped at the edge of the road across from a seemingly endless field of tobacco where the slaves were working almost a hundred feet in, and a dozen feet back from them, Philpot and Ben, with nearly forty feet between each other, were passing through the rows of plants. With three cracks of Ben's whip, the slaves stopped and turned to walk toward the cart.

The heavily perspiring and heavily breathing Philpot met the three at the cart, greeted them without a smile, and took his dome-covered plate, cutlery, and a cup of cider. He frowned when he noticed the brace on the cart's right front wheel, and after Becky described the incident, leaving out that Oink was driving the cart, he told her that the next morning he would leave behind their two carpenters to replace it with one of the few extras he believed he had. After he told Oink to join him when he was finished eating, the boy said he would and watched the man walk to a wooden chair shaded by a wide parasol that amused him since, like an umbrella, it was considered womanly.

While Ben sat on the back of the cart quietly eating his chicken and vegetables with his fork and knife, Becky used a large ladle to pour stew into wooden bowls that she handed out to the slaves, who then sat at the edge of the field eating with their fingers. When Ben finished and the slaves were again working their rows, he told William to follow him into the field.

"This is the most tedious of our tasks, and we do it for more months than the harvesting and felling combined," Ben said with disdain as he stopped five feet from a woman using a short knife with a guarded plate at its end to cut off a small part of a plant's top. With William following, he turned and gently squeezed through a row of three-foot-tall tobacco plants.

"It could feel less tedious if we had a man playing the fiddle," William said, offering his brother's suggestion from when they were cleaning the ship's floors.

"That'll *never* happen," Ben smirked, and then seeming to have forgotten what he had told the newcomer the Saturday before, said, "We cut their tops every few weeks to force the leaves to grow larger at the top, but the common task is removing the worms. Today they do both, and today we check for both worms and make certain the tops are cut as we pass through the rows. If I find a worm, I crack the whip once to signal to the one working that side that they missed one. Crack it twice if the top isn't cut. If we find another missed, we whip them." Looking back at William, he noticed the shock on his face. "I try to crack it an inch or two from them. Looks like they've been struck and they act like they were, and Philpot's content. More reason to learn the whip well. Anyone can crack it, but using it with skill takes practice. *But* if I find the boy or girl missed one three times, I *must* strike them, but seldom need to."

Walking through several rows, William did as Ben did and checked the leaves. Spotting a worm, he discreetly picked it off and crushed it beneath his shoe.

Stopping, Ben turned to him. "What do you tell a slave

with fresh wounds on his back?"

"I-I don't know."

Ben grinned. "Nothing, he's been told twice already."

Bored, Oink sat on the ground next to Philpot's chair while the man stared at the tiny figures of William and Ben slowly passing through the rows, and looking for something to do, he asked if he could join the slaves in their work.

Taking a moment to accept what he had heard, Philpot huffed and shook his head. "Overseers oversee the work. They don't perform it. We make sure they're doing it, doing it quickly and properly, and we can't do that if we're performing the task with them." Yawning, he added, "No, you shall stay with me and observe."

Five minutes later, the man was snoring in his chair while Oink sat on the ground struggling to stay awake through his boredom.

While Philpot took his afternoon nap and after Ben explained to William that they seldom had to tell a slave to work faster, the two silently passed through the rows ensuring the tops had been removed and no worms were left nibbling the leaves.

"How often do they rest?" William asked.

"Rest? Every couple hours for water and to relieve themselves, but not in the field, at the side of it," Ben said before picking a worm from a plant, crushing it under his boot and cracking the whip, causing those working a few rows to the left and the right to look to see whose row it was. "Let's move up closer to see who missed that one. No good if we don't know who it is. Also, can shorten the distance between them and us."

"What are you two doing?" an out-of-breath Oink asked.

"Overseeing slaves," Ben replied coldly before passing through another row. "If you're joining us, mind the plants when you pass through a row."

"What do we do?"

"Explained it to your brother. He'll explain it to you when you're tall enough."

Passing through a couple dozen more rows, Ben found another worm, cracked the whip, and walked up closer to the slaves, making William believe that if he had never found a worm, the slaves would be almost out of sight.

"Have any tried escaping from the field?" William asked to Oink's curiosity.

"None of ours. Others tried, but nowhere to go. Last spring, on the other side of Williamsburg, some escaped with two indentures acting as their masters, but they too were found. I know of one they never caught and expect he perished. Ran in January a few years back and probably froze."

At the last row being worked by the giant of a man who was impossible not to recognize, the three walked deeper into the field until they were several feet from King, and as they turned to again pass through the rows of plants, Oink asked, "Is this it? Is this all you do?"

"Yes, and now we walk to the other side," William frowned.

"Back and forth?"

William nodded.

"All we do until harvesting," Ben added.

Having a tough time believing they would have to do something so boring for the full day every day, Oink told them, "I'm going to find my whip."

Turning to him, Ben said coldly, "Won't be practicing here. You'll confuse them. If you must, you can practice at the house."

"I'll do that," Oink said as he turned around and walked toward the road. "I expect you prefer the mines now, Willy!"

The next three days, from dawn until dusk, during sun and light rain when Philpot's parasol acted as an umbrella, William with his unconditioned legs aching followed Ben through Lord Chalmers' rows of tobacco plants examining the slaves' work, and to his relief, Ben never had to strike one.

That Friday the two worked Philpot's smaller scattered fields while Philpot worked his others, and with Philpot demanding his meal be delivered first, requiring Becky to pass William and Ben to deliver them, the meals for Ben's team were cold by the time they arrived. But Ben didn't mind, telling William that it was a small inconvenience for being away from the man, and he took advantage of it by not bothering with the whip and occasionally leaving William to walk the field alone as he took a nap on the back of their long cart.

Each morning while waiting for Philpot to leave, Oink walked the parameters of the garden with his whip in hand, and a few minutes after Philpot left, he joined the children in their work.

When the work in the garden was finished for the day and the children had vanished into their cabins, he joined Becky in bringing the meals out to the field, and after returning with her to the house, he spent a few hours unknowingly annoying her by practicing a more difficult crack of the whip that Ben had shown him, one that with two quick arm movements, he cracked it to his left and then to his right. Easily cracking it on his left, it took some practice before he could consistently crack it on his right without striking himself.

CHAPTER 22
William's Solution and Becky's Questions

That second Saturday, after he and Ben had taken thirty minutes to harness the two groups of six horses, William worried it would take him more than an hour when doing it alone that coming Friday after Ben had retired from the plantation, and thinking he could reduce that time by at least half if a slave or two were to help, he asked Ben why it was that only they harnessed them.

"Philpot doesn't want them learning a faster way to escape."

The response made no sense to William. He was sure that those cleaning the stalls while they harnessed the horses would've seen it performed hundreds if not thousands of times before then.

"And remember, you'll be doing it alone after I leave Thursday evening."

"Why not leave Friday morning? Why leave after dark?"

"Prefer it. Rather not stay a minute more than I must. Also, Philpot demands it. As eager to have me gone as I am to be gone."

After he woke Oink and the three ate, William did as Ben said and picked the twenty men and ten women, and by the women's reactions, it seemed as if his taps had burned them.

"Hold back, girls," Ben said before turning to William. "The boys are good, but these girls aren't. The older, fatter ones may be attractive to you, but they aren't to the men on our route." Then, as he tapped another ten women, he said, "If so, they would've requested them. For us, it's the younger, slimmer ones."

When Ben held the belt of two pistols out to him, William traded his disappointment with being discovered choosing the less desirable women for his disappointment with having to wear the firearms.

"Never had to use them during my seven years. Their threat's all that's required, but I suggest always wearing them into Jamestown, wearing them openly. Philpot even wears his waistcoat of six when going there. That's how you know he's going to Jamestown. He's as fearful of that place as he is of the slaves."

After William had put the belt around his waist and King had stepped up onto the cart, Ben passed the reins to William, who rode the cart away at a casual pace. Thirty minutes later, as they came to the end of the second half of Chalmers' field, Ben seemed to relax as he did when leaving it that previous Saturday, but William tensed up knowing that the renting would soon start.

"Going to be hot and dry today," Ben said.

William looked up at the sky and nodded.

"Remember the route?"

He shook his head.

"I'll guide you and you guide the horses. Driving the cart

you're certain to remember. Had six weeks to learn with my predecessor, but the roads were busier then and with more distractions. In a few weeks, the roads'll be crowded with those moving their harvests from their fields to their curing barns, and later crowded still with the moving of the hogsheads to town." With William saying nothing, Ben looked over at him. "Something picking at you?"

William nodded.

"With child?" Ben laughed. "That'll add two years to your contract."

"I want to rent the women."

"Rent a woman?" Ben asked, surprised. "Didn't take you for… didn't expect that, but we can bring one to the stream if you truly desire it. Won't rent them all… but you said women? More than one?"

"All," William said before looking over at a puzzled Ben. "Not for bedding."

"Then what for?"

"To make certain they're not bedded."

Then even more puzzled, Ben asked, "Want to use your sterling on the women?" and when William nodded, he said, "You're truly unusual, but I don't see why not. It's something you must keep to yourself, and you needn't worry about me speaking of it for the brief time I'm here."

William switched the reins to one hand and with the other reached into the pocket of his sailor's trousers and pulled out the loose coins he had earlier prepared for the occasion. "Ten shillings," he said as he handed them to Ben, who pulled out his coin sack and dropped the coins into it.

"How much do you have? How many Saturdays do you intend to give the man your sterling?"

As neither noticed the whispers of the eavesdroppers on the cart's bed passing on what they had just heard, William replied, "I may have enough until October."

"And after that?"

"I haven't thought that far ahead."

"Could rent enough boys to have no room for the women. Philpot's indifferent to who works the field and more concerned with Saturday's sterling. But don't become too excited," Ben warned. "If he sees an opportunity to rent more, he could have you take two carts of them. I tried finding more renters for the men but most ordered me off their plantation, and some even threatened me with lead... all because I'm Philpot's man. Those who rent them are desperate for the labor or don't know of Philpot's reputation... or don't judge him for it, but most are only desperate for the labor.

"I'll admit I worried I'd become like Philpot and had to check myself occasionally. This place can change a person, but not as much as Philpot can, and I have to admit too I'm curious to see if you'll feel the same as you do now after a month of being on your own, curious if you'll still want to pay for the women. There are moments when I feel I left my soul on the edge of the plantation, and it only returns when away from it. It doesn't help too that we have no one to talk to for seven years. There's no conversation to be had with Philpot. We only hearken to him."

"I have my brother."

"That's true, and there's a good chance he too will change for the worse... because of his age."

Taken aback by Ben's words, William had never considered the place would negatively affect Oink. Having hoped to hide its negative aspects from him, it worried him that over time he wouldn't be able to, and it worried him too that the changes he was experiencing in himself over such a short time could also change his brother.

With William adding the new concern to his short but growing mental list, the two avoided the plantations that rented women, and at each plantation that rented men, Ben did all the talking while William, who felt drained of energy, only greeted the landowners.

Twenty minutes later, after renting twelve men, a galloping horse approached them from behind. "Oi! 'Ave ya forgots where I be?" a topless and shoeless Benton growled from his weathered saddle. "I'll be takin' a girl!"

Ben smirked when William shook the reins to have the horses trot, forcing Benton's horse to trot along with them, and his smirk grew to a smile when William avoided looking at the man as he said, "They're all spoken for. Have a blessed morning."

"What?" the man asked. "Who's takin'em?"

"Just as I'm certain you wouldn't want us telling others you take them, I'm certain others wouldn't want us telling you they take them," William said, continuing not to look at him.

Benton cursed and halted his horse. "Bring more next week!"

"Not possible," Ben yelled back. "No room and all are taken for the rest of the year. Have a better time in Jamestown. Remember, they're four shillings there, and that's for a mere hour, but they're English." Grinning, Ben looked at William. "I truly dislike that man, but even so, this much enjoyment has to be a sin."

After William nodded, Ben went through his sack of coins to offer three shillings back to William, who offered him a confused look.

"Best to keep the sterling as it normally is," Ben said. "Rarely rent them all, and as I said before, if it appears you are, Philpot could force more on you." Taking the coins, William thanked Ben with a nod as he pushed them into a pocket. "We'll have a better time at the stream today. The last time for me, and I brought celebratory drink," Ben grinned as he pulled a waterskin from his long coat. "Sammy will be thankful for the ten women and whatever men we have left, but let's not tell him of my possessing a bit of Philpot's good rum. The godly man doesn't believe in drink, and on any day but today, I'd respect that."

After they filled the buckets with fish, the three sat near the stream's edge sharing the bread and cheese that Sam had gifted them before he was surprised to learn they brought him many more women to work his fields. As King and William shared the bottle of cider, which William showed King how to properly drink from, Ben drank the rum and was soon talking about whatever entered his mind. He talked about the bugs buzzing around them, the fish they had just caught, which Philpot called Mackerel but Ben thought was something different but didn't know what. He told him how he had found a case of wine stuck in the stream, how he had found on the stream's bed the lead cross that he proudly wore around his neck, and after pulling it out from under his shirt and showing it to William, told him how he had come across the body of a child at the end of his second year there. "Anything floating down this side of the York River is pushed down this stream." Then, after speculating on what William might find in the stream during his seven years there, Ben decided to guess

King's given name and offered a dozen guesses, with the last being Mark Henry Jonathan Hamilton the Fourth, which caused William to laugh at the confused look on King's face.

"Is it James? Do you remember being called James?" William asked.

King stared at him for a moment before nodding, "He me say James."

"What?" Ben shouted, startling King. "I offer a dozen guesses and you find it on your first!"

"King James," William nodded. "The first name I thought of after your guesses. All the guesses I would've had before that, you had guessed… except for your last."

"Not good at lying," Ben smiled. "You'll have to learn to do it well when being around Philpot. Have to control those eyes of yours. They bounce about when you lie."

"You saw through me," William frowned. "I was going to guess your last guess too."

After Ben released a roar of laughter, surprising both William and King, he told William that with all the awful rumors attached to Philpot, he does and doesn't treat slaves any worse than others do, which to Ben worked out to be about the same. "He might not clothe them well, especially during the winter, but he feeds them well, and they don't have to cook their meals since Mary and Ann do it. Not much variety in the meals, but they're healthy. There are fewer now than when I arrived, because of the pox, and there could have been even fewer. Lost more than half the children, but only three adults. Philpot handled it well, though. Put them in a curing barn as soon as they showed signs, them and his daughter. Several adults survived, but only one child did, and the man hates the boy for it because his daughter died. But he allows them to form families and gives them their privacy with the individual cabins. But those cabins are also there to stop them from planning an escape or an attack, or that's what Philpot believes. Locks them away in those cabins to make it difficult to organize, but if they want to, they'll find a way. And that battle room is more impressive than practical. They can lay siege to the house and starve him out while avoiding the cabin's side, making the shutters' slots useless. He would eventually have to escape through the hatch and be caught." Then Ben shook his tipsy head. "No, he relies too much on that room with that bloody door."

"Must they stay in their cabins when he's at the house, or is it by choice?"

"Both. If they're not working, Philpot doesn't want to see or hear them. And if he's in a bad way, drunk or angry or both, he'll act on it if he sees one. I heard from the previous apprentice that Mary limps because he almost beat her to death, and Ann doesn't speak because he cut out her tongue, of that I'm a witness. A night close to six years back, he came across her after his Sunday night with the Carters. I was in bed when I heard it, and you could hear King screaming louder than her from his barred cabin. The beast tried to break down his cabin door, and he may have if her screaming lasted more than a minute."

"Why would he cut out her tongue?" William asked, not hearing anything Ben said after that, and though he didn't want to know the details, he felt he needed to.

"She always spoke when spoken to. Philpot complained about it but also seemed to make a game of it, a game to see how many times she would reply, even when told not to, and then she never spoke again. I've said it before and I'll say it again. Philpot's not one you want to be on the bad side of."

"And Becky accepts it, condones it?"

"Becky? She hasn't been on the plantation for more than two years. Don't expect she's aware of it, especially not the renting of the women. I would never tell her, and I doubt Margaret would've if she even knew of it herself. Could scare Becky away. I expect it took some persuading from Margaret to have her agree to be the child's governess, seeing how she was certain to know the rumors concerning Philpot."

"Governess?" William asked.

"Governess," Ben nodded before telling him about the rumor of Philpot killing his first wife and later killing his son and two daughters who were threatening to offer witness to the crime. "Nothing's proven. Only a rumor he pushed her into the well and a rumor he set the house ablaze to conceal the murder of his son and daughters. Then there's the salting of crops. Poison the crops to force the landowners to sell for much less than they would for a healthy field. Nothing could be proven, though I expect nobody bothered. Far too many bad things happen here for anything to be done about them. And then there's the—"

"We should be leaving. They'll need to prepare the fish in time for his return," William said, then agreeing with Becky that he didn't want to hear the rumors.

"But I only started. There's more to be said, much more."

"I don't think my paining head can take any more."

"Paining head? Should've joined me in drink," Ben laughed before taking five gulps to empty the skin. Placing it aside, he said, "Before we go, let's fire those pistols. Be my last time for a while, and you should experience it too. Hand one here."

Taking a moment to consider handing the intoxicated man a pistol, William reluctantly pulled one from the leather hoop on the belt and handed it to him.

"Even Becky fired one, a long gun. Almost hit Harry Carter, and Philpot laughed when he heard about it." Then, with a question mark on William's face, Ben said, "They're charged. All one has to do is pull back this hammer and make sure this metal thing is down." Holding it out, he pointed it at the trunk of a large tree a dozen feet away. "Might want to cover your ears," he said, and with neither William nor King doing as he suggested, he pulled the trigger. The hammer slammed down and caused a spark but no blast came from the gun. Continuing to point it at the tree, he said, "A fail. Have to wait a moment to make certain it isn't going to explode." After a few seconds, he pulled back the hammer and again pointed it toward the tree. Giving it a slight shake, he pulled the trigger, and after a quick flash, the burst from the barrel stunned both William and King. "Missed. Poor weapons. Rarely hit where you point unless you're only feet from it. Don't beat the arrow. They strike where they're meant to and faster to repeat. Pistols are as effective as Philpot's battle room. Don't understand why one would want one over an arrow, except maybe face to face it's more effective than a knife. Now you fire the other."

"Later," William said. "We should be leaving."

Handing the spent weapon back to William, who returned it to his belt and noticed the barrel's heat against his thigh, Ben said, "I'll show you how to charge it when we return."

**

After they finished weeding the garden, picking off the insects, and replanting the vegetables used earlier that week, Oink thought he would befriend the children *and Sophie* by playing games with them. Gathering them near the kitchen, he suggested they play Hide and Seek, with them doing the hiding and him doing the seeking.

In the kitchen and hearing him explaining the game's simple instructions to the apprehensive children, Becky's eyes almost jumped out of her head, and with Mary and Ann just as shocked, she left the kitchen to join the group. "Oink, it would be best if they seek you."

"Seek me? All of them? That wouldn't last more than a few minutes."

"That may be, but they won't be comfortable being seeked… sought."

Oink stared at her for a moment before it occurred to him it would be as if he was searching for runaway slaves. "Your way would be better," he nodded, embarrassed. "You seeking me would be better," he told the children whom he had yet to hear speak a word. "Turn and face the house, and I'll run and hide while you count to a hundred." And with the children doing as he said, he ran toward the rows of cabins.

Becky couldn't help but smile at the boy's assumption that the children could count to a hundred and she said, "I'll do the counting, and I don't believe you'll need to search the house for him."

When she reached a hundred and told them to search for him, she watched them casually walk away, forming small groups and whispering among themselves as they disappeared into their cabins.

Hiding in the pigsty under the shade of its covered section and with neither pig showing any interest in the boy lying behind them, Oink gave no thought to the déjà vu he experienced as he listened for sounds of the children searching the sheds. After ten minutes of not hearing them, he guessed they were searching the house, and after another ten minutes and with still no sounds of them, he was fighting off asleep.

Twenty minutes later, he woke to the sound of slapping hooves and a rolling cart. Groggy and expecting William to have returned with Ben, he struggled to his feet just as Becky was opening the gate of the pigsty.

Surprised to find the boy standing there rubbing his eyes, Becky was reminded of him sneaking aboard the ship by hiding in a crate of pigs and wondered if he had a strange interest in the animals.

"Is William back?" he asked.

"No, it's a delivery."

Walking through the opened gate, he heard the snorts of pigs coming from the long cart moving ahead so its back was near the gate and asked, "Those are for Master Philpot?"

"Two dozen. They're replacing the ones that died last fall from disease," Becky told him. "They've come from England."

"England? These could have been on The Colonist!" Oink said with his eyes lighting up.

"Could have," Becky said, smiling at the boy's excitement.

Oink tried to control his excitement as he watched two men step down from the cart, and after each struggled to remove the sideboards and the pigs cautiously stepped away from the edge of the two-foot drop, they lowered the tailboard and made a ramp from the sideboards. As they placed ropes around the squealing pigs' necks and led them down the ramp and into the pigsty, a hopeful Oink made two short whistles, and much like a person recognizing the bark of their dog, he thought he recognized Gibby's squeal and was surprised and then overjoyed to see a pig running down the ramp, tumbling onto the ground, and after getting to its feet, rushing toward him.

Watching Oink dropping to his knees and holding his arms out to the animal with a gibbous mark on its side, Becky wasn't sure what to make of the boy hugging the pig, which in its excitement was dripping pee while shaking its curly tail.

"This is Gibby, my pig! Well, not mine, but my friend. May I keep him with me?"

"You… you may, but if he runs off, Philpot will demand he's kept with the others," Becky warned him. "Uh, perhaps you can ask Mary for some vegetable scraps."

As Gibby, with his curled tail still shaking with excitement, followed an excited Oink to the kitchen, neither the boy nor the pig noticed the children, some carrying brown-faced dolls, peeking out at them from behind several opened cabin doors.

**

On their way back to the plantation and to William's amusement, Ben had fallen asleep against him, and then forced to steer the cart with one hand while keeping an arm around Ben so he wouldn't fall forward, William impressed himself when he found the way back on his own.

At the house, William had King put Ben's arm over his shoulder, and together they walked him toward the back door.

"Where we goin'?" Ben asked with one eye open and his feet inches from the ground.

"To bed," William replied.

"It's time?"

"It is for you."

After William and King gently placed him on top of his

bedsheets, Ben appeared to fall asleep, but as they were leaving the room, he said through his inebriated state, "You're a good... a good man, William Lovely, a lovely... a lovely man. A friend I'll miss, and I'll be certain to let him know, as He is my wit... my witness, let him know you're—"

"Sleep well. I'll wake you in a few hours."

Though he didn't share his excitement, William was as surprised as Oink had been to learn Gibby had been delivered to their plantation, and like Becky, he told him not to lose the animal. "He might be your friend, but he's Lord Chalmers' property."

William and Oink spent the rest of that afternoon unknowingly stressing the slaves with the cracking of their whips, and while William practiced *almost* striking the onion, trying to stop an inch short of it, Oink, who had become bored with bursting it every time, took Gibby out into the cow field where he made the pig sit a safe distance away while he practiced the figure-eight crack Ben had shown him the evening before.

When William decided he had enough of the whip, he joined Oink in the field, and after being impressed with his brother's ability to crack it to his left and right in two quick motions, he did as his brother asked and stood several feet from him to toss onions into the air so the boy could practice striking them as they fell, which he could do on almost every third toss.

At seven o'clock when William went to wake Ben to collect the slaves, he found him as he had left him, and as he went to shake him awake, Ben said something in his sleep. Curious, William bent down to listen in on what he was saying.

"…introduce you to my love, Rebecca Rowling. Becky, if you will… yes, it's a pleasure to be home, Michael. A pleasure to see you and Joe well… yes, he arrived safe and with his brother… trespassed aboard the…"

Deciding not to disturb him, William left Ben to his dream and went alone to pick up the slaves.

He remembered where the first seven were, but after twenty minutes, he couldn't remember if he was to take the second or third left. Stopping the horses, he asked the slaves sitting at the back if they knew which turn he was to take and found it interesting that they whispered among themselves before answering, not discussing directions but discussing who would tell the new overseer his error. After a few seconds, a thinner man cleared his throat before finding the courage to tell him he had missed the turn and had to turn around to take the first right they came to. Then thinking he would have to ask at least once more during the trip, William asked the slave to join him on the bench, and after the man nervously climbed over the back of the bench to sit beside him, he was confused by William offering him the reins. "I believe you should drive. You know the route, and I can learn from you," he said, and then he smiled when the man looked back at the shocked slaves to toss them a smile before taking the reins. Driving the cart, the man held the smile until he noticed William smiling along with him.

Parked near the log cabins and with the slaves slowly stepping down from the back of the cart, several women and men looked as if they were struggling against saying something to William still sitting on the bench, and with him not wanting to be thanked for something that should be done, like offering a starving man a meal, and not wanting to give them hope that it would be permanent when he didn't expect it could be, he tried to hurry them off the cart faster by imitating Gorge, "Off, the lot of ya!"

Philpot didn't hide his surprise and laughter when discovering on his return from working his fields that the story the boy had told him about the pig was true, and he told Oink he could take the pig from the pigsty, but only after finishing the gardening, warned him that if the pig ran away, it would stay permanently in the sty, and as if reading the boy's mind, added that the pig was to stay out of the house.

**

The next day, Becky held herself back from slapping Philpot as she lathered his face with froth and she didn't give any concern to nicking him when she gave him an unusually fast shave, and when she gave Ben his shave, rather than spreading the froth about in her usual gentle manner, she slapped it on his face several times before purposely nicking him several times. And when William and Oink sat on the stools for their shaves, she disappointed Oink by telling him he didn't need one for another three or four weeks and disappointed him further by telling him to wait outside, and then alone with a nervous William, she stropped the blade longer than necessary as she tried to calm down.

Earlier that morning, when entering the kitchen to collect the meals, she walked in on Mary confirming with Ann what she had heard the night before. Hearing the woman say, "None were bedded. He wouldn't allow it, and even offered his sterling to stop it," Becky asked, "Who weren't bedded?" and when a blushing Mary tried to change the subject, Becky became more curious and asked again, feeling justified since they had no issue inquiring about her life.

After Ann gestured sternly to Mary, the large woman reluctantly shocked Becky twice, a bad shock and a good shock. She was shocked to hear that some of the women rented were being bedded, and she was shocked to hear that William had avoided renting them the day before by paying for them himself.

Becky wanted to berate Mary for never telling her about the bedding of the rented women, wanted to kick herself for never considering that some of them would be bedded, wanted to ask how long it had been going on for, and wanted to ask what else was being kept from her, but with William not there to answer question at the front of her mind (why did he pay for them) she could only ask which bowl of porridge was Philpot's before leaving to deliver the morning meals.

Sitting across from William, she was eager to know if he had the sterling to pay for the slaves again that next Saturday, and if he did, was he planning to do so, and if not, what did he plan to do to avoid renting them again? And there was again the question as to why he did it. She was considering asking him when she found him alone, but then it occurred to her that with him not knowing more than her first name, her questions might scare him into doing as Philpot expected him to do, and the only way she could discuss it with him where he wouldn't feel threatened was to earn his trust, and she could only do that if he became familiar with her, which at that moment didn't feel like such a bad thing.

Becky ate little as she struggled not to stare at the newcomer, and five minutes later, when she gave up on eating and allowed her eyes to bounce between Ben and Philpot as they ate, she was engulfed by a wave of anger so intense and unfamiliar that it caused her to hear every furious beat of her heart, making her thankful that Philpot said nothing during the meal since she was sure his voice would've made her lose control, would've made her throw some harsh words at him or something heavier like the empty brass candleholder in the center of the table.

Now alone with William, she laid the small blade on the table beside him, rubbed her hands with the soap, and gently lathered his face much longer than necessary, only stopping when William's eyes asked her what she was doing as he squirmed uncomfortably on the stool.

"That… that should help avoid any nicks this time," she said while forcing her staring eyes from the face that couldn't look any more attractive to her, even when covered in froth, and when she slowly shaved him, she felt as if she was revealing its full beauty with each pass of the blade.

Disappointed with having finished shaving him, she wiped the blade, placed it on the table, and instead of handing him the towel around his neck, she gently wiped his face dry with it. "See, no nicks," she smiled, holding the cloth out for him to see there were no tiny spots of blood.

William could only nod before awkwardly standing up and rushing out of the shed.

A couple of hours after church and with both Philpot and Ben leaving the plantation, Oink finished practicing with the whip, and as he was coiling it, he heard the deathly squeal of a pig. Fearful and with Gibby beside him, he searched for the source of it.

In the first shed he entered, where flour sacks of dirty clothes hung from hooks on the wall, a woman was using a long paddle to move about the slaves' clothes soaking in the steaming sudsy water of a short but wide wooden washtub and another was tightly twisting the rinsed clothes with her hands to force out the water. Noticing the boy, both froze before forcing a smile and offering a bow of their heads, and with the sound not coming from there, he returned the bow and left.

In the next shed, a woman was removing jars from a pot of boiling water and placing them on a table where another poured boiled fruit into them, and like the women in the previous shed, they too froze for a moment before greeting him with a bow of their heads.

In the third shed, where several slabs of salted meat hung from the ceiling, Oink found three women with their backs to him standing at a table rubbing salt over large sections of meat, and his heart raced when he saw a fourth woman in a blood-covered apron struggling to drag something through the door at the back. His jaw dropped when she dragged the body of a dead pig to the side of the table, and he and Gibby were gone before the women noticed him.

As Becky cut meat into cubes, Mary chopped herbs, and Ann mixed something dry in a huge wooden bowl, all three stopped to stare at the watery-eyed boy with a pig standing beside him.

Smiling at the boy, Becky said, "The meal will be late. On Sunday, there're many chores to do before we prepare it. It should be ready in two hours, and it's pork stew. We all eat the same today."

"Please don't kill him!" he begged, pointing down at Gibby while his eyes jumped from woman to woman. "You'll know him by the gibbous mark, the three-quarter moon on his side there."

Exchanging glances with Mary, Becky said, "No one will hurt Gibby. Everyone knows he's your friend."

"I… I thank you," Oink said, relieved, and then taking a large breath, asked, "When will the meal be ready… and what is it?"

**

Returning from reading to King and thinking Philpot might take the candlelight from her bedroom window as an invitation to annoy her again, Becky struggled to push her dresser against her bedroom door, and content that he hadn't returned when she closed her book and snuffed out the candle, she woke two hours later to the man requesting a *kissy* from behind her barricaded door. When his requests went unanswered and he finally stumbled off to his bedroom, she reconsidered Ben's warning, but only for a moment before she fell back to sleep.

CHAPTER 23
The Letters

Late Monday morning as Oink helped the children with the gardening, Becky left on the small cart to pick up the brothers' clothes and boots, a half dozen sacks of flour, a dozen of pig feed, a dozen of chicken feed, and couple bottles of the good rum, and just over an hour and a half later, she was carrying a wooden box containing the clothes and boots and the bottles of rum to the Town Hall where, with the all spaces near the shops taken, she had been forced to park the cart. Excusing herself, she passed through a crowd taking up the walkway in front of the building, and as she placed the box on the back of the cart, her eyes were drawn to two figures sitting on the bed of a small cart rattling past her. With the two frightened Black men wearing only a cloth wrapped around their groins, Becky shuddered. Even if they were better dressed, she would still know by their hands tied behind their backs and one's ankle tied to the other's that they were new arrivals, the less expensive slaves who were auctioned off at Port Anne. It always affected her more to see the new slaves than it did to see the second or more generations of Virginian slaves being auctioned off in town. Though both were treated just as poorly, her heart broke more to see those, who months before were living a free life, arriving in Virginia by obscene circumstances, terrified and not knowing the language. The only comfort to her, if it could be one, was that the new arrivals were usually mixed in with English-speaking slaves who would teach them the language and duties while making certain they understood escape wasn't an option in this land an ocean away from where they came.

The ringing of the Town Hall's bell reminded her she had to hurry, and as she walked to the front of the cart, a soldier pulled a sobbing and topless young man to the whipping post where his hands were tied to its ring. Curious to know the crime the gentle-looking man had committed, she untied the reins and eavesdropped on a well-dressed older man saying to a well-dressed older woman, "Heard they caught him making a run from Francis'. Heard too Francis only maltreated him to force him to run and see another two years added to his contract."

"He's a cruel man that Francis is," the woman said. "I don't want you giving him your sterling. I'm certain there's another you can use."

"Now, Harriet, the worst is over for the lad. I don't expect he'll be as cruel to the boy as he has been now that he has the extra years, and I'll tell you too that as rough as he is, he's still a fine blacksmith. Only saying what I heard, not what I believe. Come, Kat, we don't have to see this."

"Don't have to see this? Then why did you stop us?" the woman complained as they continued down the walkway.

As she stepped onto the cart, Becky recalled Oink saying his friend was an indentured servant to a blacksmith, and wondering if that was him, she rode away as a man standing near the whipping post announced both the crime and the punishment with a shout. Trying to ignore his words, she trotted the horses toward the grain shop's warehouse, and a minute later and almost three blocks away, she heard a crack of a whip immediately followed by a scream. Stopping at the wooden two-story structure, she ran into the building, hoping to escape the next four strikes.

**

To the right of the inkwell and quill were several sheets of blank paper patiently waiting for ink, and to her left were several more sheets covered in irregular lines of pencil writing so large that with better penmanship two pages could easily fit on one.

With the log walls muffling the constant cracking of a whip, Becky picked up the pages Oink had given her minutes after she had returned from delivering the afternoon's meals. On the first sheet, she read his apology for causing his family to worry and his justifying it by writing that if he hadn't boarded the ship, William wouldn't have survived the journey, but instead of describing the incident with the pirates, he only wrote that it was too long a story to tell in their first letter, and added, 'And Willy insisted we not mention it since it would cause you all far too much worry.' Cracking a smile, Becky considered crossing out the last part but then decided against it since she was asked to put it to ink while correcting the spelling and grammar.

Struggling through Oink's poor grammar and spelling, she read on as he told his family how he came to board the ship, how he and William had worked as sailors so both would be indentured to the same plantation, and he told them about the work they did and the friends they made, including Gibby. He ended the paragraph by telling his family their sea names and about the captain offering him a position on the ship, but he had to refuse it since he was 'needed to watch over Willy.'

Slowly making her way through Oink's details of the plantation, she cracked another smile when she read how he had met many slaves his age and expected to befriend them, including Sophie whom he would marry when they came of age. After he had described meeting an Indian named Jacob, who delivered the post and dressed like the English, her smile grew when he described William's work as only walking back and forth through a field of tobacco plants.

After finding it sweet that he included a pound sterling for pencil sketches to be sent back as a reminder of their faces until they saw each other again, her curiosity was tickled by her name repeatedly jumping out at her from the next paragraph. Reading it, she learned she had been 'torturing William,' who couldn't look directly at her because her warm brown eyes would draw him in like a moth to a flame, making it impossible to break away from them, and the boy wrote that William had repeatedly told him her voice was like that of a siren, making him want to kiss her whenever she spoke. To William, her small ears looked to be as delicate as soap bubbles, never to be touched, but only looked at with fascination. Her straight Roman nose with its small nostrils resembled something a sculptor would create when short of clay. Her hair was as fine and shiny as threads of silk blowing in the wind on a sunny day, and her lips were the perfect size for his. Then Oink caused her to laugh when he ended the paragraph with his wish for her to wear a sack over her head so he wouldn't have to hear William talking about her so often.

Surprised to find herself flattered by the older brother's

attraction, she belittled it by reminding herself he had only recently met her and knew almost nothing about her, and she further belittled it when it occurred to her that with the long voyage not including women and with her being the only English women on the plantation, his attraction would've been exaggerated, and in the next week or two, he would come to his senses.

After Oink ended the letter by wishing his family well and asking forgiveness for what he promised would be the last of his impulsive acts, her mind was still on the previous paragraph, and curious about what the older brother was seeing, she took the last page of the letter to the bathroom.

Looking into the round plate of polished pewter, she examined her eyes and saw nothing out of the ordinary besides the few hairs between her eyebrows that she then plucked with her fingernails. Examining her thin lips, she puckered, smiled, and frowned, and saw nothing interesting with them, but then William had only said they were the right size. As for her nose, it was straight, but she didn't consider it small, and after struggling with the mirror to look at her 'soap bubble' ears, they seemed small, but there was nothing special about them either, nothing resembling soap bubbles. Then wanting to kick herself for her interest in the newcomer's attraction to her, she reminded herself that he was an apprentice overseer of slaves, and when his contract ended, he would *be* an overseer of slaves.

Back at the desk, Becky took two and a half pages to write out what Oink had written on five, and when she reached the part about her, she skipped it and felt she could do so since it was about her.

Having written out the boy's last lines to his family, she

paused to consider an idea, and then with as few words as possible so as not to go beyond the third page, she wrote a short paragraph to the Lovely family explaining that she was the house servant putting Oink's letter to ink, telling them that the brothers were adjusting well to Virginia, the plantation, and their duties, and that William was making certain the slaves were safe, healthy and happy.

**

That Wednesday evening, Philpot was curious to learn he had received a letter from Lord Chalmers when he didn't expect one for two more months.

Sitting at his desk after the evening meal, he cracked the letter's wax seal and straightened out the single sheet of paper, and after reading it and being perplexed by it, he read it again. Still perplexed, he placed it on the desk to reflect on it.

It was the first time in over two decades of overseeing the plantation that its ledgers would be examined and the property and everything on it would be counted and valued, and sometime in September, he was to expect a visit by an agent of C. Hoare & Co. to perform the task, giving him several weeks to prepare for the unwelcomed guest.

He found it difficult to believe Chalmers' reason for the agent's visit. If it were for taxes, as the man stated, then he would have been told to expect a visit from a Virginia tax evaluator, not from an agent of a bank in England. No, Philpot expected the true reason for the inspection was to determine either its worth as collateral on a loan, which wouldn't concern him, or its worth as a potential sale, which would concern him since it would threaten his own tobacco crops by removing access to the plantation's slaves, equipment, and curing barns.

But why would the man lie about the reason if it were

merely to assess its value as collateral?

Believing then that the absentee landowner's need to lie meant he was planning to sell the plantation, Philpot banged his fists on the desk.

Sitting up on her bed, Becky heard the bang and assumed the letter Philpot received contained bad news, and she hoped hers didn't. She folded back the single sheet, and by its horizontal and vertical lines of writing, she immediately knew which member of her family had written it.

Her brother wrote that her mother had recovered from her cough, wrote that he and their father had finished expanding the master's stable, and after mentioning that the two pure-bred Arabian horses they were intending to breed had arrived from The East as males, he informed her that the governess position he had earlier wrote about had been filled. He ended the short letter with his hope that Margaret was doing well and his wish for Becky to soon join them.

Knowing then what was to come in the next few weeks in response to her inquiry regarding the governess position, Becky refolded the letter, laid it near the edge of the bed, and wasn't sure how she felt about the position being filled. She expected to be disappointed, but she wasn't. She wanted to join her family, needed to join them, and she was confident she could book passage for the next week, but without knowing why and not wanting to search her mind for the reason, she thought it best to wait another month.

**

That Thursday, after he had changed into a set of clothes he had received as part of his contract's completion, Ben placed the whip, charged pistols, and sword in their usual places, and handed the pocket watch and long leather coat to William, who placed the watch on the small table between the beds and hung the coat over the sword that he would try to hide from his brother who, if he discovered it, was sure to want to practice with it.

"I'll be certain to write to you, and you can take that as my word. Not like Jeremiah, who promised me the same and never did," Ben said as he adjusted his waistcoat.

"I look forward to your letter, and I'll reply."

Placing a shoed foot on his bed, Ben adjusted his stocking. "You'll have to learn to write first." Changing to his other foot, he adjusted its stocking too. "Must admit, I'm envious of you. There'll be changes here, and any change would be a good change."

"How's that?"

"Can't say now. Only a… a feeling. Still, I don't have to worry about you. More than a few indentureds don't make it through their last year. Accidents happen to some so their masters can avoid payment. No, Philpot's a lot of things, but he's not one of those," Ben said before offering his hand. "But let's have our farewells now rather than in front of his *Lordship*."

"It has been short, but I'll still miss your company," William said, shaking his hand.

"You'll miss it more when it's only you and *him* on the morrow. I'm certain of that."

"I expect that's true, and I would've liked to have given you a proper sendoff, a celebration."

"Philpot would never permit it, but I appreciate the thought," he said before startling William by hugging him tight and with his voice cracking, added, "If we had more time, we would've become staunch friends."

"I… I agree," William nodded as Ben released him.

Then with both slightly uncomfortable, both cleared their throats.

"Would say you remind me of myself when I first came here, but can't. Wasn't as naive," Ben smiled before his eyes enlarged. "Oi, I almost forgot!" Hurrying over to his flour sack of clothes, he took a few seconds to search through it before pulling out something wrapped in a handkerchief with its corners tied together. Returning to William, he held out the small bundle. "Takes this. Ten pounds in small coins to help pay for the women. My penance… or part of it."

William shook his head. "No, you'll need it."

"No, I won't, and I'll explain why in my letter," Ben said, and with William still not taking the bundle, he tossed it onto William's bed. "Come. Let me humor that fat man one last time."

With Becky having left with the dirty dishes and Oink having left with the excuse of going to the privy as a chance for a quick second or third dessert, William waited for Philpot and Ben to finish their desserts.

The room's almost constant tension seemed thicker that evening, and wondering if it was only him feeling it, he decided it was when he looked at Ben contently putting the last spoonful of his rice pudding into his mouth and then purposely annoying Philpot by rapidly scraping his pewter spoon around the pewter bowl to collect the remaining bit of cream. After Ben put what little he had collected into his mouth, William had to force down his smile when the young man again whipped his spoon around the bowl for several seconds.

Dropping his spoon into his bowl, Philpot belched and said, "I say I do hope you don't think worse of me for making you walk. William would drive you if not for him needing his rest for his first day alone on the morrow. The drive itself would take more than an hour each way, and add to that the time to harness and—"

"I understand, and I *can't* think any… don't think any worse of you," Ben said, tossing a smirk at William just as Becky entered with the red bottle of rum and a short stack of pewter cups.

As she placed the bottle in front of Philpot and set out the three cups, the man asked, "Where's the boy?"

"He'll be along soon," she said, covering for Oink who was amusing Mary and Ann by spooning down the last of the rice pudding from a small pot.

As she took her seat, Oink rushed in to sit next to her, and before Philpot could say anything to the boy with cream at the corner of his mouth, she placed a small wooden box in front of the man.

"What's this?"

"We know next Sunday is your birth date, and since this is the last time Ben will be with us and the gift is from all of us, we decided we would present it to you now."

More surprised than Philpot, the others watched him pick up the box and slide out its top. "I say it's a snuffbox," he smiled as he pulled out the small covered dish. "A pewter one, and one with my initials engraved into it. This is truly a splendid gift! Bless you all for thinking of me on my twenty-fifth. I shall be certain to take this to town whenever I'm about. I tend to fear someone might try pinching my silver one, but now you have removed that fear."

With all not sure how to take the man's words, Becky said, "We expected as much and expect it will work as well as the silver one."

"I expect it shall too, and I thank you all for this gift, but as we shall be sharing this rum tonight and with you being a woman and the boy being a… you're a boy, I say you two may retire early."

Oink was about to say he had experienced rum when Becky said, "Oink, you can join me in cleaning up the kitchen, but before I leave, Ben, allow me to wish you good fortune."

Ben stood up from the table, nodded, and with his eyes seeming to plead with her, said, "I thank you, and I-I wish you the same."

Becky shook his offered hand. "Have a safe journey to Williamsburg and again, good fortune to you," she said before leaving the room.

After Oink stood and offered out his hand, which Ben shook, the boy said, "Good fortune to you, and I thank you for your lessons with the whip."

"And I, you. It was my pleasure, but do mind your brother. He's the apprentice now."

"Don't ask me to do what you know I can't," Oink laughed as released Ben's hand and hurried after Becky.

When Ben sat at the table again, Philpot asked, "Have you packed your belongings, gave the lad the pocket watch, coat, whip—"

"I have," Ben nodded, annoying the man by cutting him off. "My sack is near the back door."

"Good, and you should avoid the trails. You have more coin than a few indentures would—"

"I will. I know the route best by the roads and could lose

myself by the trails."

"And be sure to avoid any strangers wanting to distract you by conver—"

"I will. I'm wearing a long blade to support my words if I need to use it."

"A-a blade?"

"This dagger," Ben said, pulling it from the polished sheath hanging from his waist and laying it on the table near Philpot. "Stronger and sharper than any man's words."

"When did you receive this?" Philpot asked as he examined the long double-edged blade before placing it on the edge of the table in front of him.

"Purchased it a week before William arrived."

"W-well… uh… then let's drink to the… the end of your contract." After pouring a couple of shots into his and William's cups and almost filling Ben's, he slid the cups in front of the two, raised his, and said, "To good fortune to come."

After holding up his cup and repeating the man's words with Ben, William watched the two empty theirs.

"You didn't drink?" Philpot said, glaring at William. "When we tap cups, we drink."

"I would prefer not to," William said, shyly.

"I would prefer you did, and it's what I prefer that's important, yes?"

Ben placed his empty cup on the table and grinned. "I'm fine with it. He prefers cider, soft rather than hard."

"If I say you are to drink, you *shall* drink!" Philpot growled. "Now we shall have to do this again." After he poured two more shots into his cup, added two more to William's, and again almost filled Ben's, he raised his cup and again said, "To good fortune to come."

After the two joined him in raising their cups and repeating the words, Ben gladly emptied his second cup of rum and William struggled to drink the liquid that tasted worse than it smelled. Successfully fighting back a cough, he placed his empty cup on the table and hoped it was the last.

"Better than the cheaper rum, yes?" Philpot asked Ben, who responded with a nod. "But the next time you feel the need to take it with you, bring the bottle. That waterskin you used last Saturday will smell of rum for several weeks. I know of it because I used it days later, but I'm not angered by it. No, I say I would've done the same if I had less than a week remaining on my contract," Philpot smirked. "And with that, let us have one more."

The man poured out two more double shots for himself and William, and again, almost filled Ben's cup. "To William's health and a safe next seven years," he said, and as the two forced themselves to empty their cups, he placed an arm over the dagger and slid it onto his lap. "If you want to reach the inn by the eleventh hour, I say you should be off now, lad."

Ben nodded and stood up from his chair. "Philpot, it was an… an experience working with you these long seven years," he said, and after Philpot, who stayed sitting, shook his hand, he offered it to William, who stood to shake it. "It was a pleasure meeting a man of your mettle, and I do hope someday we'll cross paths again."

"I do too," William nodded. "Be safe and mind your journey to Williamsburg."

"I will."

After watching Ben leave the room, the two listened to his

footsteps fading down the hall and then the back door shutting.

"I say that boy loses all manners when he drinks. Called me only Philpot, he did, and said it was an experience, not a pleasure!" Philpot hissed to William.

"I'll… I'll retire for the evening, if I may."

"You may," Philpot nodded, and as William left, added, "And don't be following that stripling's habit of using a waterskin for rum!"

**

That Saturday morning after he unbarred the cabins' doors and shutters, William had the first few men he came across help him harness the horses, and as he expected, all knew how to do it, taking less than thirty minutes to have six horses attached to each cart.

After William ate alone in the dining room, he chose the men and women for that day's renting, and the first man to raise his hand when William asked who knew the route for renting them was the man who proudly drove the cart.

At Sammy's, with an additional two men and ten women to help in his field, William and King filled the buckets with fish, and then as the two sat on the grass sharing the apple cider, bread, and cheese, William tried having a conversation with him, but after receiving a few blank looks and a couple of semi-coherent responses, he felt as if he was talking to the wind and gave up.

Later, as they were about to bring the fish to Mary, he asked King if he knew the way back, but when the man nodded, William had second thoughts, and said, "Good… good to know," and kept the reins to himself.

**

That Sunday morning, as eggs boiled, bread baked, porridge

simmered, and smiles covered Mary and Ann's faces, Mary told Becky that William had again paid for the women, and then, with Ann impatiently gesturing to her, said, "He appears to have the temperament to be a proper husband."

Relieved by the news, Becky smiled at the woman's hint and nodded, "Yes, he does, from the little we know of him, but if you're expecting me to have an interest in him, remember he's still a slave overseer, though perhaps a gentler one, and if he was to marry, it wouldn't be for seven years when his contract ends."

Mary nodded before joining Ann in frowning. "Yes, that is a long time to wait, and much can happen during that time," she said, reminded that Becky could be gone within weeks. "Still, I have to say he'll make a woman happy when his time is finished here… if he hasn't changed for the worse."

"Yes, if he's not changed for the worse."

Sitting next to Philpot, William feared a repeat of the uncomfortably intimate shave he had the week before… until he saw Becky quickly shave Philpot, nicking him twice.

After sliding the bucket of water over to William and placing the cloth around his neck, Becky's racing heart confused her since she didn't expect it would when she was aware of his interest in her, even if it was only a temporary infatuation.

Lathering up his face, she struggled to pull her eyes from his that were dancing about at everything but hers. Straightening up, she stepped away to strop the blade until she calmed down, and as she did, she realized she had no other opportunity to become familiar with him besides his weekly shaves and monthly haircuts and she believed it could take many short conversations during the shaves and haircuts, maybe even a year of them before he was comfortable enough with her to respond unguarded to her questions regarding the renting of the women. Then struggling to search her mind for a more frequent and longer opportunity to be alone with him without seeming as if she was trying to court him, she stropped the blade faster.

About to slide the blade down his cheek, she asked him how he was and smiled when his eyes purposely avoided hers as he said, "Fine."

As she shaved his cheek while he closed his eyes, trying to imagine his mother doing it, an idea came to her and she said, "Oink told me you can't write. Is that correct?"

"Yes," he replied, catching himself from nodding.

"Can you read?"

William wanted to say he could read some, but with the razor sliding down his neck, he went with the shorter and, from what Ben had told him, the safer reply of, "No."

"One can only write after they're able to read," Becky said, breaking a smile when he opened his eyes to find hers looking at his and quickly closed them again. "I expect reading and writing would be a requirement for an overseer, every sort of overseer. Would you agree?"

"Yes," he whispered as the razor ran down the small area under his nose.

"Oink said you left school at twelve to work in a mine, so I expect you can read some," she said before moving on to his chin. "I expect too that you know your letters and only need practice recognizing the words. Is that correct?"

Not knowing why she would have an interest in his ability to read and write, William nodded, "Yes."

"Careful. I almost took off your *soap bubble* ear," she warned as she shaved his other cheek, and with William thinking it was a strange way to describe an ear, she asked, "Would you like to practice with me?" Only getting a puzzled look from his opened eyes, she snuck a large breath before forcing out, "Would you like to join me while I read to King? You can practice by reading to him too… and I could help you along."

Both surprised and excited by the chance to be alone with her, William said through his almost closed lips, "I would like that."

"Then… then that's what we'll do. You can join me on the morrow night after Master Philpot retires but don't mention it to him… or Oink. He mightn't be old enough to hold his tongue about it."

"I won't, and he isn't."

After laying the blade down and gently wiping his face with the towel, she straightened up, wiped the razor with the towel, and said, "We'll meet at the kitchen near ten after Master Philpot retires."

"You're reading the fairy tales to him?" William asked, hoping the words would be simpler.

"We are, but not to Master Philpot. He can read them to himself," she smirked, causing William to smirk too.

**

Pipe smoke filled the room like a dense fog, blurring the light of the few oil lanterns mounted on its walls of bare wood and highlighting the late afternoon's rays entering through its several high and narrow windows at a forty-five-degree angle, and with most of the tables taken, Harry stood at the bar. "I'll tells ya again, that there's not it," he complained while pointing at the two columns of numbers written in chalk on the board mounted on the wall behind the barman. "I didn't 'ave no four P's, and six Q's! I only 'ad four quarts, I tells ya! And I never drinks no pints!"

The barman rolled his eyes at the bowlegged man's weekly attempt to lower his tab. "Harry, you know if there's a problem with the count, you're to state it when you see it or at the end of the night, not when you return with little memory of it."

"I knows, but I couldn't. Can't never do that. A'ways three sheets to the wind by then."

"Listen here," the man raised his voice. "I'm not in the mood for this game today, not in this heat, so I'll repeat what I tell you every week. If you can't mind your P's and Q's, have someone mind them for you, perhaps one of your brothers. They've never had a problem with theirs. Now if you don't pay what's owed, you don't drink, not yours or anyone else's."

"Robbin' me, I tells ya!" Harry growled as he reached into his pocket and counted out several coins. "Take it from that an' give a pint 'ere, ya 'ighway robber!"

With the ceramic mug in hand, Harry caused the smoke to swirl about as he approached a corner table where his brothers sat with Philpot.

"Were you successful?" Robert asked over the many voices filling the room with a low rumble.

Harry huffed as he sat down. "No! Not a give to the man. Not even an offer 'o one less P or Q. What's comin' o' this town whens they won't offers no consideration for me pa'ronage! I thinks we should make 'im miss us, We should take Charlie out to the other one for 'is celebration next week?"

"Which other one?" Stuart asked.

"Don't matter none if we takes 'im to Jamestown," Harry said before he and the others spat on the floor. "What say ya to that, Charlie?"

Hearing his name, Philpot pulled his mind to the present and asked, "To what?"

"To your birth date celebration in Hell Town," Stuart said.

"There could be a time to be had there," he nodded before picking up his large ceramic mug, "And I say with the news I received this week, I could use a good time, and it's been some time since I've been with a woman."

"News?" Robert asked, picking up his pint.

"The bastard Chalmers intends to sell the estate. He has a banker coming in September to record all on the property and examine its ledgers. I'll cover the ledgers, so there's nothing to be questioned there, but I'll be damned if I'm giving him all there is there. I'm considering taking much of what's not nailed down, and if I do, you three shall store it for me. When he leaves, I'll return it until Chalmers sells the place. I figure ten pounds will tickle you to do the task."

"Only ten?" Harry asked with raised eyebrows.

"I say it's not as if I'm having you bury someone," he hissed. "But speaking of it, it went well?"

"Went well?" Harry asked with a smile. "That's this comin' Thursday, yeah?"

As his face turned red, Philpot barked, "It bloody well was last Thursday!"

With the three brothers laughing, Robert was the first to stop. "Harry is jesting. It went well."

"I say you're the amusing Carter, you are," Philpot said to Harry, sarcastically.

"'E was feelin' no pain, an' 'e felt none," Harry grinned slyly. "'E couldn't even walk straight."

"Yes, I expect his state made your task easier. He had a dagger on him, and after applying some rum, I relieved him of it. You are welcome."

"That explains the empty sheath. And he also had this here," Robert said as he pulled a folded letter from his waistcoat and passed it over the table to Philpot. "With my reading not respectable, I figured you might want to see if it's important."

Curious about the letter, Philpot looked at it, and not able to read it in the dimly lit room, he stood up and left the brothers to their drinks. Outside and after a man entering the tavern nodded a greeting to him, Philpot went to the side of the building to read the letter.

With only *BEN CARLSON* written on the outside, he thought it strange that the letter would've been one of several sent in a package, and folding back its two sheets, he was surprised to read that all on the estate were eagerly awaiting Ben's return, that Joseph had arranged his bedroom just as he had left it, and that the man was dusting it weekly in anticipation,

Return? The boy wasn't going home. Why would it read as if he's going home… and to an estate with servants?

Realizing he knew nothing about Ben's family, he looked at the third page to learn who the author was and only seeing the name Michael, he still didn't know. Continuing to read the letter, the author wrote that it would be his last letter but requested another from Ben to confirm his passage to London and his opinion of his replacement. When Philpot read that Ben was to receive a hundred pounds from Francis Bradbury and read that the writer was sure Bradbury would appreciate an end to their meetings, his face reddened.

Francis Bradbury, the tobacco agent?

Then Philpot's knees almost buckled when he read that the author was longing for Ben's return and was eager to discuss how they would deal with 'Philpot's misdeeds', how they would ensure less abuse by the next overseer, and with the full use of the plantation's slaves, how much land they could expect to clear in the next five years and its estimated increase in the harvest. Then the large man had to lean against the wall of the tavern when the author ended the letter by thanking Ben for taking a seven-year charge that he didn't want and ensuring him his time was 'not for naught' since it would finally push the plantation's growth out of 'its near stagnant expansion.'

Nonplussed, Philpot folded the letter, placed it in his waistcoat, and walked back into the smoke-filled tavern to sit with the Carter brothers, who stared at him as they waited for him to tell them what was in the letter that had obviously affected him poorly.

"Did ya finds out 'e was your lost son?" Harry laughed, breaking their silence.

Opening his pewter snuff box, Philpot removed the tiny spoon attached to its side and took two sniffs of the grayish-white powder, and after several seconds, he said as if talking to himself, "They never accepted me, shall never accept me as one of them. I say I dress better than most, talk better, and have far more sterling than most, and yet I shall never be one of them. No respect and no loyalty, not even from an indenture, not from that halfwit Ben Carlson, the damned ambidexter!"

"The one ya 'ad us bury?" Harry asked, smirking. "No

loyalty from 'im, ya say?"

"It matters not what came of him! My point is he wasn't loyal!" Philpot barked. "He was informing Chalmers of my actions from the first day he arrived! Chalmers isn't selling! He's replacing me, and I expect he's making a list so I don't walk away with anything!"

Stuart cleared his throat. "You should've had us oversee them. You had us do the other tasks. Why not the proper ones?"

"Because He didn't create you three cumbergrounds for constant and consistent work! You work as one and take the sterling of three!" Philpot hissed.

"Let's stop looking back and let's look forward," Robert said before clearing his throat. "I'm assuming now you'll be taking a different path than planned, knowing you as I do... now that revenge is part of it."

"I believe you're correct, but I shall reflect on it when I can think clearer," Philpot said as he unbuttoned his waistcoat. "At this moment, I only want to burn the place to the ground!"

"We'll need over ten pounds for that," Stuart grinned.

The large man glared at him. "Speaking of pounds, how many did you find on the stripling? My guess is you each saw forty for your hour."

"Had almost a hundred on him," Robert nodded. "Did he steal it from you?"

"No, he would never have found where I buried my coin. Chalmers gave it to him for betraying me, but I shall consider your newfound wealth when you join me in whatever I decide to do." After taking a moment to empty his quart, he added, "But with next week being my birth date, I shall not permit this matter to disturb my mind. No, there's plenty of time to consider the proper action."

**

Becky woke to Philpot banging on her bedroom door barricaded by the dresser and was taken aback when he didn't ask for a kissy, but demanded one. As the door opened a crack, pushing the dresser back an inch, she jumped out of bed to sit on it, and after the next several pushes had little effect and his fourth demand went unanswered, he stumbled down the hall toward the stairs.

CHAPTER 24
Reading and Waxing

Bathed and changed into the clothes he had worn to church that previous morning, William sat on his bed anxiously waiting for Philpot's snoring to belittle his brothers, and with nothing to distract his mind, he wondered why Becky would offer to help him with his reading. From what Ben had told him about Philpot not wanting his apprentices to read, she must have known it was contrary to the man's wishes, just as she knew he wouldn't approve of her reading to King, and he questioned if she enjoyed discreetly rebelling against the man and if helping him practice his reading added to that enjoyment. Then it occurred to him he might have to read aloud that first night of reading practice, which he wasn't comfortable doing, and he became even more anxious.

When Philpot's snoring began to resonate through the walls, William's anxious state forced him from the bed so fast that his shoes landed hard on the floor. Freezing where he stood, he listened for the snores to stop, and when neither did, he rubbed his sweaty palms against the legs of his breeches and left his bedroom to creep past the snores and descend the steep steps two at a time, pausing with each loud creak.

Holding a leather-bound book in her hand, Becky had been standing outside the kitchen for ten minutes waiting for the candle in his bedroom to be snuffed out as a sign that he was on his way, or after several more minutes of not seeing him, that he had changed his mind. With the candle still burning in his room, the back door opened and he walked out.

"My apologies. I had to wait until Master Philpot was asleep," he whispered over his furious heartbeat.

Becky couldn't help but smile at him looking as if he was attending his first day of school, but she dropped her smile when she realized she too had changed for the occasion. "No need to apologize. If you had arrived a minute sooner, I would be the one apologizing," she whispered back. "Come, we're going to read Little Red Riding Hood," she said as they walked toward King's cabin. "Have you heard of it?"

"No."

"It's about a little girl being followed by a hungry wolf."

"That's a children's story?" William asked, not understanding how a story about a wolf chasing a little girl would be something a child should hear.

"It is."

After William unbarred the small cabin's door and followed her in, his presence startled the man sitting on the bed.

"King, Master Lovely is joining us to practice his reading. He's going to read you Little Red Riding Hood. You enjoyed the story, yes?" she said, causing William's heart to race.

With a nod from King, William sat on the dirt floor to face the bed, his back against the log wall, and when Becky joined him, her shoulder touching his, he became more nervous, but she didn't. Having the day to prepare herself for that evening, she was able to view it as a governess and her ward.

"When you come across the older, less common words, such as *durst*, try to replace them with their common equivalent, such as *dared*," Becky said as she opened the book to the first page of the first story and handed it to him. Picking up the candleholder resting on King's table, she held it up so William could see the words better.

Not having heard of *durst* and therefore not knowing it meant *dared*, William was wondering why the writer wouldn't have just written *dared* when Becky said, "You may begin reading when you're ready."

William cleared his throat and paused to try to calm his heart. "Ohnce. Up—on. A. Time."

"Once," Becky corrected him. "It's pronounced with a W sound rather than the long O, like the word *one* is pronounced… the number one — O, N, E."

William nodded, embarrassed. "Once upon a time, there lyved…"

"Lived, like *river*. The I is short."

"There *lived* in a… a Ker—tayn"

"Certain. The C is soft when followed by an E."

"*Certain*," William nodded. "There lived in a… a *certain* village, a little cooontry… country girl."

His reading went slow, slower than either had expected. After twenty minutes of correcting almost a fifth of the words and covering only the first two pages of the five-page story, Becky was amused by King's snoring but disappointed when she realized their time with King would give them little opportunity to talk. Then an idea came to her, and after the two walked back to the house, where William wished her a blessed night before heading toward the stairs, she said, "We're not finished. We'll spend an hour reading the next story so we won't lose King's interest on the morrow night."

"More practice? Where?"

"In the dining room. We'll read The Fairy."

After William followed her to the table and sat next to her with the chandelier's candles burning above them, Becky opened the book to the second fairy tale and told him that if he slid his finger along with the words he was reading, it would help him track his pace and her to know which word he was stumbling over.

Turning the pages back to *Little Red Riding Hood,* William blushed when he told her he wanted to know how the story ended and asked her to read on from where he had stopped since it would take him far too long that night to read it and the next story too.

After Becky agreed, and feeling as if she was reading to a child, she slid her finger along the words as she slowly read the rest of the story to him while giving the wolf and Little Red Riding Hood different voices, amusing William as he discreetly tried to admire her facial features.

When she finished, he said, "The wolf ate her? I doubt anyone would sleep well after hearing that."

"It's a fairy tale, not a bedtime story," she smiled. "And for King, I changed the ending to the grandmother's big, brave houseboy killing the wolf. The message of the tale is to dissuade children from talking to strangers, or from trusting them before knowing them."

William smiled back. "I don't believe it's a message King needs to hear. I don't expect he'll be talking to many strangers."

Becky's face went cold as she turned the page to *The Fairy*. "You shouldn't be making jest with the way he speaks."

William blushed. "I was referring to his size, not his speaking. Most strangers would be afraid to speak to him, I expect."

"I suppose that's true," she said, sliding the book over to him. "Now let's begin the next story and hope we finish it before the sun comes up."

"That's at least five hours away."

"It is and we should start now so you might finish before then."

As William struggled through the larger words and some smaller ones, proudly correcting himself when he figured out on his own the word he was mispronouncing, his patience impressed Becky. After the first half an hour of slow reading, she would've expected him to become frustrated with the task and/or himself, as Beth would, but he forced himself through it.

The next evening William wouldn't be as nervous as the night before, and since it would be his second time reading *The Fairy*, he kept the giant's attention through its six pages and only needed help with the few words he didn't immediately recognize from the evening before

Then that Sunday night, sitting at the dining room table after having read to King, Becky slid the closed book over to William and asked him to read *Cinderella* by himself sometime between Monday's evening meal and his reading to King, and not understanding why they had sat at the table if she was only going to give him the book to read on his own,

William stood up from his chair and picked up the book.

"How are you finding it here compared to your home?" she asked him.

"Uh… it's… it's much like being on a deserted island," he said, hoping not to offend her. "Here, the neighbors are some distance away compared to back home. There the furthest neighbor in our village is only a twenty-minute walk."

Becky nodded. "It can seem like being alone on a deserted island. I was raised on a much smaller plantation but it felt like that to me too," she said before telling him she had only spent time with others her age when their neighbors visited her parents and brought along their children or her parents visited the neighbors and took her along. If she didn't like the children, she was forced to spend hours with them, like one boy who tortured her during the entire visit by chasing after her to pull her hair, and if she liked them, she only had a few hours to spend with them and might not see them for years afterward if they didn't attend the same church.

Returning to his chair, William listened to her describe her chores on her parent's plantation, which had a few animals but no slaves, and tell him that her only regular escapes from 'the island' were their weekly church service and their occasional trips to Williamsburg, which had changed little since she was a child. She talked about her brother whom she considered a dreamer and never short of ideas to earn sterling, like when he came up with using dried tobacco stalks for fire kindling, where the smoke might relax folks, as roof material, and as stuffing for ticks, with none catching on, though not for his lack of trying, and she smiled when she told him that Oink reminded her of her brother, "But my brother's not so gifted with things that move."

After she had told him that her family once had over a dozen indentured servants working their field, told him about some of the memorable indentured servants that had worked for them and what some of them were doing now, like owning their own businesses and plantations, and then told him how her family had spent much to send her to Boston for schooling while her brother worked the plantation, she realized she had spoken for close to half an hour and realized too that she was comfortable around him, and then wondering if he had become comfortable with her, she asked him about his time in the mine.

William hesitated before telling her there wasn't much to tell. It could be dangerous work but was mostly repetitive, and when the agent came around and he was of age, he saw it as a chance to escape it. Then thinking he said too little, he described his sisters and parents and explained that he had chosen the overseer contract because he was told it wasn't repetitive work and was a responsible and respectable position.

When he paused to search his mind for more to say that might interest her, Becky decided to ask him about his paying for the women, but before she could, the slamming of the back door followed by a clatter, a heavy thud, and then a moan caused each to stare at the other's puzzled face before her eyes widened. "He's back!" she whispered in panic. "He might come to my chamber door, so stay here and don't leave until he's climbed the stairs. Sleep well."

Wondering why Philpot would go to her door, William watched her rush from the room.

After quietly closing her bedroom door, Becky was trying to drag her dresser up to it when it opened to reveal a grinning Philpot standing in his opened waistcoat of six pistols. With his trousers stained at the knees, he swayed slightly as he struggled to say clearly, "Thhhere she is. I shhhall be… be needing me… my kisshhhy."

"M-master Philpot, it's late. You need your sleep for on the morrow."

"Balderdashhh," the heavily intoxicated man said as he walked into her bedroom. "Come, I shhhall need two kisshhhies. One for my birth date and… and a shecond for a… for a b-blesshhhed night."

"No!" Becky yelled, her face growing red with anger at his expectation. "I've never given you kissies and never will! Go to bed before this night embarrasses you on the morrow!"

Continuing to sway, he lost his grin. "A kissh is what I require, and a kissh is what I shhhall resheive," he said as he grabbed her forearm. "You shhhall give it or I shhhall take it!"

"Leave her be!"

Tightening his grip on her, Philpot turned around to find William standing at her door. "Shhhtripling, you besht be gone or… or for all intentsh, con-conshtructionsh and purposhesh you shhhall find yourshelf buried!"

"Unhand her and I'll be gone."

"Then buried it shhhall be!" Philpot growled.

As Philpot grabbed a pistol from his waistcoat and pointed it at William, Becky tried to pull her arm away, causing the large man to stumble to the side and fire the pistol into the wall several feet to the right of William, filling the room with the blast and a bit of smoke.

Cursing, Philpot dropped the pistol, released his hold on her arm, and pushed her to the floor, and as he was going for another pistol, William rushed him and punched him in the cheek, sending him to the floor next to Becky. After helping

Becky to her feet, both stared down at the man lying on his back, snoring.

Pulling her eyes from the man, Becky picked up the spent pistol and placed it back into the man's waistcoat. "I-I suppose we must put him to bed."

"Must we?"

"What!? We can't leave him here, not where I sleep! No, we have to move him to his bed."

Embarrassed, William nodded his understanding, and as he bent down to grab Philpot by his arms pits, Becky crouched down and struggled to put a leg over each shoulder. Then, after several times straining to lift the man, she carelessly dropped his legs. "Perhaps we should each take an arm and drag him down the hall."

"That would work for the hall, but not for the stairs."

"Who discharged the gun?" Oink asked as he stood at Becky's bedroom door in his nightshirt.

"Master Philpot was… he was showing them to William before he fell asleep," Becky said.

"He fell asleep there? Is he drunk?"

"He is," William nodded, "And seeing how you're up, you can help us carry him to his bed."

"No, I have another idea," Becky said. "I'll only be a moment."

After watching her rush out of the room and then hearing the back door close, Oink looked William up and down. "You're dressed? You went to bed when I did… and you weren't wearing those."

"Uh… yes, but I… I was needed for something," William said, hoping the questions would stop there but not expecting them to.

"And you changed for the occasion?" Oink asked, smirking at his brother's eyes darting about. "Help with what, kissing? I know enough to know it takes two."

"I… I asked her if she would help me practice my reading."

Oink's smirk grew to a smile. "And?"

"She said she'll consider it."

"That took a couple of hours? It's at least that since I went to bed."

"And we talked."

"Kissed?" Oink asked, continuing to smile. "Did you kiss her? Did you?"

"No!"

"But you wanted to."

"I want to read better."

"More so when it's *her* helping you, yes?"

"Yes," William nodded, blushing.

"Read first, kiss second," Oink said, smirking again.

Before William could respond, both heard the back door shut, and a second later, Becky entered her room with King following her in his stained shirt and shorts. Trying to catch her breath, she said, "King will put the master to bed."

King crouched down and easily placed the man over a shoulder. Standing up with the man's arms hanging down behind him, he followed the three down the hall, up the stairs, and into Philpot's room, where he dropped the man onto the bed.

"We thank you, King," Becky said as Philpot resumed his snoring.

"Me go?"

"Yes, and sleep well."

With King descending the stairs to the back door, William asked Oink not to ever mention what had happened so as not to embarrass Philpot, and after Oink agreed, the boy wished both a blessed night and returned to his room, grinning.

After waiting for his brother's door to close, William whispered to Becky, "I don't expect to sleep well tonight. This could continue on the morrow."

Looking up at him, Becky shook her head. "I'm certain it won't. He's more inebriated than he normally is on Sunday nights. If there's no sign of it when he wakes, he might never be reminded of it. And if he does remember, I expect he'll be too embarrassed to mention it," she told him. "It's not the first Sunday night he came looking for a… a kissy, and on the days after, he's never mentioned his disappointment with not receiving one."

"Now I'm strangely jealous," William smirked. "He's never requested a kissy from me."

"There's always next Sunday."

Then standing there looking at each other, both waiting for the other to either say something more or leave, Becky wondered if William's actions that night were brave or stupid, and as both felt the growing awkwardness, both looked down at the floor before again looking at the other… until William forced himself to wish Becky a blessed night, she returned the wish, and both headed to their bedrooms.

Lying in bed with her mind refusing to close down, her shock at Philpot firing the pistol at William returned, making her fear what could've happened had the man's pistol found its mark. Then forcing her mind away from what could have happened, she struggled to come up with a way to make sure it couldn't happen again, and her first thought was to remove all the firearms from the house, but that would be noticed almost immediately. If she couldn't remove them, then maybe she could make them impossible to fire. Knowing better than to try to empty the firearms' powder and balls packed into the back of their barrels and knowing better than to remove the bit of powder from their tiny pans beneath the frizzens, since at some point both would be noticed, her mind went through the parts of a pistol. And after she struggled with how she might break their triggers and then struggled with how she might make the hammers unable to be pulled back, her mind reached the frizzen and she was hit by an idea so hard that it forced her to jump from her bed.

In her shift and in the dark, she ascended the stairs, and with each creaking step, she tried to make herself lighter. In Philpot's room, standing near the still snoring man, she held the bottom of her shift out, and with each of his snores, slid a pistol from his waistcoat and placed it carefully onto her shift. After removing all six, she held the pistols in her shift while she carefully made her way down the stairs, where she hurried down the hall to enter Philpot's study.

After sliding the pistols onto the desk, she used a candle from the dining room's chandelier to light the two candles hanging on each side of the study's door, and after lighting the small, thick candle on the desk, she blew out the chandelier's candle and picked up the pistol smelling of burned powder. Dipping her finger into the hot transparent wax of the desk's candle, she rubbed it against the rough striking surface of the pistol's frizzen, and after applying a second coat, pulled back the hammer, dropped the frizzen, and squeezed the trigger. The small piece of flint snug in the jaws of the hammer snapped against the frizzen's wax-coated surface and failed to produce a spark, and after only sparking on the third try, she was satisfied and reapplied the wax before applying it to the frizzens of the other five pistols.

After returning the weapons to Philpot's waistcoat, she returned to the study to clean the wax drippings from the top of the desk.

Tired but proud of herself, she yawned and stretched out her arms and legs.

The snapping of the door's release surprised her. The loud echoing bang of the heavy door slamming shut stunned her, and as its echo faded away and the candle hanging to the right of the door smoked from being blown out, she realized her foot had struck the lever under the desk. Taking a moment to shake off the shock of having locked herself in, she considered trying to open the door herself but quickly dropped that impossible idea, and after a few seconds, realized the only escape from the room was across from her, and she slid the heavy chair to a window, stepped up on to it, opened the pair of iron shutters, and climbed headfirst through the opening. Softening her fall with her outstretched arms, she landed in the tall weeds separating the house from the road leading to the back, and after brushing the dirt from her shift, she headed to the back door that she had forgotten to bar after King had left.

A few minutes later, while standing over him with a candle lantern in her hand, she took a moment to admire the peaceful profile that showed no sign of a pistol having recently been fired at him, and she was only able to resist the urge to tickle his nose when it occurred to her how inappropriate it was to be standing over him as he slept.

Waking to a light shake, William was startled to find

Becky looking down at him with bits of weed in her long, straight hair. Not able to imagine anything more beautiful, he thought he was dreaming until she whispered, "I need your help. I locked myself out of Philpot's study." Then expecting a dream to make more sense, he realized he was awake and reached over to the small table under the window to pick up the pocket watch, and after struggling to make out the position of its arms by the light of her lantern, he said, "It's… it's past midnight. You haven't gone to bed?"

She shook her head, "No," and then pulling him by the arm of his nightshirt, she said, "Come, we'll only be a minute."

Shy with being seen in his nightshirt and then more shy when he realized she was in her shift, he stood and said, "W-we should wake Oink. We could use help with that door."

"No. He might ask questions I would rather not answer."

"Like why you were in his study at this hour?"

"Exactly," Becky nodded while poking him in the chest with her index finger. "Questions much like that. Come."

Outside the window of the logged section of the house, she placed the lantern on the ground and told him to give her a boost, and doing as he was told, he laced his fingers so she could place her small bare foot in his cupped hands, step up, and climb through the opening, and as she struggled to get her stomach past the window frame, he gave a push on her bottom and then cringed to the crash of a chair falling over and the thud from her hitting the floor.

A moment later, her eyes looked over the windowsill. "I'll join you on the other side of the door."

After she closed the window's shutters and returned the chair to the desk, she only had to wait a few seconds for him to join her on the other side of the door.

"Are you there?" he asked.

Wondering where else he would expect her to be, she spoke loud enough to be heard through the thick door, "I am. I'll tell you when I have the two bolts pulled back." Stretching an arm above her, she pulled down on the top bolt while using her big toe to painfully force the bottom one up. "Push!"

William grunted as he pushed against the door, and after it opened a couple of inches, she pulled on the door's handles. Slowly the door opened, and with William using the door frame as leverage, they opened it enough for the bottom bolt to drop into the small hole in the floor, locking it in place.

As Becky caught her breath, William said, "I should be… we should return to our beds."

"Yes, you go ahead. I have some… something to finish," she lied, worrying that while walking with him to her room, he might ask what she had been doing at the desk, and when William suspiciously eyed the almost bare top of the desk, she distracted him from his questions by hugging him and saying, "I appreciate your help."

Then William surprised himself and her when he dropped his head to hers and gave a quick kiss to her cheek as he would to his mother or sisters. "My a-apologies," he said as his face turned a dark red and he broke their hug.

"I-I thank you for your help," Becky whispered, and then in her physically and mentally exhausted state, she dropped her inhibitions to pull his embarrassed face down to hers to kiss him on the lips… and he kissed her back.

Forcing herself to break their kiss, the dark color of her face matched his as she whispered, "My… my apologies."

William thought he should say something, but suddenly at

a loss for words, he could only nod.

Disappointed that he said nothing, Becky nodded too before watching him leave the room, smacking his shoulder against the doorframe before stumbling out and disappearing down the hall.

"Are you hurt?" she asked, loud enough for him to hear.

"Never been better," he said. "Have a blessed night."

Minutes later, while thinking of their kiss, he fell into a profound sleep.

Back in bed and thinking about their kiss instead of the incident with Philpot, a wave of guilt was preparing to charge at her, but it retreated when she considered that with what she knew of William so far, Peter would like him and would understand and even approve of her attraction to the noble young man.

**

The next morning she woke unusually happy and proud of herself for both tampering with the firearms and kissing William... until she panicked when she realized she had forgotten to tamper with the other pistols and long guns in the house. But she was pacified when she reminded herself that they were seldom handled and the only time she knew of them being used was when she used them.

When a tired Philpot joined the brothers at the table in only his nightshirt, a shocked William and a curious Oink couldn't help but stare at his face.

Noticing the looks, the man broke his usual morning silence by asking, "What's so interesting about my face?"

With William's eyes dropping to the table, Oink said,

"Your eye's bruised. Were you in a battle of fists? Were you punched?"

"Battle of fists? Punched?" Philpot rubbed his right eye and squinted at the slight pain. "I presume it happened when I left the tavern, though I have no memory of being struck there… and I expect my face now matches my soiled shirt and breeches."

"You soiled your breeches?" Oink smirked, causing William's eyes to widen.

Philpot stared at the boy for a few seconds, which seemed like minutes to William, before he cracked a smile. "Yes, but not that sort of soiled."

Becky entered the dining room with four bowls of porridge and four cups of cider, and after smiling at William, who confused her by turning his eyes away, she almost dropped the tray when she saw the thick red and blue mark covering the bottom of Philpot's eye.

"Yes, Becky, it seems I have an additional gift to mark my birth date, but as I was telling the lads, I have no recollection of being gifted it, but while I'm reminded of it, collect my clothes and have the girls wash them today. I fear I may lose a fine shirt if I allow the stains to linger, and, Oink, after the midday meal, I shall have you oversee the slaves with William. And, William, to address this headache, I shall lay my head down after this meal, and until Oink finishes with the garden, you shall be on your own, but I expect you're competent enough to oversee the full complement for the short time."

Where William appreciated the chance to work alone in Chalmers' field that morning, Oink was disappointed to be losing both his time with Gibby and his time practicing the whip, and he was more disappointed when Philpot added, "But why stop there? It seems better to have you work with him every afternoon. I say with you overseeing both the garden and the field, you shall understand the workings of this estate better than your brother. It shall do me good as well. I can bring my ledgers up to the moment and the several changes I'm planning for the estate shall take me away from the field over the next few weeks."

CHAPTER 25
William and Becky

That evening his heart raced much like it did when meeting her that previous Monday, but this time it was because of the excitement of being alone with her after their first kiss. With nothing in the field to distract his mind from the night before, he had been longing to be with her, but fearing Oink might notice their attraction and later mention it in front of Philpot, he had forced himself, almost painfully, to avoid eye contact with her. Then seeing her waiting by the kitchen, his heart raced faster, and he had to control his walking so as not to rush over and scare her off like a small bird.

Questioning if the kiss had been premature and wondering if forcing it on him revealed a level of boldness that he might consider unattractive, Becky waited anxiously near the kitchen door not sure if he would join her that night after having avoided eye contact with her during the day's meals. Then seeing him leave the house and walk toward her, her heart skipped a beat, and she wanted to meet him halfway and embrace him, but by his casual walk, she held herself back, fearing she might scare him off like a small bird.

With each hoping the other would mention the kiss while

they resisted the urge to grab the other's hand, they greeted one another much like they did the week before, and on their walk to King's cabin, only discussed their appreciation for the cool breeze.

Sitting again shoulder to shoulder on the dirt floor, each discreetly appreciating the other's touch, it surprised Becky with how many times she had to correct his reading before he had finished the third page of the fairy tale. "Did you have time to practice on your own, to read it on your own?" she whispered so as not to wake a snoring King.

"I-I did between the evening meal and now, but it seems to have done little for me. Without you there to correct me, I didn't recognize the more difficult words," he whispered back, leaving out that he also found it difficult to focus on the words because his mind was on her.

Leaving King to sleep and with the stronger winds bringing a drizzle, they walked back to the house, and in the dining room, the two focused only on William's rereading of the tale.

With both still waiting for the other to mention the kiss, neither did, and both went to bed disappointed that they didn't discuss it... or repeat it, and over the next four nights, still neither mentioned the kiss, convincing each that the other thought little of it or was ashamed of it.

That Saturday night in King's cabin where William expected to reread the previous night's fairy tale, Becky surprised him by telling King he would hear a story about two slave brothers saving a ship's crew and passengers from pirates, and after explaining what a ship was, what pirates were, and described the two slaves as one being a large slave, coincidentally named King, and the other a younger, smaller slave named King's Brother, she shocked William by asking him to tell the story.

After an awkward William took a moment to accept that he would tell it and took another to decide how to tell it, he described the work the two brothers performed (the emptying of the heads, cleaning of the pigsty, cleaning the floors, swabbing the deck, polishing the brass pieces, helping the cook, and cleaning the captain and first mate's quarters) and then told him that on a dark, cloudy day, as the brothers were swabbing the poop deck, they noticed a pirate ship following them.

He was content to find Becky as interested as King when he told him about the smaller brother coming up with the plan and the ship's crew acting on it, but when he reached the point where the small boat of chests was threatening to flood by listing too much, he paused to find the courage to recall his experience, and just as he decided he would skip that part of the story, Becky surprised him by telling King how the older brother, King, risked drowning and sharks by jumping into the rough sea to save their plan, and after telling King what sharks were, she told him how he fought them off while swimming to the small boat, how he balanced the chests in the boat, and after he had swum away from it, how the pirates took the chests and soon after, their ship exploded. She ended the story by telling how King's Brother ordered the crew that was then subservient to him to sail back for his brave brother, and when he was safely aboard, how all on the ship praised the slaves for their courage and quick thinking.

"Will that story help you sleep?" she asked.

"No," King replied, surprising both.

"You don't like the story?"

"Me story like. Story me no sleep."

Becky exchanged a puzzled look with William and asked, "The stories don't help you sleep?"

"Me stories like," he said before shaking his head. "Stories me no sleep. Here you, me sleep."

Realizing then that it was their company that helped him sleep rather than the stories, Becky told King that William would read *Little Red Riding Hood* to him the next evening, and he would add the wolf's voice while she would add the little girl's. "Would you like that?" she asked.

King nodded, and when he looked at a confused William, it startled the apprentice overseer to see what he thought was a slight grin on the large, round face.

"I can't read as you do," he whispered to Becky.

"You can. You've read it three times now, and if you read it to yourself several more times after church on the morrow, you might have it memorized."

"We're not practicing tonight?"

"No. I thought we would take advantage of the clear sky and cool air and sit on the wharf for a few minutes before bedding down."

After the two wished King a blessed night, William followed her to the wharf, and doing as she did, he sat at its edge with his feet hanging inches from the water.

"The river's higher during the spring," Becky said, trying to make small talk as she looked out at the river glistening in the moonlight. "They build the houses out here on short legs in case the water rises above its banks."

"It's on legs? This plantation's house?"

"Many. They're hidden by the siding, and they're the

reason he's able to have that hatch on the floor of the study."

"Has it ever happened, a flood?"

"Twice that I know of, but little damage. Both times were in the early spring before they transplanted the tobacco seedlings."

Then sitting silent while staring out at the water, both struggled with how they might mention the kiss, until Becky said, "It shocked me to see his eye bruised. Is striking someone in the face a habit? Have you practiced it? I ask because it's the second time, that I know of, that you struck someone, and you sent Philpot to the floor."

"No, it's the third time I struck a man in as many months, but the second to the face, and I expect it hurt me more than them. I hurt my wrist each time."

Using the excuse of looking at his wrist to touch him, Becky took his left hand. "I suppose hitting a head would be like hitting a wall."

"I don't know," William said, as he took his hand back. "I never punched a wall. Never been threatened by one, and I'm fortunate Master Philpot remembers nothing of it," and then offering his other hand, he said, "It's this hand... this wrist."

Looking at the reddish, swollen wrist, Becky realized it must have been painful for him to have helped her open the study's door the night of the incident, and gently rubbing it, she asked if it still hurt.

"It's sore to move, but not so much when touched."

"I think, to avoid a repeat of what had happened last Sunday, we shouldn't spend too much time together on Sunday nights... but I thank you again for your help that night."

"You thanked me more than enough with that... that kiss."

Finally, he brings it up!

Becky looked at William for a moment before saying, "That kiss wasn't me thanking you. I may have kissed you after thanking you, but it wasn't for that."

"Then I believe you haven't thanked me enough," William said, and then surprised himself by adding, "I've been thinking of that kiss every moment since it happened."

"You have?"

"I have," he nodded.

"I thought you thought nothing of it… or were ashamed of it."

"I thought you thought nothing of it or were ashamed of it."

"Why didn't you mention it?" she asked.

"Why didn't you mention it?" he asked.

"Because you ignored me every day since we kissed… since I kissed you. Avoided looking at me during the meals."

"I did," he nodded. "But only because I was afraid Oink would notice and mention it near Philpot."

Enlightened and strangely relieved, Becky said, "I thought you were regretting it."

"I thought you were regretting it," he said as he stood up. "I'll only be a moment. I need a rest from you repeating everything I say."

"You're repeating everything I say!" she said, pretending to scold him as he hurried down the wharf to disappear into the darkness near the stable.

After a minute, she was considering following him when she heard his footsteps approaching, and seconds later, after sitting down beside her, he held a white flower up against her face. Not satisfied with it, he dropped it into the water, and then holding up a blue one, he frowned and dropped it too into the water.

"Are you teasing me with flowers?" Becky smiled. "Offering them and then discarding them."

"No. I thought they were pretty, but when I held them up to you, they weren't."

"What!?"

"I'm not insulting you," William smiled. "Your beauty is greater than theirs. I'll have to find a flower that can hold its beauty next to yours and then I'll gift you as many as I can find."

Thinking that they couldn't be any more comfortable with each other than they were at that moment, she asked, "Did you pay for the women today, too?"

Shocked, William had to force himself out of it to ask, "Pay… pay for the women?"

"I only learned of them being rented for what they might be rented for when Mary told me of you paying for them so they wouldn't be rented for… for that."

"Does Master Philpot know?" he asked, worrying that if she discovered he had paid for them, then Philpot might have too.

"No."

"Then yes, I… I paid for them today too."

"Why?"

"Why?" he asked, puzzled.

"Yes, why? Why would you give your sterling to save them from being rented?"

"Because I… I can't rent them for the purpose some want them for. It's not Christian, not right. Even if only a few of the women being rented are being bedded, it's safer if I don't rent any, better if I pay for them myself, so none are at risk of being bedded," he said. "It was a... a different feeling. I felt I had lost part of my soul the first time I rented them with Ben."

Then even more attracted to him, she asked, "How many more weeks can you rent them? I don't expect you to have much sterling... I mean to say with you being an indentured servant."

"I don't, but with what I have and the ten pounds Ben gave me, I expect to be able to pay for them for the rest of this year and a good part of the next. But before then I hope to find more who'll rent the men so there's less room on the cart for the women."

Curious about Ben giving him sterling, which she would never have expected, she took his hand. "You truly are a good man... and perhaps Ben too. And you make me want to do it again, but I'm not going to, not this time."

"Not going to do what?"

"Kiss you. I kissed you and you never mentioned it until now, almost a week later. No, I'm not doing it this time," she said, trying not to smile.

"But I kissed you first."

"You kissed me on the cheek like you would your grandmother, but I kissed you on the lips."

"You're telling me you're *not* going to kiss me?"

"I'm telling you I won't be doing it, won't be kissing you on the lips."

"I should be the one to kiss you? Kiss you on the lips? Because I'm the man? Kiss you like this?" he asked before twisting her to him, and with both closing their eyes, he gently slid his lips over hers, sending a chill up their spines and goosebumps over their arms.

With her heart trying to escape from her chest, Becky

forced herself to pull away and instinctively took a large breath to calm down. "Yes, like… like that. Who taught you to kiss like that?"

"Oscar."

"What?"

With a grin covering his face, William said, "I jest. Yours are the first lips I've touched, ever."

Becky grinned. "Do you still consider them the perfect size?"

"Consider what the perfect size?"

"My lips."

"I suppose, but I never gave lips that sort of thought."

Then realizing what Oink was doing by adding that paragraph about her in his letter, Becky laughed, soft at first and then harder.

"What's so funny? What did I say?" William asked, confused.

Getting control of herself, she continued to smile as she said, "You said we'll have to do it again, kiss again before we part for our chambers."

"No, I didn't."

"You didn't?" Becky asked, feigning disappointment.

"I… yes… yes, I did, and we should hurry because I can't wait a minute more!"

Standing up, he helped her to her feet and pulled her grinning behind him as he hurried to the house where they would have a longer kiss, but not long enough for either of them.

CHAPTER 26
Philpot's Wrath

At a corner table in the half-filled tavern, Philpot sat alone leaning back in his chair with his back to the wall, his mind in deep thought, and his hands wrapped around an almost full quart of beer resting on the top of his large stomach.

"You're early," Robert said as he and Stuart placed their pints on the table. "Much earlier," he added when noticing the three empty quarts in front of the man. "You might want to slow down if you don't want to be as drunk as last week."

Startled, Philpot straightened up in his chair, laid his quart on the table, and hissed, "I say four quarts to me are the same as four pints to you, considering my size!"

"I expect the quarts are the reason for your size," Stuart grinned, causing Robert to laugh. "Why so early?"

"I left the others to walk to church while I went to MacDonald's, but it's been some time since I've been there and forgot he opens later on Sundays. My plan to grab four firkins of oil and be gone has been delayed. If everything went as planned, I would've been back here about now."

Sitting at the table, Stuart took a drink of his beer and wiped his mouth with the sleeve of his shirt. "Then if I were you, I wouldn't allow myself to be too comfortable here. He also closes early on Sundays. Opens in ten and you have but two hours before he closes again."

"I hope you're planning on purchasing oil lanterns from him too," Robert said. "Without those, he might think you were planning to burn something to the ground."

Philpot leaned in. "I plan to do exactly that, burn down everything and everyone," and then straightening up, he nodded, "And I believe you're correct. I shall make oil lanterns the cause of the accident. With them returning to the estate before I, I shall need the lanterns to justify the oil."

As Harry sat down with his pint while cursing the barman, Robert leaned in to look curiously at Philpot. "Who gave you the bruised eye?"

With Harry and Stuart leaning in to get a look at the six-day-old bruise that had lightened but still stood out in the dimly lit room, Philpot said, "The stripling struck me."

"Struck you?" Robert asked.

"Last Sunday night, he had the jump on me. Sent me down, and I say I don't know how they managed to move me to my bed. And the next morning, I had to feign not remembering the strike. Mentioning it would only put the stripling's guard up and perhaps threaten my plans."

"It must o' killed ya to let it go. I'd've expected ya to be askin' us to dig another 'ole," Harry laughed. "If it was me, I would've beaten the devil out o' 'im. That one can't weigh more than seven stone"

Robert cleared his throat. "Let's hear your plan, your plan to burn it to the ground."

"This Friday, we shall burn the whole bloody thing, and with them in it," Philpot said as if boasting. "After we go into

James... Hell Town to celebrate Harry's birth date, they'll retire and sleep so profoundly they won't wake when we return to spread the oil. But before putting a flame to it, we shall load a long cart with all I want to take, and as the plantation burns, we return to Hell Town. If we must, we shall cause a commotion to make certain we're remembered there, and when I return to the estate, I shall be distressed to find my years of work destroyed. Then, with no one alive to harvest the crop, it shall rot on the stalks. The land shall be worth no more than half what it is now. Stuart, you'll take the cart and join us in town after you hide it."

"Hide it where?"

"I'm sure you'll find a safe place. Perhaps hide it at your father's. I'll decide in a couple of weeks where it goes from there."

"You know you'll have no one to harvest yours too," Stuart warned him.

"I do, and it concerns me not at this point. It's earlier than I planned, but I shall retire to Boston to be near my son and daughters. I'll either have an agent rent what I have and be an absentee landlord or have him sell all I have. I'm fine with either, and it's not a decision I need to make today."

"Sons an' daughters? I 'eard they died in a fire," Harry said.

"Son and daughters," Philpot corrected him. "I say it's a rumor. The burning of the house and their not being around afterward caused some to assume the worst. They left weeks before then. After my wife's death, they left to live with my brother and his wife in Boston to be raised and schooled there, and now they're married and still there. They gave me eleven grandchildren, seven I've only seen once. The fire was my doing. Too much drink and too little care with the oil."

"And Becky?" Robert frowned. "Will you take her with you?"

"Becky? No! She's as disloyal as the rest! I expect she's also communicating with Chalmers and shall meet her end too!" Philpot growled before taking a gulp from his mug. "Robert, have your chemist put together enough sleeping powder to put several, let's say six, into a profound sleep. Bring it to me Thursday afternoon at the latest and be discreet. We don't need Becky's eyes and ears picking up on the plan."

"I can do that, and he prefers being called an alchemist. But why only six? You want only to put the English to sleep?"

"I do," Philpot nodded. "The slaves shall be barred in. Shan't be leaving their burning cabins."

"Then why not use an inheritance maker, like nightshade?"

"I need them to bar the cabins while we're seen out. They'll go to bed at their usual time, and as I said, they'll sleep profoundly through the fire. As for your... your alchemist, he can call himself anything he wishes, but if the powder fails its task, he shan't be calling himself anything but dead when we're done with him."

"Why six when there are three?"

"To make sure they ingest enough of it. I shan't be spooning it to them. I shall put it in their... why am I explaining the parts that don't concern you? Enough of the questions! You need only do as I say!"

Robert sighed. "Still doing away with all those souls is not the same as doing away with one, and it'll cost you a thousand pounds for the deed."

Straightening up, Philpot glared at him. "It's three, three English who shall not require holes, and the slaves are merely property and add nothing to the body count. And as for the sterling, I shall give you two hundred. Not for each of you, but divided… since the task takes merely a couple of hours."

"So ya stays for a few weeks, and then be gone?" Stuart asked.

"That's the plan, and it shall do me good to be rid of you three," Philpot smirked. "Harry, fetch me another two quarts and have a pint on my line. I say the company of you three can cause a man to drink himself to death."

"That's what I tells Archibald there," Harry said as he stood up. "'E should be payin' us to drink 'ere."

**

A little after four in the afternoon, the children rushed off to their cabins when a scowling Philpot drove the smaller cart up to the barn to unload four large sealed buckets and two dozen oil lanterns.

Curious, Oink quickly coiled up his whip before he and Gibby joined the man. "What's in the firkins, beer?" he asked.

"No, whale oil. Boy, move those lanterns to the barn and be certain to separate those that hang from those that don't," Philpot ordered. "And where's your brother?"

Curious with the sound of the returning cart, William had closed the book of fairy tales and rushed from his bedroom to join them. "I'm here, Master Philpot."

"Grab the firkins and set the bloody things in the barn!"

As Philpot climbed up onto the cart's bed to slide a large covered bucket to the edge, Oink quickly grabbed two of the ceramic lanterns encased in a square cage of iron.

"Be careful with those! They're as fragile as they are expensive!"

After Oink brought the last of the lanterns into the barn

and William, walking much like Harry Carter, struggled to carry the last firkin in by its wooden handle, Philpot headed toward the house, and a few seconds later, Oink chased after him. "Master Philpot, may I show you my skill with the whip?" he asked, hoping to bring the man out of his poor mood by impressing him.

"The whip?"

"I've developed quite a skill with it," Oink said proudly.

"You have, you say?" he said, stopping at the whipping pole between the kitchen and the house.

"I have," Oink nodded, and after he shouted to William to grab three onions, he said, "William has been helping me master a strike I expect will impress."

While William reluctantly walked to the garden thinking it a bad idea to try to entertain the man who didn't appear to be in the mood for entertainment, an annoyed Philpot seemed to confirm it when he asked, "Onions? Three? Are you planning on juggling and cracking the whip at the same time?"

"That would be impressive, but no, I'm... I'm only going to strike them."

"On the whipping pole as Ben had practiced?"

"No, this is more impressive than that, I believe."

"Well then, I say you've tickled my curiosity."

William returned with three onions, and knowing what Oink wanted him to do, he stood several feet from the two of them.

With Philpot turning to look curiously at the older brother, Oink took a couple of steps back, flicked the whip behind him, and with Gibby sitting at his side, said, "Toss it."

William did as he was told, and with a crack, the onion exploded in the air.

Then as Gibby ran over to eat the pieces of onion, Philpot let loose a loud belly laugh. "I say that was impressive!"

"I can hit the other two too. I never miss when William tosses them as he did, and if I miss, it's his fault," Oink smiled.

"Then instead of watching you do the same thing three times, I say we make it more interesting. William, throw it straight up so it comes down on you."

"I... I haven't... we haven't practiced that, Master Philpot," William said.

"Practice? I say it's only above you rather than away from you. What practice is needed? Throw it above you, lad."

After the brothers exchanged nervous nods with each other and Oink readied the whip, William tossed the onion above him, and after a loud crack and as pieces of onion dropped on his head, William opened his eyes and released the breath he was holding.

Philpot slapped a thigh and laughed again. "Impressive indeed! A foot lower and you would have struck your brother, perhaps scarring his face for the rest of his days. I say that gives me an idea. Let's make it more impressive yet. Lad, place the onion on your head."

Before William could confirm what he had heard the man say, Oink protested, "What!? I can't do that! We never practiced that!"

"Indeed you have," Philpot smirked. "You've practiced it on the spike, and this is only slightly different."

"But if I miss, I'll—"

"Then don't miss!" Philpot growled. "Stripling, I said to place it on your head!"

Believing Oink was practicing the whip, Becky found it strange to hear Philpot's voice when she didn't expect him to return until later that evening. Curious, she left the kitchen to find William standing near the whipping pole while trying to keep an onion from rolling off his head.

Seeing a perplexed Becky looking at him, William offered her a smile but failed to include his eyes with it.

"Oink, strike it, but do keep in mind your brother is standing beneath it," Philpot chuckled.

When William closed his eyes and Oink took several deep breaths before nervously shuffling his feet a little to the left, fear covered Becky's face and she ran over to them. "Master Philpot, is it not reckless to include William in such a dangerous whip trick for only your amusement?"

"Girl, it will do you good to mind your pl—"

"I can do this," Oink said, trying to console her. "If I miss the onion, I'll be certain to miss him too."

Philpot growled, "If you miss, you will do it until you don't! Now strike it!"

Wiping away the sweat sneaking down from under his cap, Oink steadied himself with several more deep breaths, cocked his arm, and with a crack, the onion partially split as it rolled from William's head.

"Impressive!" Philpot laughed. "Now, while I'm in the house for a moment, collect all the boys and girls. All should see this," the man said with a smile covering his face as he walked to the back door.

With anger replacing her relief, Becky didn't have the chance to berate William for allowing Oink to strike the onion from his head. Before she could approach him, the rush of adrenalin had sent him rushing off to collect the slaves.

Minutes later, as Mary, Ann, and King joined Becky near the kitchen, Oink looked curiously about the semicircle of bodies five deep. Spotting Sophie in the group, her terrified expression frightened him.

Returning just as the rest of the slaves joined them, William was taken aback to see Philpot leave the house in his waistcoat of pistols, and doubting that Oink could avoid his head a second time, he asked Philpot if he should pick three more onions.

"No, we shan't be wasting more vegetables. We shall make this a practical exercise," Philpot said, standing at the whipping pole and smirking as his eyes searched the group. "Boy, Devil Child, come here!"

Several women moaned as Thomas stepped out from the group to walk to the whipping pole. Confusing William, Oink, and Becky, he removed his shirt, dropped it on the ground, and turned away from them to reach up and grab hold of its ring.

"Boy, each time you drop your arms, you shall receive an extra lashing."

"You… you want me to whip him?" Oink asked, thinking it couldn't be as it seemed.

"I do, and you shall. You can't consider yourself familiar with a whip until you've drawn blood with it, and I say it's been too long since I reminded them of its bite."

Shocked by the man's words, William fought his way through it to say what Oink was about to. "He's done nothing wrong, nothing that requires being whipped."

Pulled out of her shock by William's words, Becky added, "Master Philpot, you are abusing Lord Chalmers' property."

Philpot turned to her. "Am I? Abusing him, you say? No, my dear, we are about to present the boy with a taste of what he can expect when he breaks the rules of the estate while at the same moment giving Oink a taste of what's expected of him when they do. No, I say there's no abuse, only a quick lesson." Then with King's chest growing noticeably larger with each breath, Philpot watched Becky grab his large hand and whisper something in his ear. "And keep that giant child in line!"

"No, I can't do it! I can't do this!" Oink exclaimed.

"You can't? Indeed you can! Only minutes ago, I witnessed you strike an onion from your brother's head!"

"I can, but… but I won't!"

"That's more accurate. Devil Child, pick up your shirt and join me."

All watched with relief as Thomas turned around, picked up his shirt, and walked over to Philpot, who grabbed him by his thin arm.

"Oink, remove your shirt and grab the ring. William, you shall deliver the lashes."

As Oink took a moment to take in what the man demanded, William said, "I won't. He can strike me. I'll take his place if you feel he must experience whipping someone."

"No, you'll whip me!" Oink said with his voice rising, and then dropping his whip, he began unbuttoning his shirt.

"I won't," William shook his head. "I'm older. I'll take the whipping."

"NO, YOU WON'T!" a shirtless Oink shouted with tears coming down his cheeks as he walked to the pole and grabbed the ring. "THIS IS MY FAULT!"

"NO, ITS NOT! AND YES, I WILL!"

"NO, YOU WON'T!"

"I WILL!" William shouted as he unbuttoned his shirt and walked over to Oink to push him with some force away from the pole.

Laughing as he watched Oink get to his feet, Philpot said, "Oink, whip your brother, or I shall finally send this one to his grave." Tightening his hold on Thomas' arm, he pulled a pistol from his waistcoat and pressed its muzzle against the side of the boy's head, causing a moan from the crowd.

At a loss for words, Becky wiped an eye, gripped King's hand harder, and questioned if her tampering with the pistol's frizzens would work. Then finding her words, she said, "Master Philpot, this has gone too far to be justified!"

"It's more justified now than it was. Both have failed to follow my orders, and I say they're fortunate only one will feel the whip," Philpot said without looking over at her. "Stripling, grab the ring, and, boy, ready your whip."

Shirtless, William grabbed the ring and while waiting for the first strike, he experienced a strange wave of serenity wash over him. Knowing he would be the only one to feel the strike of the whip that day, he didn't fear it. He welcomed it.

Oink turned his head to Philpot, hoping the man would say it was all in jest, but when the man said nothing, Oink's eyes dropped to Thomas, who impressed him by calmly keeping his head up against the muzzle while his dry eyes looked at the ground ahead of him.

With the crowd not making a sound, as if all were holding their breaths, the double click of the pistol's hammer being pulled back forced all to shudder.

"Boy, give the first lash!"

Oink's hand shook as he picked up the whip and he didn't bother fighting back the tears as he flicked it behind him.

"Now!" Philpot ordered.

Oink froze. In his mind, he saw the end of the whip strike William's back and blood rush from the wound. Overwhelmed by the sight, he dropped the whip.

When Philpot hissed, "Pick it up and whip him," King startled Becky by pulling his hand from hers before walking over to William, picking him up by his waist, and moving him away from the pole, and after he unbuttoned and dropped his shirt, he grabbed the ring to revealed his back covered in the raised scars of some two dozen lashes.

Not a sound was heard, not the chirping of birds or the clicking of squirrels, until Philpot broke the silence by saying, "He shall do. William, whip him or cause this boy's death!"

Defeated, William walked over to Oink, picked up the whip, and as Oink took a few steps away from him, he took a step back before sending the whip behind him.

"WHIP HIM!"

As William took in a large breath and lifted his arm, Oink, Becky and the slaves turned their heads away just before the end of the whip cracked an inch short of King's back.

"Too short," Philpot said through his laughing at the group looking away. "We shall blame it on the boy's whip being shorter than you're used to. Close the distance and try again. And, you lot, stop looking away or each one of you shall feel the whip if it takes the rest of the day and the three of us to perform the task! Watch, I say!"

With his desperate plan failing, William reluctantly moved several inches closer to King, and as all closed their eyes, he swung the whip with much less force than he had practiced with, causing it to just slap King's back.

"Boy, you will whip him as expected. We shall hear it crack! WHIP HIM AGAIN!" Philpot yelled.

"Whip him again," King parroted, confusing the brothers.

Oink, Becky, and the slaves again closed their eyes just

before the whip cracked, and not hearing a scream, they opened them to what they assumed was another miss but instead saw a fresh three-inch gash on the giant's back.

"Again!" Philpot ordered.

"Again," King parroted.

With wet eyes, William again struck King, who again gave no reaction to the strike.

Lowering the hammer and sliding the pistol back into his waistcoat, Philpot released Thomas' arm, and as the boy remained standing where he was, the man yelled, "AGAIN!"

"AGAIN!" King parroted.

William struck him again.

"Again," King said.

Wiping away his tears, William struck him again.

"Again," King repeated.

William struck him again.

"Another!" Philpot ordered.

"Another," King parroted.

Then, with his arm shaking uncontrollably, William missed King's back.

Moaning, the giant grabbed the back of his head and dropped to his knees.

"Boy, you want to strike his back, not his head!" Philpot barked and then shaking his head, he added, "I say this shall do for now."

As King stood up dazed, William dropped the whip and walked to the back door.

"Where are you going, stripling?" Philpot hissed.

"To my chamber."

"So be it. Now back to your chores, all of you!"

William dropped himself onto his bed, wiped his eyes, looked up at the ceiling, and wondered if that was the worst of it, and if not, how could it possibly be any worse? And just as he was reminding himself that King had taken the lashings for him, a red-eyed Oink entered the room to lie down on Ben's bed.

"My apologies."

"You have no reason to apologize," William whispered.

"It would never have happened if I didn't try to impress him."

"We don't know that. If not today, it could've happened on the morrow, and if not, then the day after that or the day after that. The worst anyone could blame you for is hastening the inevitable, but not causing it."

"Perhaps, but I still feel it's my fault," Oink said as he stood up from the bed and left the room.

While the older Lovely was reflecting on King taking each strike of the whip on his back as if it was nothing more than a mosquito bite, Oink returned with a small pile of clothes. Dropping them on the floor, he opened an empty dresser drawer. "I'm still surprised King took your place at the pole. I never expected that. I assumed because he doesn't speak well, he doesn't think well, but he had to have known what he was doing when he offered his back for yours."

"I was thinking the same thing, and I don't know how I can repay the act," William said as he struggled to fight back the swelling behind his eyes while watching his brother carelessly shove clothes into two dresser drawers before hanging the rest in the wardrobe. "I-I left your whip on the ground."

"The ground can have it. I don't want it with King's blood

on it," Oink said as he rested on Ben's bed and looked up at the ceiling. "Did you finally kiss her?"

William took a moment to consider whether he should lie to his brother, and deciding against it, he said, "I did, but it's for naught. I expect she'll not look at me again after today."

"I thought you did. I see the way she looks at you when you're not looking, which is almost always, and her looking at you today didn't say she blames you for striking King. She looked as if she was feeling your pain just as she was feeling King's."

Changing the subject, William asked, "Should you bring your chamber pot? No one's going to use it over there."

"No, it's full."

"Of course it is. I wonder who filled it."

"Can't be certain, but I expect Philpot's been visiting my room to use it."

Where William would normally have smiled at Oink's joke, he didn't. "Wouldn't be the worst he's done."

"No, it wouldn't, and I don't think this is something we'll include in our next letter." Then noticing the book on the table between the beds, the boy asked, "Is that what you're reading, practicing reading?"

"It is. It's a book of fairy tales. Some of them are horrifying," William said before a thought came to him on how they might distract their minds from the whipping. "Would you like me to show you how well I read?"

"You want to read me a fairy tale?"

"It may take your mind off what has happened. Have you heard of *Little Red Riding Hood*?"

"No," Oink smirked. "Have you?"

"It'll be my first time reading it," William lied.

Wanting to console William, Becky didn't see Oink in his room as she passed its opened door, and as she approached William's, she heard him reading *Little Red Riding Hood*. Stopping near his bedroom door, she formed a faint smile when he made a low voice for the wolf and then a funny high-pitched one for the little girl, and her smile grew slightly when he ended the story with the grandmother's house slave chasing away the wolf who then boarded a ship to England.

**

Still wearing his waistcoat of pistols, Philpot was sitting alone at the dining room table when Becky, who had spent the remainder of the afternoon tending to King's wounds, entered with two bowls of pork stew.

"Did you taste it?"

"I did," she lied.

"Where are the brothers?"

"In their rooms. I expect neither feels the need to eat after what you forced upon them."

"I forced them to do their task… or one of them to do his task, and I say they shall eat tonight and they shall eat here. I can't have them performing their duties on the morrow tired because they missed this meal," he growled, and then forcing a smile, he softened his tone. "Do collect them so we may eat together."

Minutes later, after Becky suggested it would be best for all if they joined the man at the table, a reluctant Oink and William sat down with Philpot who was eating his stew, and without exchanging greetings with the man, both waited for Becky, who entered a minute later and after setting out their stews and cups of cider, sat down and ate with them.

Ten minutes later Philpot wiped his mouth, and as the three continued slowly eating, he said, "I won't apologize for my actions. It was what was needed to have you… force you to experience the worst of your tasks, the whippings. There's a reason you have the whip, but there shall be few formal whippings over the next seven years, far fewer than were necessary when I began overseeing this estate, but I say a reminder does some good for all… and your whip is on the chair next to William. Take it with you when you retire for the evening." Watching Oink lay his spoon in his half-empty bowl and stare down at it, he asked, "Why so melancholic? The giant lives and he barely noticed the strikes. I expect the past whippings have numbed his flesh."

"I feel bad for him, but I'm worried about Gibby," Oink said, continuing to look at the bowl, "He's run off. I couldn't find him after the… the… and I forgot to put him back in the pigsty."

"Run off? No, he's in front of you," Philpot said before smiling at the three's enlarged eyes.

"I-I ate Gibby?" Oink asked, his voice cracking as his face went pale.

"We all did," Philpot continued to grin.

The dizzy sensation Oink was experiencing left as fast as it came, and with his face burning a dark red, he stood up and rushed from the room.

"Boy, I didn't say you could leave! You shall eat your pudding at this table!"

Without a word, Becky and William left the room too.

"You two can take the dishes with you," Philpot laughed.

Startling Mary and Ann as they wiped down the kitchen table, Oink rushed in with tears running down his cheeks and grabbed a shielded knife from the counter, and as he spun around to leave, Mary asked, "Master Lovely, I have to ask what you intend to do with that."

The woman's calm voice forced him to stop and turn around. "I'm going to kill the bloody bobolyne!"

"And how do you intend to commit such an act with *that* knife?" she asked as Becky and William arrived at the kitchen door.

Realizing his error, he looked at the knife and whispered, "He… he killed Gibby… my Gibby."

"No, he didn't. Master Philpot ordered us to use him for the stew and to salt the rest, but we did neither. We all know he's your friend," Mary said, and looking at the three confused faces, she added, "We've hidden him in the last curing barn, but I have to say I'm not sure where we'll hide him during the harvest, but I have more than a few weeks to decide on that."

"You saved Gibby?" he asked, wiping his eyes.

"*We* did," she corrected him before the boy startled her with a hug.

Releasing her, he gave her a puzzled look. "Why not tell me before now?"

"If we did, you wouldn't have reacted as you did and the master would know of our deception. There would be more whippings, and Gibby would not be so fortunate."

Taking a moment to consider her words, he smiled and said, "I thank you, Mistress Mary."

"You are welcome, Master Lovely… Oink. But I have to ask you not to carry that smile into the house. It'll announce our actions… our inactions."

Oink was about to say he wouldn't when Ann approached and held out a bowl of rice pudding to him.

"I thank you, but I'm to eat at the table."

Mary smiled. "It's the master's pudding, and she wants you to spit in it."

Then with William just as taken aback as him, Oink said, "I don't understand."

"It'll make you feel better, better than when you thought we cooked Gibby," Mary said before explaining their daily draws for the opportunity to spit in the man's meal, which enlightened Oink to the brief appearances of the various faces at the window during their meals.

After all five had spat into the pudding and Becky placed it and three others on a tray, Oink reminded her not to forget which was Philpot's, and with the three about to leave, Mary asked them to wait a moment before she searched through a tin bucket of vegetable scraps, found a few pieces of onion, and told them to close their eyes. Squeezing the pieces and rubbing the juice over their eyelids and cheeks, she said, "We can't have you three returning with dry eyes."

Walking down the hall with their eyes watering, Becky and William had to hold back their laughs when Oink whispered, "On the morrow, we should pee in his soup," and when the three entered the room with nearly the same expressions they wore when they left it, Philpot told them the pudding would put smiles on their faces, and he would've been correct if all three didn't force them back when he took the first spoonful of his five-spit pudding.

**

Becky, William, and Oink entered King's cabin to find him face down on his bed, topless and with light-brown mud covering his back's several opened gashes, and then when William took the burning candle and leaned in for a closer look at the gash at the back of King's head, he cringed at the size of the mud-covered wound made prominent by the area around it being shaved clean.

"King," Becky called to him.

With no answer from the sleeping man, Oink asked about the mud, and after Becky told him that the women used a special mixture of bark and herbs to help reduce the chances of blood poisoning, William suggested they stay for at least an hour in case he woke. "I need to apologize to him. I need him to know I didn't want to do what I did."

Becky sat down on the dirt floor with William, took his hand, and said, "He knows you didn't, and I'm certain he offered his back because he didn't want anyone being whipped… especially not you."

Then feeling like the third wheel on a two-wheeled cart, Oink left the two and went to the farthest curing barn where inside its huge open space was a bucket of water, a bucket of dried corn, a small area covered in hay, and an excited pig running toward him.

That late at night there was little to do with Gibby but walk around in the dark, and after half an hour of that and feeling bad for the pig confined to the building, it comforted Oink when he realized he didn't have to be constantly confined to it. When Philpot left the estate the next morning with William, he could let him out until the midday meal, when he joined William in the field.

On his way back to the house, Oink peeked into King's cabin to find Becky and William sitting shoulder to shoulder, holding hands, and asleep. Believing they were together because of his letter's extra paragraph, he smiled proudly and left them to wake on their own.

CHAPTER 27
Philpot's Wrath... Again

When Oink and William returned from the field the next evening, the smell of burning whale oil reminded them of home. Candles still burned in the iron chandeliers, but oil lanterns had replaced the candle lanterns hanging from the walls of the house, and they would later learn that oil lanterns were also placed in the cabins.

Preferring to go hungry rather than eat with the man, Becky and the brothers forced themselves to sit down at the table with Philpot who talked throughout the meal and continued for some thirty minutes after it as if nothing had happened the day before, making Oink, who couldn't imagine spending the next seven years with him, wish they were back on *The Colonist*.

While Philpot snored behind his barred bedroom door, William and Becky sat in King's cabin giving voices to the characters as they reread *Little Red Riding Hood* to King, who was forced to work the field as his wounds healed, and with Becky deciding they would reread the same book of fairy tales to him until William had almost memorized them, each night after his reading, she had him practice his spelling with the small chalkboard she had used with Beth.

The spelling practices went slowly. Both had a difficult time focusing on them through their need to touch and trade short kisses and their greater need to talk, sometimes cutting the practice short to share moments of their pasts, compare their opinions on whatever came to mind (including their agreeing on slaves having souls) and discuss their life's goals and expectations, but neither was ready to mention how they saw the other in them. Once, William had asked Becky about Peter, and when she tried to tell him through her cracking voice and wet eyes how she had met him, they ended up sharing a long hug that William felt guilty for appreciating since Becky paid the emotional cost of it.

While William and Becky spent time together, Oink released Gibby from the curing barn and, in the light of an oil lantern, played fetch with a roll of bread that Ann had purposely overbaked for the occasion.

**

That Friday afternoon, as Mary and Becky were chopping the last of the stew's vegetables and Ann was forming mounds of dough, the light in the room dimmed, and when the women looked toward the open door to find the reason for it, all froze at the sight of the large man's silhouette.

"Becky, I'm in the mind for a change and would like my chamber's furniture moved to their opposite walls."

With it being the first time she saw the man in what she considered her sanctuary, Becky nervously placed her shielded knife on the table and wiped her hands on her apron. "I'll have your furniture moved before you return and please pass on to Harry my wish for him to have a safe birth date celebration."

"I shall tell him, but I want it moved now so I may approve of it before I leave. I would rather not risk being disappointed with the rearrangement when I return. Mary and Ann may help you with the task," he said as he walked in to look down at the large pot of stew and the small pot of soup hanging over the wide fire. "And I believe the meal can be left alone for the short time it takes, yes? It shouldn't take more than twenty minutes, I say. Also, I plan to give my older clothes to charity, so I'll need five sacks, or perhaps ten, left in the room. I may not sort through them on the morrow, but I would prefer the sacks ready for when I do."

Hiding her annoyance with his immediate need and her confusion with him giving something to charity, Becky forced a smile and a nod, and after Philpot stepped aside, Mary and Ann removed the two pots from the fire and stirred them before following her out of the kitchen.

Taking the shutting of the back door as his signal, Philpot pulled a leather pouch from his trousers' pocket and poured the light-green, almost tasteless powder into the smaller pot of bean soup. Stirring it in, he was satisfied when the soup's color changed only slightly.

In the house, the sounds above made him confident he wouldn't be disturbed, and with a spade in hand, he made his way down the hall to his study, where he unbolted and opened the hatch to step down and dig in the dirt. Finding a small chest, he shook the loose dirt from it and struggled to step out of the hatch to place it on his desk. After pulling out a ring of keys from the pocket of his trousers, he unlocked the chest to find a twelve-pound sack of coins. Unlocking the desk's deeper drawer, he pulled it out and dropped the sack onto an assortment of small items, including an eye patch and a leather-corded lead cross. No longer hearing furniture being moved about, he closed the drawer, locked it, and after throwing the spade into the hatch, closed it and left the study, giving no thought to the empty chest resting on his desk.

**

In only his trousers and with his stomach warm and his head feeling light, as if he had just drunk rum with Captain Humphreys, and strangely much more tired than he normally would be at that hour, Oink left the curing barn and almost dropped the oil lantern when he stumbled. Fearing he might stumble again and cause a fire, he lowered the lantern's burning cord until the flame died, and then only using the light from the three-quarter moon, he made his way to King's cabin, where in the light of its lantern, he found William and Becky sitting on its dirt floor sleeping shoulder to shoulder while King snored in his bed. Quietly closing its door, he stumbled twice on the short walk to the house, where he found the stairs to the second floor difficult to climb. Dropping onto his bed, he was snoring almost immediately.

Almost two hours later, the four rode up to the stable and after placing their horses in the stalls, they stood outside as Philpot unbuttoned his waistcoat of six pistols. "I say tonight is a good night for it. Clear and by that moon, it's not as dark as it could be, but even so, you two shall require a lantern to harness the horses to the cart. Come and take one from the house," he whispered. "Harry, you shall find the four firkins in the barn there. It's unlocked and I've loosened their tops. Use the ladle I placed with them to splash the walls of the curing barns, and from there, splash the barn, cabins, and sheds, in that order. And when you're finished, pour oil about the house, inside and out."

"Why does I 'ave to spread 'er?"

"Lower your voice! We need not wake the slaves!" Philpot hissed.

"And what o' me lantern?"

"You don't want one when handling the oil and don't need one to see the wall you're splashing. Now, while you three do as I said, I'll gather my clothes and bedding. Stuart and Robert, when you have the cart ready, bring it to the side of the house and move everything from my chamber and the study onto it, and take the long guns from behind the bookshelves in my study. When we're ready to burn the place, we'll take the horses we rode in on. Hence why you don't wet the stable with oil, Harry. It'll catch a flame well enough on its own when we're gone. And, Stuart, tie your horse to the cart and join us after you hide it."

William woke to a rough shake and King saying, "Here master. Go you." Groggy, it took a moment for his eyes to adjust to the dim light of the thirsty lantern's low flame, took a moment for him to realize he was in King's cabin, and took another to realize King was standing over him telling him Philpot had returned. Then realizing Becky had fallen asleep next to him, he gently shook her on the shoulder, and not getting a response, he shook her harder.

Her head lifted. Her eyes opened slightly, and she mumbled, "Blessed morning."

"I don't believe it's past midnight, or if it is, it's not long past it," he said, feeling like he and Philpot had shared rum again, but much more of it.

"Here master. You go."

After nodding his understanding to King, he was about to ask Becky if she had closed her bedroom door, but then realizing she always did, he relaxed… until it occurred to him that the man might visit her bedroom for a *kissy*. As he was about to tell her they had to hurry back, she closed her eyes and dropped her head. With another shake, she opened them to see King's knees. Looking around, she realized where she was, who she was with, and that her head hurt. "We fell asleep?"

"Yes," he said, getting to his feet, pulling her to hers, and leaning her up against the wall. "And Philpot's back."

As Becky's sudden panic helped her to wake up, William opened the cabin door and peeked out. Pulling his head back in, he said, "He's… he's attaching horses to a cart, a long one, and four are harnessed now… or maybe he's putting them in the stable."

Becky looked out of the small window to the right of the door. "I don't remember him leaving with a cart." Squeezing her eyes closed and rubbing them with her fingers, she looked out again. "I thought he left on horseback."

William peeked out past the door toward the footsteps near the barred cabins and saw a dark figure a few cabins down struggling to carry something. Pulling his head back, he said, "I think I saw a man with one of the four firkins Philpot brought back on Sunday. Stay here. I'll be only a minute."

Gone before she could tell him to be careful, each second of waiting caused her anxious state to grow until she decided she had waited long enough and almost bumped into him when he rushed in and closed the door.

"It's not Philpot. Two men are harnessing the horses, and Harry, the man I struck in Williamsburg, is splashing oil on the cabins," William said through his panic while struggling to keep his voice down to a whisper. "By his walk, it must be him and must be oil. If he's planning to set fire to the cabins, they must be stealing the cart and horses."

"The Carter brothers?"

"I-I only know of Harry by his walk," he said. "You should wait with King while I inform Philpot, and it's probably better to come out after they've left, so it appears you joined us from your chamber." He was about to open the door when he stopped. "Or should we confront them and put an end to it now?"

Becky took a moment to consider his question. "If they're intending to burn the cabins and those inside them, I don't expect them to stop because we asked them to. No, I believe informing Philpot is better, and when we confront them, we should do it with the long guns from the study."

"Then I'll inform Philpot."

After grabbing him, kissing him, and telling him to be careful, she watched him leave, and several seconds later, struggled against joining him.

With his heart racing, William crept from shed to shed until stopping to hide in a shed's moonlight shadow, where he watched Harry struggle to move the barrel to the next cabin in the row, set it down, scoop out oil, and carelessly splash it over the walls. When the man moved on to the back row of cabins, William crept to the back door and into the house, and not wanting to risk waking Oink and involving him, he tried to reduce the creaking of the steps by taking each one slowly.

Looking into Philpot's bedroom lit by the light of an oil lantern resting on the dresser, William saw the man with his back to him and was about to inform him of the Carters' actions when he was confused by the sight of a half dozen bulging sacks on the floor, the naked bed with its tick folded over, several piles of neatly folded clothes resting on the tick, and the large man in his waistcoat of pistols stuffing a sack with clothes. Then believing that the man's actions were connected to the stealing of the cart and the oil being splashed on the cabins, he was about to return to Becky when the snoring coming from his bedroom reminded him that Oink was in the house.

Creeping into their bedroom, he quietly closed the door, kneeled next to Oink's bed, placed his hand over the boy's mouth, and shook him. After several shakes, each rougher than the next, the boy tried to mumble something, and when he realized he couldn't, he woke in the darkness with wide, confused eyes and grabbed at the hand. With the hand pressing harder over his mouth, Oink panicked more until William whispered in his ear to calm down and told him all that he had just seen. Removing his hand from his brother's mouth, he had to put it back when Oink tried to speak. "Shhh! He's in his room packing his clothes!" William whispered. "We'll decide what to do when we're outside. Nod if you understand."

Oink nodded, and with his eyes adjusting to the darkness, he got up from his bed, and curious about what his brother was doing, watched him place the clothes from their wardrobe under their bedsheets. When he was finished, the older brother looked at his work and decided to add more from the dresser to those under Oink's sheet, which would have offended the boy if he were fully awake.

The footsteps coming down the hall forced him to pull Oink to the hinged side of the door, and hearing the double click of a pistol's hammer being pulled back, he placed his hand over the boy's mouth. With their hearts beating hard, the door opened and a few seconds later, it closed, and with the footsteps fading down the hall, William took a deep breath as he removed his hand from Oink's mouth. "We'll wait a moment before leaving," he said, not wanting to admit he needed to calm down.

A minute later, William took the soft banging of Philpot striking the bed's side rails from the slots and dowels connecting them to the footboard as their opportunity to leave without being noticed, and just as they were, footsteps on the creaking stairs forced them back in.

Sweating, Philpot laid the footboard on the floor and waited for the heavy footsteps to reach the top of the stairs.

"Where do you want us to start?" Robert whispered from the entrance of Philpot's bedroom.

Philpot wiped his forehead with his hand before turning around and whispering, "The study, and as I said, the desk, clock, and the guns behind the bookshelves are coming with us. You shall have to remove the desk's top from its pedestals of drawers to fit it through the door. It's held on with dowels. Force it off, but watch the noise so as not to wake the girl... and I say be mindful of the lever beneath the desk. Hit it and our plan is ruined... and you shan't see your sterling."

After Robert descended the stairs and while Philpot struggled to beat the rails from the headboard, William removed his shoes and stockings, whispered to Oink that they should step with each of Philpot's bangs, and was annoyed by the boy stuffing his coiled whip into the waste of his trousers. Closing the bedroom door behind them, they quietly passed Philpot's door, where Oink stopped to watch the man with his back to them disassemble the last of the bed. Curious about how the bed was put together, he was trying to figure out how he could get a closer look at how the sideboards fit into the headboard when William pulled him along, whispering that they would have to take the stairs slowly. At the bottom of the stairs and with more light banging coming from the study down the hall, the two hurried out the back door.

Worrying for William and feeling useless waiting with King, Becky worried more when she heard the cart roll away. Telling King to stay in the cabin, she opened the door and peeked out before leaving. From the sheds, she saw between the first row of cabins a figure moving awkwardly among those of the second row, and after the two Carter brothers parked the cart at the side of the house, whispered between themselves for a few seconds and then headed toward the back door, she moved across to the first row of cabins for a better look at the figure then easily carrying a bucket while moving awkwardly to the next cabin, watched him use a ladle gleaming in the moonlight to splash oil against the side of it, and after hobbling around it to splash its other logged walls, he went to the next cabin where he raised the bucket to pour the last of its oil against the front wall. Dropping the bucket, he walked towards the barn and returned a couple of minutes later struggling with a full firkin. As he carried it to the side of a cabin, Becky was pondering what she should do when her mind jumped to what she could do and she crept off to King's cabin.

Deciding not to waste time on words, she took King by the hand and led him out of the cabin, and a minute later both returned with King easily carrying the last firkin of whale oil with only one hand. She took a moment to try to calm down, but unable to, left again to check on Harry, who was splashing oil around the pigsty and laughing when he splashed it on the pigs. Expecting him to be at King's cabin in only a few minutes, she returned to it and again led the giant out by his hand. After barring its door, she led him beyond the cabins and the slaves' privies to the far end of the slaves' unmarked graveyard near the edge of the tree line, where she whispered above her furiously beating heart for him to stay hidden in the woods until she came back. Walking away, his footsteps forced her to turn around, and before she could tell him again to wait in the woods, he said, "Come me."

"Stay here where it's safer."

The giant shook his head. "Come me."

Not sure how she could convince him to stay, she said, "Then you must stay close to me and do as I do."

After nodding he would, King followed her to the nearest cabin in the second row where she removed the beam blocking its door, opened it, and was silently greeted by two adults curious about what was happening outside. With the couple creeping towards the graveyard with their four children, she barred their door and unbarred the door of the next cabin. At the fifth cabin, she made its occupants freeze at its door when she heard Harry's footsteps beyond the first row of cabins, and when hearing him enter the barn, she had them run toward the graveyard.

Seconds after emptying the cabins in the second row, she heard Harry complaining loudly to himself about there being no more oil, and with her hard breathing and racing heart refusing to take a rest, she peeked around the back of a cabin in the first row to watch him hobble toward the house.

Minutes later, as she and King were about to empty the front row of cabins, Harry, with a lantern in hand, was again heading toward the barn. "Look again, I says!" he mimicked Philpot. "I looked a'ready! But no, I 'ave to look again!"

As she waited anxiously for him to return to the house, a hand was on her shoulder, and before she could scream, another was over her mouth.

"It's us," William whispered before taking his hand away and noticing King standing in a shadow.

After Becky had taken a moment to calm down and after she told them through a whisper that she and King had sent the slaves from the second row of cabins into the woods beyond the graveyard and that they had hidden the last firkin of oil in King's cabin, William told her about seeing Philpot packing his clothes and taking apart his bed. Then with all knowing that the Carters and Philpot were working together, they anxiously watched as Harry passed them on his way to the cart where his brothers placed one of the desk's pedestals of drawers on its bed.

Creeping to the corner of the cabin, William peeked out to see the overseer join the brothers.

"It takes two of you to carry that?" Philpot hissed as he placed four bulging sacks on the cart. "I'm thinking you're going to need the three of us to carry its top!"

"It's no good exerting ourselves after drinking as much as we have, more so when it took all we had to quietly remove its top," Robert whispered. "We don't want to return sweating more than we should. It might cause questions."

"Not there, I tells ya," Harry said, hobbling to the cart with the lantern in his hand. "There ain't no more firkin's in the barn, I tells ya. None there, there ain't."

"There were four when I left this evening, four," Philpot growled. "It's somewhere on the grounds… or perhaps Becky left it in the house after filling the lanterns. Go check the house."

After Philpot and the Carters entered the house, the four rushed to release the last of the slaves from the first row of cabins.

When Philpot climbed the stairs, Harry turned down the hall to check the bathroom and then the dining room where the short candles in the chandelier continued to burn. After checking the empty room next to Becky's, he opened her bedroom door to find the firkin wasn't there... and neither was she.

Meeting Philpot coming down the stairs with more stuffed sacks, Harry told him the firkin wasn't there. "And Becky ain't too."

"What?"

"'Er bed's empty."

"The bloody hell it is," Philpot hissed as he dropped the sacks, took Harry's lantern, and left him standing there as he checked for himself. Seconds later, he returned. "Out of my way!" he ordered before climbing the stairs.

As Robert and Stuart passed with the top of the desk, Stuart asked, "What's the problem?"

"Becky's not in 'er bed. Never was from the looks of 'er."

"Probably not here," Robert said as he gestured to Stuart to keep moving. "Changes nothing except she too will find the place in ashes."

Peeking into the brothers' room and content with seeing both in their beds, Philpot was about to close their door when a thought came to him. Entering the dark room, he walked over to Oink, who should've been snoring, poked him with his finger, and finding it too soft even for the chubby boy, pulled the sheet away to reveal a pile of clothes spread out on the bed. Pulling William's sheet away, he found the same thing and tried to make sense of it.

With Robert and Stuart carrying out the pendulum clock, Philpot joined Harry waiting downstairs, and not wanting to distract the Carters from their tasks, said, "The brothers are sleeping, and I forgot Becky was visiting friends. She shan't burn up, but she shall find herself without a position and only the clothes on her back. Harry, I'm going to find the fourth firkin. Be useful and start clearing out my chamber. Your brothers will be up there soon enough to help with the armoire and the dresser."

As Harry slowly headed up the stairs, placing both feet on a step before taking the next, Philpot ignored the sacks on the floor and headed to the barn while listening for any sounds besides the Carters'. Not hearing any, he entered the barn and took a quick look around. Not seeing the firkin, he pulled a pistol from his waistcoat, pulled back its hammer, and left to search the sheds in the hope of finding the oil, Becky, and the Lovelys.

Hiding behind the cabin in the middle of the first row, Oink pulled his head away from the corner to whisper, "He's looking for us! He has a pistol in his hand!"

William shook his head. "That makes no sense. If they knew we were out of the house, they would all be looking for us."

"Does any of this make sense?" Oink asked.

Wanting to see what Oink was seeing, Becky peeked around the corner. "I don't know what to make of it, but the pistol might not do him any good if it's from his waistcoat. I coated the... the... whatever they call those things that the hammer strikes. I coated them with wax the night he discharged one at you, but I can't be certain it'll stop all from discharging on the first try."

With William impressed and Oink wondering when Philpot had fired a pistol at William, Becky moved out of Oink's way so he could again peek around the corner.

"What's he doing now?" William asked.

"I don't know. He headed to a shed. I can only see a little light from his lantern, but I think he's checking them."

Hearing the sheds' doors opening and closing, the three crept to the back of the last cabin in the front row to watch Philpot make his way to the curing barns.

"He's going to find Gibby!" Oink whispered in panic, and then with William grabbing his arm to hold him back from going to the pig, he whispered, "Let me go! I can go around the back and let him out!"

Becky whispered, "It's too late for that. He'll hear you coming."

A few minutes later, as they waited anxiously for Philpot to return, Oink gasped at seeing him walking Gibby by a rope toward the three Carter brothers waiting at the cart.

Then understanding why the boy hadn't grieved for his pet after the night he had learned they had eaten him, Philpot laid his lantern on the bed of the cart and said, "Harry, hand me your blade."

Curious about what the man with the pig was going to do, Harry unsheathed his knife and handed it to him.

"Remind me later to show you how to hand a knife to someone you're not trying to stab," Philpot growled, not caring that his voice rose. Kneeling, he grabbed Gibby by the scruff of his neck, causing him to squeal and try to shake off the grip. "Robert, it seems your chemist's powder did nothing. The three are out there watching us now."

"Ya saids they's in bed."

"I said that so they wouldn't know we knew they were out there, and now we have a hostage who shall make them come to us rather than us going to them, or one will and the others will follow."

"This ruins our plans," Robert said, frustrated.

"It ruins nothing, and there's little change to the plan. Merely a brief delay. First we find them and then we decide what to do with them," Philpot hissed, and then raising his hand to show the blade of the knife gleaming by the light of the lantern, he raised his voice to say, "Oink, I know you're out here. I only want the oil. What happens to you three concerns me not. The four of us shall find the last of the oil, *but* if you save us the bother of looking, I shall let your pig live. If you don't, I shall kill it. I promise no harm shall come to him or you if you come out and tell us where it is."

"Ya think he'll come?" Harry asked.

"You have until I count to five. ONE!"

Oink looked at Becky, who shook her head.
TWO!
After looking at William, who shook his head and again

grabbed his arm, Oink struggled to decide what to do, and when William winced at the pain of the kick to his shin, the boy pulled his arm from the weakened grip.

THREE!

Rushing toward the cart while making sure his whip was still snug in the waist of his trousers, Oink shouted, "DON'T HURT HIM! I'M HERE!"

When the topless and shoeless boy joined the four at the cart, the grinning man released Gibby and stood up to grab Oink by his arm. "Where's your brother and Becky?" he demanded as Gibby rubbed his ear against Oink's leg.

"Who?"

"Don't play this game with me, boy!"

"They left… went to find help."

"No, they didn't! I know the stripling well enough to know he would send you rather than leave you here, so I'll ask again, where are they?"

"Who?"

"You insist on trying my patience, do you?" he said before handing the knife back to a smiling Harry, pulling a pistol from his waistcoat, and pulling back its hammer. "Where's your brother and where's the oil, the missing firkin?"

"What oil?"

Philpot pointed the pistol at Gibby's head. "Where is it?"

"You said you wouldn't hurt him!"

"I said I wouldn't hurt him if you told me where you hid the oil, and you haven't done that."

"It's… it's… GIBBY, RUN!" Oink yelled as he kicked the animal's behind.

Gibby took a few steps forward, stopped, and looked back

at Oink, as if confused, and as two short whistles caused him to turn his head toward the cabins, the pistol's slamming hammer failed to cause a spark.

"GIBBY, RUN!"

When a frustrated Philpot shook his pistol and pulled back its hammer again, two more short whistles caused Gibby to run toward the cabins, dragging the short rope behind him. As he disappeared behind the cabins, the pistol failed to fire again, and believing it was the one fired two Sundays back and never reloaded, Philpot cursed and threw it to the ground.

"And now we know where his brother is," Stuart grinned. "Behind those cabins there. The first row of them."

"Of course they are! That's where the boy came from!" Philpot growled. "Harry, go make a torch for when we're ready to burn the place to the ground. We shall go forward with our plans while dealing with the three."

"Why nots go after'em?" Harry asked.

"It'll do no good chasing them in the dark! Now go make that torch!"

"Make a torch?"

"Yes, a torch. I say it'll be faster to set each aflame with a torch rather than a candle."

"'Ow?"

"How what?"

"'Ow does I make one?"

"I say your generation doesn't know the simplest of things! Been spoiled by the easy life! Wrap the top of a pole with a grain sack and cover it in oil. A grain sack... a corn sack, not a flour sack. It's a different cloth. You'll find a pile of empty ones in the barn."

"But we don't 'ave no oil for it."

"You can use the oil from a lantern in the house. And once you've done that, empty each of its lanterns onto the floor. We shall do without that last Firkin. And, Stuart, take the boy and hold him over there by the pigsty so his brother may see him, and if he tries to escape, cut his throat."

With Stuart grabbing Oink roughly by his hair, Harry grinned and kicked him in the groin, causing Oink to moan and drop to his knees. "'Ow's that feels?"

Laughing, Stuart lifted Oink to his feet by his hair, pulled him over to the pigsty, pulled out his knife, and put it against his neck, terrifying the boy who struggled to maintain a brave face through the pain of being pulled by his hair and kicked in his groin.

Alone with King and unable to come up with a way to stop Philpot from doing what he intended to do, William could only hope they would release Oink before setting fire to the plantation.

As he watched Harry pass the cabins on his way to the barn, Becky joined him and placed her hand in his, calming him slightly. "Mary's minding Gibby," she said, trying to sound calm. "Do we have a plan?"

"I... I have nothing. We can't pass them to grab the pistols in my chamber, though only one is charged. The shorter brother, not Harry, is keeping Oink there with what looks like a... a knife, and Harry just went to the barn, but I don't know what for," he said, defeated.

Philpot yelled, "William, Becky, if you don't come out, Stuart shall kill Oink there. I don't want to hurt him... or you, but I don't want any interference with my plans." Turning to

Robert standing next to him by the cart, he whispered, "Make certain the long guns are close. There should be six there from the study," and with Robert doing as he was told, Philpot yelled, "You have to the count of five to join us or the boy dies. ONE!"

"I'll go," William said. "You and King join the others."

TWO!

"No, we'll go together," Becky told him. "King, go the others."

THREE!

"Come me," the giant said.

"We're coming," Becky yelled as they walked out from beyond the shadow of the cabin.

Philpot smirked when he saw Becky holding William and King's hands as they walked toward him, and he smiled when he saw Harry following behind them carrying a spade with a sack wrapped around the top of its shaft. "Robert, the giant is with them. Ready yourself with a long gun," he whispered before saying to the three, "Stand out of our way. Stand with Oink by the pigsty there, and we'll release him when we're finished."

"Let him go now!" William demanded while doing as they were told.

"I shall permit him to go when I permit you to go."

"Then tell this man to remove the knife from his neck."

"When we're finished. Until then, it would be best to do as I say or he shall use it."

"Why are you doing this?"

"Why? I expect you know our Lord Chalmers plans to

remove me from my position and take my years of work, but after this night, he can't take what isn't there."

"And the men, women, and children? What of them?"

"Yes, those, the horses, the pigs, the chickens shall all burn. All the animals shall burn."

"Oi, I owe ya a punch," Harry said as he approached William, punched him in the nose, and continued to the house.

"Why are you beating them?" Philpot barked as blood rushed from William's nose, flowed down over his mouth, and dripped from his chin.

"For strikin' ya on the eye," Harry lied as he entered the house. "Yer we'come!"

"Don't expect more sterling for it and don't light that torch in the house! We don't want it to go up until we're ready!"

Noticing King's breathing getting stronger, Becky whispered in his ear to calm him down, and then pulling a handkerchief from William's pocket, she gently pulled his head back and wiped his face with it. Giving it to him to hold under his nose, she said, "Master Philpot, you must know you can't distance yourself from this. They will find you and charge you."

Philpot smirked. "Merely another rumor to add to my collection."

"And you, Robert, and you, Stuart, you don't expect to be caught?" Becky asked before it occurred to her they wouldn't leave any witnesses.

Stuart smiled. "They won't know cause there won't be any—"

"We'll be gone before they start searching for us," Robert said, receiving a confused look from Stuart.

"It's done," Harry said proudly as he came out with the

makeshift torch.

"Light it with this lantern here," Philpot said, grinning at the spade/torch. "But be careful. Your trousers are dark in areas, and I expect that's oil waiting to catch a flame."

Doing as he was told, Harry lit the torch, brightening the area, and holding the shaft near the spade's blade, he proudly held it up.

"Start with the cabins," Philpot told him. "I shall enjoy hearing the screams of the slaves as we leave."

With the knife at his neck, Oink found the courage to feel for his whip's handle partially sticking out from the waist of his trousers, and as Harry began walking toward the cabins, the boy said, "Harry."

Harry stopped. "What?"

"You kick like an eight-year-old."

"Then let me try again," he said as he hobbled toward him.

As the bowlegged man closed the distance between them, Oink pulled the whip from his trousers, and with two quick motions of his arm, it cracked as it tore the back of his hand, causing him to scream, drop the torch, and grab his bleeding hand, and as the torch landed at his feet, his shoes caught fire and flames engulfed his trousers.

"The water's that way," Oink said, pointing to the river.

With all but Oink shocked by the man on fire, Harry continued screaming as he ran toward the river much faster than anyone would have expected.

Hearing the splash, Oink said, "Stuart," and not getting a reaction from the man who had loosened his grip on his hair and lowered his knife, Oink nudged him. "Stuart, can your brother swim?"

Stuart pulled himself out of his shock and looked at Oink

as if it was a stupid question. "Of course not!"

"Can you?"

With his eyes widening, Stuart released Oink's hair, dropped his knife, and ran toward the river. "Harry, I'm coming!"

Red with anger, Philpot walked over to the burning torch lying on the ground, but he stopped short of picking it up when King took two steps toward him. When Philpot stepped back, King stepped back too.

"Kill them all!" Philpot barked at Robert.

Standing at the side of the cart's bed and more than willing to kill the one who had set his brother ablaze, Robert aimed the long gun at Oink, and as the slamming hammer sparked and the pan flashed, King was in front of the boy to catch the explosive burst. Hit in the chest, King took a step back into Oink before recovering his balance and stepping forward toward Robert, who picked up another long gun from the cart, pulled back its hammer, and fired it. As King continued walking toward him, he picked up a third and fired it into the chest of the giant who stopped, dropped to his knees, and fell backward, shocking Oink, William, and Becky.

"Now the rest!" Philpot ordered after shaking himself from the amazement of seeing it take three shots to drop the giant, who was lying on his back struggling to breathe. "Let's finish this now!"

When Philpot pulled another pistol from his waistcoat that failed to fire at the three still in shock and Robert grabbed another long gun, Gibby strolled out in front of the two confused men and stared at them. After pulling their attention from the pig, Robert readied the long gun, Philpot grabbed another pistol from his waistcoat, and the two paused when they heard an army of footsteps coming from their right. Taken aback by the thirty-plus topless men rushing out to stand between them and Gibby, all armed with either a small or large axe, Robert's shaking hands fired the musket over their heads.

"HOW COULD YOU BLOODY MISS!? THERE'S A WALL OF THEM!" Philpot shouted, and then with that pistol also failing to fire, he shouted, "BLOODY HELL! ROBERT, DRIVE THE CART!"

Dropping the gun, Robert grabbed the lantern from the cart's bed and ran to the front of the cart.

Then with his fourth pistol failing to fire into the wall of men, Philpot climbed onto the cart's bed just as the six horses took off at such a gallop that it would have slid him off the cart's bed if he hadn't grasped onto the sideboard, and as the horses put some distance between the slaves and them, he was relieved to see the group not running after them.

As the cart disappeared into the woods and the women and children joined the men, Becky kneeled and cradled King's large, round head as he struggled to breathe.

"Hell go me?" he forced out before coughing up blood.

"No, you're going to heaven, to the good place," she said with tears filling her eyes. "All slaves go to heaven. They... they all go to heaven."

Oink and William kneeled with Becky, and giving no concern to the tears running down his cheeks, Oink's voice cracked as he whispered, "You're a... a hero."

"Hero?" King asked.

"Like... like the brothers and the pirates we told you about," Becky whispered. "You saved us like... like they saved the ship."

"Hero me," King said… before closing his eyes and exhaling.

Sharing the long cart's bench, neither Philpot nor Robert spoke for several minutes until the large man looked back at the cart's bed and asked, "You didn't take the armoire?"

"With all that happened, your mind is on the wardrobe?" Robert asked as he used the light from the lantern to follow the road.

"Yes, and it's an armoire! It's from France!"

"We didn't finish loading the furniture. We were taking a break when you came back with the pig."

"I thought you had finished."

"No, and we didn't say we did… and you never asked. We only had the wardrobe… the *armoire* and your paintings and such remaining," Robert said, and then grinning, he asked sarcastically, "You want to go back for them?"

"Far too late now," Philpot replied, disappointed.

"We'll have to hide for a period. Wait for Harry and Stuart before we find a way out of this."

"Hide? Not at all. We committed no crime. Merely killed a slave that was attacking us."

"We stole that," Robert said, gesturing with his head toward the back of the cart.

"Stole? Who's to know? Who's to know it's not mine? They would have to go back many years to find the records of purchase if they even exist. I say I could return to the estate and nothing changes, but I wouldn't, not with those slaves waiting for me and those three letting them do with me as they wish. No, I'm done there, even if Chalmers wanted to keep me on."

"So what are we going to do now, now that your plan failed?" Robert asked, coldly.

"I shall still pay you as agreed, and I say we shall still do as planned. Hide the cart and go into town. If they want to accuse us of something, we shall have many witnesses on our side to make their accusations balderdash."

"How are we going to do that, go into town? We left behind our saddled horses… and my brothers."

"I didn't consider that, but still, you have six horses now. Three more than you had, and I'm certain your brothers shall be fine, but perhaps we should turn around and head to your father's now. We can borrow his horses, yes? As it is, we should hide this nearer to Williamsburg, not further from it, not where we have to ride past Chalmers' property to dispose of it later."

"I have a more secure place. We'll empty the cart there and then drive it to my father's. We shouldn't risk him being caught with Chalmers' furniture," Robert said as he took a wide turn onto a path cutting through the forest that after a minute ended in the forest.

"It's going to be a struggle to back out, seeing how you can't turn around."

"It will be slow, but possible," Robert said, taking the lantern and stepping down from the cart. "Come. Let me show you my property."

"Yours?"

"Mine."

With Philpot following him into the woods, Robert said, "Purchased it three weeks back, almost three pounds an acre."

"From Hall? This was his land, yes?"

"It was, and it's thirty acres," Robert said as they came to a small clearing. "I intend to build over there. I laid out the pegs for the house, a log house from the trees I'll be felling."

"It's much work. You're starting from nothing, and I expect you paid too much per acre, considering you can't plant anything for some years yet."

"It is much work, but you're failing to consider its distance from Williamsburg. I'm paying more for the location."

"Yes, but there's the cost of clearing it."

"The cost is merely time, but tell me, are you still planning to leave?"

"I am, but sooner now. I haven't seen my revenge, but I expect the crops will fail with only the stripling overseeing it."

"I can't say we'll be sad to see you go, and even less so after this night. We'll be worried about you more than missing you."

"You need not worry about me. I can take care of myself."

"We're not worried about your health. We're worried about you talking like you worry about your indentures talking, talking of your misdeeds. We know how much you enjoy talking, and there's much you can say about us, much more than your indentures could say about you."

Seeming not to have heard him, Philpot looked curiously at the five-foot-deep rectangular hole. "I say you went long for your privy. Planning on a three-seater, are you? One for each of you?" he laughed. "That pile of dirt there will be in your way, too. I say it's best to move it as you dig it. It's more work to pile it there than on a cart, twice the work," he said before another reason for the hole occurred to him. Pulling his second last pistol from his waistcoat, he pulled back its hammer and pointed it at Robert. "Planning on burying me, are you?"

"We were, and now I am. We expected to do the deed

within a week, but since you are here now—"

"I say everyone betrays me," Philpot sighed as he shook his head. "Ben with Chalmers, William attacking me with his fists, and even Mary with that pig. And now... and now you, you who I believed was loyal, whom I trusted more than any other. I say I would expect your brothers to do this, but not you. I expected you to keep them in line."

"It was Harry's idea, perhaps the first good one he's had. You decided we would part ways, but Harry reminded us we can decide how, and there are far more reasons to bury you than there are not to. As to loyalty, one can only have loyalty when one gives it. Yours is only to sterling... and so is ours. We're loyal to that sterling you locked in that drawer, made obvious by the soiled chest you left on it."

"You removed the sterling?"

"We did. Much easier to access through the top than the outside. Once the desk's top was off, we had only to remove the top drawer and pry off the board beneath. You put far too much trust in that locked drawer, just as you do in that study of yours, or battle room as you call it. We hid it in one of your sacks there if you want to check."

"No, I shall check after I drop your corpse in that hole. But I say you're rather calm for someone who's about to meet their maker. I don't expect your brothers shall be as calm when I catch up with them to have them join you, and I say the irony of you being buried in a hole you dug for me is rather amusing," Philpot said with a smirk before pulling the trigger, and with that pistol failing to fire too, he looked at it, confused.

Robert grabbed it, smacked him in the face with it, and as Philpot stood there holding his bleeding nose, Robert used a fingernail to scratch at the pistol's frizzen. "They waxed your frizzens. It didn't occur to me why your pistols refused to discharge until our drive here, when I recalled your third pistol had scratched something from its frizzen, spit something other than a spark, something flaky."

"Waxed the Frizzens?" Philpot asked as Robert pulled the hammer back two clicks and pointed it at him, causing him to take a step back. "I-I say I have far more than what you found in that drawer, far more. I can lead you to it. Bring you to all I have for only some consideration."

"I'm certain you have much more coin, but it's not worth the trouble… a bird in the hand, as they say."

Robert pulled the trigger. The pistol fired and the large man fell backward.

**

Oink, Becky, William, and the slaves were working into the early hours of the morning cleaning up the oil from around the house, cabins, and sheds, soaking it up with cloths and then scrubbing it with soap and water, when an anxious Mary walked in to tell them that Robert had returned with the cart. More curious than fearful, the three walked out to see the long cart stopped in front of the cabins and those who had been cleaning the oil from the cabins and sheds' walls staring at the man, with two of them pointing pistols and another pointing a long gun at him as he sat on the cart's bench while holding up his hands.

"I suppose we should have taken the powder, balls, and stuffing with us too," he said when seeing the three coming toward him.

"You should have," William said, "And Philpot shouldn't have had Ben show Becky how to reload them."

"What do you want? What are you doing back here?"

Becky asked, trying not to let her anger show.

"A trade. I return what's yours… Chalmers', and you allow me to take my horse, or horses if Harry and Stuart haven't returned."

"They haven't!" Oink barked. "And you can walk away with nothing or die where you—"

"You can take the horses. They're in the stables, dressed as you left them, and if we see you on this land again, you will be trespassing and we will take action," William said calmly while ignoring the puzzled look from his brother. "And do know that the law will be looking for you regarding your part in the murder of King and the attempted destruction of this plantation. I expect that will involve a hanging."

"It was only a slave," Robert said, and then remembering those pointing guns at him were also slaves, added, "But I understand, and I'll reimburse Chalmers for the boy."

"He's more than that! He's our friend!" Oink barked, "Was our friend!"

"Where's Philpot?" Becky asked.

"You'll not see him again. I expect he's on his way out of Virginia."

"Take your horses and leave," William said. "You have five minutes. Any longer and we'll consider it trespassing, and I'm sure the men here would enjoy discharging their guns in your direction."

"I-I thank you," Robert bowed to the three before stepping down from the cart. "And my apologies for the incident."

After Robert rode off with two dressed horses tied to his horse, Oink asked William why he had let him go.

"He returned what they took, and we shouldn't keep what

isn't ours. I also respected the fact that he returned the cart of six horses and furniture to only see back his three."

"He could've come back to see what we were doing, to see if he could attack us again, and the trade was only a reason to do it."

"Perhaps, but seeing how we're prepared for an attack, I expect he has dropped any plans he may have had. To his sort, the only thing more frightening than an armed man is an armed slave."

Appreciating his opinion matching hers, Becky said, "I expect you're correct," and put her arms around him and kissed him. "And today you have proven you can keep them safe and healthy. Now you only have to keep them happy."

"*We've* proven it, and I hope you're correct," Oink said, walking away, "And if you two continue kissing as you are, I'll soon be an uncle!"

Becky released William and gave him a confused look. "Does he think—"

"I expect so. Father told him that in jest, and I don't believe anyone has yet to correct it. I know I haven't."

"You should… as his big brother."

"Yes, I should," William smirked and nodded. "Perhaps in ten years."

Becky smiled. "Has anyone told you you're easy to love?"

"My mother," William joked before it occurred to him that her question was a statement of her love. "Has… has anyone told you that … that you're easy to love?"

Hugging each other again, each looked over the other's shoulder to see the smiling faces around them, including Mary and Ann, and both blushed.

**

Several days after the incident, Sammy discovered Harry Carter's bloated body in the creak at the edge of his land, but no one found Stuart Carter's body and it was assumed he had drowned trying to save Harry.

Charles Philpot was never seen again and nothing more was ever heard about him, and without him there to face charges, none were brought against Robert Carter, whose defense was that he was only following Philpot's orders and believed the man when he told him the two brothers, whom he had never seen before, were trespassing on Chalmers' land, giving him the right to shoot at them. As to the killing of King, Robert saw no fine since he was also following Philpot's orders to perform a mercy killing. The first shot was an accident while protecting the land from what he believed were trespassers, and the next two shots were out of mercy.

Two days after his death, they placed King in a casket and buried him six feet under his cabin that would act as a mausoleum, and a short time after that, Oink took the time to carve into the cabin's door,

HERE LIES JAMES (A.K.A. KING)
A FRIEND TO MANY AND A HERO TO ALL
HIS SOUL IS IN HEAVEN

CHAPTER 28
Virginia, May 13, 1716

At a far end of Lord Chalmers' field, a group of thirty slaves, mostly women and older children, was bent over working the rows of tobacco plants no taller than a foot, and on the other side of the road, beyond the stumps and a line of fires turning branches to ash, two Black men swung axes against opposing sides of a thick tree, three more used small axes to remove a felled tree's branches, and a Black man and a White man shared a long saw to cut the felled tree into manageable sections. All topless and all glistening with sweat.

Sawing through the tree, causing the cut ends to rise slightly from the shift in the weight, the two men placed the long saw with its large teeth on the ground and stretched their backs. Straightening up, William swiped away a flying insect before pulling out a string from his pocket, handing an end to his partner, and walking passed the men removing the branches. Stopping when the string stretched tight, he waited for his partner to join him with the saw.

A yell of, "HO!" caused all working the felled tree to look toward the two who had lowered their large axes and were stepping back from the tree that slowly leaned, cracked, and then fell with such a crash that it shook the ground.

"You two can help us clean this one before felling another," William said as he bent down to take his end of the saw. "Together, it should take less than ten minutes before we're rolling it to clear its other side and you're felling another."

"Perhaps longer without your help. It seems you have visitors," his partner said as he straightened up to look toward the road where a stopped four-horse coach was taking the attention of those on both sides of the road who had seldom seen such an extravagant vehicle.

"Don't believe I do. I don't know anyone who could or would rent anything such as that. I expect they've lost their way... and prefer us to go to them," William said before walking past stumps and fires to the black coach with its polished brass lanterns, its brass door handle, and brass trim glowing from the sun's afternoon rays. "Blessed afternoon, my friend," William said to the long-coated driver standing near the coach's door. "I expect you're lost. Williamsburg's in the opposite direction."

Before the driver could respond, the passenger poked his forty-something head through the opened window and smiled. "Am I correct in presuming this is Lord Chalmers' estate?" he asked in a naturally aristocratic accent before opening the door and stepping down the wooden block of steps that the driver had placed beneath the door. With his jacket, waistcoat, and breeches matching the cocked hat resting on his white curly wig, the overdressed, smiling man looked as out of place as the coach.

"You are. It's his plantation," William replied, curious.

Continuing to smile, the man offered his hand. "And I

presume you are William Lovely."

Then more curious, William shook the hand. "I am."

"My apologies for failing to inform you of my coming. A letter would only have reached you as I stand here," the man said, releasing William's hand and bowing humbly. "I could have said all I needed to in a letter, but since I have some rare business in South Carolina, I thought it proper that I stop here along the way for a tête-à-tête, as the French would say. I also apologize for taking as long as I did to come, but with the winter's ice, I could only leave England the first week of March." Looking William up and down, he added, "And if you would permit me to say, I am pleased to find you in good health."

"I thank you, Master… Master…"

"Chalmers, Michael Chalmers, at your service," he said with a bow of his head.

Taken aback by the man's humble disclosure, William returned the bow. "I-I thank you, Master… Lord Chalmers."

"If you please, my pleasure with your health is not to be thanked. No, not at all. It is much too selfish on my part to be appreciated. Where would my estate be without your good health? I believe burned to the ground and sold for the mere bones of a cow, only enough for some broth and gelatin. But enough of my talk on what would have been," he said, wiping his brow with his fingertips. "If you would permit me to ask, may we have a conversation in the coach's shade, perhaps with a drink?"

"We can do so at the house if you would accept apple cider and a tour of the grounds."

"Then hard cider and a tour it will be," the man said, playfully slapping William's shoulder.

"It would have to be soft if you please, and if you would grant me a moment, I'll inform the men of my leaving."

"Then soft it will be, and yes, please do. I shall be waiting in the carriage."

Several minutes later, a nervous William in a dirt-stained shirt entered the carriage to sit on the leather-padded bench across from Lord Chalmers. With his back against the leather padded backrest, he looked around and felt out of place. The walls were covered in an embroidered cloth and the glass of its two windows was sanded and polished to remove the wavy patterns. A table was waiting to be pulled down between them and the railed shelf above it held several expensive glass cups and several ceramic bottles of liquor.

With his boyish smile disarming the uncomfortable young man, Chalmers picked up the brass-handled cane lying beside him and hit the ceiling three times, causing the driver to move the coach forward, turn around, and put the horses into a trot.

After a moment of looking fondly at William, Chalmers said, "I must thank you for the letter you sent after the incident assuring me you would see the harvest through until another overseer is found, and while my mind is there, permit me to compliment you on your fine penmanship, and more so when considering I had been informed you cannot write."

"You're welcome, but though the words were mine, mostly, the penmanship was Becky's. But she is teaching me to write."

"I would ask then that you pass on my appreciation to her, but permit me to say also that my tobacco agent, Francis Bradbury, tells me you are a quick learner and driven, and it appears to be accurate. I see you have planted the next harvest and are clearing the forest that I understand has been standing there for far too long."

"Yes, we've transplanted the seedlings and are clearing the land, but I can't admit to being a quick learner. The men and women are the ones who educated me, and when needed, remind me of what they taught me."

"The men and women?"

"The slaves."

"Oh yes, of course," the man said, obviously ashamed at his confusion. "Still, I expect your empathetic personality has surrounded you with competent people, including the slaves. Being my indentured, I knew of you before you sailed here. The agent informed me he had found the young man whom I sought. One who was both inexperienced with slaves and naive regarding the duties of an overseer. Someone whom I hoped would lean away from cruelty rather than one aware of the harsh duties and eager to perform them. And the agent's excellent choice was confirmed by a visit from our mutual friend, Captain Humphreys, who wasted only a day after unloading his ship to inform me of you and your brother's characters... and adventure. The good man begged me to send a letter to Charles insisting he treat you well, you and your brother. Humphrey had words with the man, but he believed it would have more powder if I added some words to it myself. But I didn't. I thought it was unnecessary. I was planning to replace Charles, and any words from me regarding you and your brother may well have exposed my plans. I only informed him of the itemization of the estate's property, and once that was done, I was to decide when and how to replace him and consider charges for his actions against the estate, actions like his overstating its expenses for his benefit and his taking from the harvest hundreds of barrels each year over the last seven years, at the minimum. That is to say, he was keeping a portion of my hogsheads for himself beyond his per centum of the harvest. But alas, he discovered my plans, though I know not how. But none of that matters now that I sit across from my estate's savior, or is it the plantation's? I never know which to call it."

"I-I believe it's a plantation. Master Philpot called it an estate but referred to the fields as a plantation, but Ben, the previous apprentice, felt referring to it as an estate was pretentious when he believed the whole was a plantation… and I agree with him."

"Yes, I believe my issue is having not been on a plantation to have the term stay with me," he said before pausing for a moment to reflect on something. "Since I'm both curious and confused, would you permit me to ask why the few slaves I saw minutes ago were barefoot when Bradbury showed me last year's expenditures with one being for their boots, a cost of close to a hundred and eighty pounds?"

William cleared his throat before nodding. "That's correct. They are barefoot. During the winter, the slaves only had shoes made from flour sacks, and I thought it safer for them to have actual boots. They all have them now, including the little ones, but only wear them when they feel they must. Almost everything is produced on the plantation, including their clothes, but the boots were their first purchased items and… and they're overly protective of them, preferring to go barefoot when they can so as not to ruin them."

"They won't wear them unless they feel they must?" Chalmers asked with a grin. "I'm no longer curious and confused, but now fascinated and impressed. Those boots should last many more years than they would otherwise. But speaking of the slaves, whom did you leave to oversee them, your brother, Oscar?"

"No, no one."

"No one? No one overseeing them?" he asked with a puzzled face.

"That's correct," William nodded, trying not to reveal his pride through a smile. "They're formed into groups of six or seven and spaced nearly fifty feet apart to make it safer for all. One man leads each group, and each group fells, clears the branches, and saws them to their proper length. It works well. They even have competitions to see which group can fell the most trees in a day or week… safely."

Laughing with a higher pitch than what William would have expected from a lord, the man said, "It appears you have come close to forcing yourself from your position."

"It appears as much, but by working with them, we set the pace… if necessary."

"Working with them, you say? Interesting, very interesting. And I see you don't carry a whip."

"I see no reason for one," William told him. "I believe its use will only slow the task already being performed as efficiently as it could be." Then thinking the man might understand his thinking better if he described it in Philpot's terms, he said, "A rider's horse can only run so fast, and whipping it when it's at its fastest will only slow it down."

"True," Chalmers said as he dropped his smile, "Though I do not see slaves as horses."

"Neither do I, but it seems some in these parts do."

"I expect you are correct, and I expect also the lack of the whip could make them more content."

"I expect they're more content than they were. They were

forced to isolate themselves, but now we encourage them to socialize. We have a dozen fire pits encircled with stools of logs so they can eat in the cool air rather than in their hot cabins. We also stopped barring their cabins at night, though the only reason we barred them was for Philpot to sleep better with his belief they couldn't attack him. I expect there's more that can be done to make them more content, but even with treating them as people rather than beasts, how content can they be as slaves?"

Hoping to hear the man's response, William was disappointed when the carriage stopped and Chalmers grabbed his cane and stood up. "It is the nature of the place. Labor is scarce and too expensive to make a crop worth the effort," he said as they heard the block of steps being placed by the door that then opened. "I expect to be only half an hour," Chalmers told the driver as William followed him out of the carriage to learn they were at the side of the house.

With the last of the children rushing into the cabins and their doors shutting, Chalmers whispered, "A shy group, yes?"

William didn't want to explain their instinctive reaction to visitors, so instead, he only nodded. "Yes, they are."

"I believe a swine is making a run for it," Chalmers warned as a full-grown pig ran toward them. Raising his cane, he spread his feet and bent his knees. "Back, you rascal!"

Holding back his laugh, William stepped in front of the man to kneel and pat the excited animal.

"You let your pigs roam the grounds?" the man asked, lowering his cane and relaxing his stance.

"They're your pigs, and only this one's free to roam about. The others are content in the pigsty. His name's Gibby. He was Oink's pet, but now he's everyone's pet." With Gibby rubbing his ear against the thigh of his trousers, William stood up. "He has the run of the estate but never leaves it. He sleeps where he wants, usually downstairs with Oscar or in one of the cabins. Oscar befriended him on the voyage here, and as it was, he was in a group of a couple of dozen sent to this plantation."

Chalmers gave another high-pitched laugh before saying with some excitement, "By Jove, that's the pig he informed me of! I plum forgot about the beast!" And before William could ask who had informed him of Gibby, Chalmers calmed down as he looked about and said, "This is my first visit, and I don't expect my father made the voyage seeing how he gave little care for its performance. But before we sit down to cider and my reason for being here, let us have that tour."

"Of course," William nodded. "The sheds lead to the barn and stable near the river, and if you'll follow me, I'll explain their purpose as we walk there."

After William pointed out the two rows of the slaves' cabins to their right, Chalmers asked to see the inside of one. Looking into the cramped quarters, the man greeted the pregnant woman and her two small children, who all froze where they were with their eyes toward the dirt floor. "Very shy, indeed," he said before leaving the living statues to follow William to the pigsty. "Those pigs are a spoiled lot," the man laughed. "Shaded here and opened there."

"The shaded area closes in to give shelter during the winter," William informed him before pointing out the chicken coop which the man insisted on seeing as well.

They visited the laundry shed, the milking shed, the butchering shed, the barber's shed, the cannery, and the smokehouse, and when they came to King's cabin, William explained the reason for the message carved into its door and the reason for King being buried under it.

Chalmers was disappointed that he would never meet King, and when he asked to meet Oink, he was disappointed more to learn he was bringing logs to the wood mill, but his disappointment disappeared when he learned he would see a small income from the sale of the logs, something he told William he never saw from Philpot.

At the stable, Chalmers inspected the two horses in it and was impressed by their health, and when William pointed out the row of curing barns, the man had no interest in visiting the huge, empty edifices but was pleased to hear that since Philpot wouldn't be using them, the plantation was ready with the extra curing space for when the cleared land was eventually growing crop.

William ended the tour by bringing the man into the kitchen, where his face showed he was impressed by its size.

Introducing Lord Chalmers to the three women, Becky fought through her surprise at discovering she was looking at the Lord of the plantation and offered a curtsy. "Welcome, Lord Chalmers."

Mary and Ann tried to imitate Becky by nervously grabbing their robes and lifting them slightly, but after awkwardly placing their right foot behind their left, they dropped to where they were almost kneeling on one knee.

Lord Chalmers laughed. "Ladies, there is no reason to curtsy. I'm a Lord, not a Stuart… or I should say Hanover now, yes? And Rebecca, if you will permit me to say, you are as handsome as I've been told."

With Becky surprised by him having heard of her, William said, "Becky, we'll be talking in the dining room, discussing the… the…"

"The state of the estate," the man said, continuing to smile.

"Yes, the state of the estate," William repeated as he picked up a wooden tray from the counter.

"What is it you need?" she asked.

"I'll be bringing two cups of cider with us."

"I'll bring them," she said, taking the tray from him.

"Bring us four, if you would," Chalmers said. "My thirst will require two, and based on Master Lovely's dry lips, I expect he could use as many."

Embarrassed that his throat was not the only thing dried by his nervous state, William led the man to the steps of the house where he pointed out the garden and behind it the eight fire pits, each surrounded by a dozen short logs firmly planted in the ground, and behind those, the several grazing cows

After William pointed out Oink's room, Becky's room, the bathroom, and the log-walled study, the two sat across from each other at the dining room table, where Chalmers removed his hat, pulled a small silver box from his jacket, and asked, "Snuff?" With William shaking his head, the man said, "As you wish," before snorting in the powder from the tiny spoon. "It relaxes one but yet picks one up when tired, and though it's not needed here, it does well to hide the offensive smells for a short time. I will admit I prefer sniffing it rather than smoking it."

Becky entered with a tray, and after placing a plate of bread and cheese between the two and placing an empty plate, two cups of cider, and a knife in front of each, she nodded to the men who thanked her.

As her footsteps faded down the hall, Chalmers took a cup and emptied it in several quick gulps. "I don't exaggerate when I say she is as handsome as he said... as he wrote."

"Who? If you don't mind my asking," William asked, afraid to take a drink in case he choked on it.

"Rebecca."

"Yes, but who wrote to you about her? Philpot?"

"Philpot? No, Ben," Chalmers said before realizing his error. "My apologies. I assumed Master Bradbury had informed you of Ben being my confidant, or more accurately, I being his. Since my father's death, I wanted to better understand the workings of the estate... of the plantation, understand why the harvest expanded only slightly year over year when there was unused land to be cleared, and eight years back, when Charles requested another indentured to replace the one retiring, Ben agreed to come here as my trusted eyes and ears under the guise of an indentured servant. He is family... was family. His father works on my estate. I had known the lad since he was a toddler, which makes my guilt for what had happened to him so much stronger. I failed to consider that seven years with the man would change him as much as I now believe it did, and I presume it was the reason for his suicide, whose fault I consider entirely mine and something I must take with me when meeting Saint Peter."

"Suicide?" William asked the then watery-eyed man.

Chalmers cleared his throat. "My apologies for using you as... as my confessor. I expect some tasks he was forced to do had an effected on him, affected him badly, and sometime between sending his last letter, in which he informed me of you, your brother, and his trespassing on the ship in England, he performed the unholy act that would sentence his soul to transportation, transportation to hell. Of course, there is no evidence of such an action, but I see no other explanation for his disappearance."

With the man looking down at the table, William picked up a cup of cider and took a sip. Placing it back on the table, he discreetly moistened his lips with his tongue. "I believe he's in heaven since I expect it was murder, not suicide, and if you would allow me a minute, I'll explain why that is."

"Of… of course," a curious Lord Chalmers nodded as he watched William leave the room.

Two minutes later, William returned to his chair and placed on the table an eye patch with an eye painted on it and a leather-corded lead cross with a bent arm. "Oscar found those in a drawer of Philpot's desk, along with other items no one here recognized. I believe these are his mementos, mementos of his murders. From what the men told me, the apprentice before Ben wore this eye patch. Something I doubt he would leave behind, and this cross is Ben's. We also discovered Becky's fiancé's ring, and when he was found… found dead, he wasn't wearing it."

Chalmers took a deep breath as he picked up the lead cross. "Are you certain? I fail to remember this, and I would remember it… with it being merely lead."

"Yes. He found it here in a stream and would never have given it to Philpot."

The man stared at William for a moment. "Would he kill to keep him quiet, to keep *them* from speaking of their time here?"

"I believe so, and I believe… no, I know he wanted Becky for himself. And there is no reason for him to have Peter's… her fiancé's ring."

"I suppose from what Ben had told me of the man, he was more than capable. Even so, I never considered he would do such a thing. May I give this to his father?"

"Of course."

Placing the cross in his waistcoat pocket, the man said, "It doesn't do much more for my soul to know he was murdered rather than having committed suicide, but permit me to put this behind me for now and say that I find you much more confident and competent than Ben had informed me, though he only had a short time to become familiar with you while you were adjusting to the plantation. However, he did write that he both liked and respected you, which is quite the compliment coming from Ben.

"But let me get to the reason for my being here. Before leaving Williamsburg late this morning, I had a conversation with Master Bradbury, and he has agreed to take some time to show you how to place entries in the ledger for this year's expenses. He shall also issue you a four-hundred-pound advance to have on hand for expenses, but you would have to forecast the expenditures so as not to find yourself short before the next advance. You shall also have to start a new ledger each year, and with you not being able to write, I expect Becky can help you with the few words it requires. Now before I find I am ahead of myself, do you have any questions?" he asked as he picked up his second cup of cider.

"I believe I'm capable of using the ledger when I've learned how, but I expect the new overseer of the plantation will want to take charge of it. Do you have a date for when we might expect him?"

Chalmers lowered the cup from his lips and stared curiously at William for a moment. Then his eyes enlarged and he released his high-pitched laugh, splashing cider from his cup. "Here I was concerned with rushing ahead of myself when I had already done so! My friend, you are the overseer of the plantation… that is if you take the position." With William confused by what he was hearing, Chalmers laughed again. "My apologies. I shall have to go back even further and state that I see no one better to oversee this… this plantation than the man who has shown both his integrity and his ability to perform the duty, and of course, that man is you. William, I wish to end your indentured contract and offer you the position. I would pay out the amount agreed upon at the signing, which I believe is a few pounds and two sets of clothes, and you would become the overseer of the plantation, overseeing it as you feel best suits my interests. You decide all, and at the end of the year, when Master Bradbury takes possession of the last of our hogsheads, he shall give you your share, but I would want to handle our expenses differently than I did with Charles. Any labor besides the slaves would be at your expense, and that includes Becky as the housemaid, at five shillings a week or twelve pounds a year. What do you say to that?"

Instead of agreeing, a surprised William asked, "And my brother?"

"Yes, your brother," the man nodded, having never considered Oink. "I shall end his contract also, but his work here would be at your expense. Before leaving for Boston, I shall have Bradbury draw up the papers terminating the contracts for you and your brother and draw up a contract for you overseeing the plantation. I'll also have him give you that four hundred pounds sterling in tobacco notes, but I think we should make it an additional two hundred, considering your personal expenses… such as new shirts."

Confused by the advance of sterling, William asked, "Two

hundred for my expenses?"

"Yes, as an advance, considering it's your first year, and a year is a long time to wait to see your share of the harvest."

"An advance?"

"On your per centum of the harvest. Charles would have earned nearly six hundred pounds for his fifteen per centum, but seeing how he will not be seeing it, I gifted it to Ben's father as an inheritance from the lad."

"Six hundred pounds? Fifteen per centum?" William repeated back, his mind refusing to accept what he was hearing.

Chalmers frowned. "My dear friend, I may go as high as eighteen per centum. Shall we agree on eighteen?"

Still trying to force his mind to accept what he was hearing, William asked, "Eighteen?"

Chalmers shook his head and sighed in frustration. "Twenty is as far as I shall go, can go, and only because you shall save me the effort and risk associated with replacing Charles with another of whom I would know nothing of."

"Twenty?" William asked, and then seeing Chalmers' face covered by more frustration, he said, "Yes, I-I'll accept twenty."

Chalmers sighed. "You have a natural skill with negotiation, natural indeed. You know your worth, and now I sit here more than confident with you as a partner." Standing up from the chair, he emptied his second cup of cider, placed it on the table, and put on his hat. "I shall be off, and as I said, I shall instruct Master Bradbury to have the contract drawn up for you to oversee the plantation at a… a twenty per centum and to draw up the termination papers for you and your brother's indentured contracts. Sometime next week, he shall come to see you with the advances and inform you and Oscar where to be measured for your finer clothes." With William joining him in standing, Chalmers added with a smile, "If it pleases you, I can see myself out. After all, it is my home as well."

After the two shook hands and wished the other well, Chalmers picked up his cane and, as he was about to leave, said, "I do hope that the slaves won't become too comfortable with your consideration and relax their effort."

Not having a response for him, William said, "Have a safe journey to South Carolina," and returned to his seat to reflect on what had just happened. Then considering the massive amount of sterling he would see at the end of the year, he thought he would have to place much of it in a bank and bury the rest somewhere safe for when it was needed quickly. When he was considering how much sterling he could send home, he was hit by a sudden joy. Being free of his contract, he neither had to ask Chalmers' permission nor had to wait until he was twenty-four to marry Becky.

"The coach has left," Becky told him as she placed the empty tray on the table, sat down on Chalmers' chair, and took William's hand. "Did he mention when the new overseer is arriving? Has he told you anything about him? Mary and Ann are working each other up about the character of the man replacing Philpot, and I'll admit I have my concerns too."

William gave her hand a gentle squeeze. "I don't believe they have to worry about his character, or I hope they don't since I'll be replacing Philpot," he said, smiling when he saw the woman he loved drop her jaw.

After William went through the details of their conversation, telling her about Ben being Chalmers' informant, Chalmers being pleased with their harvest and pleased to see the clearing of the land going well, the man ending his and Oink's contract, and twice out of a misunderstanding, raising his percentage of the yearly harvest's profits, Becky realized they could be married without needing permission or having to wait almost five more years, but she said nothing of it, preferring to let him realize it himself and propose when he was ready.

Twenty minutes later, two long carts with a group of seven men sitting on the beds of each rolled through the grounds to stop near the stable. As the men dropped from the carts, Oink stepped down from one of the carts' benches. "After you remove the harnesses and stable the horses, take some cider. We'll be joining the felling in twenty," Oink told the group as he adjusted the waist of his field trousers that were an inch too short.

Near the side of the kitchen where an upright barrel rested in the shade, Oink twisted the sweat from his red cap before lifting the barrel's top, and with the ladle hanging from it, scooped up some cider and gulped it down. He was taking a second scoop when Mary's laughter forced him to drink it as fast as the first.

"What's the good news?" he asked the ladies bouncing around the kitchen as if they were given their freedom.

"Lord Chalmers was here! He came to see the plantation!" Mary almost shouted.

"He was? He did?"

"Yes!" she nodded excitedly. "You should talk to your brother. You should hear it from him rather than us."

"He's felling?"

"He's in the house with Becky."

In the house, Oink found William and Becky sitting at the table and using several of the previous years' ledgers to forecast the plantation's expenses.

Noticing Becky smiling at someone behind him, William turned around to see his brother curiously looking at them. "I expect all went well at the mill," he said as he stood up from the table.

"Mary told me Lord Chalmers was here."

"He was, but only for a short time, and he left maybe twenty minutes ago. You probably passed his coach on your way back."

"We did pass a coach, a rich one."

"That was him. Come, let's leave Becky to continue with what we're doing and I'll tell you about his visit."

With questions piling up in his head, Oink followed his brother out the back door, past the garden, and took the short, upright log next to him when he sat near a fire pit of ash.

"What was he like? What did he say? Did he mention me?"

"He wasn't as I expected a Lord to be," William replied before telling him of their conversation.

Oink's face showed his surprise when learning their contracts would be terminated, and he showed his excitement when learning he would earn twenty-four pounds yearly. "I'm rich!" he exclaimed before calming down to ask, "Did you ask about the fiddle to make the work less dull and about training Geoff and Mark to play it, and did you ask about the sterling for the men and women?"

"I did, I did, and I did," William lied. "We can have the two of them trained if they still want it, and we'll be giving the men and women a shilling a month, two shillings for the group leaders."

Almost two weeks later, after Becky and William went over her corrections to the writing she had assigned him the day before, William dropped to one knee and held out half a coin, but in his nervous state, he couldn't remember a word of what he had planned to say, so he asked only, "W-will you?"

Staring at the half coin for several seconds, Becky dropped down to hug and kiss him, and with tears running down her cheeks, said, "You… you know it's not a piece of eight, yes? Now it has no value."

"At this moment, it has all the value of the world."

**

As a fiddle played a slow tune, Oink peered through the dining room's small far window to look toward the field beyond the garden and fire pits. His stomach growled when he thought of the massive amount of meat, cheese, bread, biscuits, cakes, sugar-topped buns and such spread out on a line of makeshift tables and covered by freshly laundered sheets to keep out that June's rays and insects. Beyond the food, the patiently waiting slaves stood in their freshly laundered clothes forming a wall from the first table of covered food to the last, making it impossible to see the twenty or so English guests standing beyond them.

After placing his shoed foot on one of the dining room table's chairs and tightening its buckle, William Straightened up to adjust his jacket that matched his breeches and waistcoat, one of the two sets of clothes that Chalmers had insisted Bradbury spare no expense on so they would look no worse than a prince on an off day. "Do you expect all are here, best man?"

"I believe so," Oink said, also dressed in one of his two sets of new clothes, "And I told you I prefer being called your second."

"And I told you I'm marrying Becky, not dueling her."

The boy turned away from the window to look at his brother. "Not now, but seeing how you two are far too alike, I expect that after a few months, there'll be times when you'll feel you are, her with a pistol and you with a sword."

Nervously standing near the kitchen table in her burgundy gown covered in a pattern of yellow flowers, which to her seemed overdressed for any occasion other than a wedding, Becky looked past Mary to the opened door of the kitchen hoping to get a glance at her husband-to-be.

"That's as good as I can make them," Mary said as she secured the last tiny bundle of Virginia Bluebells to Becky's hair. Standing back to admire her work, she added, "But I have to say it's impossible to expect flowers to make you more beautiful than you are. They'll only distract from it."

Trying not to shake her head with her laugh, Becky said, "You sound like William."

"Then I have to say I sound intelligent," Mary smiled. "Handsome and intelligent."

"Do you think they've all arrived?"

"I do. Now let's go to the field. We kept them waiting too long as it is, and I have to say if we keep them waiting any longer, they might start leaving."

"Mary, I don't remember ever seeing you so anxious. We have to wait until Oink signals Master Carmichael to play *Ave Verum Corpus*, and then we have to wait until William is standing in front of the minister," Becky reminded her friend just as the fiddler started playing the tune.

Unable to control herself, Mary rushed to the kitchen door to look for William, but only saw Oink disappearing into the back of the house.

The closer William got to the back door, the harder his heart beat, and by the time he was outside, he was feeling dizzy. Trying to ignore Oink's teasing whispers behind him of, "Left foot, right foot, left foot," William passed the faces he recognized from the congregation and those he had personally invited, like Sammy and his short wife, Charity, whom he almost didn't recognize because of their formal attire, and he was surprised to see Philip with his shirt filled out by ten additional pounds of muscle and whom he didn't expect to be there since he didn't know Oink had rented him for the day. When he stopped in front of the minister and Oink stepped to his right, he could no longer feel his heart beating. He couldn't feel anything. It was as if his soul had suddenly left his body to stand with the others behind him.

Becky's tensing facial muscles forced a smile across her face, and she would've been much more nervous, maybe frozen by it, if Mary hadn't distracted her by repeatedly telling herself to slow down her limping so as not to bump into the back of Becky.

As Mary took two steps to the left, Becky joined William, who slightly relaxed at the sight of her staring at him, and when he returned her large smile, hers grew even larger to where it hurt.

Forcing their eyes away from each other to look at the

minister, whose words seemed to be only a hum to them, William felt his heart beat again and Becky's face relaxed.

To the two, the minister's hum only formed coherent words when he looked at William and asked, "Wilt thou have this woman to be thy wedded wife, to live together after God's ordinance in the holy estate of matrimony? Wilt thou love her, comfort her, honor her and keep her, in sickness and in health; and, forsaking all other, keep thee only unto her, so long as ye shall both live?"

"I will," William said.

Turning to Becky, the man asked, "Wilt thou have this man to be thy wedded husband, to live together after God's ordinance in the holy estate of matrimony? Wilt thou love him, comfort him, honor him and keep him, in sickness and in health; and, forsaking all other, keep thee only unto him, so long as ye shall both live?"

"I will," Becky said.

When he was told to look at Becky, William gladly obliged while repeating after the man, "I, William Henry Lovely, take thee, Rebecca Catherine Rowling, to be my wedded wife, to have and to hold from this day forward, for better for worse, for richer for poorer, in sickness and in health, to love and to cherish, till death us depart, according to God's holy ordinance; and thereto I give thee my troth."

Trying to fight back her tears after hearing William say, "wife," Becky struggled to repeat after the minister, "I, Rebecca Catherine Rowling, take thee, William Henry Lovely, to be my wedded husband, to have and to hold from this day forward, for better for worse, for richer for poorer, in sickness and in health, to love, cherish, and to obey, till death us depart, according to God's holy ordinance; and thereto I give thee my troth."

When the minister asked for the rings, the bride and groom turned to watch the crowd open up for a small Black girl in Beth's poorly mended dress standing next to Gibby with a pillow tied to his back, and after the two slowly walked up to the couple, the young girl picked up the two posie rings from off the pillow, gave one to each, and both turned to join the front of the crowd.

William's voice cracked as he repeated after the minister, "With this ring I thee wed, with my body I thee worship, and with all my worldly goods I thee endow: In the name of the Father, and of the Son, and of the Holy Ghost. Amen," and with his hands shaking, he slid the ring onto the finger of Becky's shaking hand.

Becky too repeated after the minister, saying, "With this ring I thee wed, with my body I thee worship, and with all my worldly goods I thee endow: In the name of the Father, and of the Son, and of the Holy Ghost. Amen," and with her hands still shaking, struggled to slide the matching ring onto William's still shaking hand.

Grabbing his hand, she squeezed it gently as the minister said, "Forasmuch as bride and groom have consented together in holy matrimony, and have pledged their love and loyalty to each other, and have declared the same by the joining and the giving of rings, by the power vested in me, and as witnessed by friends and family, I now pronounce you husband and wife."

William pulled Becky close and the two kissed to the claps of the crowd and the wheat, oats, and barley raining down on them.

Breaking their kiss, Becky whispered, "I was worried

they'd throw tobacco leaves."

"Oscar wanted to, but Mary talked him out of it," William whispered back.

Notes Regarding the Dialogue

1) For ease of reading, in most cases the modern order of words was used in the dialogue rather than the order more commonly used during the period, such as using "He did not go to the Market," instead of, "He did go not to the Market."

2) Also for ease of reading, the use of the contractions that were going out of common use during the period, such as *'twas*, *'Tis*, and *'twere*, and words such as *whilst* and *wherefore* were seldom used in the dialogue, instead those that were becoming more common during the period were used.

3) The pronouns that were becoming less common during the period were avoided, such as *thou* and *thee*.

4) Where it would cause little to no confusion, the period's proper terminology was used, such as *jest* instead of *joke*, *whipped* or *lashed* instead of *flogged*, *larboard* instead of *port* (changed in the mid 1800s to avoid confusion with *starboard*), *cocked hat* instead of *tricorn hat* (when they went out of style and returned almost fifty years later), *Master* and *Mistress* instead of *Mister*, *Miss* and *Misses*, *trespasser* instead of *stowaway*, *overseer* instead of *manager*, *apprentice* instead of *assistant*, and *Indian* instead of *Native American*.

5) Words that came after the period or words that had a different meaning for the period were avoided, such as *rifle*, *nickname*, *OK* (common in the 1800s for *all correct* and *all clear*), and *hello* (came with the telephone.)

Notes Regarding the Dialogue (Cont.)

6) Because the modern names for meals (breakfast, lunch, dinner, and supper) didn't yet exist during the period, or did but had a different meaning than today, they were instead referenced by *morning meal, midday meal* and *evening meal* in both the dialogue and the narrative.

7) Some words that might cause confusion were avoided, like *let* for *rent,* as in, "He rented the slaves," rather than, "He let the slaves."

8) With the colonists of the period referring to themselves as English, the practice was repeated for the story.

9) Because there is little record of how the slaves spoke during the period and the two references found (letters) mentioned Virginian slaves speaking as well as the English, the slaves in the story speak as well as their masters.

About the Author

Michael Kroft is from Halifax, Nova Scotia, and writes novels about the relationships between complex and lovable characters. Having completed his first four-book series, *Herring Cove Road*, he's now working on his next series, *The Lovelys' Family Tree*.

Current Works

The Not-So-Nuclear Family Saga Series, *Herring Cove Road*

1) On Herring Cove Road: Mr. Rosen and His 43Lb Anxiety

2) Still on Herring Cove Road: Hickory, Dickory, Death

3) Off Herring Cove Road: The Problem Being Blue

4) Before Herring Cove Road: Ruth Goldman and the Nincompoop

The Family Saga Series, *The Lovelys' Family Tree*

1) Indentured Bonds: The First Generation, Circa 1715

2) Family Bonds: The Second Generation, Circa 1735 (Coming August 2023)

www.michaelkroft.com